MURDER & THE MIDNIGHT DISEASE

Marcia C Gerhardt

ISBN: 1979664234
ISBN 13: 9781979664233

For Charlie Gerhardt, Alfred and Marie Chalk

ACKNOWLEDGMENTS

I must thank Mary Lou Smith for helping me get access to the scene of the crime and Judy Omar and Susan Hawkins for their encouragement and editing skills.

Also my critique group: Chris Rogers, John Oehler, and Chuck Brownman for their never ending help and encouragement.

March 10th

Firecrackers shoot skyward. A few pop quickly with an irritating bang while others snake their way into the dark before exploding with a soft whoosh of shimmering iridescence.

An onslaught of cordite-filled smoke reaches a lone woman poised on one of several balconies strung high outside the tenth level of Houston's Reliant Stadium. She wears cowboy boots and hat, her wide skirt blowing against her thighs. The Rodeo finished its evening performance a little more than thirty minutes ago and crowds are still streaming out onto the grounds, necks straining upward towards the fiery display overhead, small children in hand or asleep on their parents' shoulders. The young woman watches carelessly, finishes her cigarette and grinds it into the concrete floor with the toe of her cowboy boot. A slow-turning Ferris Wheel catches her eye, its seats swaying, empty of passengers. She thinks there is nothing as forlorn as an empty carnival ride. Unless it's a woman scorned. Her vision blurs and she burns with outrage at what his cowardice had done to her.

Several months ago, still shaky from her visit to the clinic, she submerged herself in a steaming bathtub. Trails of blood spiraling from between her legs turned the bathwater the color of coppery ink. This reminder of her loss brought renewed self-loathing. But it hadn't been all up to her. He shared the blame. Weeks of tortured guilt had consumed her. Failing to shake off her gloom, she figured if she had only used her razor under that hot bloody bath water, she wouldn't have felt a thing. But she hadn't done it then, and she wouldn't do it now. *He* should pay. He should pay with his life. Not her.

A familiar ache reverberates inside her head. Those below are rushing home while she is consumed, not with energy, but with the powerlessness of seething hurt and anger.

The fireworks stop and the sky darkens to a murky purple. She sways slightly, clinging to the balcony railing, and feels again a churning despair that has nothing to do with her visit to the doctor.

She should leave, join the crowd. Instead, she remains, gazing across the parking lot. For a moment she sees herself as a child, her head heavy against her father's shoulder as he marches her away from a day at the rodeo, her sleepy self dreaming of horses on the long drive home.

Soft air brushes her cheek and her reminiscing stops as she shivers in the cooling night, a renewed determination infiltrating her mind. She will do what has to be done. She won't tell him why yet. Not until he's arrested, maybe even behind bars, and she can watch his expression as it dawns on him why she ratted him out.

And then, as if mere thoughts could create reality, he's behind her. A familiar smell of tobacco and citrus envelopes her as he leans close. And with his smell, her body responds, not with the hatred she expects, but with longing. Anticipation even. With his warm breath against the back of her neck, she feels her heart thumping while his knuckles softly caress the curve above her collarbone. Her body awakens with a desperate, flooding heat and she hates him for this but hates herself even more. He murmurs he's missed her.

He reaches under her arm and gropes for the snaps on her shirt, chuckling as he finds and gently rubs the tip of her breast until her nipple hardens. She shivers again and neither of them speaks.

Then she groans, "No," but he only shushes her softly, as he would a child who really doesn't mean what she says. And he's right. She doesn't. With his head against her cheek, he pulls her hair away from her ear and begins to lick her earlobe. With every stroke, her green cactus earring sways, its cold beads dancing against her neck. Her heart hammers and she starts to lean into him when he catches her around her waist, twists her to face him and sets her up on the balcony railing, his motion as smooth as a dance partner executing a well-practiced move.

She glances over his shoulder while lights from the corridor dim. The balcony sprouts shadows. Seeking equilibrium, she places her hands on his shoulders.

He drops to his knees, bunching her wide skirt up toward her waist and lowers his head. She moans, leans forward. Raking her nails through his hair, she shudders as tremors work themselves through her body. Instead of shoving him away, she sighs, her hair falling around her cheeks.

She hears a distant shout.

"What the hell?"

He pulls away quickly, abandoning her to an aching desire. Instinctively, she grabs the railing to steady herself. Her mind begs please don't leave, but he is already gone. For a few seconds she's blinded by longing, and from somewhere in front of her, hears him yell, "Stop!"

Hands slam into her shoulders and suddenly she's plunging through the air, distant screams trailing her descent. One part of her mind asks who's screaming while the other part says to shut up and try to keep your skirt down.

1

My brother, Robby, was crouched on the roof of his boarding house, threatening suicide. The hysteria in his landlady's voice traveled straight into my Bluetooth and I almost ran off the road.

"Get over here. Now." Mrs. Cathcart said. "He's going to jump, dear God. I just know it, Ms. Faulkner!"

Why now, little brother? Why now when I'm hurrying to the most important meeting of my career?

Her screams hot-wired every nerve in my body. Turning the wheel of my Civic toward the curb, horns honking all around me, I glanced in the rear view mirror and saw a truck, wheels big enough to house a family of four. Its driver shot me the finger. Another life-threatening traffic blitz in Houston, Texas.

I screeched to a stop, engine running. The last time Robby had threatened suicide, I dropped everything, drove like a maniac, heart racing, to talk him down off the roof. Promised him this time his life would turn around and everything would be better. I needed his help, I'd said, but I couldn't have him work for me when he continually wove a cocoon around himself, wrapping his crazy demons in layers of mental gauze until he succumbed to voices inside his head, convinced I was his biggest enemy.

1

Whenever I failed to notice Robby was off his meds and intervene, his hysteria would churn itself into a marathon of scribbling on paper 24/7 until exhaustion brought on suicidal drama. This was neither the first nor would it likely be the last time Robby climbed to the roof, scaring his landlady, Mrs. Cathcart, half to death. Sometimes I wanted to kill him myself.

Picturing the roof of Robby's boarding house, flat and surfaced in small pebbles, I reasoned it couldn't be more than twelve feet off the ground. He could break his neck, but it was more likely to be an arm or a leg. And, he'd never actually jumped before. Calling 9-1-1 was not the optimum solution right now, but it was my only one, even if it meant emergency medics would restrain Robby and rush him to the mental ward. He hated that, but the hospital would insure he took his meds. Also, I reminded myself as I swung my car back into traffic, downtown Houston Police headquarters was only minutes away. Emergency personnel would arrive at Robby's far quicker than I could. And, being late for my appointment with ex-boss and current adversary, Captain Lamar Hightower, was not an option.

Pressing the accelerator, Bluetooth stuck firmly in my ear, I shot into speeding traffic, yelling at Robby's landlady. "Hang up and call 9-1-1." I disconnected, realizing that Robby's constant breakdowns had unwillingly taught me to disassociate myself, to mentally shelve his chaos and craziness. At least for a couple of hours. This ability allowed me to reason that both Robby and I would benefit from my new case, and the upcoming meeting with Lamar could make it or break it. The captain wasn't the type to give me a second chance to look over his files.

I turned onto Memorial Drive and headed downtown. Up ahead, heat rose and shimmered above the pavement, pulsing diabolically, or so it seemed. Ninety-five degree heat, coupled with ninety percent humidity in mid-September, had tempers shredded to the bone. While a car screeched past on my left, the memory of Mrs. Cathcart's hysteria echoed in my ear. All of Houston felt off-kilter.

Nearing police headquarters, I searched for curb parking before pulling into the lot across the street. Reaching underneath the driver's seat, I checked the lock on my storage box where I stashed my scandium revolver. Whenever I needed my tiny, 12 oz. gun, it rode inside my pocket with no hint of a bulge. Its kick was brutal, but other than that, it suited me perfectly. Satisfied the weapon was secure, I locked the doors and handed the parking attendant my ignition key and six bucks.

Smiling and nodding at whatever the parking attendant said to me over the noise of jackhammers, I turned away to cross the street, eyes tearing against strong winds whipping dust in my face. Downtown had been under construction so long, it wouldn't be Houston without it.

A woman with orange hair and a pained expression sat behind the reception desk. After glancing at my ID, she photocopied it before picking up the phone and mumbling my name. I signed the register. This lady wasn't someone I recognized, but then it had been years since I'd worked here.

"Captain Hightower will see you," she said, looking up at me, her tone more fitting for a funeral parlor.

When the elevator stopped at Homicide, I made my way down the hall, heart pounding, toward Lamar's office. After making captain, he'd moved to a spacious corner spot with a view from his wraparound windows of an ugly building's brick façade. I couldn't help feeling it was more than he deserved.

His secretary, Angie, wasn't at her desk. I knocked on the captain's closed door, determined to keep this meeting short.

"Come in."

I couldn't tell if his voice sounded friendly or not. Stepping quickly inside, I closed the door behind me. He continued to write, head down as he waved a finger in the air for me to sit across from him. I obeyed.

His office still smelled musty, attributable, I'd always thought, to the moose head mounted on his wall. The guys used to hang string bikini underwear on its antlers when they'd wrapped up a case. Nothing hung there now.

Lamar continued to write. His "I'm ignoring you" tactic was typical when confronted with a suspect, but I wasn't used to being treated like a suspect.

When he finally glanced up, it was obvious from his crooked smirk that I wasn't the only one wanting to get this meeting over with.

"Seems as if your client and our chief are kissin' cousins. Congratulations. You've moved into the big league."

I refused to rise to his bait and kept silent.

"The chief wants me to open the Callahan files for your scrutiny. I agreed, but you may not copy them or take anything with you."

After four years, his pale hair was thinner on top and his jowls looser. He sounded tired. When working with him, I'd grudgingly admired Lamar's dedication and bull-headedness, just not when the latter was turned against me. It was true I'd wanted a quick meeting, but not one with a cloud of animosity floating between us.

"I really appreciate this—"

"I thought I'd seen the last of you." Lamar looked up quickly, eyes narrowed, before fixing his gaze somewhere over my shoulder.

All my conciliatory feelings fled, and with as much sarcasm as possible, I drawled, "Aren't *you* the lucky one," and waited for his reaction.

The captain and I went back a long way. The path we'd forged was at times smooth but had ended on the rocky side of a figurative cliff. I jumped off and apparently he'd never forgiven me. Even though I'd make the same decision today, the more forgiving side of me regretted parting on a less than amicable note. Especially now that I needed something from him.

He ignored my sarcasm and shoved several thick manila folders across his desk.

"I don't have a choice about turning over these files and you know it." Leaning forward, still smirking, he said, "You *appear* sane enough to understand this case."

His use of the word "sane" set my teeth on edge. My spine grew stiff as concrete.

Before I could snap back, he added, "Guess you haven't caught your brother's craziness . . . yet." He grinned. "You had me worried there for awhile."

"Thanks. I must say I've missed your insults." After leaving the police force, I dreamed for years Lamar was screaming threats at me, eyes bulging as he brandished his .38.

Without acknowledging my comment, he assumed his lecturing tone.

"Boots Callahan has everything all wrong, you know. His sister was despondent. She had gambling debts she couldn't pay. She was in constant pain from a fall off her horse years before." He leaned back, his hands cradling the back of his head. "LeeAnn Callahan was a nut case. She killed herself, pure and simple."

When he'd called me, my client, Boots Callahan, had expressed great love for his younger sister. We both shared a deep devotion for our siblings. LeeAnn had died when she was only twenty-four. Robby was twenty-eight, seven years my junior. He was my only family. Being responsible for him could drag me down at times, but if he ever succeeded in killing himself, I'd never be the same.

I must have paused too long, for Lamar piped up, "You of all people should recognize nut cases, now wouldn't you agree?"

Determined to sound cool and unperturbed, I took a deep breath, settled back and asked, "Is that what I'll find in these files? Proof of what you say about LeeAnn?"

His desk phone rang. Instead of answering me, he lifted the receiver. Suddenly he stood, yelling invectives while red splotches of anger spread across his face. I instinctively shrank, glad I wasn't the one on the other end of his conversation.

"You stay right there!" he said, and slammed the receiver. Turning toward me, his tone was clipped. "Take a look at the files. It's all pretty straightforward stuff. And," he added as he strode to the door, "I don't want any more publicity on that case and neither do I want

Boots Callahan hounding me. You'll come to the same conclusion we did—Miss Callahan's death was a suicide."

Maybe so and maybe no. His and Boots' versions of LeeAnn's mental state were diametrically opposed. One of them was wrong. Then again, was I willing to bet against Lamar?

For a little over four years I'd worked well and hard for the captain and never given him reason to doubt my abilities as an officer of the law. Then he'd ordered me off a hit and run investigation, claiming I was "too emotionally involved". When, unbeknownst to him, I persisted on the case and not only found the man responsible, but arrested him, Lamar wrote me up, demanding I see the cop shrink, take a leave of absence. Instead, I turned in my resignation. He was furious. But in my mind, I was already gone, my investigator's license squirreled away, myself transported to a place where I answered only to myself and my future clients.

But Lamar was a great detective and more often than not, dogged to the point of obsession. He could easily be right about LeeAnn committing suicide. How could Boots be so positive his sister had been shoved off the balcony following a Houston Rodeo skybox party last March? I was happy to have the retainer he'd mailed me, but his instincts about LeeAnn's blissful state of mind could prove wishful thinking. Anxious over what was in Lamar's files, I dreaded discovering hard evidence proving LeeAnn's suicide, and the ensuing moral obligation to return 99.9% of Boots' advance.

Scooting closer to his desk, I began pulling file papers, organizing them into piles. I flipped through a stack of testimonies. There were two witnesses, Brad Ewer and J.D. McGraw, both bigwigs in Houston Livestock Show and Rodeo. Also, a woman named Mary Nelson gave a short statement. She was at the party, but late to leave the stadium. LeeAnn's falling body barely missed hitting Mary as she'd walked along the sidewalk underneath the outdoor smoking balcony. After reading statements from Reliant Stadium security personnel, I put everything aside and opened a large white envelope labeled "medical examiner". Inside were scribbled notes and photos.

Making room on the desktop, I dealt out the pictures, left to right across the surface. First on my left was a picture of LeeAnn's body sprawled on the ground. Her head lay at a sharp angle against the concrete sidewalk. Her wide cowgirl skirt spread outward like a fan. One hundred feet head first was not a pretty sight.

I picked up the next photograph, steeling myself for another grue-some picture. The young woman's naked body lay on a stainless table that sloped slightly, indented along the edges to collect body fluids. Even in death the photo affirmed she'd been what my brother called "a hottie". But only from the neck down. I cringed at the misshapen skull, eyes blank and sightless as a doll's. In subsequent photos her eyes were mercifully closed.

After stacking the pictures, I shoved them back inside the enve-lope. Desperate for a living image of LeeAnn, I reached inside my briefcase for the photograph Boots had included along with his re-tainer. The scribbled date on the back was only a few months before the young woman's death.

She stood in a field beside her horse, a big grin on her face. Her blond hair was swept to the side in a thick ponytail. Healthy and fit, LeeAnn wore jeans that strained against her lean, muscular thighs. One gloved hand gripped the reins of her black horse while her oth-er hand rested on the animal's muzzle. As if in a pose of solidarity, LeeAnn's face leaned toward the horse's head. In the background, a rustic barn stood, its once red siding faded to watery rust.

So why had Lamar believed the two male witnesses? One of them could have had a reason to shove LeeAnn over and the other witness could serve as a cover-up.

Replacing the picture, I wondered if Angie, the captain's secre-tary, had returned to her desk. If not, I could sneak these folders to the copy machine a few doors down. No one would be the wiser.

Sticking my head out Lamar's office door, I peered left. No Angie. Someone walked toward me from the end of the hall on my right, but veered into an office without seeing me. I quickly pulled open the door, folders bulging inside my briefcase, and scurried toward the

Xerox room, repeating my surreptitious peek through a crack in the copy room door. It was empty.

Pulse racing, I hurried inside, flipped on the switch and listened to the copier whine as its ready light turned green.

Ten minutes later, I was almost finished when I heard the door open behind me. I turned just as someone spoke.

"What the hell you doing?"

2

A stranger stood eyeing me, arms crossed, deep frown lines etched in his forehead. He wore a uniform complete with Smith & Wesson holstered on his belt. He looked ready to use it. Or was I being paranoid?

"Hello," I said, pointing my finger up as if to say he should hold on a minute. Turning my back, I stuffed Lamar's files inside my briefcase before hiking its strap over my shoulder. When I turned around, his frown had deepened.

"Just copying something for Angie," I said, showing my dimples as I waved Lamar's file copies in the air for proof.

"Who're you?" His large frame blocked the doorway.

I'd never met this man and that was a good thing. He didn't know me either. "Just a temp helping Angie out."

"Why haven't I seen you before?"

"Why haven't I seen you?" I challenged him, knowing he could puncture my bravado at any minute.

Not waiting for an answer, I blurted, "I'm just kidding. I haven't been here before. The agency said to come in and finish some copying Angie had on her desk." Approaching him, trying for a confident swagger, I flicked my hand full of now-folded file copies for him to move away from the door. For a second or two, I wasn't sure he would. Holding my breath, I looked him in the eye. A beat passed. "I really need to get going," I said, and took a step toward him, praying he would step aside.

He hesitated a second while a tic throbbed against my neck, my expression and body language frozen into a pleasant, but hopefully determined, stance.

He took a step back. "What's your name?"

"Roberta." I strode past him into the hallway where I almost collided with Angie. She started to speak, but I grabbed her elbow and hurried her toward her desk.

"There you are," I almost shouted. "I have your copying done."

She looked startled. I shot her a don't-ask-questions look, turned with my hand still on her elbow and spoke back to the uniform standing in the doorway. "See ya."

"Yeah," he called out before walking away toward the bank of elevators. "See ya, Roberta."

Angie pulled away from me and dropped her lunch sack and can of Diet Coke on her desktop. "Roberta? What have you been up to, Giles? What copying?" She stared hard at the bundle of papers in my left hand.

A thought flashed that perhaps, after my four-year absence, Angie and I were no longer friends.

"Sorry. I was leaving Lamar's office and, uh, wanted to straighten out my bra strap. It was twisted and digging into my shoulder."

Angie narrowed her eyes, doubt swimming in them like a parent staring down a child who'd told a whopping lie.

"Really," she drawled. "Want to show me those papers in your hand?"

"Oh, gosh," I glanced at my watch. "Gotta run," I said. "Crap!" I snapped my fingers. "Forgot I need to drop something on Lamar's desk." If the captain returned and noticed the Callahan files were missing, he'd no doubt put out an all-points bulletin for my arrest.

Hurrying inside his office, I jerked out the file folders, flopped them down on the desktop and turned to see Angie leaning against the doorjamb, wearing a look of disbelief. "And I'm supposed to keep my mouth shut, right?"

"I was hoping you would. For old time's sake?" I had once rescued Angie from a drunk, obnoxious man at a bar we frequented on many a Friday night. As a result, I'd worn a cast on my wrist, stuck doing desk duty for what had seemed forever. Surely Angie hadn't forgotten.

She shook her head, her expression one of strained patience. "Get out of here before Lamar returns."

Needing no further encouragement, I practically ran down the hall toward the elevators.

"Thanks," I yelled back. "Tell the captain I appreciate his seeing me."

It was after one o'clock. Past lunchtime. As I stood at the bank of elevators, my stomach devouring itself in noisy growls, I felt a tap on my shoulder. I froze and reluctantly turned my head. A large female officer loomed behind me. Her skin was the color of tarnished copper and her dark hair grew wild as prickly pear cactus on top of her head. She wore a puzzled expression. "You Giles Faulkner?"

Wondering if Lamar had sent her, I nodded.

She stuck out her hand. Her smile was infectious. "I'm Sergeant Irma Doyle. Nice to meet you."

"Likewise," I said, grinning in spite of myself. The elevator dinged and I walked inside its open door.

"I'm going down, too," she said, as if marveling at the coincidence.

Irma stood half a foot taller than I. She scratched her head and a chipped nail disappeared into her stiff hair. "Actually, I heard you're looking into the Callahan suicide."

"Where'd you hear that?"

"I grew up in Beaumont. Boots' hometown. Small place compared to Houston."

When she cocked one eyebrow, she seemed to be asking me if I agreed.

Since she hadn't answered my own question, I remained silent. Reaching in her pocket, she shoved her card at me. I took it just as the elevator stopped and the doors opened on the third floor. Before exiting, Irma turned to me, brown eyes merry with her own private joke.

"I've known Boots nearly all my life. His sister was younger so I didn't know her as well." The doors closed between us, leaving behind a faint smell of gardenias and sweat.

I glanced at Irma's business card before dropping it inside my briefcase. She might prove an excellent contact.

Outside the building, jackhammers overpowered the usual city noise of speeding cars and honking horns. Gray clouds shrouded the mid-day sun and the scalding humidity threatened to melt my skin.

I hurried to the parking lot, sweat popping from every pore, and retrieved my keys from the attendant. Once settled in the driver's seat, I started the engine and switched the air conditioner on high, shoving my face closer to the dashboard's air vent. With my cheeks slightly cooler, I began to back up but a man clad in black leather astride a shiny black motorcycle loomed in my rear-view mirror, blocking my exit. The Terminator came to mind.

Below his half-helmet, his mouth stretched into a broad grin. He gunned the motor, a louder roar than the city construction provided.

I rolled down my window and shouted, "You gonna sit there or move?"

Houston was full of macho motorcyclists. When he didn't react, I began to back out slowly, playing "chicken" with this thug. Who would give first? His cycle looked shiny and well cared for. He wouldn't want it scratched.

As my bumper approached his cycle, the rider's grin remained plastered to his face, even as the distance between us shrank to the width of gauze. I was just thinking my revolver was a mere arm's length away when, with a final machismo revving of his motor, he tossed his head back, mouth open as if he were laughing, and roared off. Some people were easily entertained.

While headed to the nearest Wendy's, an image of my little brother being manhandled by Emergency refused to leave my brain. The
takeout line was four cars deep—too much time to imagine Robby's
panic over sirens approaching, his struggle against restraints he
would never get used to. Pulling out my cell, I pressed the speed dial
for Mrs. Cathcart. While it rang, my imagination bloomed with buried fears. Was Hightower right about me? Was I as crazy as my brother? Or merely a ticking time bomb, ready to explode in a matter of
weeks, days, years? Not that hard to imagine. Some long-dormant
crazy gene could suddenly jolt into overdrive and shove me headlong
into Robby's world. Then who would take care of my baby brother?

Mrs. Cathcart interrupted my paranoia with a cheery hello.

"This is Giles. Was Robby taken to the hospital?"

"Oh, my. You wouldn't believe it. Mr. Cathcart came outside, talked real sensible to your brother, and lo and behold, he walked right
down the ladder Mr. Cathcart done brought for him and back into
his room. Robby fell asleep on top of his covers."

"You sure?" Her husband was an ever present lump in front of the
television. I didn't remember him moving, much less uttering a word.
Ever.

"I'll go check again, if'n it makes you feel better, dearie, and call
you right back."

"Yes . . . please." Robby threatening suicide had always meant he
suffered from the downside of a manic/depressive episode. I'd never
known him to come out of this state and calmly go to sleep.

A minute later Mrs. Cathcart rang back. I answered while moving
two cars closer to Wendy's outdoor speaker box.

"Snorin' like a lamb, sugar."

Thoroughly stumped, I decided to take this at face value and not
rush into an emergency rescue. Sleep was good for Robby since he
got so little of it. Long ago, he'd been diagnosed with bipolar disor-
der and paranoia. But his teenage years brought a new affliction—
a syndrome called the "Midnight Disease". Victims spend days and
nights scribbling non-stop—a condition I'd long ago categorized as

preferable to his other afflictions. The Midnight Disease was layman's term for something not all that uncommon-*hypergraphia*. Dostoyevsky suffered from it, as did other well-known authors. But in Robby's case, it resulted more often in scribbling nonsense than literary prose. His true talent was painting. Occasionally, I was able to rescue a canvas before he destroyed it.

Such mania didn't allow for sleep, and the more Robby ignored his meds, the more often he succumbed to this exhausting routine.

Muttering thanks to Mrs. Cathcart, I disconnected. Relief swelled my chest and I took a deep breath. The fact that Robby was actually asleep was a stroke of good luck. And, if my luck held, Lamar was back in his office by now, had solved his crisis, shoved the Callahan files away, and would be in a better mood to answer a question.

After shouting my order for chili into the squawk box, I rolled into second place in line. The smell of burgers frying on a griddle wafted inside my open window. Lightheaded with hunger, I dialed Lamar, and Angie answered.

"It's Giles," I said. "Is he back?"

"He's back, all right," Angie said, "but his mood's scraping fingernails against a chalkboard."

Crap. "Will he talk to me?"

"You're either very brave or very stupid," Angie said. I heard her buzz Lamar and tell him I was on line one.

"What now?" he boomed. "You've read the files. Everything's there."

I secured the Bluetooth, then placed both hands on the wheel while I sat, car engine idling. "Yeah, I read them. But I have no clue why you believed those witnesses. One or both of them could have pushed her off the ledge."

"Yeah, right. And as soon as you come up with a motive, I'll listen. Until then, the fact she tried to kill herself when she was eighteen, the fact she'd been in therapy for depression, the fact she'd told her best friend she was going to "end it all,"—all of the aforementioned point to a woman determined to do herself in. And those witnesses you read about are successful men, deacons in their church, who both happen to lead the kind of exemplary life you and I would envy. But, hey, go talk to 'em. Earn your money before you throw in the towel." He hung up.

Double crap. Since when did Lamar believe that leading an "exemplary" life meant you couldn't murder someone then go back to sanctimony? And where was the contact information on her shrink or her best friend? Not in the files I saw.

Snarling to myself, I coasted to the pickup window. I didn't feel like waiting for the captain to enter the human race and make access to suspects any easier for me. Headquarters for Brad Ewer's company, Hammerly Insurance, was only a couple of blocks away. I could down my cup of chili on the way. Somehow a nice, hot cup of chili had a way of cooling me off. Maybe it was a born-in-Texas thing.

Ewer's office was on the 71st floor of Chase Tower. at 75 stories. It was the tallest building in downtown Houston. Feeling lucky I'd found street parking only half a block away, I felt my ears close, then finally pop, as the tower elevator neared the 71st floor.

Heights don't agree with me. In my previous life as a cop, while in this same tower in an office only one floor lower than Ewer's, I'd felt the building sway in the wind, my body tilting like a dashboard figurine in moving traffic. I plunked myself into the nearest chair, prayed I wouldn't vomit, when out the window a Goodyear blimp floated past. At that point, I placed my head between my knees. Two gentlemen undergoing questioning for bookmaking rushed toward me, which, under normal circumstances, would have caused me to reach for my gun. Instead, I asked for a glass of water.

Today was also a gusty day. My stomach dropped when I stepped off the elevator and felt a familiar sway from the building. The entire 71st floor was devoted to Hammerly Insurance, a Texas-headquartered firm with offices strung around the country. A massive reception desk lay ten feet across from the elevator and was curved to match the mahogany paneled wall behind.

A girl seated at the desk drawled good afternoon, her smile exposing impossibly white teeth. As I approached, feet cushioned by pale green carpeting, I noticed large gold lettering on the wall behind the receptionist that spelled out— "Hammerly Insurance & Trust, Texas Owned and Texas Proud." You betcha.

I stopped in front of the desk. "Hello. I'm Giles Faulkner. Captain Lamar Hightower recommended I speak with Brad Ewer. Is he in?"

A slight frown furrowed her young brow. "Do you have an appointment?" The brass nameplate on her desk read "Dana Young".

"No, Dana. But Captain Hightower thought Mr. Ewer should speak with me." I felt my nose growing longer.

She looked down at her open desk calendar. "Mr. Ewer has an appointment in fifteen minutes. I think he's real busy getting ready." She shrugged at me, mock disappointment not convincing enough to hide her smug pleasure over her role as gatekeeper.

Wooden double doors were barely visible in the wall beyond her desk. This young thing would not be Brad Ewer's personal secretary.

"I'll just check with his assistant," I murmured as I hurried past and pushed open the door. Dana was right behind me, voicing her protests.

A smaller version of the receptionist's curved desk sat in front of a panoramic view of downtown Houston. The woman seated behind the desk could be anywhere from her mid-forties to mid-fifties. Smartly dressed, she had strong cheekbones and straight silver hair that curved around a square-jawed, intelligent face. She, too, was frowning at me as Dana began her apologies for the interruption.

"Go back up front, Dana," the woman snapped, "and call Security." There was no nameplate on her desktop.

After Dana closed the door behind her, the silver-haired woman turned to me and stared, her dark eyes boring into mine.

"No need to call Security," I blurted. "Police Captain Lamar Hightower sent me." My palms were sweaty and I tried to look anywhere but out the massive window. As my stomach flipped, I swore the floor took a sharp tilt.

I swallowed, badly in need of a chair, and prayed this woman would order Dana to forego calling Security. Surely I looked like a sane professional, who, thanks to a recent breath mint, no longer smelled of spoonfuls of spicy chili gobbled in the short car ride over here.

"I'm Giles Faulkner," I said, returning her stare, marveling at those unreadable eyes. "I understand Mr. Ewer has an appointment, but I'll only take a minute of his time."

"And this pertains to?"

I was going to respond when a door on my right opened and the man I'd seen only in newspapers entered. "Jan, I thought the num- bers for Amarillo . . . " Brad Ewer's sentence trailed off as he spotted me.

He looked back at Jan and raised his eyebrows.

"Mr. Ewer, this woman just appeared. I have no idea what she wants."

I strode toward him, my hand extended. "I'm Giles Faulkner and promise I'll only take a minute of your time. It's about LeeAnn Callahan's death."

A flash of irritation surfaced then disappeared as he studied my face. He did not shake my hand.

"Hold my calls, Jan, but buzz me in five." He opened his office door and, placing his hand against the small of my back, ushered me inside.

Before Ewer closed his door, I heard his assistant buzz Dana and order her to call off Security. My breathing returned to normal. Sort of.

I stood inside his office. Whatever decorator they used preferred scimitar-shaped desks. Ewer motioned for me to sit opposite his. I did, but again looked out over a vast expanse of nothingness, the sky a sheaf of cloudless pale the color of skim milk. The tops of a few buildings peaked above the windowsills like glass and steel peeping

Toms. I felt anchorless, swallowed hard and tried to focus on Ewer's face.

Unlike women who, at the same age, scrambled for Botox, men such as Ewer grew distinguished gray-tipped sideburns and a few craggy lines that appeared manly rather than aging. Ewer was square as SpongeBob, with a wrestler's neck and a chiseled jaw line. A turquoise-inlaid cow-skull bolo lay snug against the collar of his starched white shirt. He looked ready to direct a meeting of the Houston powerful, particularly those who controlled the Houston Rodeo.

His desktop displayed a black and white of himself with one of the most famous of the previous governors of Texas, arms casually slung around each other's shoulders. No doubt about his political persuasion.

Ewer hitched his cuff, glanced at a micro thin gold watch.

"Thanks for seeing me," I said. "I'm investigating the death of LeeAnn Callahan." I whipped out my PI business card and slid it across his desk. "I understand you were one of the last to see her alive."

"Get to the point, Miss . . . " He glanced at my card.

"Faulkner," I said. "LeeAnn was a guest at your Reliant skybox party the night she died. I was hoping you could give me more details of your friendship with her, also about any other friends she had, a boyfriend perhaps, and if you knew whether she was seeing anyone for her depression?"

He pursed his lips and leaned back in his chair. "Lot of questions to answer in so short a time. You act like a cop. Were you?"

I imagined his mind ticking off the seconds before he would stand and leave.

"How intuitive of you." I tried dazzling him with another smile.

"You didn't like being a cop? They discriminate over there at HPD?" His lopsided grin was charming, but the undertone was too silky, too oily for comfort. I half expected him to uncoil and strike. He was not succumbing to my charms.

"Yes," I said quickly. "I liked the force, but I like being my own boss better." My tone suggested I was through with that topic. "I'm here to find out how well you knew LeeAnn Callahan."

Ewer glanced away, his mouth pursed as if deep in thought. "We both attended'Lakewood Church. And years before, she was on the Rodeo's 'Horse-pitality Committee' that I chaired. Charming young lady." His eyes, now back on mine, grew wide as if to emphasize he had nothing to hide. "I can't recall the name of a boyfriend or any of her lady friends. Sorry." He spread his mouth, lips closed, and again glanced at his watch.

I wasn't impressed with his mention of Lakewood—Pastor Joel Osteen's mega church. It boasted over 40,000 weekly worshipers, not counting the millions who watched via TV satellite. Hardly a chummy place where you were on intimate terms with the other members. Neither did I buy his lack of knowledge about LeeAnn's boyfriend. "And yet you told the police she discussed her personal life with you the night she died."

Without warning, he was up, circling his desk. He took my forearm and led me to his office door, his other meaty hand hard against the small of my back. "It's all in the police records. Whatever I knew about her death is there. Nothing else to tell." He must have signaled Jan because she was as smooth as her boss.

She gripped my elbow and led me out, past the reception desk and a smug Dana, and then to the bank of elevators. As she grimly punched the down button, I pulled away, suddenly remembering Ewer's testimony from the police files. It was Brad Ewer's secretary who'd taken ill and asked if Mary Nelson, the woman who'd barely missed being hit by LeeAnn's falling body, could take her place on the guest list at the rodeo party that night.

"Mary Nelson is a good friend of yours, I understand."

Her look was at first puzzled and then leery.

"Never heard of her," she said as the elevator arrived and the doors opened. With one foot, she stepped inside and punched the down button, her other hand now back on my arm. "You know how to transfer elevators, I assume." She released my arm, stepped back into the hall and stood watch as the elevator doors closed, her expression pleased as someone who'd just squashed a large cockroach.

3

I braced myself for the plunge to the 35th floor where I'd exit and take a different elevator to the lobby. I'd learned nothing from Ewer except he'd been anxious to get rid of me, while disclaiming he'd been close to LeeAnn. That in itself could be construed as information.

Even more interesting was Jan's reaction when I asked about Mary Nelson. I would swear she told the truth. But how could she not know Mary Nelson if she'd asked her to attend Ewer's party in her place?

Seconds after I turned my ignition key, a thunderbolt cracked, sending tremors through the Civic. Fat raindrops splattered the windshield. Pulling away from the curb, I switched on the radio weather channel and listened to a drone of forecasts. Last night's news had warned of a hurricane building in the Gulf, with no information about where or when it would strike. Within minutes, I grew satisfied that the storm remained perched miles away and had a fifty-fifty chance of fizzling. Nevertheless, in frequent downpours, Houston's poor drainage could swell the streets within minutes. I didn't want my car engine flooded. Picking up speed, I figured I'd be home in fifteen minutes if traffic wasn't heavy. But when wasn't traffic heavy in downtown Houston?

Within a few blocks, gray clouds overhead had turned an ugly black. As I switched the headlights on high, dual worries swept over me. My crazy brother, Robby, and the dread of a hurricane. I'd seen many images of hurricanes on television. You can't live near the Gulf Coast without intimate knowledge of a storm's malevolent eye, pointed out, just in case you missed it, by your local weatherman. Glowing neon on your television screen and surrounded by swirling clouds, a hurricane works itself into a fury as it moves across warm, open waters.

It occurred to me that Robby and I were a lot like a circling storm. He danced in my periphery, avoiding his big sister. I moved closer, wanting to protect him from himself. Neither of us wanted to hit land.

Suddenly the sky opened, gushing streams of water. People out on the street ran, holding objects over their heads as they dashed for cover. Even though I was snug inside, the jitters had hold of me.

My cell rang; caller ID registered Mrs. Cathcart. Her reedy voice was high with stress or excitement; it was hard to tell as she spoke my name.

"What is it?" I shouted over the sound of rain drumming against the roof of my car. "Is Robby okay?"

"Jes' remembered he picked a flower for you. Showed it to me after he come down off the roof. Thought you ought a know. I'll keep it for you, sweetie."

The woman was a saint to allow Robby in her boarding house, but sometimes I suspected she relished the drama of boarding a one-man psych ward.

"Has he eaten?" If Robby was hungry, he wasn't off his meds. At least not for long.

"Well, he did eat breakfast, but he's still asleep."

Breakfast was good enough for me. When I told his landlady I'd check on Robby later, before I went to bed that evening, her subsequent goodbye sounded disappointed. I snapped the lid on my cell phone and concentrated on the traffic. Fifteen minutes later, I pulled into the circular drive of my building.

With my brother back on my mind, I rode the elevator up to my apartment. Robby could have flushed his daily meds down the toilet.

His suicide attempt could point to that. Which meant he'd soon start to break apart—quit eating, quit sleeping, and either begin scribbling or again threaten suicide. Voices in his head would take over, followed by ranting, then aggressive behavior.

One sign of impending doom could be the walls of his room. Last week they'd been covered with neon pink, lime-green and yellow Post-It notes, their bright squares splattered with illegible ink scribbling, their loose ends dancing in the warm breeze from his open window. I'd never seen him do that before. But then, he'd never pleasantly come down off the roof before and headed to his room to sleep.

Yet Robby had eaten breakfast, proving he had an appetite. If he also ate after awaking, I could pronounce him okay for the time being. For the second time that day, I forced my thoughts away from my brother. I had a case to solve. Besides, Mrs. Cathcart would call immediately if Robby refused to eat, her voice filled with drama worthy of a Shakespearian tragedy.

When the elevator stopped three floors from mine and took on an elegant couple I vaguely recognized, my distracted "hello" was barely acknowledged. They carried on a soft conversation while the woman's Joy perfume wafted through the enclosed space. My aunt Eunice had worn Joy, even on her death bed. The rich do smell different. They exited at the next floor, the smell of perfume lost with the closing elevator door.

I got off on the 14th floor, the top floor. This high-rise apartment building on Kirby Drive was definitely out of my league. All were spacious and split level. Building staff parked your car, delivered your groceries, arranged your pet's day at the pet spa, and protected you from anyone who otherwise might intrude on your cushioned and well-insulated life. I hadn't picked it or purchased it. After Aunt Eunice died, I discovered she had willed it to me.

My aunt led what could only be described as a pampered life, and by the time she grew ill, she had only a fraction of her fortune left with which to pay the enormous monthly condo fees. Fellow owners included the mayor, an ex-Enron executive, several ex-wives of oil magnates and an abundance of society women who wouldn't have life any other way. I never could decide whether I was envious, scornful, or indifferent.

Although it had been seven months since I'd moved here from a shabby rental house, I still felt uncomfortable--like I'd stumbled into the wrong movie set. I didn't belong here.

Inside my apartment, I shed my jacket, bounded up the stairs and changed into a T-shirt and pull-on pants. Why didn't I immediately put this pricey beauty on the market, pocket the proceeds and take a long-needed vacation? Reason one—I had a weakness for fully equipped exercise rooms and indoor pools. Reason two—my aunt left her cat, almost as elderly as herself, to my care, and was adamant that I live here, with her cat, at least until the cat died. Cats were high on my list of allergies, but Suzy was a sweetheart so I took lots of antihistamines. Feeling trapped since my aunt's bequeathal, I never added Robby to the list of reasons why a vacation was not in my future.

Suzy pounced from nowhere and, with a piercing howl, wrapped herself around my ankle. She was a rare and costly purebred Siamese with startling blue eyes. I picked her up and headed downstairs, happy to hear her purring.

With painful arthritis, my aunt wasn't able to climb these circular stairs to the master bedroom and used instead the small downstairs guest room, now my study. The walls were painted the color of boiled cabbage. Her furniture was all in the King Louis-something style— gold and beige, rounded and puffed as starched petticoats.

Our family came from good German-Irish stock, middling-income ancestry at best. But Aunt Eunice had been an extremely attractive woman and used it to her advantage. She'd buried three husbands, all oil-rich. And she'd adored me, swearing I looked more like her than my own mother. Our mutual Irish genes were strong, but I secretly disagreed with her. My face lacked the symmetry of my aunt's or the stunning contrast of bright green eyes, pale skin and the blackest of hair belonging to my mother.

Before she grew sick with cancer, my mother was even more beautiful than my aunt. I didn't think I was ugly, but my mantra had always been intelligence counted for more than beauty.

My biggest problem with my aunt was the inheritance she'd left me. It was supposed to pay the fees and the taxes on this apartment as well as support Robby. After less than a year, the money was dwindling fast.

I hurried into the kitchen, plopping Suzy on the floor. She immediately ran to the refrigerator and began another terrifying cry. I stepped around her and opened the fridge. "Just a sec, Suz. Food's coming."

After dropping small pieces of chopped liver into the cat bowl—another of my aunt's requirements—I washed my hands, grabbed a piece of bologna with a slice of Swiss cheese, rolled them together and ate hungrily.

I was glad my lady-like Aunt Eunice couldn't see me wolfing down such a delicacy while standing at her kitchen sink. After two of these breadless sandwiches, I opened the freezer and took out a Snickers bar, chopped it in two, and returned half to the freezer, popping the other half in my mouth while walking into my study.

Seated at my computer desk, soothed by the sound of rain hitting the roof, I took a minute to think before committing anything to paper. Although Boots' suspicions might not require a lengthy investigation, his problem at least involved a dead body instead of a cheating spouse or insurance fraud perpetrators. LeeAnn's death could easily turn out to be suicide. I could prove or disprove she'd been abused by a boyfriend, which was Boots' theory, but I doubted I could prove she'd been driven to suicide because of abuse, at least not beyond a reasonable doubt. Boots wanted someone to blame, someone behind bars. He might not get what he wanted. I began entering a list of questions.

Two hours later, the rain had stopped. I stood and stretched. Outside the study's glass patio doors, a wrap-around balcony overlooked Houston's downtown skyline. I never stepped outside. Perhaps if Aunt Eunice's apartment had been on the first or second floor, instead of the top one, I could enjoy being out on the balcony.

Thirst drove me to the kitchen for a glass of water. The phone's message light blinked red. Surprised I hadn't noticed it before, I pressed the button. My sudden sneezing jag kept me from hearing. Fumbling for antihistamines inside a kitchen drawer, I gulped two pills, then hit the replay button.

It was Robby. "You forgot your flower. I picked one for you and you forgot it. Are you mad at me?" He breathed into the receiver before screaming, "Bitch!" and clicked off.

My skin broke out in a cold sweat. With deliberate calm, I hung up the phone and forced myself to head upstairs for a cold shower. Obviously my brother was awake.

Clear your head, Giles, untangle the brain cells. Give Robby time to forget. Frequently, his meds caused amnesia and he simply forgot any recent tirades. Besides, I reasoned, he was safe at Mrs. Cathcart's.

Thirty minutes later, refreshed from my shower and re-energized over Boots' case, I returned to my study and logged onto a search engine. Who was LeeAnn Callahan besides a much-loved little sister? Scrolling over death notices as well as articles about her suicide, I finally spotted an article in the Beaumont newspaper that shed light on Boots' grief.

When she was only fourteen, LeeAnn had been the youngest female to win the teen-level state barrel-racing championship. As a high school junior, her dazzling smile as queen of the Neches River Festival was hard to miss, even on my ancient computer monitor. But the most telling was an article about LeeAnn's instigation, at age eighteen, of a nonprofit group whose mission was to help handicapped youngsters learn confidence, and hopefully a few skills, from riding horses.

I scrolled through photographs of smiling children, some with leg braces, pale and thin, wearing helmets astride horses, their reins held by strapping teenagers who wore clown outfits, fireman's caps, Batman masks and Spiderman capes. I swallowed hard.

Whoops! My finger had almost hit the close button when something caught my eye. It was a photo of LeeAnn and her parents standing beside her uncle, Ramsey Tilman, arms around each other at his campaign headquarters after he'd won his second term as congressman to the Texas State House of Representatives.

Ramsey Tilman headed the powerful state insurance committee. Why wasn't Boots in that photograph?

I organized and entered case notes for another hour. After printing them out, I shut down the computer and shoved my findings inside the desk drawer. It was late evening, but I dialed Robby's rooming house anyway. His rent, paid by yours truly via Aunt Eunice, was high enough to include my right to call any time, day or night. Besides, lots of folks were up at 10:00 p.m. Mrs. Cathcart answered, sounding tired, but dutifully agreed to check on Robby. When she returned, she told me he'd eaten the tray of food outside his door and was again asleep on top of his covers, fully clothed.

I thanked her, hung up, and realized I'd been holding my breath. But if Robby were manic, he wouldn't be asleep. If he were depressive, he'd be on the roof again.

I'd go for a late-night swim before bed, hoping to be too tired to dream of a young woman with a big heart shoved from a balcony a hundred feet off the ground, and landing with her head splattered like a watermelon over the sidewalk.

4

*F*lowers are for peace and Giles wants peace and I try to give it to her. But she only wants me to take my medicines and I hate them. She'll never discover my new trick, never, never, never, never, never, never. She says she loves me and wants what's best for me but if she really loved me she'd want me to feel good and feel brave and feel alive and I am not like that at all when I take my pills and I want to feel good and brave and alive.

My sister won't listen. She never listens. But the other one listened to me. At first, anyway. The other one. The beautiful other one. The other, the other, the other one.

Beauty is in the eye of the beholder. The eyes of the beholder are beautiful. **She** said I was beautiful and laughed after I said **she** was beautiful and her hair swung like corn silk as she turned away from me and I started to grab her but said no grabbing to myself, I said it to myself, because the president grabbed and said it was okay but I know it's not okay to covet what isn't yours and the next time I brought flowers and they were red because **her** lips are red but I should have brought blue flowers like **her** eyes.

Gandhi spoke about peace but I had no peace and dreamed **she** lay beside me and we were full of peace and **she** could give me peace but President Clinton brought no peace and now I think he was very bad and bad for us and bad for Monica and I won't be bad. I mustn't be bad but I was forced by Clinton who said I could return day after day after day and watch **her** practice.

When she wasn't happy and cursed herself I knew better than to approach her with flowers or to say nice things because her blue eyes turned black as midnight and she turned away as if I weren't there in spite of the flowers and one time she threw them on the ground.

Maybe that's what Giles did with my flower I picked for her. Threw it on the ground. She just thinks she loves me. Bitch, bitch, bitch, bitch, bitch.

5

Fourteen gargantuan concrete busts of US presidents stood around the vast gravel parking lot. The artist who'd rendered these likenesses worked at the end of a row of warehouses near my office. It was almost as if, each time my tires kicked up dust in the presidents' faces, I expected a giant's hand to reach down from the clouds and move them around in some private game of chess. But the heads were at least twenty feet tall and made of concrete. The giant would have to be God himself. Or Herself.

With the Civic's tires slinging bits of gravel, I pulled in opposite the likeness of Gerald Ford and parked. My favorite was Teddy Roosevelt, but Gerald was the closest to my office door. Whoever had built this string of warehouses on the north side of downtown must have figured that if these huge spaces remained empty, the tiny, one-person office near the end was highly rentable.

Rain the previous day had cooled the air. Probably the reason my dour mood from yesterday had vanished. I hurried inside, switched on overhead lights, and then flipped the window air-conditioning switch, my upbeat mood unspoiled by its intrusively loud motor. Boots was meeting me here. I'd grown anxious on the drive over to match his voice with the man himself.

Feeling professional in a lightweight worsted black jacket and slacks, I was comforted by the tiny revolver resting inside my pocket.

Boots had sounded distraught over the phone, not crazy. Still, wearing a piece served as my pacifier. I could reach for it if needed.

My conscience nagged me to phone Robby, though he wasn't likely to remember he'd called and yelled at me last night. He'd probably accuse me of bugging him. And, according to Mrs. Cathcart, he had fallen asleep. Sleep was a good sign, even if Robby hadn't changed out of his street clothes. He should be okay.

I slung my briefcase on the floor beside my desk chair. Decorated in Early Aunt Eunice, the office was barely large enough for my desk, the size of a refrigerator. It had been a legacy from my aunt's first husband and it would undoubtedly outlast me as well. A matching maple file cabinet and one wing-back chair, its blue-flowered pattern faded against a yellowed background, constituted the remaining furnishings. If it hadn't been for a large skylight in the ceiling, this office would be dark as a tomb. But, I'd grown fond of it, even tolerating the ten minutes or so before the window unit cooled the space enough so I could drop the fan speed down to an almost-quiet level.

Behind my desk, a sink and a toilet were hidden by a fabric screen that didn't pretend to block sound. A small Formica countertop was just big enough to hold a coffee maker. I ducked behind the screen and while scooping the last of the Folgers, heard something over the noise of the AC.

Boots stood inside the doorway, wearing khakis, a starched white shirt, and a black Stetson hat. His mouth moved but I couldn't hear, so I hurried over to the wall by the door, flipped the air switch to low and caught the tail end of his sentence. "—so I can wait outside if you're busy."

"No, no. Come in." I motioned for him to sit in the wing chair as I peeled off my jacket and closed the door. His glance around my office was noncommittal before he sat, his muscular frame sprawled across the flowery fabric.

He swept off his hat and quickly fingered furrows through his hair. When he looked over and said "Mornin', ma'am," I could have sworn he winked at me.

After dropping my jacket on the back of my desk chair, I again disappeared behind the screen. "Want coffee?"

"Sure thing. Black, please."

The coffee machine, unlike other furnishings in my office, was new. Thankful it would stop in mid-brew, I removed the canister and poured two, almost full, mugs. I placed one in front of Boots.

A shaft of light against his hair intensified sun streaks any woman would envy. Long enough to call attention, his hair swept away from his face, ending in waves against the back of his collar. I don't know what I'd expected, but this Marlboro man across from me was not your average looking guy.

He sipped his coffee, seemingly relaxed. Pale blue, almost color-less eyes looked at me between fringes of blue-black lashes. Wearing starched white shirt and khakis, he could have been any Houston businessman, except for the tooled leather belt, the armadillo-sized brass buckle etched with a Texas Star, and his black cowboy boots. An urban cowboy uniform, perhaps.

I took a sip from my cup. "You said you looked me up because of Houston's Police Chief."

Boots dropped his head, picked at an imaginary piece of lint on his slacks. "The chief, he was real busy like, but he gave me your name. Said you were a real good cop before you started your own firm."

My own firm? One PI and her crazy brother who took photos? Why had the chief remembered me? I'd only spoken to him once.

"The chief's a family friend," Boots continued. "He knew 'bout my sister's death last March and, well, I'm pretty upset about the way they handled it and all. Hightower's office, I mean."

The soft hum of the air conditioner filled the room as Boots looked over at me, his eyes now clouded with pleading. "You said you had to look at the files first, and you did that. Right? So you'll investigate her death, won't you?"

"I got your check. And I'll do some preliminary work for you. But if I discover that your sister's death was a suicide, I'll return any deposit money due back to you."

After he nodded, I quoted him my daily rate, shoved my standard contract across the desk, and pointed out the inclusion of his thousand-dollar deposit. He didn't flinch at my hourly rate and scribbled his name at the bottom of the document.

"The police determined your sister's death was suicide." I said, placing the signed contract in my desk drawer.

Boots wore his attachment to his sister on his sleeve. His voice broke as he visibly struggled with his emotions.

"Suicide? Ha!"

I felt my own throat close in sympathy. "The captain says your sister was depressed— "

He shot forward in his chair—"LeeAnn was the most fun, life-loving gal you'd ever hope to meet! I swear to that. If she jumped, somebody had to have helped her, one way or another, ma'am."

"Call me Giles."

When he nodded, I rushed ahead with a speech only slightly rehearsed. "Do you maintain your sister was physically helped over the edge or mentally, due to abuse by her boyfriend? Because if you think she jumped to escape abuse, she would have been mentally disturbed enough to warrant medication, be undependable at work, cause her friends to be so worried they called and talked to you, and/or be under psychiatric care. Did your sister fit any of these scenarios?"

Boots looked away, his fingers drumming silently on the padded arm of the chair. "I tol' you she had a black eye."

"How many times did you see her with a black eye?"

Boots glared at me for what seemed several minutes before his face crumbled. When he dropped his head, I prayed he wouldn't cry. While he massaged the padded arms of the wingback with his thumbs, the room grew silent. Even the air conditioner lowered its hum.

When he finally looked up, I'd almost forgotten my question.

"Only once. But if it happened once, I figured it happened more than once. I only saw her ever month or so. She lived here. I'm ninety miles away." This last revelation held an undertone of defensiveness.

I needed to change tactics. "I agree. If her black eye was inflicted by her boyfriend, it undoubtedly wasn't the first time." Before the light in his eye grew too bright, I added, "But what proof do you have this boyfriend was the culprit?"

Boots straightened, his voice when he spoke was rigid and flat. "That's what you're going to get for me."

"Why? So you can go after him? From what you've said, there's nothing to prove her alleged suicide was prompted solely from abuse, even if I discover evidence to that effect."

"You let me worry 'bout that. Just do your job. Find out who turned my cheery little sister into a dead person."

I didn't want to be responsible for the boyfriend's murder. On the other hand, I could pick and choose what I reported to him. "Tell me about LeeAnn."

He nodded, appearing to gather his thoughts. I heard a soft whistle, like a sigh escape as he leaned back and began to speak.

"LeeAnn was real special. Happy little girl. Only twenty-four, like I tol' you. She loved horses, rode hers like she'd been born on its back. Like its dip weren't meant for a saddle, just her butt." He shook his head as if in deep admiration. "She was a champion barrel-racer before she graduated high school." He paused and his shoulders drooped, as if suddenly deflated. "I never saw any black eye on her 'til after she moved to Houston."

If he thought LeeAnn had been abused, why hadn't he tracked down the boyfriend already? Beaten him to a bloody pulp? I paused, pencil perched above my notebook. "Did your sister ever explain why she wouldn't tell you who her boyfriend was?"

"My sister was private. We both are...were, I mean. We come from a small family. Real small now that our parents died a few years back."

After stating he thought her boyfriend was someone she'd met at work or maybe the Houston Rodeo, he reached inside his back pocket and withdrew a wad of cash. He slid off the money clip, licked his thumb and peeled off half the bundle.

"This is for you 'til you use it up. That happens, let me know. Not enough hours in that retainer to let you work very long." He slapped the wad on my desktop, a money-green fan unfolding like a magic trick. "That retainer I gave you was just to let you know I was serious."

For the moment, I ignored the green bills on my desktop, and asked one more question.

"Did the police ever mention your sister's boyfriend?"

A mixture of disbelief and scorn crossed Boots' face. "The police say LeeAnn didn't have a boyfriend. That I'm making it up. What for? I got better things to do." He shifted uncomfortably in his seat. "Now her best friend, Sandra Connor's, taken off. She'd know about the boyfriend, but I can't find her. Maybe you can."

After verifying the spelling with Boots, I made a note of the girl-friend's name. This information should have been in the police files. Had I missed it?

I found myself staring at Boots' stack of money. Typically, my clients were prepared to write me a check. I even took Master Card or Visa, but I'd never had anyone slap cash on my desk.

As I picked it up and thumbed it, I saw only one hundred dollar denominations. Good old Benjamin Franklin. The bills in my hand made a sizeable wad, and Boots had peeled off half of what he'd had on him. Crap! Had my money problems grown a tad smaller?

After dropping the money inside my briefcase on the floor, I tore off a clean sheet of paper from a tablet on top of my desk.

"How much cash did you give me?"

"Twelve," he said.

Twelve thousand. I almost fainted. I'd guessed five. Scribbling him a receipt, I quickly passed it across the desk, squelching a cat-ate-the-mouse grin.

Surprise flicked across his face as he folded the paper, leaned forward and shoved it down his back pants pocket. Showing trust right up front usually resulted in a better client relationship. Of course I'd carefully count the cash as soon as he left.

"I'll give you regular reports by phone and weekly in writing. I need to know how to contact you."

Boots scribbled a phone number and an address on the back of one of my business cards. Beaumont was ninety miles east of Houston, home to oil-wealthy families and poor farmers. I already knew which category Boots fit. He might talk like a country bumpkin but he had a powerfully connected uncle, who, I noted, he'd failed to mention as part of his family.

6

While driving to Robby's boarding house, my thoughts stubbornly remained on my new client. I began to meld Boots' story with what I'd read in the captain's files.

LeeAnn had been Brad Ewer's party guest. She'd fallen from an outdoor smoking balcony across the corridor from one of Reliant stadium's eighth-level hospitality suites. I knew the layout of the stadium, and although I'd never been up to the private suite levels, I'd been inside the stadium more than once and driven past it countless times.

Large corporations leased the private suites. Being on their invitation list meant you had something they wanted. These costly suites, or skyboxes, were used judiciously to impress, to bring in new clients, generate more business, more money. If business was good, corporations renewed their annual leases during rodeo season as well as sports events. Not that a rodeo didn't qualify as a sports event. Anytime healthy young Homo sapiens risked their necks for a trophy and big bucks, it was sport.

From the incident report, I recalled that a Houston Police Lieutenant named Abury had responded first to the call from a security guard. At least four security guards were employed for every level of Reliant Stadium during Houston Rodeo.

At my desk last night, I'd read the *Chronicle's* version of Ewer's testimony. He had walked LeeAnn out to the smoking balcony after the others in their party had left for the evening. She was upset and had been crying.

The other witness, J.D. McGraw, was quoted as saying that when he reached his car in the V.I.P. parking lot, he realized he'd forgotten his jacket. He decided to retrieve it and, after exiting the private elevator that stopped on the top level, had headed down the corridor. He watched Ewer walk out of his suite and cross the hallway toward the balcony, a box of Kleenex in his hand. McGraw stopped short when he spotted Ewer's horrified expression while gazing out at the balcony.

Ewer dropped the Kleenex, McGraw ran up beside him, and both men watched as LeeAnn thrust her arms over her head, clasped her thumbs, then executed a deliberate swan dive, as if into the deep waters of the Gulf. That ending poetic touch was courtesy of the *Chronicle* reporter.

If those men were to be believed, which was the crux of my investigation, it took less than half a minute for LeeAnn to dive to her death.

Drawing closer to Robby's boarding house, I stopped my musings and boxed them away. While idling at a traffic light, I called Robby on my cell. Since my brother didn't own a cell phone, I'd have to follow up with his landlord if he didn't answer the phone in his room.

"What's up?" Robby sounded almost chipper.

"I'm hungry," I said. "Want me to pick you up for a bite?"

"I'm on my way to the café."

"I can swing by. I'm fairly close."

"Nope. Got a ride."

"Oh?" Robby didn't like me to question him, but I knew no friend of his who owned a car.

"I'll meet you there in ten minutes," I said. The café Robby mentioned was several blocks from Mrs. Cathcart's. An easy walk in good weather. While my thoughts were lost in the Callahan case, lengthy smears of dark clouds had invaded the sky outside. Looked like another downpour.

Robby loved storms. He followed the weather as skillfully as a meteorologist. Frequently, he painted watercolor scenes of storm-besieged landscapes, waves crashing against seashores, storm clouds severed by lightening bolts. He was a good enough artist to win a scholarship to the local community college.

But any aspirations that Robby could handle college disappeared with a puberty consumed by epileptic fits plus trial-and-error medications to ward off bipolar behavior. As an adult looking back, I realized Robby's condition ruled our household as effectively as a dictator.

While a young child, he'd been blatantly favored; the son my father prayed for after years of Mother miscarrying. I was seven when Robby was born and learned only later what his birth had cost her. Given a choice between removing her cancerous uterus or carrying the baby to term, my mother chose the baby.

When Robby was two months old, Mother died. It still surprised me that neither my father nor I felt resentment toward Robby over Mother's death. He was the reward, if you will, for all her suffering. He was the bright, beautiful shining star we both adored. Yet the empty ache I felt over Mother's death haunted me. Almost every night, I dreamed of her, but Robby refused to listen to stories about our mother. Finally, I realized Robby already had a Mother—me. I was the one who'd always been there for him.

My brother cried a lot as an infant. Merely a child myself, I fought our housekeeper for the right to hold him and soon became the only one who could soothe him. I staked my claim by filling two roles: that of Mother as well as sister. When he was two and spoke his first word, it was my name he spoke. Or a version of it. Father always called me by my initials, G.L. For toddler Robby, these initials turned into Jelly.

Images of baby Robby immerged from a world lost long ago. I shook them off. The grown man he'd become was much harder to please and ten times as difficult.

Robby's favorite hangout, Café Artiste, had stood in the same location for over fifteen years. Easy to spot, the café sported a bright mural painted on its wooden exterior. It played the part of maverick on a block of drab cottages built in the forties. This coffee house functioned as a hangout for those out of the mainstream. Robby felt at home among its struggling patrons, who could count on him to applaud their latest poem, view their recent art works, or hear about rewrites of graduate theses long overdue. When not scribbling madly, my brother appeared to be a good listener.

After parking on the curb, I went inside the cafe. Young couples and a few singles sat reading newspapers or books spread open before them. Their tattoos, body piercing, and neon hair screamed "I'm artistic" or perhaps "I'm different". Like most of us, the café crowd was, in the end, conformist. I accepted this. We all housed warring egos—desiring distinction while simultaneously seeking the comfort of belonging.

I spotted Robby at a table near the far wall. He was with a man I didn't recognize. But I knew Calvin, the waiter behind the counter. When he motioned me over, I maneuvered myself through crowded tables toward the bar.

Calvin was a graduate accounting student at the University of Houston. A cute kid, he looked the part of California surfer, with a pale blond cowlick and year-round tan. He kept the books for the owner, and was the only employee who allowed Robby to run a tab.

Calvin leaned toward me, hands twisting a dishtowel inside an oversized white coffee mug. "Robby's been low on cash for weeks. He owes the house twelve bucks."

I dug in my handbag and retrieved a twenty from my billfold.

"Keep the change," I said. "Just let me know when you need a refill."

Calvin groaned at my pun, but his hazel eyes smiled. I turned from the counter. Who was that man talking a blue streak at Robby's table? My brother's ability to focus on another person was amazing, as if he had no peripheral vision. I might as well be invisible.

I walked toward him, the familiar dance in my stomach heightened with tension as I recalled his manic telephone message from the night before, as well as his threats from the roof top. My *modus ope-randi* was too ingrained for me to change, and I fervently hoped my searching for telltale signs Robby was off his medications would not appear overly obvious. My brother and I looked a lot alike, and seeing him teeter on the edge of drowning in his demons was unnerving, like observing my own destruction through a mirror.

The man at Robby's table stared at me until Robby turned my way. My brother was a tall, good-looking man of twenty-nine. With thick black hair and classic features, he could have been a Ralph Lauren model, if his torso wasn't like a heavyweight boxer's. Yet my personal history with Robby blocked me from appreciating his outward appearance, leaving others to admire his physical beauty.

Approaching his table, I saw a grin split his face. He hopped up and grabbed an empty chair from the table beside him. "Come on, Sis. Meet my new friend, Tony."

Tony remained seated as he stuck his hand toward me.

The café sported an odd assortment of chairs, and mine had an uneven leg. When I sat, I slowly tipped sideways while reaching across to shake his hand. It felt dry and scaly while his round, fleshy cheeks looked slick, as if he'd just come from a sauna. A monk's ring of thinning mouse-colored hair surrounded his balding head. His dark eyes darted at me, across at Robby, and then down into his coffee cup. All the while, he pursed his lips with theatrical exaggeration.

"I've been telling your brother all about holistic medicine. Herbs can cure anything."

I noticed a zippered pouch on the table. Several pills of different colors had escaped and lay scattered across the table top. A salesman? A drug dealer? My instincts screamed <u>shifty</u>.

Tony giggled suddenly. "I just have to say you two sure look alike. Same gooorgeous black wavy hair and green eyes. Could be twins. Anybody ever tell y'all that?" He looked more than pleased with himself.

Too weary of that comment to respond, I noticed Robby beam. "I know I'm good-looking when I see my sister coming at me."

"Toward me, Robby, not 'at me.'" I couldn't help the rude comeback. But then it wasn't Robby's fault that creepy Tony was setting my teeth on edge.

Calvin switched off public broadcasting of bad weather ahead and for a few seconds, we sat in total silence. I tried to gauge Robby's mood, studying his pale, lime-flecked green eyes. Like those of a sorcerer, they could enchant you one minute, freeze your insides the next. With hands that remained controlled only when he smoked, part of him appeared always in motion.

When Calvin turned on recorded music, I heard the sounds of a mandolin. A rhythmic strumming from *Zorba the Greek*. Robby let out an "All Riiiight!" He pushed back his chair, hopped up on the table and threw his arms high above his head. I grabbed at the coffee cups while creepy Tony threw his head back and yelled encouragement.

Robby began to spin. Others in the café stared silently until Calvin began loudly clapping to the beat. Slowly, others joined in the rhythm as Robby danced, occasionally stomping his feet like a reincarnation of Anthony Quinn. Tony yelled out a loud "yee haw" as if Robby were doing the do-si-do.

I had to admit Robby was graceful. Beautiful, even. His eyes glowed. His smile while he danced was that of an enchanted child. Throwing his head back, he was in total control. I swelled with pride and felt close, too close to a Mother's delight over her progeny. Dancing with unbridled enthusiasm, Robby was a joy to watch. He seemed to swell at the crowds energetic approval, glowing in their appreciation, and performed all the harder.

These episodes of high excitement usually ended in stark depressive mode. I had no idea if he was on the upswing or the downswing. Either one was bad.

7

Calvin stopped the music, maybe fearing an accident. Patrons booed and continued clapping for another thirty seconds before petering out. Instead of getting angry at Calvin, Robby stopped dancing, hopped off the table, pulled his chair up and said, "Fun, huh?"

The patrons returned to their own conversations. Strains of Elton John singing *Nikita* dropped the previous uproar down several notches.

Robby smiled, showing his dimples. "I did that for you, Sis. You always like to see me dance."

He was remembering long ago when his spontaneous dancing didn't signal a melt-down.

"You were great," I reached out and patted his arm.

Impulsively, Robby leaned over and gave me a hug. With a heart shattering from dread, I hugged him back. Sometimes I could stall an explosion and sometimes not. I turned to Tony. "Do you mind if I visit with my brother alone?"

Robby opened his mouth to respond, but Tony stood, scraped the pills, some of them flattened by Robby's dancing heels, inside the zippered pouch and looked down at me.

"Course not. I can take a hint. See you around, Robby. Think about these herbs. Could solve all your problems." Tony turned with a jounce, showing a rear end both unfortunate and unmanly in its jiggle.

"What's he selling?" I asked Robby.

"Just some stupid herbs he says will change my life forever."

"You believe that?"

"Do I look that dumb?" Robby shot me a get-real look.

Thinking that Robby shouldn't feel he had to talk with weirdoes like Tony for company, I said, "A female companion would be a nice change."

Immediately, I regretted my statement. Why did I persist in the belief a girlfriend would help stabilize Robby? Take my place as policeman over his medications and bring some joy into his life.

"I had a girl I liked," he said. "I just never let you meet her."

My heart jumped and I swallowed a dozen questions. "Oh?" Robby couldn't be rushed, so I tried for a friendly, not too nosy, expression.

"Don't get too excited. It's not like we dated or anything. It's kind of hard to date without a car."

"You can borrow my car anytime." I leaned back, still practicing the casual approach. "What's she like?"

Robby looked shyly down at the tabletop and my pulse quickened.

"She was pretty. I think she liked me. We had a lot in common."

I noticed the past tense. "Where'd you meet her?"

His sharp glance told me I'd lost any opportunity to learn more. "None of your business."

Robby was most likely delusional, which worried me even more. "Did you hang out with her?"

"I said it's none of your business!"

Quickly changing gears, I asked, "Do you have any photos for me?"

I let Robby take pictures of routine case investigations such as a workers comp claim that the company suspected was bogus or an irate spouse who thought the other was cheating. Robby hid himself with a telephoto and tried to capture the sick or injured claimant engaged in strenuous, non-sick, non-injured activity, or a spouse meeting up for illicit sex. I paid him by the hour, and Robby enjoyed the work.

"Oh, yeah." He smiled. "But I left them back at my apartment. Sorry, Sis."

"That's okay. We'll get them when I take you home. What do you have?"

"Donald Rayburn finishing up his concrete patio. Got some real sharp ones."

He looked at me for approval and I gave it to him with a high five. Robby slapped my hand, shot me another smile and I almost thought I'd imagined him turning manic.

Suddenly, thunder cracked, shaking the café walls. A distant car alarm started a rhythmic two-note wail as hail struck the café's tin roof. Another storm was not welcome.

Robby jerked in his chair and his smile disappeared. He drummed his thumbs against the tabletop.

"If it doesn't stop raining, your car's gonna flood." His eyes darted between a worried glance down at the table and back up at me.

"We'll go now, then," I said, using my best soothing tone.

"No. I'm not ready. Why do you want me out of here?"

Crap. I needed another diversion. "I like this café, too. We'll stay if you want."

Robby looked dubious while I frantically scrolled though topics in my head.

The overhead lights flickered and died. Darkness descended. Someone screamed briefly, while nervous giggles echoed around the room.

Under the cover of shadows that purpled the room like a giant bruise, Robby began a tirade about how nosy I was. How I shouldn't have chased off Tony. How I'd chased off his high school girlfriend and he'd never let me do that again.

Not true. The young girl in question had dropped him the first time she experienced Robby without his meds.

The same thing was highly probable with his no-longer "girl-friend" that he "didn't date".

"Don't panic," Calvin shouted above the sound of chairs scraping against the floor. "Just overloaded the breaker, folks. Lights'll be on in a sec."

The atmosphere inside the café crackled in imitation of the storm outside. Slowly, as if in silent agreement, patrons gathered their things and left, singly and in pairs, allowing the smell of rain to slip inside. I reached for Robby, his silhouette barely visible across the table, and grabbed his arm. I felt his clammy skin, the trembling beneath my fingers.

"You okay? You love storms, remember?"

He didn't answer.

We listened as rain hit the roof, the hail apparently over. Sounds of thunder also abated. But after my eyes adjusted to the dimness inside the cafe, my heart sank. Robby's upper lip twitched, and the fingers of both his hands fluttered over the tabletop as if he were playing piano keys.

"You followed me here, didn't you?" Robby said, his voice hoarse with emotion.

My brother's feelings for me were like biker tattoos on each hand. One read "love", the other "hate". Sometimes, playing the role of critical parent widened the gap between us, and I feared there'd come a time I'd be unable to repair the damage. I often wondered whether he'd be better off if I could only leave him alone.

"Robby," I said, "have you been taking your medications?" My voice stayed low, my tone even. Four plastic bags of pills stayed on top of his dresser, all labeled. Two pills in the morning and two for the afternoon. Robby took an anxiety drug, an anticonvulsant for epileptic fits that had returned in his early twenties, and anti-psychotics.

Over the past twenty years, with too many psychiatrists and neurologists to count, Robby's drug regimen was constantly on the move. I had hoped this last cocktail would keep him, if still occasionally stuck in manic-writing mode, at least reasonably sane.

Dr. Winthrop was my latest lifeline as far as Robby was concerned. According to Winthrop, it wasn't the hypergraphia, or "The Midnight Disease," that was Robby's biggest problem, but its common partners of mania and paranoia. I agreed with Winthrop that Robby could scribble all he wanted as long as he was eating and sleeping. This compulsion to write twenty-four-seven could ruin another's life, but for my brother, a normal life hadn't been his baseline since age ten.

The lights in the café sprang to life. Robby and I were the only customers remaining. From behind the bar, Calvin shot a thumbs-up in our direction.

Robby glanced at me, his face full of malice. "Of course I'm taking my pills. And you're keeping me from my work. I don't just take pictures for you, you know."

Robby's "work" meant scribbling or painting.

"Why don't I drive you home now so you can work?" Once in his room, I could spot if he'd told me the truth by counting the number of pills remaining.

Since I'd given Robby shots in the past, Dr. Winthrop supplied me with syringes. If Robby needed more than one injection due to a non-stop writing jag, Winthrop would refine Robby's medications. What I'd never told the good doctor was that if Robby needed a shot and had been off his meds for more than two days, I'd need to call for help. We might resemble each other, but my brother was six-feet-two, muscular, and outweighed me by more than seventy-five pounds.

I smiled and stood. "Let's see what's happening with the storm. You can listen to the weather band in my car."

"This's just the sideswipe," Robby said. "It's heading to Louisiana." His look told me I must be really stupid, but he stood, the twitch in his eye no longer obvious, his nervous hands now shoved deep inside his jean pockets.

"Want to come home with me, get something to eat?"

"I'm not hungry," Robby mumbled.

"You guys leaving?" Calvin called out.

I forced a laugh and swatted Robby's arm playfully. "Calvin can handle this storm without us, can't he Robby?"

My brother smiled and I exhaled. We were on the same team again. I wanted to hug him, but restrained myself. He liked hugs but only if he initiated them.

After the dash to my car, we sat, rain-soaked, in the front seat. As sheets of water streamed outside the windows, Robby flipped the radio dial, listening intently to the robotic sound of the weather man repeating the forecast for Harris and surrounding counties. After a minute, he sank back into the passenger seat, hands resting on his thighs.

"See? I told you. Those folks off North Carolina are in for it. We just got a little sympathy storm here, Jelly. Not really worrisome."

I flipped on the windshield wipers. Louisiana. North Carolina. What the hell, he'd called me Jelly.

8

It was late in the afternoon when I stepped off the elevator of the hi-rise, a cup of chili inside a Wendy's sack. I hurried down the hallway and into my apartment, trailing the smell of spicy meat and beans in my wake. A pink sticky-note greeted me at my front door, its top right corner stenciled with a red Christmas tree.

I peeled it off and let myself in. My neighbor from across the hall, Santa Henderson, hardly ever phoned, preferring to leave me notes. Naming your only child Santa was strange, but she'd explained to me that her mother loved everything about Christmas, especially the trees. She'd inherited her mother's tree collection and constantly added to it. Concocted from various materials, both natural and man-made, miniature Christmas trees grew like mold over every surface in Santa's apartment.

Lightheaded with hunger, I waited for the microwave to sizzle my lunch. Chili needed to be almost hot enough to burn my tongue. Same with coffee. Thirty minutes before, I'd watched Robby take his afternoon pills, the correct number remaining in his pill bags. The photos he'd taken would make my insurance client very happy. I felt almost chipper.

There was one phone message from my father—his weekly phone call, timed on Tuesday or Thursday evenings when I taught class. It was my third year to teach a continuing education class on family violence to young cops. The extra money was great, but I was anxious for my business to take off and devote full time to investigation.

I deleted Father's message without listening, gave Suzy some cream from the fridge, grabbed the can of Folgers Columbian and made myself a pot of coffee. While it dripped, I shucked my jacket and poured the chili into a real porcelain bowl and, after a fleeting ladylike flush of self-congratulations, said to hell with it and crumbled saltines on top. Still, I placed bowl and napkin neatly on the kitchen table and sat down to eat. Otherwise, I knew I'd take it into my office and spill chili on the keyboard.

I forced myself to read Santa's note. "Crisis! Call me." Her signature was a round-faced Santa Claus with a pencil-slash frown.

I disliked these childish drawings, but worse, I abhorred the guilt I felt for avoiding Santa when she needed to unload. Her husband had moved out almost a year before, two days after her third miscarriage. I didn't blame her for feeling down. She had good reason. But I found it difficult not to insist she get a grip and forget about the bastard. File for divorce. Heartless, no doubt, but Santa's husband, Martin Henderson, M.D., a student of the famous heart surgeon, Denton Cooley, was a self-centered bastard whose ego could put Donald Trump to shame.

Finished eating, I bounded up the stairs to change out of my "suit of the ruling elite," as a lawyer friend referred to his daily wardrobe. After inspecting for chili stains, I hung jacket, slacks, and blouse neatly in my bedroom closet, then pulled on cotton sweat pants and a white T-shirt. Briefly considering tennis shoes, I opted for bare feet, a habit Robby and I'd adopted early, most likely because it irritated our father. I stuck Santa's note on the bedside table, a reminder to call her after class that evening. Toes liberated, I ran down the steps, stopping to pour myself a cup of coffee before settling into my den.

It took thirty minutes to transcribe Boots' ramblings about his sister into the computer. In doing so, I discovered holes big enough for a gorilla to jump through. Boots never mentioned his sister's previous suicide attempt or her depression. According to Boots, his sister had been happiness personified. She loved her new job as insurance adjuster, her increase in salary, and she had a boyfriend but refused to talk about him. The only contact he had given me was LeeAnn's best friend, Sandra Connor, who had disappeared.

I reviewed my copy of the police files. More holes. I began to type a list of questions. Lamar had interviewed only one of LeeAnn's neighbors. Apparently LeeAnn kept to herself and the neighbor had never noticed a boyfriend around her place. Nothing about attempted suicide. And if LeeAnn had been treated for depression, the doctor's name was missing. Just as I'd remembered, there was no record of a second interview with Mary Nelson, the woman at the party who'd been walking on the sidewalk when LeeAnn's falling body barely missed her.

The police report had a few paragraphs from LeeAnn's two previous bosses, one in Beaumont, one in Houston. There was a lapse in employment between the two insurance companies. I noted the dates with question marks. Also missing from the coroner's report was whether LeeAnn was pregnant or not at the time of her death—standard autopsy notation when age and gender appropriate.

Considering Lamar's current mood, I opted to call Boots with my questions and dialed the number he'd given me. Instead, I got his recording and left a message for him to call, that I needed to ask him a few more questions.

I did have the name and number of the Houston insurance company LeeAnn had worked for. Her boss, Mr. Ramon Martinez, VP of Alliance Insurance, had warranted four sentences in Lamar's files. As I dialed the number, I doubted I'd get much more.

"This is Martinez."

From the sound of his voice, he could have been from the South or the Midwest.

"My name is Giles Faulkner and I'm investigating the death of LeeAnn Callahan. I understand she worked for you."

"You with the police?"

"Captain Lamar Hightower suggested I talk with you and gave me your name and number." I wasn't above being obtuse, especially if it worked.

"Well, I've already told you guys what I knew of Miss Callahan. She was a good worker and was never late."

As if the poor woman needed a reference. "I've read the files, Mr. Martinez, and I understand she was a recent hire, only four months on the job before she died. Is that correct?"

"Sounds about right."

"And she worked in Beaumont before coming to work for you?"

"I'm sorry, but I'm very busy."

"Is there someone in your personnel department who would have that information?"

"Call Dinky Patterson." Martinez gave me the extension, mumbled something about a meeting and hung up. I dialed Dinky's extension and got a fax signal. Was Martinez jacking me around? Then, feeling I'd jumped to paranoia too quickly, I almost called back thinking I'd misdialed when another thought struck. Jerking the business directory out of my desk drawer, I found the main number for Alliance and dialed. This method was often quicker than waiting for the internet to come up. A perky female voice answered.

"Alliance Insurance."

I asked to be connected to LeeAnn Callahan.

A small gasp traveled over the line, followed by a pause "Who is this?"

"I'm her school friend, Becky, from Oklahoma. I don't mean we went to school in Oklahoma cause I moved there 'bout two years ago and LeeAnn and me talked sometime around Christmas but then we just lost touch, you know how that is, and I just couldn't let that happen and I had this wedding to come to in Houston. Perfect opportunity to catch up on old times." I sucked my breath and held it.

"Oh, dear I hate to be the one to tell you this, but LeeAnn passed away last March."

"No! She couldn't have! What happened?"

"I'm sorry. Becky, is it? I didn't know her all that well. She'd only been with us a few months, but I heard she committed suicide."

"Suicide? That's crazy!" I paused for maximum drama. "Say, would there be anyone there she worked with, any friend she had that I could talk to?"

The woman hesitated. "Well, maybe Juliet would speak with you. They worked in the same department and I saw them leave together once or twice."

"I'd sure appreciate you giving me Juliet's—what did you say her last name was?"

"Juliet Ralston. But don't tell her I gave you her name or extension. She's kind of a strange bird."

Strange or not, I scribbled Juliet's number and uttered a heartfelt thank-you to the nameless receptionist, when another question popped into my head. "Could you remind me where LeeAnn worked before she started with Alliance? It might be more likely I'd find a really good friend of hers there since I sort of remember she'd worked one place for several years before switching to Alliance, and I . . . " choking my voice as if struggling not to cry . . . "could hear about the last months of her life and all."

"Oh, you poor thing. Now that you ask, I remember hearing she'd worked at an insurance company in Beaumont. Ramsey Tilman's company, and then almost a year at Hammerly. Mr. Martinez was so happy about all her experience in the insurance business."

Hammerly. Brad Ewer's company. Now why wasn't that tidbit of information in Lamar's files? And why hadn't Brad Ewer mentioned this as a better reason for knowing someone than a mega-church with thousands of members?

As I punched Juliet's number, I felt elated. Lucky. Then I got a recording. Crap. Juliet's voice was clipped, all business. I tried to sound the same as I left a message that I was investigating the suicide of LeeAnn Callahan and would appreciate a return call.

My doorbell and cell phone rang at the same time. I punched the talk button. "This is Giles," I said, heading to the door.

"Boots, here. Your message said something 'bout more questions for me? Sure would help me out if we could take care of this over the phone."

"Hold on a sec."

I looked out the peephole. It was Santa, tears streaming from swollen eyes. Reluctantly, I opened my front door. From the looks of her disheveled red hair, hunched shoulders and aura of despair, I predicted her visit would not be a short one.

"Actually, I don't recall your saying where Sandra Connor had worked?" I spoke while opening the front door and motioning for Santa to come inside.

Boots grunted. "She worked in personnel at U of H. But you won't find her there. She left town about a week after LeeAnn died" He added that even if he couldn't track her down, that didn't mean I couldn't.

"Okay," I said, "but there are other questions I'd prefer to discuss in person." After shoving the door shut with my shoulder, I turned the lock. Santa had disappeared inside.

"Well, I'm staying the night in Houston. Guess I could meet you for breakfast before I head back to Beaumont—you like the IHOP on 59 South? It'd have to be early. Eight o'clock okay?"

I said fine, clicked off, and with some measure of dread headed into the kitchen for two wine glasses and a bottle of Pinot Gris. Santa liked wine, but even if I were taking antihistamines, it gave me a headache. The same wasn't true of martinis, but my current supply of gin was non-existent.

At the moment, I at least needed the pretense of sharing a drink with my neighbor. From past experience, I knew if I appeared to be imbibing, she'd loosen up and cut to the problem a lot quicker.

Santa resembled one of St. Nick's helpers more than the big guy himself. She was petite, maybe five-foot-one, and wore her bright red hair in a short, spiky shag. With hazel eyes that appeared perpetually dewy, prominent cheekbones and slightly enlarged front teeth, she looked a cross between an elf and a beaver. Yet the visual impression of this young woman was pleasing. She was small boned but curvaceous, and on first meeting, I'd expected her to be as soft and cute as she looked.

"That motherfucker filed for divorce!" She began a long wail straight from her wounded heart as she plopped heavily on "her" chair, the only comfortable one in the living room. Santa had claimed it on her first "welcome-to-the hi-rise" visit.

I wasn't surprised at her statement and wished I could strangle her soon-to-be ex-husband. Instead, I opened the bottle and poured two glasses, handed one to Santa where she sat dwarfed by the overstuffed chair like a miniature Alice in Wonderland. After returning the wine to the refrigerator, I switched my cell phone to vibrate and sat across from her on the sofa, Aunt Eunice's Schefflera looming behind me. The six-foot tall glossy-leafed plant endured my surreptitious wine-watering now and then. A quick glance outside showed an enormous blood orange ball spearing shards of sunlight through dust-colored clouds hugging the horizon. I'd have to leave for class soon.

Sitting back, I waited for Santa to begin. I'd been around Lamar too long to open my mouth prematurely.

While tears streaked Santa's cheeks, I thought about her husband. Even though he was a total scumbag, more disgusting than bird-shit, I knew he was the whole world to her. The man who'd knocked on my door one night, drunk and demanding, thinking he was the answer to all my pent-up sexual needs. Bette Davis once said there's nothing lonelier than a turned-down toilet seat. In my book, there's nothing lonelier than being married to a jerk.

After kicking him in the balls, I'd helped Santa's hubby down the hall to the elevator, all the while whispering in exquisite detail what I'd do to him next time he showed up at my door. But I'd never told Santa and still didn't know whether I should. Would she think I was making it up? Would she blame me?

My phone vibrated. Flipping it open, I watched as Santa dug in the pocket of her mini-skirt for a Kleenex. She gasped loud, ragged breaths, then blew her nose with a prolonged snort as I strained to hear my caller.

"Is this Giles Faulkner?" The woman's voice was low and clipped.

Had I failed to identify myself? Santa must have unnerved me.

"Yes, this is Giles."

"You called. This is Juliet Ralston."

I sprang off the sofa, held up a finger as soon as Santa glanced my way, then retreated inside my office.

"Thanks for returning my call. I'm looking for someone who might have known LeeAnn Callahan while she worked at Alliance. A friend. Someone she confided in."

"And you thought that was me?" Juliet responded.

My heart sank. "I was hoping it would be you."

9

The sound of the refrigerator opening and closing was worrisome. Santa couldn't weigh more than ninety pounds and I'd poured her a hefty glass.

Juliet breathed into the phone.

"You two had lunch occasionally," I said, forcing my attention on my caller.

"Who told you that?"

Suddenly Santa appeared in the open doorway, her small frame backlit by the kitchen lighting. She held only the neck of the wine bottle. "That sum bitch is the hemorrhoid of the medical profession. A shit-eating maggot!" She tilted the bottle to her lips. I hurried over, grabbed it and pushed her back toward the living room, cell phone tucked precariously between my ear and shoulder.

"You did have lunch with her several times, did you not?" I was repeating myself, distracted, furious and frustrated at the same time. Trying to look stern, I shoved Santa down on the chair and headed back to my office, this time shutting and locking the door behind me. Silence on the other end of the line. Had Juliet hung up? I started to say her name when she spoke.

"Monday through Friday at ten, two, and four I'm outside the building on a smoking break."

The line went dead.

Great. I stared at the phone in one hand and the wine bottle in the other. My front door opened then slammed shut. I enjoyed maybe two seconds of relief before concern over Santa rattled my conscience.

Still, I glanced at my watch. With thirty minutes before I had to leave, I could cram some work in before leaving for class. Seated at my desk, I shelved thoughts of Santa's predicament, logged on and organized notes and questions for Boots and Juliet. After hitting the print button, I completed a bill for the insurance company, along with notes and the photos Robby had taken, following this with a quick search for class material. There were always new developments in the psychology of family violence. I should know.

Leaning back, I let my conscience out of its cage. It would be tight, but I could spend almost ten minutes across the hall. Since I'd moved into this hi-rise, Santa had befriended both me and Robby. She'd come to me for help and the only consolation I'd offered was alcohol. Was I so used to solving problems with drugs as panacea? It worked for Robby. Not wine, but pills. Was there much difference in my intent? I signed off my computer and hurried across the hall. I had to leave in five minutes.

Santa didn't answer my knock. Knocking louder, I tried the handle. When the door swung open, I slipped quietly inside. Maybe she was asleep. As I tiptoed past the kitchen, a musky smell with undertones of spice floated past. Sounds of chanting led me toward Santa's living room. Her apartment layout was the mirror image of mine.

A lamp glowed saffron on the sofa table. I followed a curl of smoke rising from behind the couch. Santa sat on the floor, Indian style, a small brass incense burner on the floor between her and two large windows overlooking commercial shopping center lights.

I recognized the smell of burning sage. Santa appeared to be in a trance, her upper torso moving back and forth over the burner while alternating her cupped hands as they caressed the stream of smoke, wafting it closer to her nostrils. From her throat came guttural, atonal sounds, as if she were performing an Indian ceremony all by herself.

She swiveled her head slowly in my direction and smiled dreamily. "Hellooooo, my friend."

I squatted beside her, smoke stinging my eyes.

"Whatcha doing?" Brilliant question, Giles. "Want to get up now, let me put you to bed?"

As her body continued its sway, she spoke in a low, raspy whisper. "He said ashamed of me, don't know how to dress, how to act, am too crude, need to grow up." She giggled and fell against the back of the sofa. "These colors are sooooo bootiful."

That did it. I grabbed her up and pulled her into the downstairs bathroom. It's hard to strip clothes off a rag doll. What worked best was for me to bend over Santa and pull off her skirt and T-shirt. When I peeled off her underwear, Santa's laughter built to a high before dissolving into sobs.

I turned on the shower and shoved her inside. She collapsed in the corner, her legs tucked underneath her. Pale as a cotton ball, her body almost vanished against the snow-white tiles. If not for her brilliant hair, she would have dissolved before my eyes.

A pot of coffee was still a good idea. I left Santa and headed to the kitchen. The good doctor had replaced all the kitchen appliances with the most exclusive brands money could buy—quite sensible since neither of them cooked. After switching on the light, I spotted a white enamel pan on top of the sleek stainless stove. Removing the lid, I glanced at murky brown liquid and breathed a familiar smell. Immediately, I was transported into another world—one of tents, sand, oriental carpets, and turbans—Opium.

When I was with HPD, I'd gone to a drug seminar in Miami and was introduced to an entire gamut of stimulants. How could I forget the most unusual, the least encountered method of getting high? Opium tea. Boil poppy pods in water and you get a bitter tea that induces long-lasting intoxication but is rarely addictive. How did Santa get hold of poppy pods?

She was unlikely to sober up any time soon. I went back to the bathroom and stopped at the door, my heart suddenly squeezed. Santa lay curled in a ball on the shower floor blocking the drain, arms hugging her knees, her body trembling in a shallow pool of water.

Somehow I managed to dry her off then dragged her limp body to the bottom of the stairs, my intent to get her up to her bedroom. Ninety pounds had never felt heavier. Suddenly, I remembered Santa had a twin bed in the downstairs bedroom. I turned and as we staggered toward it. I recalled that this room had been optimistically turned into a nursery. Had they removed the twin bed?

Switching on the light, I was relieved at the sight of a narrow bed draped in a fluffy white duvet with matching bed ruffles. But relief fled when I spotted a white wicker cradle with snowy, dotted-Swiss ruffles cascading to the floor. A wooden mobile was suspended above the crib. I watched in disbelief as a dozen intermingled green and white Christmas tree cut-outs swayed with every blast from the air conditioner. This baby equipment should have been dismantled a long time ago.

Deciding that she shouldn't wake up with her lost baby's cradle beside her, and worried I'd be late for class, I managed to push-pull her up the stairs, then rolled her onto her king-sized bed where she lay, small and pitiful. I pulled the covers over her, watched her breathe, lips slightly parted, the lids of her eyes fluttering as if she were running from someone in her sleep. There was a time I admired her eyelids—the color of pale lilacs as if she were wearing violet eye shadow. But Santa never wore make-up and now her eyelids just made her appear bruised and fragile, stretched far too thin.

With a sigh so loud I feared she'd awaken, I asked myself for the hundredth time what to do for someone like Santa? Hers was a landscape I'd never visited; a need for her husband, Martin, and for babies worn on her skin, visible to all who knew her. Softly I pulled her bedroom door closed and crept downstairs.

My hand was around her front doorknob with the door partially open, when I sensed someone's presence. Aunt Eunice and Santa had the only apartment units on this floor.

I jerked the door open, half expecting to see her smarmy husband. No one was there. I hurried around the corner of the hallway and glanced toward the elevator at the end. It was an inch from closing on itself. The lighted floor buttons above read the number one with a star beside it. Lobby floor. Who was it and why had they changed their minds about seeing either me or Santa?

After grabbing my set of Santa's keys, I locked her front door.

I left for class but not before stopping at the front desk. "Has anyone signed in to see me or Santa Henderson today?"

"No, Ma'am," he said "No guests for either of you."

10

Sitting in morning traffic, I gazed at the crystalline sky, mustering positive energy for my breakfast appointment with Boots. There was a hint of fall in the air. Dry almost, and miraculously lacking the ton of invisible poundage typically added by high humidity.

My sliver of optimism came from an internet search last night after class when I'd managed to locate a woman who might be the Sandra Connor, LeeAnn's best friend. The trouble was, Sandra worked in the personnel department at Florida State University in Tallahassee. I didn't have time to fly there and talk with her. Hiring a teaching substitute would not be a problem, but it would eat into my profit margin. In case I had to return it, the money from Boots could disappear at any time.

I might have solved the dilemma of who'd been wandering the hallway last night. An ancient tenant, who belonged in a nursing home, lived on the 10th floor. With a sizeable bank account and history tied to Houston's rich and powerful, she'd never be forced out of the building. Her name was Bitsy, bestowed on her by an energy mogul of a husband who'd snatched her from a New York debutante ball over seventy-five years before. More than once, Bitsy ended up confused and wandering the hallway of the 14th floor, always with pearl button earrings and a silk blouse, vivid red or purple, matching bow tied at her neck. With every move of her walker, several long strands of pearls swung gracefully away from her bony frame.

Sometimes Santa rescued her and took her down to the 10th floor, depositing her back with the nurse she'd escaped. Sometimes it was my duty. I reminded myself to quiz the night guard about Bitsy. She could have exited the elevator in the lobby or the guard might have noticed the elevator doors open and close with no one stepping off.

The remaining puzzle stirring at the back of my brain was the identity of Robby's one-time girlfriend. If he'd actually had one. I vacillated between skepticism and thinking if he'd actually had a girl-friend, he could always get another.

When the blue metal roof of the IHOP appeared ahead, my mind clicked back into client mode. I exited 59 and pulled around back, parking my car on a huge square of concrete, no trees in sight. With plenty of eclectic, neighborhood cafes, why pick an IHOP near a free-way overpass where speeding traffic was the only view? Then I re-membered Boots was heading back to Beaumont.

My client wasn't inside, so I took a seat in a booth with a view of the front door. After waiting ten minutes, I signaled the waiter. A skinny young man with a dangerous looking Adam's apple sullenly approached my table, pad in hand.

"Take your order?"

His slouch and bored tone annoyed me, underscoring my need for another cup of coffee.

"Black coffee," I said.

He grunted and turned away just as I was thinking a more pleas-ing shade of orange uniform might improve IHOP's staff morale. Thank God Boots came through the door, waving and smiling when he spotted me. One cheerful person bringing me answers.

"You're looking mighty fine this morning." As Boots slid into the seat across from me, a perky blond girl popped up beside our booth, pencil poised to take his order. I couldn't blame her. Boots was a handsome man.

Lit by sunlight pouring through the restaurants' windows, his blue eyes now appeared pale-gray. "I'll take coffee," Boots turned his gaze on the waitress, "and fried eggs over easy. Then, little lady, I'll add some sausage and biscuits with gravy." When he handed back the menu, he winked at the waitress and I thought for a minute she was going to crawl in his lap. Boots cocked an eyebrow my way, but, shaking my head, I pointed at my coffee just arriving.

"Shall I plunge right in?" I asked, drawing notes from my briefcase. Yesterday morning I'd felt we were partners in mutual affection for our siblings and that we'd developed a rapport. I hoped my questions about LeeAnn weren't going to offend my biggest paying client.

Boots waited for cutie-pie to slip his coffee onto the table and leave, his head turning briefly to admire the young girl from behind. "What's up?" His pale eyes swiveled to mine as he tapped his index finger on the tabletop, a reminder he'd accommodated me on short notice.

"I have some questions we didn't cover yesterday."

"Say." He stilled his finger and leaned across the table, eyes suddenly alight with mischief, "Do you always wear black?"

Was he trying to throw me a curve ball? "I thought you were in a hurry to get to Beaumont." I slapped a stack of papers on the table and continued. "First question. Where would I find LeeAnn's papers, her computer, her bank account statements, monthly bills, insurance policy, etcetera?"

"Why d'ya need all that?" Boots' teasing manner fled, leaving a vacuum in his eyes.

"If your sister didn't accidentally fall to her death, but was pushed, I might find some answers in her personal papers. Or if money was a motive, in her business papers, emails on her computer, that sort of thing."

He nodded as if deep in thought. "Course you got to go through that stuff. I had storage come get it and told 'em to take her clothes and things like that to Goodwill. She had some file cabinets and a computer, for sure. We didn't email much, but she could have to other folks."

"Which storage?"

"The one up the road aways, Jake's Moving and Storage. Got the key in my pocket."

Just then the waitress placed his breakfast down. "Hot plate, sugar. Don't touch it, ya hear?"

Boots turned to me. "I've been meaning to clean it out but it's too soon. Know what I mean?"

As if food were his salvation, Boots dropped his head and dug in. My stomach flipped as he poked the yokes of his eggs, twin mounds erupting into viscous flows of gilded lava. I never did like the smell of eggs fried in grease.

I moved on to question number two. "Did Sandra Connor attend LeeAnn's funeral?"

Boots was polite enough to swallow before answering. "Nope. I told you Sandra disappeared right after my sister died. Had an unlisted number, so I tried calling her at work. They said she hadn't called in and hadn't showed. I kept trying. She never did show back up. I didn't know who else to ask about where she might be."

"So LeeAnn falls and Sandra disappears." I wrote myself a note, more convinced than ever that Sandra had willfully disappeared and wouldn't welcome a detective's questions.

"And there wasn't a funeral for my sister," Boots said. "She didn't want one."

"She didn't want a funeral?" I took a sip of lukewarm coffee before pushing it aside. How would a brother know the last wishes of his twenty-four year old sister? That would indicate compulsive planning to the extreme. I should have let Boots eat in peace, but didn't. "How did you know that was her wish?"

"My sister was a real schemer. Never did a thing spontaneously. Always had a plan, an agenda," Boots said. Then as if I'd never heard of it, he added, "Our Dad was always bitchin' at us about the six p's, how 'prior plannin' prevents piss-poor performance.' LeeAnn took it to heart, but not yours truly." He winked, then paused as if waiting for my reaction. Instead, I was thinking he'd revealed something about his sister that could have a bearing on her death. What better place to fall to your death than from a balcony with a hundred foot drop?

Boots pointed his fork at me as if to emphasize he wasn't through talking. "Ever since she was a little tyke, LeeAnn thought that burying people in coffins was disgusting. When she first got Beau—golly, she must a been sixteen—she tol' me that when her horse died, she was going to have him cremated and said they'd rest together someday in a beautiful urn." He looked at me, eyes suddenly glistening. "But Beau's still alive."

So Boots *was* still grieving. "Is Beau with you?"

He avoided my gaze "I sold him."

He must have sensed my shock. "It would a been too durn painful to keep him."

Boots went back to his breakfast, not allowing sadness to dull his appetite.

While he wiped the remaining egg yolk with a hunk of biscuit, I continued. "May I borrow your key to the storage room? I'd like to go through your sister's things."

Pulling a silver key ring from his pocket, he unscrewed a shiny black key and handed it over. "Here you go. It's close to Pease on Milam. The entry code and unit number's on the key ring."

I slipped it inside my briefcase. Now for the difficult part.

"I went over the police files again, Boots. There's a discrepancy between your version of your sister's happy mental state and theirs, which leans more toward the suicidal. Captain Hightower told me she tried to kill herself when she was eighteen, and that several people at the party the night she died stated she seemed depressed."

"Those idiots!" Boots slammed his napkin on the table top. "You believe them or me?"

Leaning toward him, I lowered my voice a notch, my manner unfazed, mentally thanking Robby for teaching me how to handle those on the verge. "When was the last time your sister spoke about her boyfriend?"

He turned his gaze toward the large picture window overlooking the freeway. "It was the first, maybe second week in December," he said softly. "I remember she said they drove to Hempstead so they could cut down their own Christmas tree. She thought that was romantic."

"They could have split up sometime between December and March, when she died."

"Maybe. But that bastard was beatin' up on her!"

"One of the witnesses, Brad Ewer, stated she was very upset over the break-up. Does that sound like she was abused?"

"You're not the only one who's read psychology. She prob'ly thought he would stop. Doesn't the woman always think the guy's gonna quit beatin' up on her? Besides, that horse-shit Ewer don't know squat. You need to be questioning him."

Boots obviously saw no contradiction in his statement.

"LeeAnn must have known Ewer fairly well in order to be invited to his sky box suite."

"My sister was pretty. Ewer likes pretty women. He must of spotted her at work, back when she was at Hammerly, but she was too smart to get involved with the likes of him. Mark my words."

His comment reminded me of something else missing from the police files. "How long did she work at Hammerly?"

"Less than a year, I think. It was when she first left Beaumont. Our parents had died and LeeAnn was ready to move to the big city. Ended up at another insurance place, better money She was real happy about it."

The mention of Beaumont and insurance gave rise to another question "Did she work for your uncle?"

His glance was sharp. "You heard of my uncle?"

"Who hasn't?"

Apparently my reply was too flippant.

"He's not Jesus H Christ, you know."

I let him stew for a few seconds before responding. "No. He's just Ramsey Tilman, state representative, who happens to chair the House Committee on Insurance."

"So?"

I noted his flare of defensiveness but refused to let it go. "Your sister worked in the insurance business. Why didn't you, with such a powerfully connected uncle?"

His eyes narrowed and his lips curled into a smile. "I hired me a gul-durn detective, now didn't I? You'd think she'd be smart enough to know when to stop asking questions."

Crap. "Boots, you hired me to ask questions. I have to have answers if I'm going to find out the truth about your sister's death."

He sighed and shook his head. "My uncle's got nothin' to do with LeeAnn's death. You gotta trust me on that one. You're headed up the wrong alleyway."

I remembered the stack of money he'd paid me, took a deep breath and nodded. Round one was over. I switched gears.

"You still live in the family home in Beaumont, right? That's the address you gave me."

Boots nodded before turning to gaze at two teenage girls coming through the door, giggling at a private joke, their matching khaki shorts showing an enviable stretch of tanned legs.

Thoughts about a short attention span crossed my mind and I cleared my throat, not knowing whether to be offended or amused. "Boots. Where do you stay when you come to Houston?"

He turned back, still wearing an expression of admiration I knew wasn't intended for me. "Our folks own an apartment near the Galleria. I stay there."

"Why didn't LeeAnn live there, save some rent?"

"Our folks made it clear that neither one of us could live there, only stay for short visits."

"But you said your parents died almost two years ago. Which one of you inherited the Houston apartment?"

He sighed, looked at me as if he'd vote to hold me back a grade. "Both of us, of course. We had it on the market. LeeAnn turned down all the offers we got, said they were too low. So we took it off. She said the apartment was our back-up, in case we ever had to sell."

Curious. If Brad Ewer was correct about LeeAnn being depressed over gambling debts, why hadn't she been more anxious to sell? Besides, two years ago they would have been paid top dollar. More than it would fetch now that the country was in a huge recession.

"Did your sister gamble?"

Boots grunted. "She liked to go to Lake Charles and play some. Why?"

"Well, Brad Ewer said—"

"I'm sick and tired of that bastard! What'd he say now—LeeAnn had a gambling problem, too?" Scowling, he threw up his hands in mock retreat. "Who you gonna believe? Him or me?"

"I'm just trying to get at the truth, Boots." I waited for his anger to subside. "Exactly how frequently did you and your sister talk? See each other?"

"Maybe four, five times a year." He screwed up his face and glanced at his watch. "Hell, maybe six or seven." He flashed a smile at the waitress as she took his empty plate.

"More coffee?" she asked.

Boots shook his head, dismissing her, and stood. "I gotta go. You do still have some of my money left, don't you?" He clicked his tongue at me before turning to leave. "You can buy my breakfast." Then as if he'd been rude, he threw me a dazzling smile before hurrying out of the restaurant.

Crap. I never had the chance to ask him the name of LeeAnn's psychiatrist. But then, Lamar should know. He had a memory for detail. If he'd talk to me, that is.

On the way to the storage facility, I puzzled over my client. He definitely thought his sister was happy and well adjusted, with no mental or gambling problems. She'd been close to her powerful uncle, but

Boots clearly was not. So how close had he really been to his sister? He was looking for someone to blame for her death as long as it had nothing to do with her or their uncle. LeeAnn's abusive, nameless, boyfriend was Boots' prime suspect, and if I didn't find him, I'd be a failure in his eyes.

11

She's nosy. Too damn nosy. She has no boyfriend, so why bug me about no girlfriend? I'm not suited. I have a temper and doc says all I have to do is take my meds and breathe deep and think about storms outside me and not inside me. I hurt her and she's gone and I had no business with a girlfriend anyway. I let myself get angry and that's not right. The doc says that's not right and I cannot allow it. Definitely not allow it. I will have no storms inside me, no storms ever and if I want to paint storms I can because they are there on the canvas or across the ocean and not inside me. This is a good thing. Good thing. So I will be placid, that's right, placid. Love that word placid and if I can stay placid I won't get angry and pull myself into turmoil like what a storm does to the water or a hurricane to land. She has no right to say I need a girlfriend. She doesn't know about placid and my need to be placid. Placid goes with peaceful and peaceful goes with private because I am good here in my room and writing and private. My landlady sticks her snout in my room and my sister says that's okay, that's the deal and I must get used to it but I don't like it. I'm supposed to be nice and peaceful but she fractures my peace and especially my privacy. A man has to have his privacy.

No one lets me have my privacy and that includes Giles because she's always after me to take my medicine and that's not giving me my privacy. She's a spy. She spies on me and won't allow me privacy. Is she coming? Coming here to count my pills? Coming after me to lock me up again? She thinks I made up the girlfriend but she's invading my right to privacy. Invading my *rights, I have rights, everyone has rights and even Father has rights to go away and leave me alone but sister can't just go and leave me alone because she must stay and spy on me. She's a spy and I wonder how much the government pays her to spy on me? Plenty. I bet plenty. Plenty, plenty, plenty, plenty, plenty.*

12

Pulling into the three-story storage building to park, I stowed my briefcase and jacket in the trunk, out of sight. The parking lot was empty except for two trucks, one black and the other white.

After punching in the numbered code on the key Boots gave me, I hit the star key and entered a dimly lit hallway running right and left. Dead-end rows, each with a dozen storage units facing each other, veered off the hallway. Letters were posted above each row. The other side of the key ring read C12. I turned the hall lights on bright and spotted row C, the third row down on my left. Number twelve stood at the end and appeared to be one of the larger ones if the width of the blue metal door was any indication.

It proved to be large, but there was little furniture stored inside. Perhaps LeeAnn's rental house had included furniture.

Pristine white packing boxes bearing the storage company's logo were stacked three deep half-way down the wall on my right, while a long, rolled oriental rug, a swivel chair, and a lamp hugged the left. The movers had configured a neatly organized space with room to walk down the middle. I looked for labels that would identify the contents of the boxes, but the moving company had been neat, not helpful. There was nothing written on the boxes but the name Jake's Moving & Storage in cheerful blue.

An antique dresser with a beveled mirror stood in the back corner. Each small drawer was empty except the one on the bottom. Like a gift to a lover, the perfect imprint of a scarlet mouth clung to the edge of a folded white linen handkerchief. Pink embroidered initials were sewn directly above the lip print, *LA C.* My face burned as if I'd crossed some deep, personal boundary—a strange reaction from someone who spied for a living. But I'd never spied on a very young, very beautiful dead girl before now.

The red lipstick impression on the hanky was too perfect, too deliberate to be accidental, and why not use a Kleenex? But then, if it were intended for a lover, why was it here in the drawer? Bright red was a color only the young can wear and again I pictured LeeAnn's blond ponytail, her youthful round cheeks, one small gloved hand resting on her horse. Such a waste. I stood, arched my back and told myself to quit chasing rabbits and moved over to the boxes lining the wall.

I counted twelve boxes stacked three deep, and began by the door in a methodical search of each one. After finding only household items, kitchenware, sheets and towels, I finally reached one containing rows of file folders. Setting this box aside, I quickly went through the remaining ones, finding one other full of papers that might prove promising. But there was no computer. Perhaps I'd misunderstood Boots.

With two boxes, one atop the other, I headed outside to my car. When I opened the trunk lid, a familiar tone sounded from my cell phone. Dropping the boxes on the ground, I reached in, grabbed my briefcase and retrieved my phone. I punched in the code for receiving messages. While listening, I cleared my briefcase and jacket from the trunk and slammed the lid, but heard only breathing, followed by a loud sneeze. I flicked the phone lid closed. Most likely a wrong number.

Turning to the boxes, I noticed an edge of paper sticking out from underneath the bottom one. I threw my jacket and briefcase in the front seat, then lifted the top box into the back seat before shutting the car door. Squatting next to the box remaining on the ground, I pulled on the piece of paper. Stuck tight in a few spots, I used my fingernail to peel it away from the bottom.

When it finally came loose, I grew puzzled, staring at a string of five black and white snapshots, a couple of inches square, like those you get from a carnival booth. Two people, cheek to cheek, were dotted with white spots where pieces of their image were torn away.

For a minute, I thought this didn't belong with LeeAnn's possessions. It must have been left on the storage room floor where it clung to the bottom of the box like a stowaway. The top three frames of the strip were the least intact, showing partial images of a man and woman smooching for the camera, large sections of their profiles blotched, anonymous. My eyes froze on the bottom frame.

No longer in profile, the man and woman smiled straight at the camera. The man wore a white Stetson hat, a small pouch of flesh beneath his chin exposing him as far older than the woman. More girl than woman, the pretty blond, her bangs slightly torn away from the photo backing, smiled just as she had when she'd posed with her horse. It was LeeAnn Callahan, side by side with one of the men who'd witnessed her death—Brad Ewer.

I leaned over to pick up the box but paused, suddenly uneasy. Someone behind me sneezed, but before I could straighten, jolts of electricity tore through my back. Pain coursed through my body. I gasped, struggling to breathe. Before collapsing on the asphalt, I saw myself— in police uniform—out cold on the gym floor. As a part of my training, I'd been Tasered. No one should have to feel that numbing lifelessness—like a small death from the electric chair.

$$\mathcal{Q}$$

"Shit, man! Lady, Lady! Can you hear me? Did'ja need an ambulance?"

I struggled to open my eyes. My forehead throbbed as I squinted into bright daylight. Above me, a pale face emerged, lines shimmering on his face like heat on a desert horizon. His head appeared small. A boy?

"Kin you talk?"

I tried to sit upright. Black dots danced where his face had been.

"I got water here from my truck."

Aiming for the water bottle, I held out my hand. After several attempts, the stranger shoved the bottle into my palm. I stared at it. When it became obvious that was my best effort, he took back the bottle, reached underneath me and, propping me upright, tilted the water to my lips. Parched, I eagerly swallowed, while small tremors like aftershocks arched sporadically through my body.

"What's your name, lady?"

"Giles. I'm Giles."

By then I could see his face. He looked fifteen but was probably twenty. He wore a tan straw cowboy hat tilted back on his head and a failed attempt at a beard.

"That's real good. You knows your name, but you still might have bumped your head, have a concussion, you know. I'm goin' call you some help." Once he satisfied himself I could sit upright without assistance, he took a cell phone from his pocket, his blue eyes clouded with concern. At the thought of an ambulance, I felt a sudden panic.

I grabbed his elbow. "No, really. I'm fine. Just need to rest against my car here for a minute." I remembered the picture I'd been looking at right before I was attacked. Tenderly, I moved my head and looked around. The box beside my car was gone. No sign of the photo. "Did you see anyone?"

"No, ma'am. Someone drove off when I come outside carryin' my saddle and tack. It wasn't till after I tossed 'em in my truck bed that I saw you lyin' there by your car. Were you robbed?"

Not wanting police involvement, at least not until there was hard evidence LeeAnn hadn't willingly fallen to her death, I managed a smile. "No. Sometimes I faint in the heat. But I've never suffered a concussion." I rubbed my forehead where a small stalagmite was growing. "Do you remember what kind of car drove off?"

"Yeah. The white one parked next to me."

"What make was it?"

"It was one of those Ford SUV's. Not a real truck in my opinion." He took off his hat and swiped his forehead, eyes narrowing. A question was forming in his boyish head. He was trying to understand my curiosity about the truck if I'd merely fainted.

Time to get moving. "If you'll just help me inside my car, I promise to go straight home. I'll be fine."

"I took first aid when I wuz in high school and I'm not at all sure you should drive."

With his help, I struggled to my feet. Once behind the wheel, I looked down where he squatted outside my car door.

"I ain't leavin' until you acts normal."

I forced another smile. "What's not normal?"

"If'n I could follow you home, I would. But I gotta get to my rodeo committee meetin' or my ass is grass. Pardon the expression."

"I'm fine, really I can drive now." My vision wavered as bile rose to my throat. In truth I felt rubbery, deflated, somewhat mis-wired. I swallowed and said, "Thanks so much for stopping to help me."

He nodded and shut the car door. Desperate to lean my head on the steering wheel for just one minute, I knew I'd never escape him if I did. He raised his palm in farewell.

Slowly, I pulled out of the parking lot. The young cowboy stood chewing on his bottom lip and then called out to me, but whatever he said was lost over the sound of the motor. From the rearview mirror, I watched him amble back toward his black truck.

I looked at my watch. If I'd spent forty-five minutes inside LeeAnn's storage unit and it took five minutes after leaving to reach my car, I'd been out for only three or four minutes. Not bad, since at training, I was out cold for a little over five. Was my attacker watching me right now?

In my rearview mirror, I spotted the other box resting on the back seat. Its lid came an inch below the seatback. Whoever Tasered me must not have seen it. Yet I mourned the loss of the missing box that might have held more pictures, told more stories about LeeAnn Callahan. Crap.

Pulling into traffic, I remembered hearing, right before I collapsed in a heap, the sound of a huge sneeze. Or had I imagined it? The unidentified caller on my cell phone had sneezed. Coincidence?

No one could be convicted from just a sneeze. Houston was allergy hell. Anxious to get home and examine the contents of the remaining box, I hit the gas. I'd check caller ID on my cell later.

Sunglasses shielded my eyes from the glare. As I picked up speed, congratulating myself on being a tough broad, I looked in the rearview mirror. A dirt-splattered white SUV loomed less than a car's length behind. Too close for comfort in my much smaller vehicle. Was this the same white truck from the storage parking lot—maybe coming after the second box? Had the young cowboy scared him away and now he was going to finish me off?

The truck drew near enough for me to see the license plate number if I could only read backwards and through a layer of dirt. I blinked hard to clear my head. The driver leaned on his horn. Trapped in heavy traffic, there was nowhere to go. I thought the trucker would give up and slow down, right up until he rammed me from behind.

13

I scolded myself for being paranoid. He was just another maniacal Houston truck driver. This time I didn't let go of the wheel as I pushed the accelerator, now dangerously close to hitting the Toyota in front of me. Surely the driver would speed up. It looked like there was space for the Toyota to move a few feet ahead while my Honda and I were sandwiched tight.

Tensed for another blow from behind, I glanced at my side mirror. A motorcyclist, probably fed up with traffic, drew up between me and the cars in the lane immediately to my left. Now directly astride me, he motioned for me to pull back which was impossible unless I wanted to be rear-ended into oblivion. I willed myself not to panic as the motorcyclist steered toward my front bumper as if to squeeze behind the Toyota in front of me. Jolts of fear ran through me. I was locked in. Nowhere to go.

My eyes darted to the vehicle behind, now retreated only slightly.

Lightly tapping the brakes, I fell back, cursing the idiot on the motorcycle as well as the one behind me. Within seconds, the motorcyclist pulled in front of me, ripped off his helmet with his left hand, and tossed it back over his head. Instinctively, I ducked. The helmet sailed over the top of my Honda. Glancing in the rearview mirror, I saw it, like a black cannonball, smash into the windshield of the SUV, a crack spreading across the glass. The truck careened into the right lane; gridlock hatched and grew as the sound of metal on metal filled the air.

Ahead of me, the motorcyclist skillfully maneuvered across two lanes and took the Louisiana exit. Was his helmet meant for my windshield? Were he and the SUV driver in cahoots or had he done exactly what he'd intended?

Too shaken to follow the biker, I slowly eased over and stopped on the shoulder. After unsnapping the seat belt, I got out, knees buckling underneath me while the odor of gas fumes filled my nostrils. Crouched beside my bumper, I spotted gas leaking in a steady stream. The sirens of police cars and the wobbly cry of an ambulance reverberated in my head while I squatted, knees pulled to my chin, my fingers unconsciously rubbing circles against my pounding temples.

A police car pulled up and an officer got out. While I babbled about the white SUV, the officer knelt beside me, asked if I was part of the chaos down the freeway. I nodded. He spoke briefly into his shoulder mike then told me an ambulance was coming for me. In a voice that sounded discombobulated, I told him I was fine, I didn't need an ambulance, that some idiot had tried to kill me and maybe a motorcyclist, too, and that I had to have a car to go see my brother Robby, that he needed me and that I had work to do and had been paid a lot of money and my time was valuable and why did it hurt to breathe?

The medics arrived, placed me on a stretcher, body restrained, an oxygen mask clamped over my face. My protestations grew faint. The freeway, memories of a white SUV and a motorcyclist, floated far away.

Thank God for Aunt Eunice. As a prominent Houston citizen and an exemplary Episcopalian, she'd sat for over twenty years on the board of St. Luke's Episcopal Hospital. My name appeared on some database of the privileged in the bowels of this esteemed Houston Medical Center hospital. So it was to that emergency room I was taken and not Ben Taub, Houston's charity hospital of last resort— where Robby would have landed. I'd always wondered why my brother was exempted from this particular Aunt Eunice largesse and not me.

Lying on a gurney, I was rushed past a waiting room filled with crying children and wheelchair-bound patients and down to a room off a long hallway. After un-strapping me and carefully hefting me onto a raised bed, one of the medics told me a doctor would be with me shortly. When he asked if I needed a shot for pain, I said all I wanted was aspirin and permission to leave. They left me staring at the overhead florescent lights.

Within minutes, a doctor bustled in. From my vantage point, I peered up at a tall, angular woman with an intimidating air. Her mouth stretched thin as she glanced at her clipboard and when she shifted her gaze to me, small blue eyes sharp as glass shards bore into mine. Her touch, though, was surprisingly gentle.

After carefully peeling up my shirt, she began poking various parts of my chest and neck. Her stethoscope must have just been removed from the freezer. I couldn't tell which was more uncomfortable, the cold metal or the thumping with her hands as if my chest were a Tabla drum, asking with each blow if I could feel that and if it hurt.

After I responded yes to the first and no to the second, she finally reached a spot on my chest that elicited an "ouch."

"I don't think you're suffering from cardiac tamponade, but just to be sure, I'm going to keep you overnight." Staring at my forehead, she carefully touched it then parted my hair as if searching for more purple gems. "Hmmm. Nasty bump. Definitely keeping you overnight."

At the very least I should have reacted to the cardiac part, but my biggest fear was being stuck in this hospital for days. "Look. I can't do that. I've got to teach class tonight and have lots of work to do—"

"You really don't have a choice. Unless, of course, you're willing to drop dead in front of your students." She arched her brow and a chill ran through me that had nothing to do with her stethoscope.

"If I have to stay," I mumbled with a big question mark at the end.

"Now we're talking. Someone will come to take you for an echocardiogram and then you'll be checked into a room." She gave me a grandmotherly pat on my shoulder before hurrying to her next patient.

One hour and one echocardiogram later, I was wheeled down more corridors, dropped a few floors in an elevator and into my room and onto a bed. I felt like a product in a huge manufacturing facility that was only half-way down the assembly line, abandoned on a conveyor belt.

After an eternity, a nurse arrived. With plump cheeks and a full head of black hair, he looked far too young to be out of high school, much less nursing school. He smiled an encouraging smile. "You need to take this to help you relax." A small, oval shaped pill appeared between his pale stubby fingers.

"Okay. But first can I ask a favor?"

He looked skeptical.

"Would you please call my department," I scrambled in my briefcase some kind soul had slung near my feet, and produced my cell phone, "and tell the secretary to put a note on my class door saying class is cancelled for tonight and then call my neighbor Santa, explain what happened and ask her to please feed Suzy." I rummaged some more, found paper and pen, and wrote down phone numbers, ignoring the painful throbbing in my head.

"Also," I said, after locating my auto insurance card, "will you please, please arrange a rent car? I know it's above and beyond your call of duty, but I'll need one first thing in the morning." At that last bit, he cocked his eyebrow, put one meaty hand on his hip, and looked far more dubious than I would have liked. I didn't care.

I would leave tomorrow if I had to climb out the window and hail a cab.

Before agreeing to make any phone calls, Doubting Thomas waited while I swallowed the tiny pill. After handing him the empty water glass, I was rewarded with a brief tight-lipped smile and his promise to use the phone at the nurse's station. Before leaving, he shot back a directive to enjoy my rest. Right. Enjoy being incapacitated, behind in my class material, behind in my investigation, and worst of all, forced to miss Robby's group therapy session at eleven the following morning.

After lowering my groggy head to the pillow, a niggling doubt asserted itself. It wasn't like me to count on someone else to take care of important business. I should make the phone calls myself, not an overworked and perhaps undependable nurse.

My eyelids grew heavy. Fighting to stay awake, my brain said to find my cell phone, but had failed to explain why.

My briefcase was no longer beside me. I slid from under the covers and tried to stand, balancing myself with one hand on the bedside table. I took a step forward, legs rubbery, my thoughts clouded, moving with tentative steps as sluggish as if I were under water. I stumbled toward the closet and opened it. Wouldn't the nurse have placed it here? He had. The outline of my black briefcase resting on the floor appeared fuzzy. I blinked hard and reached for it just as the floor flew up and whacked me on the head. Double crap.

From somewhere above, I heard a deep voice. "You don't look like you should be out of bed."

I knew that voice. Not Hightower's. Not Robby's, either. Someone familiar, but my mind refused to cooperate. I smiled back at the voice and a man reached for me, the odor of sweet pipe tobacco filling my nostrils. As he carried me back to bed, I tried to force my eyes open, but couldn't. I don't remember his exact words, but I thought he promised, as he pulled the covers over me, to have a car waiting for me in the morning.

I was like spreading honey, melting into the bed sheets. Soon I was running, running with the smell of Sherlock Holmes' pipe tobacco behind me. The funny thing was, I enjoyed the chase.

14

"You must have a hard time getting around Houston. All night long you mumbled about the Keymap." A nurse, older and very female with bright orange lipstick, stood beside my bed as golden light streamed from the open window blinds. She leaned close and meticulously peeled countless heart monitors from my chest.

At the mention of Keymap, my heart drummed faster. I prayed the monitors wouldn't pick up my excitement. But I remembered the deep, sexy voice from last night and the smell of his tobacco. What had he been doing in my room? How had he known where I was?

The nurse straightened and smiled, a smudge of tangerine on her front teeth. "Sugar, your heart is strong as an ox. The doctor says you can get dressed and go home."

I swung my feet over the bed and stood. "What time is it?"

"Eight thirty and thank God it's Friday."

When I hurried to the closet and began dressing, she hesitated in the doorway. "You should wait till after breakfast. You get to choose whatever you want."

I pulled on my clothes, smiled and shut the door behind her. By eight thirty-five I wanted to be driving away from here. Driving? Crap! What if Doubting Thomas had never called my insurance company?

Dressed and seated on the edge of the bed with cell phone in hand, I was punching the insurance number when the door flew open.

"You look none the worse for wear."

I almost dropped the phone. "You're Keymap," I said. <u>Brilliant, Giles</u>.

"In the flesh."

He wasn't what I'd pictured at all. His thick waist would have been too broad if his shoulders had been smaller than the doorway they now filled. He had a wrestler's body and neck, but only from the waist up. Rather like a gorilla, his arms seemed too long for his torso. Not a short man, but then, he wasn't as tall as my brother who stood six-feet-two.

Keymap was dressed in black leather pants and jacket. It made me sweat to look at him. His untamed eyebrows, black and thick, held a smattering of silver. Swarthy complexion, dark eyes and a face that needed a shave. From a distance he appeared bald. But he wore his hair short, perhaps an inch long, its dominant color more white than dark Not a handsome man, but not ugly either. No deep lines on his face; he couldn't be much older than forty.

Like a once-wrecked car that, after repair, still appeared skewed on its axels, Keymap loped into the room, his glance sly, his mouth twitching with mischief. He perched on the corner of the mattress, turned and stuck out a hairy paw.

"We meet at last."

I shook his hand, averting my eyes from the sight of his entire lower body straining against tight leather. His grip was strong and his hands were rough. But it was his voice, deep and musical, almost hypnotic, that sent chills running up my spine. Again that fruity smell of pipe tobacco filled the space along with the pungent scent of male pheromones. I swallowed and slipped my hand from his grasp.

"Thought I'd show up in case you needed some help escaping," he said.

His teeth flashed white and my stomach dropped. I don't know how I'd pictured him from our last phone conversation, but it wasn't this primal-looking creature sitting beside me.

Keymap's real name was a mystery I'd never solved. As a rookie graduate of the Houston Police Academy, I'd been feted, or "initiated" as my seniors called it, at Joe's Cantina south of downtown. It was late, with city smog obscuring the stars, as five off-duty sergeants, Gonzales in the lead, steered me toward the entrance, its adobe façade draped in colored paper and tin cut-outs. The cantina offered authentic Mexican food and dangerously strong margaritas. My initiation as a police officer was to see how many margaritas I could down and still walk a straight line. They had jokingly started a pool.

Only after we were seated away from the smoke-infused bar at the front did I realize the other two females in my graduating class weren't joining us.

After the second round, I foolishly thought I could walk any chalk-line laid out for me, when a waiter leaned over and placed a "Grande margarita" in front of me.

"A *senor* in black leather said this is for you." He leaned closer and whispered in my ear, "He say Mr. Willard and Mr. Gonzales hold the key to his name."

I glanced around but saw no gentleman in black. I touched Willard's arm next to mine and he leaned close.

Pointing to the oversized margarita, I said, "The waiter told me this was from a gentleman wearing black leather and you and Gonzales hold the key to his name."

Willard looked surprised, stood and left the room. When he returned, his expression hadn't changed. He leaned over Gonzales's shoulder and they conferred in whispers. I grew bored with their intrigue and began a lively banter with another cop. Halfway through my drink, Willard appeared across the table from me.

Flushed with pride, enjoying the gargantuan margarita, I was glad of the camaraderie, thinking my father would be proud— if I talked to him, which I didn't—when Willard leaned over, his paunch sectioned in half by the edge of the wooden table. He glowered, then stage-whispered to Gonzales on my right. "Should we tell her about Keymap? Or make her walk first?"

"You mean Clark Kent, dontcha?" Gonzales grumbled.

I remained confused while the two exchanged furtive glances. Then Willard leaned back. "On second thought, Keymap ain't dealt with no lady cop I know of. But," he nodded at my margarita, "he obviously likes you."

Willard scraped his chair back and motioned for me to stand. "I say you walk." He pointed to a six inch wide turquoise strip painted on the rust-colored *Saltillo* tile floor. It ended with a curved arrow pointing toward *los banos*. "Chug-a-lug your drink, Giles Faulkner, then ole' Gonzales there'll make sure you don't teeter." Willard's glance was full of challenge as he added, "Step outside the blue and those of us bettin' on you lose."

Five pairs of amused eyes stared at me. No matter what, losing was not an option. I downed my drink and stood, the clatter of wooden chair legs against tile the only sound. Gonzales took my elbow and led me to the worn band of blue. I figured there was about fifteen feet that snaked toward the back of the restaurant.

With each step I took, cops stood close enough to spit on, and with each step I jammed my heel against the toe of my back shoe to steady myself. When I came within a few feet of the pointed arrow, the end of the blue line, my vision blurred and my stomach churned—too much alcohol too quickly. *Don't look at your feet, look straight ahead and breathe deeply.* I blinked and, ahead of me, the blurred outline of an amused waiter appeared.

I felt myself sway, gritted my teeth and briefly squeezed my eyes shut. I heard a snort, then someone snickered, "Bet she folds right here, fellas."

I smiled. Nobody had said anything about running. Opening my eyes wider, I took in the line as it curved, and sprinted ahead, my shoes pounding firmly on blue.

Chaos erupted as the sound of high whistles and back slapping filled the room. My ego swelled and I grew six inches taller. It turned out only Gonzales bet I'd make it. He was the one, a fat wad of dollar bills bulging from his shirt pocket, who told me about Keymap and his legendary PI abilities on our way out of the restaurant.

Vaguely disappointed, I questioned the need to ever hire a private detective for information. I was perfectly capable of getting it myself. Gonzales's knowing smile mocked me as he scribbled Keymap's beeper number on a piece of paper. "Jes hold onto it, *chica*. It could come in handy." Before turning to get inside the car, he gave me a quizzical look. "I shouldn't have to say this is private. Keymap's name and number are not for spreading around. That drink back there says you've passed muster, but jes you and nobody else."

Neither Willard nor Gonzales had ever met Keymap in person. But now, here he was beside me.

"I'm sorry." I gripped the top of the mattress. "You'll help me escape what?" Mentally grimacing, I willed my brain to click into halfway intelligent conversation mode.

"I offered to help you out of this joint. Last night you were trying to call your insurance company. You asked me to double-check on your rental car."

"I did?" Hoping it would clear my mind, I hacked out a small cough before responding.

"How'd you know I was here?"

Keymap remained silent, staring into my eyes. Then another grin briefly flashed my way—a grin that rendered my question rhetorical.

Uncomfortable at his penetrating gaze, I was startled when he abruptly stood and looked down at me. "You really ought to get married and settle down. Quit this dangerous business you're involved in." He sounded as if he were giving advice to someone very young and very naïve. For a few seconds, I thought I hadn't heard correctly.

"What . . . "

I'd long felt immediate hostility for anyone who mentioned me and marriage in the same breath. Instead of snarling that I'd like to see him happily married with two requisite children and still be responsible for someone like my brother, Robby, I stuffed down my anger and focused on his last point. What did he mean by "dangerous business"? How could he know what I was or wasn't up to? Keymap's question cut into my thoughts.

"Need any help on the Callahan case?"

I froze, my brain stuck on turmoil mode. Surely my slowness was due to hospital drugs. "I don't suppose you'll share with me how you know I was hired?"

He pushed back the cuff of his leather jacket and glanced at a chrome wrist watch, its face cradled in a deep thatch of black curly hair. "I don't have much time." He dug in his pants pocket and pulled out a set of keys. "Catch."

I did.

"Your car is parked beside valet out front. A red Camaro. You need to live a little, Giles."

At the sound of my name, I came out of whatever stupor I was in. "You still haven't answered my question."

Another flash of teeth. "You noticed." Then as if a cloud descended, he spoke, his voice rough. "You could be in over your head. I offered to help, that's all."

In over my head? Since when was I the helpless damsel to be rescued by this ape? I bit my tongue as the thought of Sandra Connor at Florida State came to mind. It was hard to be in two places at once. "How much do you know?"

"As much as you do. Probably more."

I squelched a sharp retort. "So you know about Boots hiring me? About his sister's best friend, Sandra Connor, leaving town after LeeAnn died?" I expected at least one confused look.

I got none. Instead, he nodded as if bored.

"Okay, then I could use someone to check Sandra out. She may be in Tallahassee at Florida State, their personnel department." Rattling off questions for him to ask, I stopped when Keymap curled his lips as if to say I was wasting my breath.

"You already know what I need?"

"I know the drill, just needed your permission. And my new hourly rate. It's higher for experienced PI's than for rookies."

I worried over his last statement. When he turned to go, he stopped and looked back as if he had an afterthought. "I can help you get outside before they come back with a wheelchair. Figure you wouldn't want to leave that way."

He was right but my fast mouth snapped that I didn't need his help before my smarter self could overrule.

"Then I'm off. You'll hear from me next week."

He left, leaving the room strangely void as if all its energy had been sucked into the hallway. Suddenly, I wanted just another minute in close proximity to this leather-clad primate. Even if it was only to exchange barbs.

15

After my rookie margarita initiation, curiosity about Keymap grew stronger, but I was hard-pressed to find any real information on him.

Rumor had it he was a physics PhD candidate who'd dropped out of Stanford, had three wives in three different states, and had connections to top state and federal officials as well as pimps on the street. And he wouldn't work for just anybody. But he'd returned my first call. By then, I'd left HPD and hung out my own PI shingle.

A child support dodger had fled to Mexico. I needed my teaching income and couldn't leave town. With a female client anxious for the son-of-a-bitch to pay, I wanted my fee and thought of Keymap. His trip and unofficial extradition of the skip had cost me surprisingly little. But that was three years ago. How much would he charge me now?

Behind the wheel of the red Camaro, I glanced at my watch and realized it was two hours before Robby's group therapy—enough time to retrieve my gun. Pulling my cell out, I confirmed where my maimed car had been taken—Village Car Repair.

Idling at the corner of Kirby Drive and University Boulevard, my right-turn signal blinking, I glanced in the rear-view mirror. Directly behind me, a motorcyclist wearing black leather straddled his bike. My heart jumped to my throat. Quickly pulling onto Kirby, I again checked the mirror. Was I in for another assault? The motorcyclist was waving me over as if he were a cop.

My pulse pounded. I could keep going, maybe risk his helmet in my windshield, or pull over. I pulled over in front of a hardware store on Kirby Drive. Doors locked and engine running, I sat and waited. He wheeled up beside me and pulled off his helmet.

Crap! I recognized the motorcycle that blocked my exit after I'd left Captain Hightower's building. Keymap killed the switch before dismounting his cycle. Was he also the rider who'd thrown off his helmet that crashed into the white truck's windshield? My uneasiness turned quickly to irritation.

I jerked the key out of the car's ignition and got out. "You've been following me, haven't you?"

"Guilty as charged." He withdrew an envelope from inside his jacket and held it out. "I remembered an invite you might be interested in." He nodded as if giving me permission to open it. I crossed my arms over my chest and glared.

"Okay." He flashed his blinding smile. "I'm invited to Brad Ewer's house this evening for cocktails. Thought you might want to come."

Ewer's house. Did Brad Ewer know him as Keymap or call him by his real name? My curiosity was piqued. How did they know each other? Keymap certainly moved in lofty circles. I wondered if three wives in three separate states were equally true.

"What does Ewer call you? Keymap?"

"Think about it," he said. "A chance at Ewer." He glanced down at his motorcycle boots. "Most likely his sidekick McGraw, too."

I'd already blown my chance of befriending Brad Ewer when I forced my way into his office. But talking to his right hand man, J.D. McGraw, the other witness to Lee Ann's death, was too tempting to resist.

"Cocktail attire," he spoke above the sound of a passing truck. "I'll pick you up at eight."

Any expression was soon hidden behind aviator sunglasses as he turned and mounted his cycle. With the roar from his bike in my ears, I tried to imagine myself perched behind him wearing a helmet, heels and a cocktail dress.

After retrieving my gun and LeeAnn's storage box from my car, I headed home, remembering how Keymap had handed over his catch three years before. At five o'clock in the morning he'd chained the skip, knocked out and snoring loudly, to the back door of my rent house. His phone call woke me up. In the ex-husband's pocket, Keymap said, I'd find his bill for services. He followed this with a slight chuckle that the handcuff key was in the front pocket of the guy's pants. I'd been almost sorry he wasn't there to witness how I retrieved the key without blushing, and without the man waking up.

Even more amazing was that after three years, I'd remembered the sound of Keymap's voice, deep and rich, as if he spoke from a buried well of narrowly hidden emotions—the sign of a truly sensitive man.

I shoved the Camaro into third gear. Never award sensitivity to the male species. Especially not to a man you've just met. Then again, I was looking forward to tonight. If I could consider this a date, it would be my first in over a year. Well, maybe my second.

I pulled into the drive of the hi-rise and allowed the parking attendant to carry the box inside the elevator. Congratulating myself on my memory, I retrieved my cell phone, but was immediately disappointed to see "caller unknown" for the sneezer's phone call.

I needed a change of luck. As I leaned against the elevator wall, it dawned on me—what <u>was</u> I going to wear tonight?

Robby's shrink officed on West Alabama Street, four miles from my hi-rise. On a once-residential-only street, it morphed over the years into a busy commercial thoroughfare of two-story brick cottages housing antique shops, dental and doctors' offices and the occasional restaurant. Lack of zoning laws meant that a few hardy types still lived in these houses next door to going business concerns.

Dr. Winthrop's practice was on the first floor. He lived on the second. His conference room was far from opulent, with folding metal chairs placed in a circle near the entrance and a few stuffed chairs relegated to the far end of the room. More than once, I'd wondered if the upstairs were as frugally outfitted. But then Dr. Winthrop counseled Robby, and several other clients, on a reduced fee basis. It seemed this psychiatrist cared more for his patients than his pocketbook.

Robby's group session held four other patients whose ailments, over time, grew familiar as textbook cases. Clyde, a balding man in his fifties with Asperger's syndrome, walked up the sidewalk. He turned only slightly as I drew close behind him, but refused to speak when I greeted him. He entered the house ahead of me. Over the years I'd watched Clyde struggle with socialization skills and developed great admiration for his tenacity.

Everyone else, including Robby, was already seated in the conference room when I took the one remaining seat in the circle of folding chairs. Originally, this room had been a living room and dining room. Winthrop had knocked out the partition, painted it a cheery yellow and hung bright Picasso prints on the walls. Unlike the cheery room, the occupants gave off the scent of stale odor and nervous anticipation, avoiding eye contact.

The doctor glanced at me over half-framed tortoiseshell glasses, his expression blank. But I knew this was his professional demeanor, and that his mind ran constantly at the speed of light.

After glancing at Robby seated across from me, my chest tightened. His head was hung, arms resting on his thighs, black curls glistening as if he'd just stepped out of a shower. With one hand clutching the other, Robby stared at his left thumb as it rubbed continuously over his folded fingers. I knew this gesture and it filled me with dread.

"We can begin now," Dr. Winthrop said. "Who wants to go first?"

Robby raised his head and glared at me. I knew what was coming.

"You don't belong here, sis."

I glanced at Dr. Winthrop, silently asking for support.

He looked the role of leader, dark khakis and a black T-shirt, his right ankle resting on his left thigh. As he leaned toward my brother, he assumed an expression of mild interest, tinged slightly with concern.

"Now, Robby. We agreed your sister could come. In fact, you all were invited to bring the person responsible for helping you with your condition, the one who reminds you to take your medicines. And you all signed to that effect. Besides, Robby, Giles won't talk unless you ask her to."

"I'm asking her to leave." Robby looked around the room, his look a dare to the others. Winthrop gazed steadily at him. His tone, when he spoke, was polite but resolute. "You may leave if you like, Robby, but your sister stays." He waited, but Robby sat motionless.

"Clyde." Dr. Winthrop switched his attention, "Tell us about your week."

I held my breath. Clyde opened his mouth, but then glanced at Robby first, as if seeking his permission.

My brother snapped upright in his chair, eyes burning with rage and every bit of it directed at me. "You're not supposed to follow me. You follow me everywhere. You're a spy for the government and you," he jabbed his finger at me, "better leave me alone."

My stomach twisted and I swallowed hard, struggling for just the right tone. "I'm not spying on you, Robby," I started slowly. "You agreed it would help if I came. Don't you remember last month? I missed coming. If I was spying on you, I wouldn't miss a session, now would I?"

He looked confused and paused as if rethinking his logic. Then his thumb began its rhythm again.

Dr. Winthrop nodded at a frightened Clyde, now rocking back and forth in his chair, his body bent over as if he had a stomach ache.

"You were about to say?" Dr. Winthrop urged Clyde.

Robby mouth twisted as he stared. For a moment, he looked close to tears. But my brother hadn't cried since he was five. It was as if the beginning of his mental struggles had been the end of his sensitivity.

"I made you something and you never came to get it." His anger deflated. He appeared desolate, his voice uncertain, his posture slumped. "Nothing I do is good enough for you."

Dr. Winthrop turned to the group. "Does anyone have something to say about Robby's issues?"

Suddenly, Robby lunged, punched me in the chest and I fell backward. Clyde, an uncharacteristic look of beatific calm on his face, jumped Robby from behind while Winthrop sprang toward me. The four of us landed in a tangled heap.

Dr. Winthrop no longer appeared benign. He helped Clyde to his feet, then grabbed Robby by the arm and hauled him out into the hallway, shouting for his assistant. Part secretary and part bodyguard, the big guy was an ex-wrestler and keeper of the hypodermic that rendered violent patients docile. Docile enough to be hauled off to the mental ward. Robby hated lock-up and he would blame me.

Clyde held his hand out. He wouldn't look at me, but righted my chair and helped me sit down. Still not looking at me, Clyde turned, walked across the room and took his seat. Through my tears, I called out a weak "thank you." My chest throbbed. Instinctively, I rubbed the spot, hoping to assuage the pain. Damn my brother! Would I have kneed him in the groin if we'd been alone together? He should go to lock-up. Crazy bastard!

Dr. Winthrop returned with his composure unruffled, his expression unreadable.

"Let's talk about Robby's outburst against Giles. Clyde, what are you thinking?"

"Off his meds. He's prob'ly off his meds." Clyde sat and continued his rocking.

"Anyone else?"

No one spoke. I pondered how Robby always saved his rage for me and our father, who had moved to another state—something I could never do. Besides, Robby's anger at me had always been limited to a single fist blow and never to my face, whereas our father had suffered a broken nose, broken teeth and bruises. Why did I still blame him for leaving us?

One woman in the group piped up that Robby had been cruel and Dr. Winthrop should punish him. The good doctor replied that forced hospitalization was enough punishment.

I tuned out their comments, thinking that Robby's breakdowns were not only coming more frequently but that my ability to preempt these disasters had been sorely lacking. Anger flew red rage straight through all my senses.

Clyde was right. Robby had obviously stopped his medications, flushed his pills down the toilet. It wasn't the first time. Why the hell couldn't Robby do the right thing and take his meds?

16

Desperate for something to take my mind off Robby, I sat on the floor of my study with LeeAnn's storage box open in front of me, examining each folder. Most were empty, and those with papers held only a few out-of-sequence bank statements. No telling photographs of Boots' sister. My cloud grew darker.

It appeared LeeAnn hadn't hurt for money, spending over $20,000 a month. A company called "Logos, Ltd.," had, for the only three bank statements in date order, deposited $23,000 per month into her account. Trust fund? Also, why were there so many missing statements?

I tucked the name Logos into the folds of my brain for later investigation. My heart wasn't into this enough to focus, and the best thing to combat my preoccupation over Robby was exercise. Bank statements could wait.

I pulled on my swimsuit and headed to the basement pool. With only one lane to choose from, I dove in and began a furious crawl. After an hour, I hoisted myself out, arms and legs quivering. With Robby still on my mind, I watched a man perform the butterfly stroke, slinging water into the lanes on either side of him. Like the swimmer, my brother plowed though life, oblivious to anyone within close range.

I understood why Robby flushed his medications. They carried side effects—an inability to concentrate along with an intermittent ringing in his ears that maddened him. But when he stopped taking his meds, voices from God, Jesus, Gandhi, or the Dalai Lama took over his mind, torturing him with their edicts. Sometimes he wrote down bits of their contradictory sermons. This was Dr. Winthrop's idea.

After Robby was back on medication, he occasionally shared these holy mandates with me, recognizing the humor of his affliction, but with a frustrated bitterness that tore at my heart. I stood, grabbed my towel and headed upstairs.

Forty minutes later, I was showered and dressed in sweats. Picking up the receiver, I dialed Dr. Winthrop.

"Yo, Giles," Winthrop answered. He tried to sound lighthearted, but I recalled his expression at group therapy when we all pretended not to hear Robby's rage from the hallway as he was bound inside a straight-jacket and shoved into the back of an ambulance. Winthrop's face had mirrored everyone's with a look of defeat tinged with sorrow.

"Have you spoken with Robby's doctor at Ben Taub?"

"It's only been a few hours. You know the drill. Someone will call me tonight, after rounds. I promise I'll let you know what they recommend." There was a pause followed by a sigh. "So how're you doing? It's not your fault, you know. Robby's responsible for his own mental progress."

I wanted to lash out and ask who I could blame if not myself. Who was Robby's med police if not me? There were times I could listen to psychobabble and times I couldn't. I chose not to respond.

"I've been thinking," Winthrop said, after a long pause. "Could Robby have got hold of any psychedelic drugs? His behavior at group is something I haven't seen, even the last time he stopped his medications."

Winthrop was right. I thought a bit before answering. "I guess there's always a possibility." Robby's weird friend at the café came to mind. "But I don't know how he'd pay for it. He's on a tight string, you know."

"Yeah, okay. Just wondering." He said something else about trying to forget about my brother for now and hung up.

I stared at the phone in its cradle, willing myself to take Winthrop's advice. There really was nothing more I could do for Robby. If I left the hi-rise now, I had just enough time to shop for a cocktail dress at the Galleria, Houston's gigantic indoor shopping mall. I rarely indulged in shopping therapy, but thought I might find a dress for tonight. My spirits lifted a bit as I changed into slacks and thought about my evening with Keymap.

As I pulled the car keys from my purse, Suzy howled and rubbed against my ankles. I could so easily satisfy the cat with chopped liver, satisfy myself I was a good owner to Aunt Eunice's animal, but no one could satisfy me that I was a good sister to my brother.

❧

That evening, at five minutes before eight, I paced the living room wearing, not a new dress, but a black lace strapless that had belonged to Aunt Eunice. Slightly too snug across the chest, it had a fitted waist and a flattering circular skirt that ended just above my ankles. Not appropriate on a motorcycle but surely Keymap owned a car.

I only hoped this evening would redeem what I'd already chalked up as a disastrous, unproductive day. When the concierge buzzed me, I retrieved a black satin clutch, also Aunt Eunice's. I thought again about Keymap's motorcycle, grabbed the keys to the Camaro, and headed for the elevator.

When I stepped off, I spotted him, his black tuxedoed back to me while he studied an oil painting that hung over the lobby fireplace. The painting, an original Klee, was probably grateful it was parked in Houston where fireplaces were only for show.

He turned around and I must admit the light in his eyes, coupled with a low whistle, was gratifying. I approached, momentarily flabbergasted at Keymap's outfit. He wore a black T-shirt under his tuxedo jacket, black jeans, a dyed black carnation in his lapel, and on his feet, black tennis shoes. He looked like he was headed to the funeral of a beloved rock-star.

Grabbing my hand, his eyes swiveled toward my chest. I pulled away from his grip. "Bring your motorcycle?"

To my dismay, his reply was filled with mockery. "Bring my car keys?"

For a moment I was confused. When the truth registered, my cheeks burned with embarrassment. I dug in my purse and tossed them over. Deftly, he caught the keys before they hit his chest.

Feeling foolish, I took Keymap's arm on our way out and prayed for a truce. I wanted his help and for us to be on the same side again. Yet once settled in the front seat of his Camaro, I was suddenly tongue-tied. Two passengers inside the car shrank its interior space. I grew aware of his body heat, his wide shoulders almost touching mine. Silence stretched as I struggled for something to say and then we both spoke at once.

"Thanks for the use of—"

"The man driving the white truck—"

We laughed, our eyes locking for a moment before quickly looking away. As our laughter died, Keymap swung onto Kirby Drive. An awkward stillness hovered briefly before I spoke again.

"I'll be happy to rent a car. Surely you need yours back."

"Keep it. Remember, I'm leaving for Florida tomorrow. Besides, it smells better since you've been driving it."

Better at responding to criticism than compliments, I quickly changed the subject. "How do you know Brad Ewer?"

"I don't know him terribly well. We belong to the same club."

Same club? This put Keymap in a whole different category. I grew even more curious "Which club?"

"River Oaks. But I don't want to talk about myself. Let's keep to the case at hand."

I felt snubbed. "All right. Who was driving the white truck?"

"It was a rental. The driver ran from the scene. I've got someone checking into it."

"And the name on the rental agreement?"

"John Smith." He flashed a silent 'of course' in my direction.

"How about the real name of my rescuer? The man on the motorcycle?"

"Whoa," he said softly. "I told you. Let's stick to business and my name's Keymap."

I edged toward the passenger door, stuffing down my irritation. I'd find out his real name at the party. "Will you explain why you were following me? Or did you just happen to come along right when the white truck decided to off me?"

"You didn't seem to mind at the time."

He had me there. Glancing out the windshield, I watched oak branches lit by street lamps sway overhead in a slow dance. It was a warm evening. For most of the year, Houstonians were used to air conditioned surroundings. I should have brought a wrap in case our hosts preferred frigid indoor temperatures.

"You're antsy to know why I was following you," Keymap said, "but if you don't mind, I'd prefer to skip that for now." He pressed the accelerator. The Camaro obliged by roaring ahead as if from a starting gate. "Let's talk about what you were doing right before the guy in the white truck took such an interest in you."

"I was at Jake's Moving and Storage looking through LeeAnn Callahan's things." I relayed the particulars of my visit and ended with the discovery of the photo of LeeAnn and Brad smooching for the camera.

A soft whistle escaped his lips, but Keymap kept his eyes on the road. "Do you have it?"

"No. I got Tasered from behind. Whoever did it must have snatched the photo strip."

Keymap released the accelerator, hovered his foot over the brake pedal as if he weren't sure of his next move. "You never told me that."

"You never gave me a chance."

He flipped the turn signal, slowed, turning left onto Lazy Lane. Apparently Brad Ewer was one of the privileged River Oaks residents.

His house, like the others on this street, stood well behind a tall brick wall. Guards that could be wrestlers on their off-hours stood on either side of the entry gate. We stopped and Keymap leaned out the window and identified himself. The guard checked against a clipboard, then asked for my name which he wrote down, but only after I showed him my driver's license.

A tree-lined allée like that leading to Scarlett's Tara stretched ahead as we motored through the iron gate. Lights strung in the trees glowed like phosphorescent deep-sea creatures caught out of their element. Ewer owned a significant piece of real estate. Buffalo Bayou ran behind the property. Occasionally someone reported an alligator on the banks of the bayou looking for its supper—a crime deterrent provided free of charge by Mother Nature.

Inching behind a tan Maserati, we drew closer to the house. It appeared to float on pillars, its entrance up a long stairwell as if leading to a temple. Below, attendants hurried toward cars pulling up at the circular drive. A line had formed from the portico, where Ewer and his wife greeted guests as they came up the steps toward massive oak doors.

Keymap leaned toward me as he steered toward the entrance. "Let me introduce you and stay close."

A fearful thought jumped into my head. "Did you tell the Ewers I was coming with you?"

As we climbed the steps and up to our hosts, Keymap looked down at me, thoroughly amused. "Nope," he said and winked.

Both Brad Ewer and his wife greeted Keymap. "Shoot-a-mile, Key," Brad said. "You brought yourself a date."

His eyes, when he turned toward me, were flirtatious before sudden recognition made them widen, then narrow with suspicion. His host demeanor won out and he smiled, directing his comment to Keymap. "We've met." Obviously dismissive, he turned to the couple behind us.

Mrs. Ewer, who introduced herself as Cathryn, looked stereotypical of a Texas tycoon's wife. With smooth skin tight against prominent cheekbones, streaked blonde hair and a mass of diamonds around her neck, only her outstretched arm with its slackened flesh showed she was pushing fifty. Cathryn appeared to be on automatic. The welcoming smile plastered to her face made my jaw ache. Like a mechanical doll, she invited us in a soft voice filled with lazy vowels to come on inside and enjoy ourselves.

We joined the other guests teeming inside a wide hallway that led to a much larger room. Over the din of merrymakers, I heard the sound of a string quartet. Keymap guided me around several couples whose conversation had glued them to the floor, and we entered the cavernous room filling quickly with guests. Waiters scurried as they balanced trays filled with either champagne flutes or hors d'oeuvres. The room was bone-chilling cold.

On the far side, floor-to-ceiling French doors opened onto a deck that appeared to span the length of the house. Thickly wooded, the grounds beyond sloped downward toward the bayou. No alligator could have escaped notice in those brightly-lit grounds.

Keymap disappeared while I wondered if Brad calling him "Key" meant that was his real name or just a shortening of his nickname. I looked around and tried to spot J.D. McGraw, but unless I went searching, he could be anywhere in the crowd. I did spy our city mayor surrounded by cronies, one of whom was the D.A. or his twin. The police chief was also among the huddle paying homage to our city leader.

Keymap reappeared at my elbow and handed me champagne. In his other hand he held an old fashioned glass filled with two fingers of amber fluid, neat.

"Scotch?" I asked.

He nodded and took a short sip.

When a waiter neared, I handed the champagne back.

"Madam," the waiter said as he took the full glass, "May I offer you a different drink?"

"Is there gin?"

"Of course." The waiter turned away

As he retreated through the crowd, I called out, "with a twist." Left hand balancing the drink tray, he gave me a right-hand thumbs-up without turning around.

"I should have known that," Keymap said. "Sorry."

"Why? Because you've been spying on me?"

He shook his head in disgust, but stopped short. "Your man's over there." He pointed toward the far corner of the room where a balding man stood beside a woman tall enough to be a model, if only she'd been attractive.

My pulse quickened. I couldn't decide if I should approach him alone or with Keymap. Which would seem more innocent and non-threatening? The waiter appeared and handed me a glass of gin, its surface shiny with oil from the floating lemon twist. I took it, then forgetting all about Keymap, headed through the crowd toward J.D., sipping courage as I walked.

17

He saw me before I entered his small circle. His expression was hard to read. Did he know me? Had Ewer told him about my visit to his office?

Smiling apologies to those around him, I introduced myself. "I don't know many people here, but I do recognize you," I said, looking at J.D. "You're Mr. Ewer's partner, aren't you?"

J.D.'s expression was blank, neither friendly nor hostile. He had a patrician's nose and his pale face was handsome in a Renaissance sort of way. His sharp chin carried a slice of dried blood where he'd nicked himself shaving.

"I'm the attorney for Hammerly Insurance, if that's what you mean."

His handshake was firm as he nodded at the tall woman beside him. "This is my wife, Gloria."

She glanced down at me, her expression one of complete boredom, and didn't offer me her hand. A statuesque woman, she had dark hair that appeared flat, as if it were home-dyed. She wore it loose where it framed a square face untouched by make-up. In stark contrast to the other ladies in the room, she wore no jewelry and if her straight satin gown had been a flattering color instead of mustard gold, she might have presented a more attractive figure. Admiring her lack of vanity, I said hello.

The others in J.D.'s tight circle introduced themselves. Then all chatter ceased as if they were waiting for me to leave.

Aunt Eunice was my only introduction to how the rich behaved, and she would be ashamed of these stuffy, unwelcoming party-goers. They needed an attitude adjustment and, foolish or not, I decided to liven things up a bit.

"Mr. McGraw," I said "I'm investigating LeeAnn Callahan's death last March during Rodeo and I was hoping I could speak with you in private for just a minute."

Gloria McGraw's eyes came alive, looking at me as if I were a snake who'd changed stripes.

"The police have everything on record," J.D. said. "I have nothing more to say. I might add," his eyes sweeping around his audience, "that a social occasion is hardly the time to bring up suicide." He appeared smug as if he'd scored a coup, but no one smiled.

"How about murder?" I knew I'd overstepped an invisible boundary in front of his friends. The only thing I was sure of was that someone didn't want me looking into LeeAnn's death. I had a hospital visit and a damaged car to prove it.

J.D. murmured, "Excuse me, ladies and gentlemen," as he stepped toward me, grabbed my arm and led me through the crowd toward the balcony. I didn't mind. The room was freezing. I glanced around for Keymap and spotted him close to the string quartet, a beatific smile on his face, his body leaning as if standing straight would be too much trouble.

Pushing me a little harder than necessary, J.D. led me through the balcony's French doors, shutting them behind him. I moved away, close to the railing, and gulped humid, sultry air that smelled of magnolias. Still, a chill ran through me as J.D. drew beside me. I looked down at the sloping lawn below and wondered how far off the ground we were.

Withdrawing a pack of cigarettes from his inside pocket, he shook one out, lit up, and began to smoke. I remained quiet, giving the nicotine time to do its work.

"What are you doing here?" he finally said, his tone strident in spite of his cigarette.

"I do apologize," I said. "If you prefer, I'll be happy to come to your office next week. Captain Hightower thought you might talk with me." I set my drink on the balcony railing, unsnapped my clutch, and withdrew a business card.

He took it and frowned. "Who hired you?"

Feeling a spirit of cooperation, I almost told him before deciding against it. "My client prefers to stay anonymous."

"That's alright by me. It's Boots Callahan. Has to be." He dropped the butt of his cigarette and daintily snuffed it with the toe of his brogans. "I cannot tell you in any greater detail than I told the police. I watched her climb up on the balcony and jump. Her own free will."

"Then why would her brother claim she was pushed, mentally or physically, by an abusive boyfriend?"

"He's obviously making that part up since either Mr. Ewer or myself would have to be the abusive boyfriend. We were the only witnesses."

His eyes on mine grew wary, and when he spoke again, it was as if he'd made up his mind to share with me. "If I were you . . . well I'd forget about pursuing this. But if you want to know why Boots would claim this nonsense, you need to understand the conflict between Brad Ewer and Boots Callahan. A few years ago, Boots had too much to drink at Ewer's sky box party. It was during rodeo season. Boots started to make a scene, refusing to leave. Brad cold-cocked him and dragged him out in the hallway. He hasn't been invited back."

J.D. moved closer and leaned toward me, his clothes, his breath, smelling of cigarettes. "There are folks like Boots that always think life has dealt them a bad hand. His sister inherited a bigger chunk than he did and she was named trustee over his share until Boots gave up gambling."

My mouth dropped before I recovered. "LeeAnn was withholding Boots's inheritance?"

"I didn't say that."

"What <u>are</u> you saying?"

"She let him—"

Just then, a laughing couple joined us at the railing. J.D. smiled, turned his back on me and walked away, his swagger suggesting he couldn't be happier at the unwelcome interruption.

"It sure is cold back there, don't ya think?" The smiling Paris Hilton look-alike showed perfect teeth as she sought my agreement.

I could have strangled her. Back inside the party room, I looked around. Where was Keymap? Maybe he'd be willing to talk with J.D.

I watched J.D.'s back until he located Brad in the crowd. The two men soon separated themselves, heads together. Too bad I couldn't hear what they were saying. J.D. scowled down at Brad. The look on his face, even from this distance, was frightening.

Just before glancing away, I noticed a young woman with long, wavy brown hair approach. When J.D. spotted her, he grinned broadly and left Brad standing alone. I maneuvered through the crowd, wondering about the young woman. When close enough to focus, I saw two cute young things hugging Keymap's side like bookends. I'd never thought of him as a chick-magnet. A flare of jealousy was soon replaced by a more familiar one of annoyance. I needed to speak to him alone.

He spotted me and skillfully dismissed the girls, or at least it looked that way as they left him, still giggling and waving their fingers, to search for more prey.

"Want me to refresh your drink?" He cocked a bushy eyebrow at my empty glass.

"No, thanks. Or maybe I could use another to douse Mr. McGraw."

"Uncooperative, huh?"

My attention refocused itself across the room where J.D. still stood beside the pretty young woman. "Do you know who's talking with J.D?"

"That's his daughter Peggy or Pamela. Something like that."

"She doesn't look much like her mother," I said.

"Ah, dear Gloria. Truth is she's not the mother. But then, Peggy or Pam, I think it's Peggy, is J.D.'s daughter. His first wife died. The daughter was pretty young when he remarried."

"He sure didn't marry Gloria for her looks," I said. "She doesn't appear the motherly type, either."

"Ah," Keymap smiled. "That's where you're wrong. Rumor says she'd do anything for that young woman. Probably the only thing she and J.D. share is devotion to the daughter."

"Why? They don't like each other? Divorce rumors?"

"Not at all. Gloria comes from a F-O-F, although rumor also says it may not currently be a F-O-F-W-M."

I knew what he meant. "Fine Old Family" vs. "Fine Old family With Money." They weren't the same, although their status among Houston's upper crust might be considered equally impressive. Houston was a young enough city to revere anything that smacked of a dynasty.

"So tell me what you learned from your tête-à-tête with J.D."

"LeeAnn was given control over Boots' inheritance until he gave up gambling," I replied, wondering whose responsibility it was to declare him habit-free. The more I learned about LeeAnn, the more similar our lots in life appeared. Both of us our brother's keeper.

"Also," I said, "he claimed Boots is angry at Brad for kicking him out of his sky box party a few years ago. Know anything about that?"

Keymap shook his head, chugged the last of his Scotch and grabbed my arm. "I hate to not hear the end of Borodin's String Quartet, but I'm ready to leave."

Unwilling to admit I'd never heard of Borodin, I begged to stop at the bathroom first. He pointed left off the foyer before edging closer to the musicians.

A woman stood in front of the closed door to the powder room. She smiled as I joined her.

"You'd think Cathy would have more than one guest bathroom."

A quick glance showed this woman was unlike the other female guests. She wore a black suit, a white shirt and sturdy black shoes. Her brown hair was streaked with gray and her posture was that of a woman comfortable in a body as sturdy as her shoes.

"You've known Cathryn Ewer a long time?" I asked.

"Since before she kissed the frog. Believe me, Cathy wasn't to the manor born. Wait till you see the john and you'll know what she puts up with. Brad's testimony to his virility."

I wanted to question her further, but just then a middle-aged prom queen in a snug green satin dress pranced out the door. The woman who knew Cathryn Ewer scurried inside and shut the door. By the time she came out, she looked preoccupied and I was clearly invisible.

Unprepared, I stood, my mouth agape at the powder room walls. They were covered with photographs of Brad smiling, hugging, and smooching with various dress-up cowgirls. The full-length photos showed the women, young and not-so-young, in pastel-colored western shirts, swing skirts and flamboyant boots. Inevitably, the women were blonde beneath their cowgirl hats. The photos were professionally framed, some in gold-leaf. It appeared the woman of the house had participated in this gallery of her husband's popularity.

The biggest shock was a twin of the photo I'd discovered in the parking lot of LeeAnn's storage facility. Except this snapshot was not of LeeAnn, but a brown-haired young woman with freckles spattered across her nose and cheeks, who looked very much like J.D.'s daughter.

I stood lost in thought. Did this mean Brad's kiss with LeeAnn meant nothing? That he was a show-off flirt who liked to schmooze with the ladies and LeeAnn was just another one in the long line of cooperative women?

Keymap waited for me outside the powder room. We sought out our hosts for a polite exit when I noticed Brad and J.D. conferring again, their backs toward us. Brad wore black cowboy boots, his two inch heels lifting him almost as tall as J.D.

Veering away, I steered Keymap toward Cathryn Ewer. We managed a quick thanks for a lovely evening. No use bothering the head honchos. I'd get nothing further from them tonight.

Taking one last look over the party room, I caught Ewer's eyes. His look put Gloria McGraw's fierce expression to shame. A chill ran through me that had nothing to do with the temperature of the room.

⚜

I awoke to the feel of sandpaper raking my face. Suzy's breath smelled of chopped liver and cream. When the roof of my mouth began to itch, I reached for the antihistamine beside my bed with one hand and stroked Suzy with the other. Why do I always love hazardous creatures?

Downstairs, I spooned Suzy her food while mentally replaying last night's conversation with Keymap. I'd told him about LeeAnn's bank account and Logos, Ltd. He only grunted. Then he listened to what I'd seen on the powder room walls. Still, he was quiet, preoccupied perhaps. I preferred Keymap's sarcasm to his aloofness. He did mention a legal tiff between Hammerly and another insurance company I might want to check out. When he handed over his car keys he lightly stroked the nape of my neck with the back of his hand, then mounted his motorcycle, ordering me to be careful.

Over my wake-up cup of coffee, I sat at the kitchen table and perused the morning paper. Houston Police Department's crime lab made the front page. More claims of lost evidence and another lab worker fired. No wonder Lamar had appeared stressed. Screw-ups by the crime lab had been featured by the newspaper for months with the DA, the mayor, and the police captain firing jabs at each other.

I poured a second cup, went into the study and logged onto my laptop. I wanted to learn all I could about Hammerly Insurance. After an hour in the *Chronicle's* archive, I had some answers, but by no means all. Hammerly was mired in a lawsuit. They were making demands for public records from The Fenley Group, a company holding the sub-contract for state workers' compensation insurance claims. In Texas, that translated to more than a million policy holders. An enviable contract, to say the least. If the judge ruled The Fenley Group was withholding public information, a new bidding process would be invoked and Hammerly stood a good chance of winning.

Both parties were awaiting the judge's ruling.

Not to be left out, The Fenley Group was suing a non-profit called Texans For Sound Policy, TSP, for disclosure of all their investors' contributions, claiming Hammerly was the major donor and the reason for TSP's public smear against The Fenley Group.

So how did Boots fit in all this? I knew that his uncle, Ramsey, owned a Beaumont insurance company but it was far-removed from the likes of The Fenley Group, headquartered in Austin, or Hammerly, here in Houston. But, his uncle was still chair of the state House Committee on Insurance. Taking bribes from one side or the other? If Boots and his uncle were on friendly terms, and Tilman had something at stake with The Fenley Group, Boots's reasons for embarrassing Brad as well as J.D. would make more sense than a drunken scene with Brad during a rodeo party. Which meant Boots was after retribution for the insurance war by hiring me to investigate his sister's death, knowing it would lead to questioning Brad Ewer and J.D. McGraw, principal players at Hammerly.

Leaving the newspaper archive, I began a new search. After eliminating four candidates as being too young, I noted phone numbers and addresses for two maybes. Two phone calls later, I had arranged to meet that afternoon with the woman at Brad Ewer's rodeo party last March—Mary Nelson—the one who'd barely missed a collision with LeeAnn's falling body. I also did a quick search on J.D. McGraw and discovered his daughter's name was Margaret, Peggy for short. J.D.'s wife, Gloria, was part of the Whidby family. The Whidby's endowed buildings at the University of Houston and the Medical Center. Big bucks.

I closed my laptop, bounded up the stairs and quickly dressed. I had to see Robby at the hospital, but my first stop was an appointment with the female cop from Beaumont, Irma Doyle, the woman who'd shoved her card at me in the elevator of Captain Hightower's building. Apparently, she'd known Boots from her Beaumont days and had a small window of opportunity to visit with me before she reported for duty.

18

The address Irma gave me was in the Heights, an historic area of Houston north of downtown—my old stomping ground. The Heights was slowly being reclaimed by downtown workers wanting proximity to their offices. In the process, the financially impaired, i.e., mostly minorities, were being forced out by the inevitable rise in property values. I didn't want to drive down the street where my small rental house was located for fear of finding it gone, torn down by developers. Instead of seventy-five to hundred year old cottages, the area was booming with copy-cat Victorian dwellings and huge condominium complexes. No yards, just dwellings to hide in after a hard day trading gas or whatever. Sometimes I reminded myself of an elderly curmudgeon griping about how things weren't like they used to be. Well, they weren't.

Glancing in the rear-view mirror, I congratulated myself on a new phobia—the fear of being rear-ended. But the best indication of my nervous state was my gun stashed underneath my car seat.

I fumbled for my previously-frozen Snickers bar inside my purse and happily discovered it wasn't totally melted. At 17th Street, I took a right then pulled up in front of an original clapboard cottage with a white picket fence surrounding its small front yard. Huge pecan trees on either side of a short, cracked sidewalk draped their branches up over the cottage roof, their roots sunk into plots of St. Augustine grass so miniscule they only mimicked a front yard. I opened the wooden gate and spotted Irma dressed in her uniform just inside the open front door.

"Got one for me?" Irma pointed to my half-eaten candy bar. I swallowed and offered her the rest. I was mildly surprised when she took it, then motioned me inside.

She popped the candy in her mouth and, chewing, pointed at the couch. The front room's cherry paneling was faded to salmon by decades of sunlight pouring through long casement windows. An oval braided rug covered wide oak planks. Overstuffed furniture, ruffled and cushy, fit with an ambience that spoke of times less frenzied, less whipsawed by technology. While I withdrew my notepad, Irma stood over me, smacking her lips.

"Man, I'd forgotten how good those damn things taste. I try to watch my weight. Ha!" she barked. "Watch it grow, I mean."

Irma was a big woman without an ounce of flab. She wore the summer HPD uniform of short sleeves and pants that stopped at her knees. With taut arms and calves, she reminded me of a bulldog whose body fat index was zero. Definitely a woman who could take care of herself. I wondered if she was married but there were no family photos and no wedding ring.

"Coffee?" she asked.

"No, thanks. I'm coffeed out."

"That sugar made me thirsty." Irma turned and went through an open door where I could just see the side of a white enamel refrigerator and the backs of two wooden chairs. She called out, "Soft drink?"

"I'm fine."

I heard ice-cubes drop into a glass and the pop of a soda can. She walked back pouring a can of Coke over a tumbler filled with ice. "Shouldn't have these dang things, either."

She plopped on a rocking chair beside the couch and raised her glass before downing her drink. Then she belched, banged the empty glass on the coffee table, and smiled. "That's better. Now we can talk about wild-man-Callahan."

Outside, kids shouted at each other as they whizzed by on bicycles. I suddenly realized it was cool enough to have the windows open, especially with Irma's ceiling fan turning lazily overhead. I brightened, feeling relaxed, and smiled for no particular reason.

"Is that your name for him or others as well?"

"Everybody in our high school called him that. Don't want to disappoint you, but all I got on Boots Callahan is gossip. Nothing first hand. It wasn't like we ran around with the same crowd, if you get my drift. But then Beaumont's a small town, especially fifteen years ago, and whatever trouble one of us got into, it was pretty much spread around town by suppertime."

Irma used her hands, fingers spread as if smoothing bed sheets. Her nails were long and recently polished a glossy deep red. She saw me notice and laughed. "Purple Passion they call it. That's me. Purple passion." She threw her head back and laughed a deep belly laugh. "I sure hate it when some idiot makes me break one of these doozies. Cost me a fortune."

"Okay, Irma. Tell me some gossip." I sank further against the pillows, enjoying the breeze, enjoying Irma and her joie de vivre.

Folding her arms over ample bosoms, she began to rock, eyes locked in the distance. "Rumor one: Boots loved his weed. Nothing stronger that I heard of, just weed. Rumor two: Boots loved to party. Actually, that's a fact, cause I went to a few "un-segregated" parties we were at together. Not together, but you get my drift. He was skunk-drunk fifteen minutes after showin' up. Rumor three: His parents spoiled him rotten. Boots drove a Corvette. Come to think of it, I'm pretty sure he wrecked one in tenth grade. They gave him a new one, though. Stupid rich whi—" She stopped and snuck a quick look to see if I'd caught her intention.

I laughed. "Don't worry about offending me."

Irma nodded. "Can't do what we do and not know there are stupid rich parents of all color. So where was I? Oh, yeah. Boots used to ride horses beyond what they should'a been. Only fight I heard 'bout between he and his sister was over a horse. I think the parents sided with LeeAnn over that one, though. Heard Boots gave up riding after that."

"Irma, did you ever hear about any gambling problem with either Boots or LeeAnn?"

"Hmm." She rocked back and braced herself, staring at the ceiling. "Seems as if I do recall somethin' about that Boots's senior year. He used to take a bunch of kids with him to Lake Charles. Not that far from Beaumont."

Lake Charles sat just inside the Louisiana border with East Texas. Louisiana allowed boat-gambling there off shore. "Did he ever take his sister?"

"Nah. She was a baby. Seven years younger is a big gap—she would have been only eleven to Boots's eighteen."

"So you don't think they were close?"

"I don't know nothin' about that." Suddenly, Irma shoved the rocker forward, the toes of her shoes tucked back. "Wait a sec. I do remember hearing something 'bout Boots and his folks havin' a fallin' out. It woulda been summer after graduation." She paused and thought while I held my breath.

"That's it! My cousin was in the same grade as Boots' sister, and they were casual friends. I can't vouch if it's God's truth." Irma's eyes as she stared at me sparkled with self-congratulations. "My cousin said LeeAnn was upset 'bout her parents kickin' Boots out. It was his 'bad habits' that did it. I'm quoting now, if my memory's correct. 'His bad habits.' This was when my cousin was in high school. So I guess Boots never did give up drinkin' or smokin' pot or gamblin'. Or maybe he added some other vices I didn't hear about."

Both of us grew quiet, lost in our own thoughts. Why would a young girl get addicted to gambling if that had been the reason, or one of the reasons, her older brother was booted out, and she'd been upset enough to talk about it?

"Was Boots a good student?" I asked.

"He made A's and a few B pluses by never openin' a book. Real smart, but lazy. He could a been Valedictorian instead of just Salutatorian, but I beat him to it." Irma grinned.

"You were Valedictorian?"

"Yep. A first for someone straight out of the Pear Orchard. That's the Fifth Ward of Beaumont, in case you didn't know."

The Fifth Ward was an all-black neighborhood north of downtown Houston filled with shacks, reeking of hopelessness, poverty and crime.

Irma donned a different persona, her eyes mocking as she looked into mine. "I cruise the streets, talk to my kin-folks in the Fifth Ward and they're black. Just like me. They trust me. Where would that trust go if I presented myself as a damn Oreo? I'm smart and I'm black. If you have a problem with that, tough toenails."

Shame burned my skin but I continued to look her in the eyes.

"No problem whatsoever."

Irma grinned and renewed rocking. "Yep. That Boots was real pissed off at this smart nigger. But then, you'da thought he'd have studied harder if he wanted it that bad. Pissed a lot of white students off, if you get my drift."

"Did Boots go away to college?"

"If he did, I don't know where. You know his folks were super rich. They died in a car crash about two, three years back. I heard Boots returned to the old homestead after they died."

"Where was he in the meantime?"

"Don't know. I was off at college. Reed College in Portland, Oregon. Long way from home. I could have kept up if my family'd stayed in Beaumont, but my parents moved back to North Carolina to take care of my mom's folks. I've only been in Houston going on three years now. Sorry."

"How did Boots' parents get their money?"

"Goes way back to Spindletop Oil. Lots of thick, black, gooey money."

I noticed Irma look at her watch and start to rise.

I rose also with one last question, more personal than professional. "I know this is off the subject, but what's going on with the HPD
crime lab investigation?"

"I knew some of the fired lab workers. They weren't qualified to
conduct a test on bat guano, much less humans," Irma said. "Captain
Hightower's overloaded with that political mess. Been making the
papers for almost a year now."

Nodding, I turned to leave, thinking of the holes in the police
file on LeeAnn's death. I threw out a long shot. "I don't suppose you
know anyone at the lab that would talk to me?"

"I do, but mum's the word around there. Head of the lab doesn't
want their operation catching any more stink over botched evidence."

"What if I could guarantee nothing he tells me would come back
on him?"

"You're either kidding or you're mighty naïve." Irma walked over
and opened the front door.

"By the way, you need to adjust your thinking. My friend's a," she
stopped and spelled it out for me, 'w-o-m-a-n'. Sorry. Gotta run."

I stood just outside the door. "Irma. You're a cop. You heard how
LeeAnn died. What if you thought the police report had holes in
it? Wouldn't you want to follow through? LeeAnn could have been
killed. Don't you want the killer found?"

Irma's eyes hardened. "You got good reason to think she didn't
jump?"

"Just the fact that I was Tasered and evidence stolen means someone doesn't want me on this case."

"I'll think about it." As I started to argue, she held up her palm.
"Gotta go, girl. I'll feel out the temperature at the lab and let you
know."

19

Why _two_ vents in the ceiling? Could one be for a listening device? One for air and one for spying on me and listening to everything I say? I won't talk to anybody. I'll open my mouth to eat but that's it. But I'm not hungry so I don't think I'll open my mouth at all. If I breathe very slow and very low then nobody will hear. I'll tell the nurse when he comes back. I'll tell by putting my finger to my lips and I'll point to the vents and he'll know not to say anything. If my sister comes I'll show her, too. She always thought I was clever and even says I'm too clever for my own good. That's sarcasm. I'm not stupid. Gandhi says our thoughts, our actions, and our words must be in harmony. I am in harmony. But my body is tied and I won't be able to signal with my finger and they will hear me and hear everyone. The vent listens. Maybe I should open my mouth and scream for someone to come and let me out because I can be quiet as a mouse and they don't know that.

I am saying this without opening my mouth or writing this down because they have tied up my body. I need to write and so instead of screaming out, I am going far inside my brain like I do sometimes when my mind's eye holds my pencil and writes all these words. It's good I am not writing this down on paper because they would only read it and give me lots of medicine to take and I don't want any. I can feel myself and even if I'm tied I can feel my mind thinking and reasoning and it feels alive and I'm alive and that's all I want is to feel alive.

The door opens and two men come in and my heart starts to beat very fast. They don't look at me but only at my body, but they are untying me and letting my body go free and I want to thank them but don't want the vent to hear so I remain very quiet watching them avoid looking at me. When I see the one hold up a needle I begin to struggle because I know they are putting me to sleep and I want to stay awake but they don't let me. Come get me out of here, Sis, come please and save me, save me . . .why won't you save me?

20

The Neuropsychiatric Center on the third floor of Ben Taub smelled of human stench with an undertone of Lysol. It must be difficult to disguise the smell of patients who are psychotic, belligerent and allergic to bathing. After buzzing an intercom, a grandfatherly looking nurse with a short white beard opened the locked door and escorted me to Robby's room. Visitors passed through a huge space with cafeteria-style tables scattered throughout. Patients not under lock-up could wander into the big room where nurses stationed on either side watched from behind walls of Plexiglas. Men and women wearing empty expressions sat either hunched on benches or walked paths known only to them. A dozen eyes turned toward me, eyes filled with an oppressive hopelessness, watching, always watching. As I followed behind the nurse, I felt their stares and an old familiar urge to escape.

Taking a key from a huge crowded ring on his belt, the nurse opened Robby's door. "When you want out, just press the buzzer next to the door."

"I know the drill," I said.

The slam of the heavy door behind me brought no reaction from my brother, who lay in bed, his face turned toward the wall. At first I was surprised Robby was in a room by himself. The NPC usually arranged two to a room. When I realized why he was isolated, a flash of irritation surfaced. My brother would never hurt a stranger.

The room was small and bare, hardly enough space for one person to stand beside the patient's bed. A sink and toilet positioned at the foot of the bed further cramped standing space.

Robby knew I was there. His breathing quickened as he squeezed his eyes tight, his face scrunched like an angry child's.

"Robby?" I reached for his left hand where it lay atop a gray blanket. Robby and I were both cold-natured, so I was grateful he'd been given more than a sheet to cover himself. He jerked his hand free, eyes still closed.

I began to stroke his arm and he didn't pull away. "It's good they have you back on your medications. You should be able to go home soon." Dr. Winthrop's mantra rang in my head. *Never promise a particular day.* "Won't that be good?"

Robby's pale face, tinged gray as the blanket, showed sunken eye sockets and looseness in his cheeks suggesting sudden weight loss. I smoothed black curls from his forehead where it clung in damp clumps, my heart squeezed to the point of pain.

"Are you hot? Shall I remove the blanket?"

Robby jerked the blanket higher up under his chin, his face turned toward the wall.

"I'd like to know what happened, Robby? Why'd you quit your meds? You know—" I stopped myself. What good did lecturing do?

A tear clung to Robby's eyelash before snaking down his cheek. He opened his mouth but didn't speak.

Close to tears myself, I took a ragged breath. I had to be strong. I had to sound positive. Anything else would be a betrayal. "I know it's hard, that it's not fair. But just when you think you can do without them is the most dangerous time. Remember the message I taped for you to play when you first began to think you could quit your meds? You don't have to tell anyone, just listen to the tape." I stopped talking and reached for his hand again, needing to feel him, feel his fingers in mine. Just to know he was still with me.

He let me hold his hand, but continued to face the wall. When he spoke, his eyes remained closed.

"You have no idea what it's like for me." His voice was hoarse as if he'd been talking for hours. "What the meds do to me." When he turned and looked at me, his eyes were tortured. He squeezed my hand, and I gritted my teeth.

"They kill me. I can't feel anything. Nothing. I'm in a void and I'm all alone. You have no idea what that feels like." He closed his eyes. "No idea."

"Robby—"

He whipped his head around, glaring as he jerked his hand away. "Why don't you just let me go? I'm dead inside anyway."

My cheeks were wet and I tried to steady my hand as I swiped at my face. Get a grip, Giles.

"I do understand—"

"They listen to everything. Everything. "Go away, Giles. Leave me alone."

The stench of the third floor followed me to the car along with deepening despair. My father once warned me that Robby was a repeat offender. As if Robby were some juvenile hoodlum who'd never recover. But would he ever be normal?

I cranked the engine, my heart hammering wildly. A mild breeze from the open window attempted to dry my tears. Gulping repeatedly for air, I cursed my father for leaving us, cursed the gods that had dumped my little brother into a world of pain. He deserved better.

When I grew depressed over Robby, myriad doubts surfaced. My brother would never get well. My PI business would never take off. I would never have a normal life with a man who understood the claim my brother had over me. The last doubts to surface were about my case with Boots. Why had I thought someone wanted to stop me from investigating LeeAnn's suicide? There were other, quite reasonable explanations for what had happened to me.

Being attacked in a storage facility parking lot was undoubtedly not unique. Anyone could buy a Taser off the internet, and what better place to steal belongings valuable enough to store? And the freeway accident. The man in the white truck could have been drunk. Maybe he had a DWI on his record, got a fake ID, and ran away to avoid punishment. I had no solid evidence that LeeAnn hadn't chosen to jump to her death.

My cell rang. I blew my nose before answering.

"Ho, little lady." It was Dr. Winthrop, posing as a cheery, we-can-fix-this-latest-setback, shrink.

"I just left Ben Taub, doctor, and Robby seems terribly depressed. He told me to let him go. Should he be put on suicide watch?" Growing up, Robby had threatened suicide more than once. Our father would hospitalize him, even though Robby always swore up and down he was only kidding. The therapist reassured us we'd done the right thing. That any time a patient threatened suicide, he or she was in danger and needed help.

"He's as good as under suicide watch right now," Winthrop said. "I have a nurse check on him hourly and there's nothing in his room he can use to harm himself. We even use plastic forks. But then, you know the rules. I won't dismiss him until he's better, and I'd guess that won't be for awhile."

Last March Robby had stayed three weeks before Winthrop allowed him to go back to a boarding house, and only because the landlady, Mrs. Cathcart, agreed Robby would not be issued a key to his room and that he understood she could enter his room to check his dresser drawers, the contents of his closet and anything else that took her fancy. She would insure there was nothing he could use to harm himself. I was responsible for Robby taking his meds. Not hard to figure out which woman had failed her duty.

"When will he be allowed into the big room?"

"He could go now if he wanted. It's too soon to expect him to feel social, Giles.

But Robby liked to be around people. The Café Artiste crowd could verify that. Tomorrow I'd bring Robby his tablet and pencils. And flowers. I said good-bye to Winthrop and no sooner had I closed the phone than it rang again.

"This is Giles."

"Lieutenant Abury here. I'm running about ten to fifteen minutes late. Just wanted to give you a head's up."

Before leaving home, I'd placed a couple of phone calls. One of them was to Lieutenant Abury, the first rodeo-employed cop on the scene at Reliant Stadium after LeeAnn's dive. He was doing me a favor by meeting me at the stadium. I wanted a better picture of what he'd seen the night LeeAnn had fallen, and I wouldn't get up to the top tier without him. Reliant's sky-box levels were for private clientele and required special elevator keys, easier for cops to get.

"No problem," I replied and hung up. I hoped Abury would have the name of the elevator guard on duty the night LeeAnn died. When I'd checked my notes from the police files, the guard's name had been missing.

Traffic on Main Street was stop-and-go. Otherwise I'd grab a quick lunch. Twenty minutes later, I turned into Reliant's south parking lot off Kirby Drive and pulled next to the lone parked police car. Lieutenant Abury hopped out and whipped off his aviator sunglasses, right hand extended.

Abury appeared to be in his early forties, a few inches taller than I. He was slim, with a padded jaw line that could have been a chaw. His brown hair stood up in a thick, bushy shag.

"Thanks for meeting me here," I said.

"My pleasure. I didn't call ahead, but there shouldn't be a problem. They know me."

Reliant Stadium towered over the nearby Astrodome like some giant futuristic curved glass and metal airplane hangar, reflecting a true Texas attitude of "bigger means better." While it was being constructed, I read everything I could about it. This stadium was a gadget lover's dream.

In the end, it cost taxpayers over 500 million dollars. Its near 70,000 seating capacity was built with a unique retractable roof made of Teflon-coated fiberglass fabric coupled with 12,000 tons of air conditioning for fans not wanting too hot an experience. For the protection of all-star quarterbacks, a unique three million dollar installation and maintenance system of real grass was installed. Texans had invented synthetic turf; now they reinvented real grass. When another surface was required, special forklifts removed the grass and stored it across Kirby in a hangar where a unique watering system kept the rolled and stacked grass alive until it was needed again.

As we walked to the south entrance of the stadium, I questioned Abury. "Who called you the night LeeAnn fell?"

"Old man Huber. He's been a tier guard at the rodeo ever since I was in diapers. Or so I'm told."

"How old is he?"

"Too old to be a guard." Abury said, and chuckled. "But he shows up ever year like clock work. All I can say is someone way up at the top owes him a favor."

"You mean a rodeo officer?"

"Yep." Abury opened the south entry door and we stepped inside a broad hallway. The emblem of the five-pointed star of Texas was woven into the carpeting under out feet. I followed Abury to the rodeo business office. A receptionist behind the desk wore her blond hair piled high on her head. Her navy satin bomber jacket sported the orange Houston Livestock Show and Rodeo logo as well as several brass committee badges.

Abury showed a confidence older than his appearance as he strode forward and introduced himself. "I'm Lieutenant Abury and I need the elevator key to tier eight."

The woman frowned and popped her gum. "What for?"

"We need to see the balcony where LeeAnn Callahan fell from last March."

"The police said it was suicide. Why's it still an issue?"

"That may be true, but when other questions come to light, we need to follow up."

"What other questions?"

Abury's eyes narrowed, fists on his hips. "You trying to tell me what I can and can't look at? Call Dan Oxspring."

The woman glared, reached across her desk and punched an extension. "Gary, I have a police officer here with an unidentified woman. He's asking for Dan. Wants the elevator key to eighth level." She listened a minute, her lips curling into a smile. "Yes, sir, I certainly will."

Her smirk told me she thought she'd won this battle. "Dan Oxspring is no longer with us You two take a seat. Our new head of operations will be out shortly."

Abury started to reply, but changed his mind. He didn't look pleased as we retreated to chairs across the room. I wasn't surprised at the cool reception we were getting, even if our request seemed innocent enough. Houston Rodeo was known for keeping its operations close to the vest.

A barrel-chested man with a sunburned face shoved open the door and glanced around as if ready to catch a thief. The receptionist nodded her head in our direction. He came toward us, a scowl on his face. "What's this all about, officer?"

Abury stood. "I'm Lieutenant Abury. This here," he turned toward me as I also stood, "is private detective Giles Faulkner, formerly of HPD."

"Gary Schaffer, head of HLSR Operations," he said. "I repeat. What's this all about?"

Gary's use of initials announced he was an official rodeo hotshot. Most Houstonians referred to this monumental annual event as simply Houston Rodeo.

"I've worked overtime for HLSR," Abury replied, mimicking Gary's use of the acronym, "every year for the past four years and my going anywhere in this stadium has never been an issue. Pardon me if I appear disrespectful, but, Mr. Schaffer, what's this all about?"

"This is about privacy, Lieutenant. That level is all rented out. Who goes up there is for the folks paying the rent to say. Not you or your sidekick." He jerked his head in my direction but only looked at Abury.

I feared for Abury's molars as he stood glaring at our uncooperative watchdog.

"No problem," I spoke up. "Let's go, Lieutenant."

Out on the sidewalk, a warm breeze riffled my hair. The air smelled like coming rain.

"Asshole," Abury grumbled as he leaned over and spat on the sidewalk. "I'll have to contact my buddy at the Ford dealership. His company has one of those suites." His gait quickened but I caught his next grumble. "One of these days those high-falootin' rodeo guys are gonna get their comeuppance."

21

Not knowing how to respond, I didn't. One way Houston Rodeo mania showed itself was in its 16,000 volunteers and over 90 committees. Rodeo brought in millions annually through various competitions, a kiddy carnival, food vendor rental fees, liquor licenses, and sold-out performances by big-name country and western stars. Every year, various publications trumpeted Rodeo's huge donations to educational scholarships. But trying to pin down how many millions Houston Rodeo's non-profit corporation kept to itself had gotten one local journalist suspended from his paper for several months.

The reporter had questioned the corporation's expenditure of $53,000 for a conference table and over a million on cherry veneer that served as wainscoting in corridors and floor-to-ceiling paneling in its executive suite. The rodeo, he claimed, had spent over ten million building out its 72,000 square-foot offices amounting to over $150 a square foot. The rodeo sued the reporter. Their settlement was never revealed.

Rodeo had obvious clout. I wondered if their protective, as well as secretive, nature extended to covering up murder, but kept my thoughts to myself. "Come on, Lieutenant. Let's look at the balcony from down here."

He followed me around the stadium where it fronted Kirby Drive. Standing on the sidewalk, conversation proved impossible. From a short distance, sounds of squealing brakes and honking horns filled my ears. We craned our necks upward. Abury pointed to the balcony where LeeAnn had fallen.

I pictured the young woman perched on the balcony's railing that hugged the outside wall of the stadium. Had she been startled to find herself over the ledge and falling, blond hair blowing wildly as she plummeted? I imagined her broken body at my feet and tried to imagine Mary Nelson's reaction. I prayed my afternoon interview with her would prove fruitful.

Before parting company, Abury scribbled the elevator guard's telephone number.

"Where was Huber when you arrived at the scene?" I asked, taking the slip of paper from him.

"Near the glass door leading out to the balcony. Why?"

"Just curious," I said. "How long before you got there?"

"I was a couple of levels down so I'd say no more than four, maybe five minutes. I used the elevator which took a little time."

He shook my hand again before we both got back in our cars. I sat for a minute, rubbing the fingers of my right hand back to normalcy, and thought. Five minutes was long enough for someone else to have come and gone without being seen. But how, if the guard had been manning the elevator?

As I drove up Kirby, I dialed Huber's number. A woman answered.

"I'm trying to reach Mr. Huber," I said.

"Who's this?"

"I'm Giles Faulkner. Captain Hightower of HPD thought Mr. Huber might talk to me about the death of LeeAnn Callahan last March during rodeo. He was elevator guard on the eighth level, I believe, the night she fell."

"He already tol' the police all he knows. Besides I'm fixin' to go to the hospital. His kidney stones have flared and he's trying to pass 'em. I gotta run."

"Which hospital, ma'am?"

"Methodist. But you better not bother him none. He's busy tryin' to pass those damn stones. Been the curse of that poor man's life, so you leave him alone, you hear?"

"Yes, ma'am," I said, and closed the lid on my phone. I had no intention of leaving Huber alone.

22

Walking up the sidewalk of Mary Nelson's bungalow, I hoped she'd have more information than the police files.

Glancing around the street, I noted its quiet compared to other neighborhoods, hearing only the sound of a lone sprinkler watering the lawn next door. Large oak and pine trees grew tall, dappling manicured lawns with shade. I realized how much I missed my rent house, the smell of fresh-mown grass, its small garden for puttering. There was something about digging in dirt that put most problems in perspective.

Relishing the sharp odor of pine needles, I rang the bell. When the door opened, I thought I had the wrong house. A tiny woman with grey hair pulled into a tight, thin bun at the nape of her neck, peered at me through rimless eyeglasses. Her pale blue eyes twinkled, and she chuckled softly.

"You must be Giles."

I nodded.

"You're wondering, young lady, what an old woman like me was doing at a noisome rodeo party, aren't you?" A huge grin split the woman's face. "Giles is such a lovely name. Come in."

I returned her smile and stepped inside. A second glance at Mary Nelson gave a different impression. Her posture was ramrod straight, her white silk blouse tucked tight inside the waistband of her navy slacks was age-appropriate but not dowdy, and her face was lively with intelligence. She might make a good witness, after all.

Glancing around her living room, I noticed framed pictures of horses, some with riders and some without. A faint smell of sweet decay could be traced to a glass bowl filled with brown-edged magnolia blossoms.

Mary drew up beside me and pointed with a bamboo cane. "The painting over the couch there was my horse, Blue. I grew up on a ranch near Abilene. My brothers were all award-winning bronco riders."

"Lovely horse. You also have talented brothers," I added, feeling a stab of self-pity at the pride in her voice, wondering if I'd ever sound that way when talking about Robby.

"Would you care for some tea?" she asked, cocking her head.

When I nodded, she disappeared into a hallway off the living room, presumably leading to her kitchen. Quickly cringing over my rudeness, I called out, "May I help you?"

After a cheery "no thank-you" floated my way, I took her absence as an opportunity to study the room. You can tell a lot from a person's home. Dying magnolias seemed an anomaly among Mary's modern furniture as did the lack of painted china bric-a-brac typical of some elderly women. The tables were all glass and steel. Not a lace doily in sight, only a few small stone Buddha statues. A Biedermeier-style black leather couch with matching chairs looked stunning against deep green walls and scattered antique Turkish prayer rugs. Steel-framed family photos sat atop every horizontal surface.

Mary, I decided, was a woman who enjoyed a distinctive taste in style, who cherished family, and valued her independence. On the other hand, I allowed someone else's style to dictate my surroundings.

Without disturbing the arrangements, I wandered the room, leaning over to study each group of photographs. A small one of Mary seated beside a young woman stood on a table next to the couch. The two women shared the same blue eyes and small chin. Her daughter?

"That is my niece."

I accepted a china cup filled with hot tea, and Mary retreated once more to the kitchen. With a cane, she could only carry one cup at a time. After returning, she sat on the sofa and, placing her cup and saucer on the glass-top coffee table, motioned for me to do the same.

"I won't have this thing much longer," Mary said, pointing to her cane. "Hip replacement, you know. Should be good as new in a few more weeks. Isn't my niece beautiful? Allison is her name. Not as unusual as Giles, but still quite a pretty name."

I nodded, thinking Mary was like a flitting bird and it might be difficult to keep her on topic. "Yes, a very pretty name."

"It was really Allison's friend who was invited to Mr. Ewer's rodeo party, not me. But her friend got sick and something came up in Allison's schedule and she begged me to use the invitation. She wanted photos of her favorite singer, Martina McBride. So I went and thoroughly enjoyed myself. It'd been ages since I'd seen a rodeo."

"So your niece is friends with Brad Ewer's secretary, Janet? I can't recall her last name."

"No. But Allison's friend knows her somehow. I believe the secretary's name is Janet Boyer. Allison has lots of friends. She's the one who called Janet and explained I would be going in her friend's place. Needless to say, I didn't know a soul there."

Mary Nelson was her niece's friend's substitute. No wonder Janet had looked bewildered when I inquired about Mary. I withdrew a notepad and pen from my briefcase. "You're the first person I've talked with who was at the party the night LeeAnn died," I said. "Can you give me your impressions?"

"Oh, my. You want my impressions." She sipped more tea, appearing to revel in a visitor, someone who'd listen to her.

"Lots of young, rowdy people, of course. The young lady who died appeared, if I'm remembering correctly, not to be having as good a time as the others. But then her face was mostly hidden by her cowboy hat. Black, it was." She appeared pleased, as if she'd given me a vital clue.

"Oh? She never removed her hat?"

Mary lightly touched my thigh. "The other guests did. But not her. A sign of protection, perhaps." She peered closely at me. "I can feel another person's sadness. Can you?"

I cleared my throat. "Do you have any idea why LeeAnn seemed sad?"

"Oh, my, I wouldn't have the faintest clue."

"Was LeeAnn friendly with the other guests? Did she visit more with anyone in particular?"

Mary considered my question before shaking her head. "I'm afraid I didn't pay particular attention. This was <u>before</u> she fell dead at my feet, you see?"

The sparkle in Mary's eyes told me she was enjoying her wit, but I was on a roll.

"What about after the rodeo and performance were over? Did everyone leave at once or did some guests linger?"

Mary cocked her head "Not everyone left at once. Some of the younger guests stayed and talked to each other. I believe Miss Callahan visited with another young woman for a few minutes, but then they both left."

"Together?"

"No. Miss Callahan went by herself across the corridor to smoke. Mr. Ewer joined her after asking me if I was okay or needed any help leaving." Mary chuckled. "I guess that was his way of asking me to leave, but I told him I always wait for crowds to disperse and then manage fine by myself."

"How long were the two of them on the balcony?" I asked

"When I left about twenty minutes later, they were still out there."

"Did they seem to be enjoying each other's company?"

"Oh, my. I'm not sure 'enjoy' is the right word. They appeared very animated, pacing back and forth, you know. Gesturing, as smokers will, with their cigarette, just to make a point."

"Both of them were gesturing?" I asked, scribbling on the notepad.

"Oh, yes. Both of them. And then I left. Or tried to leave but it took awhile."

"So you left the suite about twenty minutes after Brad Ewer went outside and joined LeeAnn on the smoking balcony?"

"I can't say it was exactly twenty minutes, but I'm pretty close."

I noticed Mary wore no watch. "Did you happen to notice the time?"

"No, I'm afraid not." Mary finished her tea then sat back, stuffing a red silk pillow behind her for support. "I was driven home by one of the policemen. So kind of him. I do recall checking the time when I arrived home that night and it was 11:35. I was quite exhausted."

I glanced at my notes. "You mentioned taking pictures for your niece. Did you take any of the party guests?"

Before I could reach out to help, Mary rose, using her cane for leverage. "I did and I'll get them for you."

While she was gone, I pulled out my notes of those who'd attended the party. The DA had come and gone earlier in the evening as had Ewer's wife. J.D. was there, but none of his family was listed as a guest. Other than the police chief and the DA, the rest of the names were noted in the police files as employees of Hammerly Insurance.

Mary came toward me, her outstretched hand clutching snapshots. "I'm afraid my camera was one of those disposables. Not many of these are any good, but you're welcome to them."

I shuffled through the stack thinking Mary was correct. They all were either under or over exposed. A profile of a young woman standing in a tight circle of females looked vaguely familiar. I stuck them in my briefcase then looked back through my notes.

"You said earlier that you 'tried to leave but it took awhile.' Do you mean you had trouble getting out of the stadium?"

"I meant just what I said. The man with the elevator key was not there. I waited at least five minutes for him, probably more." Mary's lips pressed downward at the memory.

Here was another five minutes with no guard or policeman in the corridors. "Did the elevator guard offer you an excuse?" I asked.

"No. He didn't even apologize, the old goat."

I murmured something in sympathy while the reason for the delay hit me. Someone with a kidney stone required lots of fluids. Huber was undoubtedly making frequent trips to the bathroom.

"Can you explain just where you were when LeeAnn's body fell?"

"I was on the sidewalk, directly beneath the balcony. Well, not directly beneath. Otherwise, I would have been squashed like a bug, now wouldn't I?" With a satisfied air, Mary's bright blue eyes peered at me.

She was right about that. Police photos showed LeeAnn's head and torso had taken the brunt of her fall onto the concrete walkway, with her legs partially positioned on grass.

"Once you were outside and walking along the sidewalk, before LeeAnn fell, did you glance up, see anything from the balcony?"

Mary stared into the distance as if in a trance. "It was my fate to witness the poor girl's death." She turned her head, her eyes boring into mine. "I believe in karma, don't you?"

Thinking of her Buddha statues sitting, pregnant-bellied, among her photos, I said, "Of course."

"Oh, good. I just knew you did. If you tell me your time and date of birth, I can work up your astrological chart."

"Perhaps another time, Ms. Nelson."

"Oh, but you must call me Mary. Everyone does."

"One more thing, Mary. As you walked along the sidewalk, did you hear anything before LeeAnn fell?"

"Oh, my, yes. She screamed."

I paused. Would someone committing suicide scream? "You're sure?"

"My dear, I'm only seventy-four years old. My hearing is quite sharp and I know a scream when I hear one."

"But you never looked up?"

"I did glance up, but that was after she screamed, you see, not before. There might have been a face in front of her as she balanced for a second up on the railing, but it was buried in shadows. I didn't think it was Mr. Ewer, but as I told the policeman, I couldn't be sure. It could have been him, after all, and everything happened so fast. LeeAnn screamed and then her body was there you see, right at my feet. I grew quite upset, as you can imagine."

"Yes, of course." I didn't understand her phrasing, so posed my next question carefully. "How could a face be in front of her since she fell head-first off the balcony? Any individual up there with her would have been behind LeeAnn, wouldn't he?"

"Oh, my, no," Mary said. "She fell backwards, my dear, screaming until she landed."

23

I drove away with my mind in a whirl. Perhaps one of my old psy-chology textbooks would delve into one's mindset during the act of suicide, but the fact that LeeAnn had screamed as she fell wouldn't appear to indicate prior planning. And why was she facing the interior of the balcony? I supposed she could be someone who, al-though wishing to die, did not wish to view beforehand her final rest-ing spot. J.D. had stated he and Brad watched LeeAnn deliberately "dive" to her death with her arms over her head. Falling backwards was one way to dive. And yet . . .

Those minutes heckled me, too. It took Lt. Abury five minutes to respond to Huber, but, according to Mary Nelson, Huber wasn't always manning the elevator. Theoretically, there could be more than one five-minute lapse when the guard wasn't around. Someone could have appeared, entered the balcony, and shoved LeeAnn overboard. That someone would have needed an elevator key which meant they were high up in the rodeo echelons. But I was still missing the motive. And, if someone else had shoved LeeAnn off the balcony, why were Ewer and McGraw keeping quiet about it?

When my cell phone rang, I hoped it was Winthrop. If anyone would know the likelihood of screaming as you tossed yourself to your death, he would. It wasn't Winthrop, but I was equally happy to hear from the caller.

"Got time to meet me back at Reliant?" Abury's voice carried an edgy undertone of triumph.

"You have keys?"

"Would I call if I didn't? I'm ten minutes away. How 'bout you?"

"Closer to fifteen," I said, turning east on Bissonnet toward Kirby Drive. I began checking my rearview mirror again. A part of me still believed someone didn't want me looking into LeeAnn's death.

When Mary talked about the rodeo party, my mind had struggled over where LeeAnn had spent the last hours of her life. I'd never been on any hotshot's guest list and, therefore, had never seen Reliant's infamous swanky sky boxes for a privileged bird's eye viewing of the rodeo and superstar concerts.

Due to traffic congestion, I pulled into Reliant's parking lot twenty minutes later. Abury hurried toward me, dangling keys and smiling broadly. With his chipped front tooth, he looked like a little boy. The likeness vanished when he spoke.

"I just hope that Gary bastard sees us," he said, taking my arm, hurrying me as if away from a fire.

We entered the same door as earlier, but instead of walking toward the rodeo office, we veered left, heading up spiral carpeted stairs until we reached a spacious lounge. Its shape followed the stadium's oval curvature overlooking the field.

"These are the Club Lounges," Abury said. The space was empty, divided by themes into bar and lounge areas fronting the stadium seats. Chairs in the first lounge area were upholstered in Texas-star imprinted fabric, the next lounge area in cowhides, and lastly a ranch-themed bar with branding iron logos etched into the backs of bar stools. Viewing stands hung over the field, perched closer than the cheaper seats beneath.

"We can go up to the seventh level." He pointed left toward a bank of elevators. "Then ride an escalator up to the eighth tier, or we can go directly to eight." He indicated elevators on the opposite side of the arena. "You pick it."

I stood for a moment, surrounded by the soft background hum of air-conditioning as it cooled the vast emptiness around us. "I didn't know there was an escalator on seven." Someone could have ridden up to eight, pushed LeeAnn off the balcony, taken the escalator back down to seven, and left the stadium unnoticed.

Assuming Abury would follow, I struck out toward the elevators leading to the seventh tier. After exiting, we rounded a bend in the corridor and there it was—an up-escalator with its counterpart directly beside it. An unspoken agreement about maintaining silence permeated our ride up to the eighth tier.

We stepped onto a curved mezzanine with glass windows hugging the outer walls. Doors opening into suites lined the inner wall to our right. I'd read there were a total of 166 private suites for rent and imagined the ka-chink of rodeo's cash registers as we passed suites booked by Houston's moneyed corporations.

"These units along here are pretty much laid out the same," Abury said, opening a door and switching on overhead lights.

I followed him inside, gaping at the opulent surroundings. No wonder Mary Nelson had jumped at the chance to be a guest. On the floor, a circle of plush brown carpeting lay bordered by Texas limestone pavers. A black granite buffet counter ended with a stainless steel built-in beer tub, empty at the moment. Cherry wood liquor cabinets hung above a large stainless steel sink. Against dark brown leather-paneled walls hung four TV monitors for those guests not wanting to open doors that led out to exclusive padded theater-style seats overlooking the indoor field.

"These suites were designed for about sixteen to twenty-two guests," Abury said. "A private restroom's behind the buffet."

Glancing at the overstuffed chairs placed around the perimeter, I mentally filled the space with drinking and partying, but not smoking, guests. If you wanted to smoke, you stepped outside and across the hall to one of the outdoor smoking balconies. I pictured guests from Mary Nelson's photographs who'd been at Brad's cocktail party—the mayor, the district attorney, the police chief. Her pictures had been grainy, but clear enough to recognize Houston's much-photographed elite.

I opened an interior glass door and walked out onto a private platform that fronted steeply sloping bleachers, roped off from those on either side. The bleachers overlooked the oblong arena. Binoculars would still be required if you wanted a good view of the show from here. But then, one could see everything, real-time, on one of the big HD screens inside the suite.

When most people think of attending a rodeo, they think up close and personal, outdoors and seated in rickety wooden bleachers, the dust from the arena blowing in their face. Houston Rodeo was nothing like that. Families came to Reliant and enjoyed first the outdoor carnival rides, cotton candy, and fried foods. Show animals from cattle to rare chickens graced indoor arenas where families viewed the blue-ribbon winners.

If you still had money in your pocket, you could buy rodeo apparel, silver and turquoise jewelry, leather goods and much more from vendors who paid dearly for a booth inside the rodeo-owned halls and meeting rooms. If the distance between these outdoor areas was too far to walk, you might hop on one of the open-sided buses provided to squire attendees from one end of the property to the next. One of the few free things to be had.

Once inside Reliant Stadium, ticket holders sat in plush seats in the air-conditioned amphitheater with thousands of others. Rodeo competitors came from all over the country, big money luring them to Houston. Spectators viewed contestants on the floor of the arena from far above and far away. How high and how far depended on the ticket price. Sitting with popcorn and hotdogs in air conditioned comfort, audiences watched giant television screens, dropped strategically from the ceiling of the stadium for closer view of the action below. When a bull pleased the crowd by bucking off its rider, the TV repeated the crucial scene over and over in instant replays while the viewers gasped in unison.

For a second or two, I imagined the stadium filled with spectators cheering their favorite bronco or bull rider, barrel or wagon racer; saw leather-vested contestants, their cowboy hats shoved down on their foreheads, coming fast and hard out of the shoots and may the best man or woman win. Not much different from ancient Rome and its gladiators.

Houstonians didn't appear to need the heat, the dust, the in-your-face tradition of small-town rodeos. After the end of competitions, the audience sat back, relaxed, and enjoyed either pop/rock bands or country and western-singers of international fame. Tickets for the most famous entertainers sold out months before the event.

I stepped back inside the suite and closed the door. At least most spectators were gone before LeeAnn's last, and fatal, rodeo attendance.

Abury locked the suite behind us and we headed down the passageway toward the middle smoking balcony. He opened the door and I stepped out onto the concrete floor.

Surrounded on three sides by glass walls, the balcony's interior was visible to anyone passing along the corridor. Heading toward the open railing that overlooked Kirby Drive in the distance, I willed myself to be fearless. Wind whipped my hair as distant traffic whizzed along like toy race cars pushed by invisible toddlers. Ears buzzing, I clutched the railing and closed my eyes. It was a long way down. I felt Abury beside me. We were both silent. Turning away, I opened my eyes and studied what I could see from where I stood. Neither the escalator nor the elevator was in sight, but fifteen to twenty feet of corridor was visible. Ample time to know who was coming to join you. Grabbing the railing, I forced myself to look straight down.

While blinking against the wind, I sucked my breath, seeking the sidewalk below. "She landed there?" I pointed to a spot below.

He moved my arm a tad. "There."

Directly beneath, the concrete walkway curved outward. I blinked again and LeeAnn was there—a tiny doll thrown by an angry child.

Her figure lay at an angle, her calves ending in black leather boots, red skirt spread like a fan around the middle of her thighs. Her torso and head hugged the concrete while the left side of her head lay flattened and bloody. Suddenly I remembered the cowboy hat. Mary had said LeeAnn kept her hat on while others had removed theirs. I strained to remember the coroner's photos. I didn't recall seeing any hat beside the body or listed in the inventory. So where was it?

I moved away from the ledge and lurched toward the door, anxious to leave the balcony. Abury was directly behind me as I headed toward the security of the inner wall, leaned against it, and let my heart slow before speaking.

"When you arrived, Lieutenant, did you see LeeAnn's cowboy hat? I think someone said it was black."

"I don't remember seeing a hat anywhere."

✷

Seated inside my car, air-conditioner humming, I scrolled through the contact list on my cell, smiling when I reached Codger. His real name was Mike Codgden, shortened to Codger and sometimes Old Codger behind his back. No one knew his age. He'd been director of the forensic section responsible for crime photos, as well as the latest in computer technology, for over thirty years. I only prayed, as I punched the dial buttons, he hadn't retired.

"Hullo."

"Is this Codger?" I asked.

"Nope. Hang a sec."

I held for what seemed a full five minutes.

"Hullo."

"Codger? Is that you?"

"In the flesh. Who's this?"

"It's Giles, Giles Faulkner. Remember me?"

"Ah," he said. "The pretty one that got away."

I had to laugh. "Not exactly 'away,' Codger. Just decided to go out on my own. I'm a PI now, in case you haven't heard."

"They tell me I'm too old to remember shit like that."

"Sure you are." That man could recite specifics on a case so far back the case files were buried under a foot of dust.

"Tell you why I'm calling. I've been hired to look into the LeeAnn Callahan suicide from last March. She fell about 100 feet from a Reliant Stadium smoking balcony. Would you have the photos taken at the time of her death?"

"Greg took those shots. I can rustle them up. Why? I thought that case was dead."

"Her brother doesn't agree it was suicide. Tell me if I'm wrong, Codger, but I seem to remember software we, I mean your department, was getting about the time I left. Sort of like the bullet trajectory software, but this was supposed to compute how someone had fallen, at what speed, what angle, etc." I was hoping he'd fill me in on the et cetera part.

"You're way behind the times, Lassie," Codger said. I'd forgotten he used to call me Lassie. My Irish heritage.

"We're on Codger Two now. Much more accurate than Codger One."

Another memory from the past. He and his cohorts always named their equipment after lab employees.

"Can you help me out? I'm not far away and I think the witnesses may have been wrong about the way LeeAnn fell off the balcony. I was hoping your equipment could prove one way or the other."

"Sure thing. We've moved. Temporarily stuck in downtown's basement."

"Be there in fifteen minutes."

24

The receptionist was warming up to me. "Back again?" she asked with a smirk.

After being screened for weapons, I caught the elevator down. Once at basement level, I got off and followed signs to the lab. The basement smelled of mold and was poorly lit. Almost spooky. Codger stuck his head out the door a few feet ahead.

"Thought I heard the elevator," he said, beckoning me inside.

I swore no matter how much space they were allowed, Codger's equipment would fill it. Computers, monitors, cameras, slide screens were stacked helter-skelter among discarded trays of foul smelling fluid dried to thin patches like parched earth.

"I keep the newest in my office," Codger said, leading me into what appeared to be a storage closet.

I entered a narrow space of peeling paint and stained brown carpeting. It held a small, scarred desk where three oversized monitors hogged the majority of the desk top. There was space for only a single chair.

"Stand behind me here," Codger sat and wheeled his chair toward the desk, pulling out its middle drawer that held a keyboard. "I pulled the photos you wanted and scanned them."

"Is this the first time you've run these photos through your program?" I asked.

"I get your insinuation, lassie. I was told, and no, won't tell you by whom, to shelve this project many moons ago. It was suicide, and that was that."

I'd only offend him by being pushy, but wondered who in the upper ranks had decided to make LeeAnn's death a slam-dunk suicide. The mayor? The Chief of Police?

While looking over his shoulder at the monitors, I viewed photos of a lit Reliant Stadium as they popped on the screens, in 3-D, no less. There were pictures from below the balconies that hugged the top perimeter as well as internal shots of the stadium's stairwell, where folks walked up or down multi-levels of concrete steps. Several photos were taken from the ground straight up to a single balcony. Ground zero.

Codger tapped on the keyboard. "Dead woman's height and weight?"

"Five feet, five, and one-sixteen."

He clicked the keys and what looked like a combo of digitally enhanced and actual photos popped on the middle monitor. Codger continued clicking and manipulating the mouse until I drew in a sharp breath.

A three-dimensional white figure, perhaps an inch tall, sat atop a schematic of the balcony railing, weird limb-like legs dangling as if seated. Something cold flew up my spine. Thank God Codger hadn't given the little figure long blonde hair.

"Weird, ain't it?" Codger chuckled, obviously delighted to show-off his latest toy. He clicked for another half a minute. "What's your concern, here? Speed? Angle? Position before falling?"

"Mostly the last one," I said, adding, "One witness says her arms were over her head and she dove head first." About to continue with Mary Nelson's opinion, I stopped when Codger held up a finger. "Give me the next one in a minute."

Several more clicks and the tiny white figure stood atop the railing, stick arms over her head before swan diving toward the bottom of the screen. I didn't quite get it until, a minute later, Codger positioned another half-digitized, half- real image of LeeAnn's body against the sidewalk.

He shook his head. "See here?" He pointed with the end of a pencil. "No can do with a dive." The little stick figure lay a foot from LeeAnn's body with her digitized head angled ninety degrees from that of LeeAnn's actual head.

"Shoot me the other scenario," Codger said.

"Sit her facing the inside of the stadium, perched on the railing, and she falls or is pushed backwards." I held my breath.

"Two different things, Lassie," Codger said. "Will do the falling backwards first."

I watched the white figure tumble back in a somersault toward the bottom of the screen. Codger didn't have to point out that the spot where the figure's head landed was significantly closer to the stadium than LeeAnn's had been.

"Now for the last." He clicked for what seemed forever. "Pushed hard or just a nudge?"

"I don't know," I said. "Try a medium push if there is such an animal."

A minute later an eerie site popped on the screen. A disembodied arm moved forward into the small white figure. We watched the tumble.

"Now see here?" Codger pointed again. "Old Codger One wasn't as precise. Three inches off, right here." He pointed to the tip of LeeAnn's boot heel.

"I gave that pusher some heft. Next I'll try a medium-light, but still deliberate push," Codger said.

He changed a few parameters and silently we watched the small white figure tumble and nestle into LeeAnn's dead body as if her spirit had returned home.

Raindrops splattered the windshield as I pulled into the drive of the hi-rise. My stomach churned. I couldn't decide if I was hungry or merely upset from viewing the re-enactment of LeeAnn's fall. I tried to imagine Ewer nudging her a mere fraction, just enough to set her in motion. It couldn't have been an angry shove. Codger had shown me that a heavy-weight push would have moved LeeAnn's entire body almost half-a-foot from where she'd actually fallen.

My ride up the elevator seemed interminable. Anxious to take a hot bath and collect my thoughts, I was exasperated when the elevator stopped at the tenth floor and Bitsy hobbled aboard, smiling vacantly, red lipstick smeared into deep pits surrounding her lips, long pearl ropes dangling against the elastic-waistband of her pink slacks. Arriving on fourteen, Bitsy started to get out with me but I murmured she was on the wrong floor, punched the down button for her floor and waited while the doors closed. I felt remiss in not escorting her back to her apartment.

Turning, I noticed Santa heading in my direction. She brightened when she spotted me, calling out, "You okay? Suzy and I were worried about you."

My overnight stay at the hospital and meeting Keymap seemed a century ago. "I'm fine," I said. "You look pretty good yourself."

It was true that my neighbor bore no visible scars from her descent into depression over her impending divorce, or her night spent in an opium-tea stupor. Her hair flamed as red as ever and her eyes sparkled with enviable clarity. Dressed in brown athletic shorts, a camouflage patterned T-shirt and hiking boots, she balanced a large backpack over one shoulder.

Santa noticed my appraisal of her attire. "I'm headed to the sweat lodge. Going to see which way to face." She grinned broadly. "Wanna come?"

"It's raining," I said, but she just stretched her grin.

"That's no excuse."

I started to mutter another rationalization, when she interrupted. "I know. Work. Little Miss nose-to-the-grindstone. And," she paused dramatically, "I have work to do, too!" With a wave she bounced off toward the elevator, her tiny butt jiggling, the clomp of her boots heavy with purpose.

She wouldn't mind the rain. I sighed, not knowing whether it was in envy of her stamina or at her stubborn determination in pursuing those ridiculous outings in the piney woods north of Houston. Repeatedly, Santa tried to get me to join her on these excursions where groups of desperate city folks followed a self-proclaimed guru into the woods and sat inside a tepee filled with heated rocks in order to examine their chakras. It was called a "sweat."

At the one and only "sweat" Santa talked me into attending, she grew depressed on the ride back to Houston because her solar plexus—the "power" chakra—had ached when she faced west.

"It means I have to accept the end of something in my life," she'd wailed. "Do you think it means I'll never have a baby?"

I told her I thought it meant dip-shit. She'd not spoken to me for the rest of the trip home.

Turning the key in my front door, I heard the sound of the kitchen phone ringing. It couldn't be my father because he only left messages during the week and never on Saturdays. Perhaps it was Keymap calling from Florida with news about interviewing LeeAnn's best friend, Sandra Connor.

I picked up the receiver. At first I was glad to hear Winthrop's voice. But then his words doubled me over as if I'd been punched in the stomach. Robby had disappeared from the hospital.

25

A man came to see me. I never saw him before and I don't like him or his ponytail but he brought me paper and a pencil and told me he'd spring me out of here if I wanted and we could go to Galveston. I told him thanks for the paper but I was waiting for Giles to come get me out. He laughed and I didn't like his laugh. He said she locked me up here, that she's the reason I'm here.

He said— I think I'll call him ponytail cause he said just call him buddy which is really stupid cause he's not my buddy and I know that's not his real name cause he paused a little to think of it. He must think I'm really dumb. So ponytail said to write my sister a goodbye note and got mad when I started my drawing. I want to get out of here too so I drew my picture really fast. My hand itches to draw, always itches to draw and ponytail has no understanding of this but he has a truck he said and would drive me anywhere I want to go. Galveston sounds nice because I like the beach and maybe I'll feel better looking at the water.

I'm bigger than ponytail and I can take care of myself and I don't feel as dead as I did feel after ponytail offered to spring me and I got to draw a picture.

Ponytail is puny. Real puny even if he talks tough.

26

The last time Robby ran away was still etched in my mind. He was eighteen. Dinner was on the table and Father yelled for Robby to join us, but my brother was engaged in scribbling on paper, a relatively new compulsion for him.

"What the hell?" Father stood in the doorway of Robby's room. His reaction reflected how little he visited my brother's bedroom or he would not have been surprised. Father didn't like surprises.

Robby sat crossed-legged on top of his bed, shoulders hunched, writing furiously on a tablet. Paper littered the floor as well as his pale-blue chenille bedspread. Instead of covering each piece of paper with his writing, Robby sat, glassy-eyed, writing only fragments before ripping pages and tossing them aside.

I hurried from behind Father and began picking up papers, gently prodding Robby with my elbow, keeping my voice low as I urged him to come to dinner. But Father never missed a beat.

He stormed across the room, lifted Robby by the collar, and dragged him off the bed. "Get your ass to the dinner table now!" Robby took a feeble swing at Father's jaw, but missed. Father's face turned into a parody of an enraged actor, his mouth curled into a menacing snarl, his eyes squinted in fury. He shoved Robby hard against the wall. Robby slid slowly downward like a thrown bucket of paint

"Quit acting crazy, you son-of-a-bitch!" He jerked Robby up and began pummeling him on the chest and shoulders. I rushed over, coming between them a little too fast. Father's fist hit my mouth. Blood spurted against my tongue as I staggered and fell.

Robby cried out like an animal in pain, twisted away from the wall and came at my father from the side, feinting like a boxer. Robby was taller than our father who'd allowed desk work to add twenty pounds of slacking gut to his shorter frame. Now Robby was in a rage, something I'd witnessed several times before. I don't know where he learned it, but Robby delivered a high chop downward against the base of Father's neck and he dropped, unconscious. Robby was sobbing loudly now, shifting his weight from one foot to the next in total confusion before he whirled and ran out the front door.

I searched for him until after midnight. When I finally crawled into bed, unsuccessful, Father flipped on the hallway light and stood outside my door. I turned to stare at him, but neither of us spoke. I looked away first, rolled over onto my side, and pulled the sheet over my head. I wouldn't let him see me cry.

When I exited the elevator on the third floor of the psychiatric ward, Dr. Winthrop stood panting as if he'd just arrived in front of the nursing stations. I hurried beside him. I'd always thought of this floor of the hospital as a jail. Lots of security and no escape. Wrong.

Winthrop's expression was grim as he nodded at me. With his arms folded over his chest, he responded to a nurse who'd joined us, asking what she could do to help.

"My patient, Rob Faulkner, was on half-hour check. How far could he go in less than thirty minutes? I find it hard to believe you weren't able to find him after you saw what he'd done."

When she replied, I recognized the head nurse, Ms. Mills. Her pale cheeks flared red. "We acted on your orders, doctor, that Robby didn't need restraint 24-7. And, on your orders, he was on hourly check, not every thirty minutes. Otherwise, this wouldn't have happened." In spite of her accusation, her voice quavered with misgiving.

I felt a spot of sympathy for the woman, but not enough. Words tumbled out, my outburst aimed at the hapless nurse. "How could you let my brother get away? How could he leave when you people had him locked in his room?" The pitch of my voice sounded too high and too loud.

Apparently I was a safer target as Ms. Mills lowered her head before darting her eyes in my direction as if I were seconds from a head-butt. "'You people', you say? I want you to know we are all trained professionals here and your brother's request for a Coke was not something out of keeping with his prior actions. Your brother was not under restraint orders. If he had been, this never would have happened."

I shuddered. I'd witnessed Robby in a straight jacket before and grew nauseous at the memory.

Dr. Winthrop sighed loudly. "She's right, Giles. I should have seen this coming." He turned to me and grabbed my elbow. "The police have been alerted. He can't have gone far."

Ms. Mills took a deep breath and motioned for us to follow. She unlocked an office door opposite the viewing stations overlooking the patients' gathering room. The same room I'd walked through the previous morning. Once Winthrop and I were seated and the door closed, she went behind the desk and punched a telephone button. "Johnny. Will you come into the consult office, please?"

She stood and shuffled papers, her head down until a short, balding man entered. I recognized him as the one who'd escorted me to Robby's room.

"Would you tell Dr. Winthrop and Robert Faulkner's sister the details of his escape?"

"He didn't hurt me," Johnny turned and looked down at us. I felt disadvantaged, as if Winthrop and I should also be standing. "Robert must have been behind the door when I entered with his soda. He grabbed me, knocked me down, tied my hands behind my back with a torn sheet then stuffed the tail of his pillowcase in my mouth. He's pretty strong. His teeth are, too," he grinned, "to split the bed sheet like he did."

I stared at the man and wondered how he ever could have been hired to work this floor. Appearing to be on the brink of seventy, his bulk appeared soft as if he used to be in good shape but had given up the effort.

"May I see Robby's room?" The question escaped before I had time to wonder why I should bother. He'd only spent, what, one night before he ran?

Johnny nodded and we said our goodbyes to Ms. Mills, who appeared, understandably, glad to see us go.

Johnny pushed open Robby's door without using a key. I realized my brother would have taken the key ring. The single bed stood empty, the top bed sheet crumpled and torn, its edges frayed. Robby wasn't himself without his medications. He hadn't been here long enough for his meds to kick in and return my brother to the promise of what he could be. I felt jagged, stuffing anger at Winthrop, as well as this inept guard by my side.

Except for the torn sheet, there was nothing to indicate Robby had ever been here. Wait. An edge of paper stuck out from beneath the pillow. I walked over. I had meant to bring him paper and pencil. Had Johnny done this for Robby?

I stared at the paper, feeling that familiar admiration whenever Robby chose to draw instead of scribble. He had a distinctive style, his characters drawn muscular under their clothes, their expressions those of wonder or surprise at something secret. I held a pencil sketch of a young woman on horseback caught in the act of racing around a barrel, her hair flying behind, the graceful lines of horse and rider straining together, elongated forward as if from a strong, invisible force. Robby had volunteered at Houston Rodeo last year. Mostly cleaning up horse stalls.

I spoke to Johnny after sharing the drawing with Dr. Winthrop. "Did a young woman visit my brother?" I thought of Robby's mysterious female friend, but Johnny shook his head. The woman probably didn't exist.

"So then you brought Robby paper and pencil?" I was prepared to entertain forgiveness for his negligence in letting Robby get away if he'd actually shown such compassion for my brother.

"No, not me." He appeared sorry, but added helpfully, "It was his cousin."

I must have misunderstood. "What did you say?"

"I said his cousin brought him paper. Said he knew Robert would want to draw. Your brother's fast, too, cause it was only twenty minutes or so after the cousin left that Robert waylaid me."

"Whose cousin are you talking about?" I demanded, blood pounding my temples, my ears buzzing as if I stood miles above the earth, battling vertigo.

A trace of worry flashed across Johnny's face. "Robert's cousin, of course."

As I began to tremble, I locked my knees, willing myself not to stumble.

"Robby doesn't have a cousin."

27

No one spoke. Winthrop and I paced in Ms. Mills' small office while she and Johnny frowned at the linoleum floor. We waited for the photo copy of the man who'd visited Robby, the man who'd claimed he was Robby's cousin. All visitors signed in and left a copy of their driver's license before they were allowed inside.

So what would this cousin look like? I prayed it was someone I knew. Perhaps posing as a cousin just for sport. But who would do that? Not anyone I knew. Robby considered Santa his friend and he'd met Captain Hightower several times. He also knew a few of those who frequented Café Artiste. Maybe it was one of those café weirdos in a joking mood.

On the verge of asking Ms. Mills to call the front desk again, I closed my mouth when the door opened and a nurse entered. She carried a manila folder, handed it to Mills, and left the room.

While Mills perused the papers in the folder, I held my breath. When she finished, she walked behind her desk, sat, and then handed the papers across to me. Winthrop peered over my shoulder as I studied the color copy of the license as well as a photocopy of his signature.

What kind of joke was this? The man who stared out at me was a stranger, but the name he'd scrawled on the guest register, the name on his driver's license, caused me to gasp "G. Legion Faulkner." My name.

⁑

"Here. I have something for you." Dr. Winthrop placed a small plastic bottle in my hand. "You need to go home and get some sleep. You're walking death."

He held the car door for me and I tumbled into the driver's seat. My body felt boneless and tired to the point of nausea. Winthrop ducked his head as he leaned over, his brow furrowed into ridges. "Want me to drive you home?"

I shook my head, turned the ignition key, and listened as the engine roared to life. Winthrop patted me on the shoulder and spoke before closing the car door. "The police will get to the bottom of this. They'll find Robby. Just leave it to them."

I waved him away and drove off. Like hell I'd leave it to the police. But tonight, I had no choice. Sleep beckoned me like a lonely lover. Thanks to Dr. Winthrop's pills, success was assured.

⁑

I awoke to the ringing of the phone. Suzy howled from under the bed. There must have been lightening and thunder during the night. She was a true scaredy-cat. I, on the other hand, had been drugged into body-numbing sleep-of-the-dead.

"This is Giles," I said, my voice throaty with sleep.

"It's Keymap. Did I wake you?"

Due to a brain thick with cobwebs, it took more than a few seconds to clear my head. When it did, I grew excited Keymap was back. "No," I glanced at the clock. Ten a.m. What had Dr. Winthrop given me?

"I'm in Florida, about to board the plane," he said. "Thought I'd check and see about getting together tonight. Go over what I learned."

I sat up. Suzy took this as a sign I needed company and pounced on my lap, digging her claws into my thighs. "Ouch!" I pushed Suzy away. "What time?"

"I'll come by about eight. Unless you have company."

Company? I got it. "No. My cat was slicing me with her claws. Eight is fine."

"I'm allergic to cats," Keymap said before hanging up.

Thinking we had at least one thing in common, I proceeded to shower and dress. After grabbing pictures of my brother and the mysterious cousin, I headed to Kinkos to make copies, convinced I knew Robby's hangouts better than anyone.

꩜

Six hours later I'd covered all the territory I knew, having canvassed the neighborhoods around Robby's boarding house, Dr. Winthrop's office, and Ben Taub. I'd dropped by for a twenty-minute visit with Mrs. Cathcart that should have taken three. Leaving her excited over the missing-person drama, I drove to Café Artiste and spoke with Calvin. Before leaving, I posted both pictures on the message board along with my name and phone number. Then I called Captain Hightower, who assured me his best officers were looking for Robby—that a picture of the man posing as Robby's cousin had also been circulated to all surrounding counties and they were running it through their facial-recognition software.

"Hang in there, girl. We'll find your brother."

Blind luck had found Robby when he'd last run away. After hitchhiking to Lubbock and back, he hid in the park near our house. When an officer hassled him, Robby admitted where he lived rather than go to jail. With torn, mud-caked shirt and jeans, elbow and cheekbone bloodied, and one eye swollen shut, he surprised me at our front door, the peace officer beside him.

"Hey, Jelly," he said before walking inside and back into his room as if he'd never been gone.

Fighting off images of Robby lying dead in a pool of blood beside the road, the cousin laughing demoniacally with a raised, blood-soaked hatchet, I drove back to the hi-rise and handed the parking attendant two pictures, one of my little brother and one of the man who'd used my name. Giving way to exhaustion, I leaned against the elevator wall as I rode up to my floor.

A feeling of doom began to swallow me piece by piece. Why couldn't I believe that Robby would return without all this worry? If I grew as unstable as my brother, who would take care of him?

Locking my front door behind me, I slowly climbed the stairs. Just as I started the hot water running in the tub, I thought of posting Robby's picture on the internet. Half-dressed, I hurried downstairs and opened the door to my office. After flipping on the overhead light, I stood frozen by the chaos in front of me. The chair cushion lay angled in the corner. Papers littered the floor. Books yanked from their shelves lay scattered in clumps. The filing cabinet gaped empty with its drawers pulled open as if displaying evidence of missing bodies in a morgue.

Suzy snaked around my ankle and yowled. Suddenly my meltdown reversed itself as adrenaline shoved purple rage straight to my brain. Crap! Who had dared break into my home and take papers from my office? I ran to the front door and examined the lock. It looked perfect, undisturbed. Repugnance, as if I'd been personally violated, seared through me. Whoever had done this would pay.

Blood pounding in my temples, I began retrieving empty file folders and papers from the floor. Willing my hands to cease trembling, I tried to visualize what was missing. It took a minute to home in on what was gone—a folder filled with typed notes on LeeAnn's background, another of interviews with Boots, Brad Ewer, and a few musings about J.D. McGraw. Also, typed transcriptions from the police files, and a separate folder related to Hammerly Insurance. Scattered about were my bank statements, school records and notes for class.

I hurried over to my desk and couldn't believe my luck. Shoved toward the back of the center drawer was my secretarial sized spiral notebook I'd used to scribble notes from LeeAnn's police file. That would help some. My relief was short-lived when I remembered my gun. When not driving in my car, I kept my gun along with my camera inside my briefcase. Only after discovering both were still there did I breathe again.

Mary Nelson's rodeo photographs lay between pages in the spiral notebook. I carried them into the living room and placed them on page eighty-five of Aunt Eunice's coffee table picture book of Egypt. Perhaps it made me feel more in control to move them.

Lamar 's experts could check my office for fingerprints. Mine were the only ones that belonged. From early on, I'd kept my office off-limits to others, and when having guests, locked my home office door just as I did my downtown office. But if you could open my front door, the same key could open my home office. I'd have to change that.

Once I'd shoved all loose papers back inside the appropriate files, I closed the file drawers, and was replacing the chair cushion, when I noticed my laptop was missing from my desk. No chance to retrieve any missing files from my hard drive! My stomach knotted and sweat popped out on my brow. This was the final blow. How would I recreate from memory everything I'd learned? I sank to the carpet, fearing I might be sick.

Gritting my teeth, I talked myself into calming down. Someone desperate to learn what I knew about LeeAnn's death had entered my apartment and made sure my files were gone for good. When? While I'd slept last night? Or after I'd left that morning to look for Robby?

28

From upstairs came a noise of gushing water. Crap! I took the stairs two at a time. The tub was within a hair of overflowing. After draining a couple of inches, I walked into the bedroom and picked up the phone.

Captain Hightower promised he'd send someone to dust for fingerprints, but it would be a few hours. I was tired of being told to hang tight.

Back in the bathroom, I stripped and sank into the hot water as if returning to the womb, certain now that someone wanted to keep me from investigating LeeAnn's death. I forced my mind into a blank, promising myself I'd think about the ransacking of my office later. Soak, Giles. Float away. When calmer, I'd question the gatekeepers of this high-security hi-rise. They had a lot of explaining to do.

Only slightly more relaxed from my bath, I was on my way to question security when the doorbell rang. It was Santa, grinning through the peep-hole. I opened the door and she held out a bottle of gin adorned with a large red bow. "I never did thank you for putting me to bed the other night."

Any other time, I would have invited her inside. But at that moment, I wasn't myself, as I quickly proved by blurting out, "Someone broke in, ransacked my office, and Robby's run away from Ben Taub. I have to question the building staff. Right now."

Startled at what flew out of my mouth, I realized that whenever my brother was involved, that thread, that mental anchor I enjoyed in my professional life rattled and came loose, leaving me aghast and forlorn, as if my own mind had declared war. The next thing I knew, Santa had backed me inside the apartment and offered to pour me a drink.

"No! I can't have a drink. I'm going downstairs to question security, and then I'm . . . I'm going out to the grocery store. I need lemons for the gin," I added weakly as she narrowed her eyes while shoving the gin bottle inside the freezer.

"I have lemons in my icebox," Santa said. "Go sit down while I get them, and then you can tell me all about what's happened while I've been out finding my true chakra."

She wouldn't leave until I was seated on the sofa, my head in my hands, thinking about escape. The door closed behind her. Did I have time to sneak out before she returned? Yes. I bolted for the door, locked it behind me and was at the elevator when I felt her tiny, but painfully strong hand grip my arm.

"Not so fast, Giles. You'll work yourself into a fit if you keep this up."

Me? What a laugh. Advice from Miss opium-tea drinker!

"I'm fine, and I'm not waiting a minute longer to talk to security."

Clutching two lemons, Santa stayed glued to my side as we descended to the lobby. "Just let me do the questioning," I said, storming across to the sign-in booth several feet from the elevators. Wilcox was on duty.

He smiled as we approached, but his grin faded when he saw my expression. My throat was tight with controlled outrage. "Someone broke into my apartment. Either last night or while I was out. I want the records showing everyone who came and went."

"Of course," Wilcox replied. He was a tall, elegant-bodied young black man with shorn hair and wire-rimmed glasses. Now he resembled a tired accountant at tax-time as he reached for the sign-in clipboard and began flipping pages.

"Let's see about last night—"

He didn't have time to finish his sentence before I grabbed it away and began searching signatures from five p.m. the day before until midnight, when a new signature sheet began. There was nothing that didn't belong. Flipping the page over for the midnight-until-seven a.m. list, I again saw only familiar friends and relatives of hi-rise owners. I pointed to one name, Timothy Landers, as someone I didn't know, but Wilcox assured me he was the stepson of the couple on the ninth level and had visited many times before.

The next sheet covered seven a.m. until six p.m. today, which was thirty minutes away. There were about fourteen names and I started at the top. I found him in the middle, his distinctive signature popping out at me like a mouse from its hole. Robby Faulkner. With my pulse skittering, I searched for the name G. Legion Faulkner but it wasn't there. "My brother signed in, it says here, at three-thirty this afternoon. You didn't tell him I'd gone out?"

Wilcox took off his glasses and rubbed his closed eyes with his thumbs like a sleep-deprived child. "He signed in to see Mrs. Henderson. Besides, Robby's your brother, Miss Faulkner. He's been here lots of times when you're out. He visits Mrs. Henderson here," he nodded at Santa, "or occasionally, just says he'll wait in your apartment. He has his own key." He stared at me, small red veins swimming in the corners of his drooping eyes. "You want me to run the camera tapes?"

At my nod, Wilcox swiveled toward a computer screen perched behind him and began clicking keys. The images appeared grainy, but when he stopped on the revolving front door of the hi-rise, there was no mistaking Robby. He wore a long sleeved shirt and slacks, obviously brought by his cohort who'd sprung him out of Ben Taub.

Wilcox froze the frame, but Robby appeared alone. After I asked for the next couple of minutes of frame, a man wearing a baseball cap, his face averted, appeared on the screen within thirty seconds of Robby's entrance. He seemed to drop something and bent out of camera range and didn't reappear. Even after replaying it several times, the three of us agreed it was no one we knew. My mystery man? I asked for a print copy and Wilcox disappeared back inside the main office.

I knew I had no business blaming Wilcox. Robby could and did come to my apartment. He also visited Santa, but most of the time I was included in their visits. In fact, I thought it was me including Santa, not the other way around. So why had she kept quiet about Robby's visit?

I turned toward my neighbor. "So how often does my brother visit you without my knowing?"

A shadow fell across her face, but she recovered quickly. "Not often. I wanted to tell you upstairs that I'd seen Robby earlier so he wasn't really missing."

"Oh? Then why didn't you?"

She shrank under my gaze.

"If he's not missing, then go get him and bring him back." I wanted to add, "smarty-pants" but thought that was a tad childish.

"I don't ever call him, Giles. He calls me. I wish I could find him for you."

"You 'wish'?"

Just then Wilcox returned and handed me a picture of the man who'd entered the building briefly. Too briefly, since he'd never signed in. Wanting to finish this conversation out of Wilcox's hearing, I grabbed Santa's arm, and without speaking, we rode the elevator back to my apartment.

It was after five and thoughts of cold gin appealed greatly, but I refused to indulge in front of Santa, who indulged herself far too often. Wondering why I should feel like her parent, I slowed down the somersaults in my brain and tried hard to appear calm.

"So did Robby seem like someone who'd escaped from the psych ward? Why the visit?"

Santa had tossed her lemons in my icebox and now stood with her back to me, gazing out the picture window onto Kirby Drive below. Her red hair shown bright with health and her taut body advertised her addiction to the gym, which only reminded me I'd let another day pass without swimming. I waited her out.

When she turned to face me, she was biting her lower lip, her eyes defiant but her posture slumped. I started to mouth off about her fading chakra but didn't.

"Robby's such a nice person, Giles. Sometimes I think you smother him too much."

Where was this going? I shoved aside anger as well as an overwhelming compulsion to defend myself.

"What I mean is . . . " She looked away.

I refused to prompt her. I would stand here all night if necessary.

"He and I enjoyed drinking tea together, that's all."

"Tea?" The word shot out of my mouth before my mind grasped what she referred to. When it did, I pounced. "Are you saying you gave Robby opium-tea? You gave a manic-depressive opium-tea?" I shook her shoulders and Santa looked close to crying. I didn't care. "You know that's wrong! You would have told me long before now if you'd thought nothing of it, but you kept it from me! You . . . you idiot! He's on medications, for heaven's sake!"

Her eyes filled with tears and she began to sob. The louder she sobbed, the more focused I became.

"Robby lives on a seesaw," I said, my voice full of venom. "His meds have been continually fine-tuned since he was five years old. He's psychotic, he's manic/depressive, and has episodes of paranoia. Opium-tea may not bother you, but I can't believe what you've done to my brother." I turned my back, my temples pounding. "Please don't tell me you let him leave here inebriated from your drug of choice!"

She tried to reply, but instead began to hiccup, her breaths interrupted by spasmodic interjections of high-pitched yelps. In any other circumstance, I might have been amused. I marched to the kitchen and filled a tumbler full of water. When I returned, Santa sat on the floor, her tear-stained face a mask of remorse.

She drank the water in one long gulp, then paused as if choosing her words carefully. "We shared one cup is all. He said he wasn't driving so it wouldn't matter. Besides, neither of us gets soused on half-a cup."

"Sounds like you two have quite a history of sharing opium-tea." I didn't give her time to respond before continuing, "Did he say who was driving him or where he was going?"

Santa shook her head.

"Did he mention he'd busted out of Ben Taub, or were you too skunked to notice?"

Defiance flashed for an instant as she blurted out, "He wasn't dressed in a hospital gown," before she resumed her pitiful expression. With giant liquid eyes staring out of a mournful face she resembled the poster child for *Les Miserables*. "I said we shared one cup. Not enough to feel anything."

"Maybe not for you, but you're not Robby." And then I wondered about the rest of the camera tapes. "What time did Robby leave?"

"Around four."

I escorted Santa back to her apartment and extracted a promise she'd call immediately if Robby returned. And if she ever served Robby opium-tea again, I'd turn her over to the authorities. She vowed she was through, proclaiming she wouldn't serve it to Robby and would never indulge again. Santa wouldn't shut her door until I promised I'd forgiven her.

I told her what she wanted to hear and firmly closed her door. In fact, I didn't want her accompanying me back downstairs for another scrutiny of the tapes. I needed verification she'd told me the truth.

With me looking on, Wilcox fast-forwarded the video. At five after four, Robby exited the elevators alone and disappeared behind the revolving door, again alone. But could I be sure he hadn't had time to vandalize my office and take my documents? The fingerprint guys couldn't get here soon enough.

Winthrop had asked me if Robby could possibly be on drugs. I'd been certain the answer was no. What else didn't I know? It could have been my brother who'd been in my office and taken all the documents about my investigation of LeeAnn Callahan. If so, why?

A more likely scenario was the cousin, whose entrance into the hi-rise had somehow gone undetected. He could have used Robby's key to ransack my apartment while Santa was busy with my little brother. Which still led to the question of why Robby would participate, cooperate with a stranger?

Prone on the living room couch, I clutched the note Robby'd left on my desk top. The note I'd missed in my panic over the rape of my office—the note a really good private investigator would never have missed. It was Robby's handwriting, scribbled in a downward pencil scrawl, so strong it tore the paper in spots. "I'm out!!!!"

I would have liked one more sentence, one without any exclamation points or torn paper. Any hint that his mania was on the downswing.

Had Robby written the note alone, or was the name-stealing cousin standing over him? Perhaps forcing my brother to leave this note for me to find? A warning to stay away from LeeAnn Callahan's death or what? Take Robby, kill him, now that he had my case files? Panic threatened to shut down my thought processes. I shouldn't have banished Santa so quickly. Surely she would have told me if she'd seen anyone, someone skilled at avoiding cameras and security. After rising off the couch, I headed across the room when Aunt Eunice's clock chimed. Half-past seven. In thirty minutes Keymap would be here.

Change clothes or not? Not. But I could wash my face and brush my teeth. In the end, I also ran a comb through my hair and put on lipstick. The face looking back at me was blurred as if through a fog. Every movement of my arm seemed flaccid, like fluid and bone had been leaked or stolen for my mummification.

Did I really not know how Robby felt when he complained about feeling dead inside?

29

When the doorbell rang, I let Keymap inside. Again he smelled faintly of pipe tobacco as he passed, carrying a large paper bag in his arms. He withdrew a bottle of gin with a flourish. To keep him from seeing Santa's red-bow-tied bottle in the freezer, I set his on the kitchen counter. It was already cold.

"Thanks," I said. "I have some really old Scotch if you'd prefer." Did Scotch go bad if not stored correctly? Aunt Eunice had been a Scotch drinker and several dusty half-full bottles were still in her liquor cabinet.

"I drink most anything," Keymap said in his sexy drawl, flashing a smile charming enough to slay the heart of anything in skirts. But then his smile faded quickly as his gaze on me sharpened.

"Something's happened. Let me fix you a drink. Go. Sit in the living room and I'll be right along. Twist of lemon, right?" He had the refrigerator door open, his hand on a lemon when he gazed back at me. His small grin grew sardonic as he nodded at the lemon-peeler I'd retrieved from the kitchen drawer. "Now go. I have everything I need."

From the living room I heard cabinets open, then bang shut. Dishes clattered while I sat in Santa's, no— my easy chair—and stared out into the night at the traffic below. In the distance, office and house lights twinkled, and I wondered, not for the first time, about all those lives locked inside their climate-controlled walls. Were theirs as crazy as mine?

When Keymap appeared, he carried a large tray I recognized. He'd scrounged up a basket of chips I didn't remember owning, a bowl of guacamole he must have brought with him, as well as a separate plate of crackers, cheese and grapes, artfully arranged, that had never lived in my kitchen.

"*Voila!*" he said, plopping Aunt Eunice's teeming silver tray on the coffee table. Before settling on the sofa across from me, he disappeared back into the kitchen and returned, carrying two glasses of gin with a twist of lemon floating in each.

Okay, I said to myself, we now have two things in common: cat allergies and gin. Which reminded me to excuse myself, run upstairs, and shut the door to my bedroom where Suzy lay snoring. When I was seated again, Keymap handed me a cracker smeared with Brie. "Take a long slug of gin, eat something, and then we'll talk."

I did as I was told, felt liquid fire travel to my stomach, hit my brain, then my extremities, leaving behind gratitude of worldly proportions. I not only ate the one cracker, I dipped guacamole like a mad woman, popped grapes in my mouth and chewed while he gazed at me, lazy-eyed contentment on his face. I could have kissed the man, but didn't. I'd had zero nourishment all day, unless anxiety contained calories.

Finally, embarrassed over my gluttony, I accepted a second drink, kicked off my shoes and curled my bare feet underneath me. Being here with him felt natural, as if we'd sat opposite each other this way before. If I shared Santa's slant on the world, I'd believe Keymap and I had known each other in a previous life.

In order to start spilling my troubles, I needed no prompting. His eyes, full of sympathy, stamped approval for a confession. This sudden compulsion to unload felt foreign and would only confuse me if I chose to dwell on it, so I didn't.

"My brother disappeared yesterday. Ran away from Ben Taub. He has mental issues. It could be he ran off with a man who used my name to get inside the hospital, calling himself Robby's cousin and bringing pencil and paper, ostensibly so Robby could draw. Wait I'll get photos."

I jumped off the sofa, found my briefcase, and extracted copies of the photos I'd been posting around town. I handed them over and resettled myself on the cushion.

Keymap studied the pictures, nodding as if he were familiar with both men before he slid them in his back pocket. By pointing his forefinger upward, he switched gears.

"I think a little soothing music is called for." He hopped up and began shuffling through the CD collection. I was thinking he certainly knew his way around this apartment when my thoughts were interrupted by the soft strains of Vivaldi's Winter Concerto.

Aunt Eunice had loved this piece and asked for it repeatedly in the months leading up to her hospitalization and subsequent death. Hot tears sprang to my eyes. My aunt, at least, had loved me, had felt sympathy for me when my father left for Florida with his new wife— leaving me alone to care for Robby.

Even if the intellectual part of me knew Father deserved happiness and freedom from a son with overwhelming mental problems, the emotional part of me resented the hell out of his abandonment. Which is probably the reason I didn't speak to him. Why was I anointed the responsible one? Didn't I deserve to live my life free of an unstable, dependent brother?

When Keymap spoke, I was startled to realize my cheeks were soaked with tears.

"Right now," he said soothingly, "I want you to lean back, close your eyes and let the music sweep through you. Take your time."

I tried to relax, swiping at my cheeks. All I could think about now was my brother. I didn't really want Robby to disappear from my life, I just wanted him normal.

I left the room and splashed my face in the kitchen sink. Robby was okay. He had to be. Surely if he were dead, I would feel it.

After reentering the living room, I sat, gaze averted from any sympathetic look from Keymap. "A minute ago, you seemed to recognize both my brother and the man posing as our cousin."

He gazed at me, eyes narrowed, head swaying as if keeping time with the music. "Is that what you think?"

"Looked like it to me," I said.

"Looks can be deceiving. Let's talk about facts."

Keymap may be sympathetic, but he still refused to talk about anything but his own agenda.

"This may not be fact, but I believe Robby was here in my office this afternoon while I was out looking for him. Either he or an accomplice removed all the files I had on the Callahan case. As well as my computer." Gulping my drink, I felt my brain teeter in a downward spiral. Without a drop of remorse, I resolved to get good and drunk.

Keymap looked worried and solicitous at the same time. He leaned toward me, elbows resting on his thighs. I fought a sudden compulsion to jump up and crawl in his lap. With his rumpled black T-shirt, and black slacks, he appeared open, vulnerable even. The total opposite of the distant man who'd escorted me to Brad Ewer's cocktail party.

"What makes you think your brother took your files?" he asked.

This new role of sympathetic inquisitor set off a warning bell, while at the same time causing a flush of warmth in a part of my body I'd ignored for years. Feeling hot, I glanced away while reaching in my jeans pocket, then silently passed Robby's note across the coffee table.

He scanned it and handed it back, his finger grazing mine. "What if Robby left this note after your office files had been taken?"

"What the hell are you suggesting?" My gin-soaked brain responded without benefit of reason. "My brother's a little cock-eyed, but he did graduate from high school, he can fix any broken motor on the planet and knows meteorology better than the TV weatherman! So he wouldn't notice the wreckage? Oh. Dear me. My sister's files are all over the floor, her filing cabinet has been emptied, her chair knocked over and all her books are on the floor. But I'm going to just write her a note and leave?"

Keymap stared without responding while my addled mind realized: yeah, my brother could do that when he was in one of his altered states. He could ignore a lot when the biggest thing on his mind was voices driving him even crazier.

I drained my glass to keep from talking. But then, Keymap might let me get away with changing the subject. I'd have to wait for the fingerprint guys, anyway, before I'd know for certain who'd ransacked my office.

I broke the silence. "Tell me about Florida. Did you find Sandra Connor?"

He hesitated, as if deciding whether he was willing to drop our current discussion. "I found her."

"So tell me." I sat up straighter, willing my brain to clear.

"She's one smooth woman, Giles." When he leaned back, apparently satisfied with our current subject, I breathed easier.

"My guess is that she was paid off and has too much money in her bank account to rat on anyone. The only thing I can tell you is that she wouldn't agree or disagree about LeeAnn being suicidal. According to Sandra, LeeAnn admitted she had a married boyfriend, but wouldn't identify him.

"Something else, too." He compressed his lips and nodded as if acknowledging his memory was correct. "Sandra said to check out LeeAnn's will and her "conniving" brother, Boots. Interesting, no?"

I nodded, puzzling over the derogatory comment about Boots until I remembered J.D.'s statement that, due to Boots's irresponsible behavior, LeeAnn had control over her brother's inheritance. Then again, it could be that Sandra, as her best friend, was overly protective of their relationship and resented Boots' claim on her. Especially if Boots were still playing the role of wild, older brother needing lots of attention. But LeeAnn herself was running around with a married man. Not that gambling and loose behavior canceled each other out. I'd look into it for sure.

Keymap watched me digest his information before continuing. "The second time I showed up at Ms. Connor's place unannounced, I managed to put a guilt trip on her. They were best friends, how could she not tell all she knew about LeeAnn, etc.,etc. But, in all honesty, it could have been my promise not to bother her any more if she'd cooperate. Regardless of the reason, she coughed up the name of LeeAnn's psychiatrist, who you know doesn't have to talk to you, and," he paused for dramatic effect, "the fact that this mysterious married boyfriend got LeeAnn pregnant."

My brain cleared instantly and I almost whooped aloud. DNA! I'd find that bastard and nail him. Then I remembered there had been no mention of a pregnancy on the autopsy report. I'd pay the ME a visit. He'd have to have it on record along with a tissue sample.

Keymap dropped his head and when he looked up again, his expression was pained. "I've already talked with the ME, Giles. LeeAnn wasn't pregnant when she died."

30

As if he'd accomplished what he came for, Keymap slapped his palms on his thighs and quickly stood. "I gotta go. You're car's ready, by the way, so I'll take mine."

When I had trouble switching gears, he added, hand outstretched, "Keys? I'll have yours delivered by morning."

Silently, I cursed myself. Instead of leaving, had I expected he'd sweep me in his arms and carry me upstairs like Rhet Butler? I scratched through to the logical part of my brain: no, Giles, you will not sleep with this man while inebriated or any other way. You must keep this strictly business. I tossed over his car keys and followed him to the front door.

He paused and gently cupped my chin with his fingers. My entire body flushed.

"Go straight to bed, Jelly." He bent over, kissed my cheek, his face warm against mine, then thrust papers into my hand before closing the door behind him.

I stood frozen, stunned. What was that all about? And how did he know Robby's nickname for me? Only family members knew it. I stared at the papers he'd handed over. Keymap's invoice and notes from his Florida trip startled me like a slap in the face. What did he mean by kissing me and then flinging me a damn bill? Was that supposed to make his fee more palatable? Jerk! He'd just reminded me of our true relationship: we were investigative partners, period.

When the doorbell rang, my heart leaped into my throat. Maybe it was Keymap regretting his abrupt departure. Gritting my teeth, I told my body to behave itself, and answered the door.

Two fingerprint officers, dressed in gray coveralls to protect their clothing, asked if they could come inside. I shoved down disappointment and showed them to my den. Standing in the doorway, I watched as they sprinkled black powder over every surface. To take my mind off the mess they were making, I retrieved the food tray and empty gin glasses from the living room, returned to the kitchen, and filled the dishwasher

While cleaning, I mentally reviewed what Keymap had learned in Florida. The name of LeeAnn's psychiatrist was a godsend and, with a professional-courtesy request from Winthrop, he just might agree to meet with me. Also, I still needed to interview Juliet Ralston, LeeAnn's friend from Alliance Insurance. Tomorrow I planned to catch her on a smoking break outside her building.

Almost an hour later, the fingerprint team left. At my anxious expression, the older one said, "Think we got some clean prints there. You'll get a call in a day or two."

I shut the door, thinking the prints could all belong to me, then dragged myself upstairs to bed. Good thing Winthrop gave me more than one sleeping pill. Gin and sleeping pills were not my usual fare, but, again, the energy to care was gone.

Over the years, I grew to recognize what I called my "Robby overload." Too much angst over my brother and I shut down with my brain refusing any more visits.

Not wanting to oversleep, I set the alarm for seven-thirty. LeeAnn's death was where I needed to focus. It was becoming harder and harder to believe this young woman killed herself. I had to find out before Boots's money or his enthusiasm for my abilities ran out. Robby was fading from my mind.

Or so I thought. Something about lying in a drugged state between waking and sleeping brought clarity, and with clarity, shame. Tonight I'd cried, wallowing in self-pity. Even I couldn't tolerate the memory of myself downstairs spilling all my troubles over my brother to a man I barely knew. Get a grip, Giles. You haven't had such a bout of self-indulgence since screaming at Father ten years before, accusing him of abandonment. But where Keymap was concerned, there was no connection to be abandoned from. This realization was followed by a slow unknotting of my stomach. In spite of a nasty throbbing in my temples, my anxiety dissipated. Keymap was one less man to fret over.

Suzy woke me the next morning before the alarm. Over a second cup of coffee, my dull headache subsided and I clicked into gear. Bounding back upstairs, I dumped the remaining sleeping pills in the toilet. One drug-dependent person in our family was enough.

First on my list was a call to the ME's office. After that was finished, I hurriedly dressed. Grabbing a jacket, I locked the door behind me and headed to the Harris County Medical Examiner's office, but only after knocking on Santa's door and getting no answer. As much as I wanted to make sure she'd not heard or seen anyone around my apartment during Robby's visit, I'd have to wait.

For me to depend on Irma to give me the name of her contact at the ME's office was foolish. So I'd used Hightower's name to get an appointment with whoever was available, and now had a scheduled meeting with one of the assistants, not the ME himself. I didn't care. Any of them could give me a copy of LeeAnn's autopsy. I could request a copy in writing, but that not only took too long, it didn't allow face-to-face when asking questions about possible missing information. Years ago, Chief Hightower had drilled me on the advantages of personal interrogation.

The ME's building was located on Old Spanish Trail, a street running behind the maze of hospitals and medical towers that made up the Houston Medical Center. I parked out front of the five-story pink-brick building. With an awareness of likely glacial indoor temperature, I carried my jacket slung over my arm. The sky overhead was cloudless, but Houston still groaned under humidity that added ten degrees to the heat index. Pollyanna, in the guise of the radio weather woman, had gloated that it was, after all, only in the mid-eighties. I'd snapped her off in the middle of her cheery report.

When I stepped inside, the smell of sterile, frigid air rushed to meet me. Approaching the receptionist, I juggled my briefcase while pulling on my jacket. She noted my name and directed me through the doors on her left and up to the second floor, where I knocked at room 212. Dr. James Blanton, Assistant ME, shouted through the door for me to come in. The first image I had upon entering was of a pale, pink circle of baby pigskin crowning his head.

"Just a sec," he mumbled. Without an upward glance, he pointed at the chair in front of his cluttered desk

I sat and removed my notebook filled with earlier scribbling from LeeAnn's police files—not as legible as the neatly-typed pages stolen from my apartment.

Dr. Blanton finished writing and closed a thick manila folder. When he glanced up, I saw a ruddy-faced man, somewhere in his fifties, with thin, sandy hair too sparse to be hanging in feathery strings to the collar of his lab coat. He dropped his pencil on top of the folder.

"This death you want to discuss is old."

I attempted to reply, but he beat me to it.

"I have it here, the autopsy report, and there's nothing to add." He rustled among stacks on his desktop and pulled a flat manila folder from underneath a tower of files. "Everything's pretty straightforward. March 10, 10:52 p.m., LeeAnn Callahan, white female, aged 24, died of blunt trauma to the brain, with multiple contusions and internal bleeding. Her fall was voluntary. The police questioned her relatives, I believe, and it was ruled suicide. Why are you taking another look?"

"Her brother wants the case reopened. He asked me to investigate." In response to Blanton's disgusted expression, I added, "LeeAnn had been pregnant before she died. Is there a possibility uterine tissue samples were taken, perhaps still stored somewhere in the building?"

"There's no mention of pregnancy in the file, young lady. Here." He passed the file across his desk. "See for yourself."

I scanned the autopsy photos and findings I'd already seen in Hightower's office. But toward the end of the report, I spotted a page with scattered, handwritten notes I hadn't seen before. The writing was small and dribbled across the page like the tracks of a dying cockroach. Blanton would never sit still while I struggled to decipher them. "I find it hard to believe no pregnancy test took place."

Blanton stared at me as if I'd thrust him into a migraine. "Without the presence of indicative tissue, there would be no sign. Especially if her presumed pregnancy had been aborted several months before her death. We aren't clairvoyant. Do you know how many autopsies we perform in a month?"

I declined to rise to the bait. He looked more overworked than guilty of conspiracy.

"Could I speak with the pathologist who conducted the exam?"

Blanton shook his head. "Why do you think I'm the one whose morning was interrupted? The mortician you speak of, Dr. Beth Doyle, happens to be out of town. Her mother's ill or something." Blanton rose. "I'll have the file photocopied for you and waiting at the receptionist's desk, if that's all."

But it wasn't. There are times in life when serendipity comes calling, and this was one. The file in my lap wasn't closed but open. When I looked down, the photo of LeeAnn's body on the sidewalk stared back at me. The realization struck me. She was lying on her back. Would someone who deliberately dove, head first with arms stretched to the sky, have landed on her back with her head facing away from the balcony?

"One more thing, please," I said and held up the photo. "Does this look like someone who leapt face forward off the balcony or fell backwards while seated on the railing?"

Blanton placed his hands on the desktop and leaned toward me without a glance at the photo. "That's for the police to say. We attend to the body."

"But surely you have an opinion?"

"No. I don't."

So much for my face-to-face showdown. I still had Codger's evidence. I stood, shook his hand, and thanked him. In danger of feeling pity when he wearily ran his hand over his bald pate, I reminded myself he was a public servant and that my taxes paid his salary. Nevertheless, it was only nine-thirty in the morning and he already looked tired.

❧

Café Artiste seemed as good a spot as any to go over the handwritten scribbles on the autopsy report. Besides, if Robby stuck to old habits, I might be lucky enough to find him there, not that I felt particularly lucky that day.

Thunderclouds rolled across the horizon as I parked the car. Another storm? Perhaps it was my anxiety-laden presence invading my brother's stomping ground that caused this misalignment in the universe. The gods telling me to keep away. Leave Robby alone. Quit hovering, as Santa had accused me. That'd work great if Robby weren't psychotic. Maybe Santa should attend one of Robby's group therapy sessions. Get acquainted with the real world of crazies.

Thunder growled in the distance as I entered the café and sought a seat away from the entrance. A few student types were scattered around the room, but of course, my brother wasn't among them. Calvin looked up from behind the counter, nodded, and in less than a minute, placed a cup of coffee in front of me. "You always bring a storm with you?"

I started to frown until I noticed his eyes sparkling with humor. A second later, he leaned over, looking concerned, "Found Robby yet?"

I shook my head, and when Calvin started to say something else, I grew anxious to change the subject. "Any blueberry muffins this morning?"

"Sure thing." Calvin hurried off, and I opened the autopsy file, flipping immediately to the back page. The ink was dark, the letters drunken and small. Typical doctor's handwriting. Vanity kept me from using them often, but I dug in my briefcase for reading glasses.

A hot muffin fragrant with cinnamon and blueberries appeared on the table beside my notes. With good graces, Calvin was gone before I could mumble thanks.

After a sip of coffee, I placed a call to information. Something nagged at me and there was no time like the present to check one more thing off my to-do-list.

Once connected to the County Clerk in Beaumont, I requested copies of LeeAnn Callahan's Last Will and Testament as well as that of her parents. The woman on the phone took down my credit card number and promised I'd have my copies within 48 hours. If that were true, I was prepared to be impressed.

Studying Dr. Doyle's handwritten notes, her *p*'s and *g*'s looked similar, but her *h*'s had solid sticks for tails and weren't looped like the *p*'s and *g*'s. I began copying the letters I could identify, starting with words scrawled in the upper left corner of the page.

The scribbling ended with a question mark and began with an *h*. In the middle, sandwiched between six or seven different letters, there was another *h*. All the letters in-between were gobbledygook It looked like *h* _ _ _ _ _*a* _ _ _ ? Taking a giant bite of muffin, I almost swooned. The combo of cinnamon and hot blueberries was practically orgasmic.

Eating every bit, I studied the last letter until it grew fuzzy. It could be a *c* or an *e*. Then again, the second letter looked more like an *e*. So that would leave a *c*, which translated to *h e* _ _ _ _*a* _ _ *c*. A medical dictionary would come in handy about now. Puzzling over the other letters got me nowhere, so I moved on to the other side of the paper.

Quickly recognizing four of the six letters, I filled in the rest to spell "anemia." So LeeAnn was anemic. Doyle's scrawl of the words *type AB*, was self-explanatory. From the letters *AB*, Dr. Doyle had drawn a line that ended in an arrow pointing toward two words at the bottom. Because they ended in an exclamation point, I grew more determined to decipher them. Jotting down guesses for a few of the letters, I stared, uncomprehending, for at least ten minutes. The first letter of the first word resembled a *p*. It was followed by four or five indecipherable letters.

The second word began with what looked like an *h* followed by another *h*, then two or three vowels perhaps, before ending in another *h*. That made no sense.

Aunt Eunice had been a fanatic player of crosswords and Scrabble. She delighted in beating me at Scrabble, but we were a good match. This exercise was enough like Scrabble to almost be fun, if it weren't so critical to my investigation. There wasn't the luxury of waiting for Dr. Doyle to reappear in Houston, so for now, fill-in-the-blank was my only option.

Playing with various configurations of consonants with long tails, I came up with *p _ _ _ ff _ _* And second word, *b l _ _ h*

The door of the café swung open, the smell of rain hitchhiking inside the café on the backs of strong winds. As I looked up, my mind was still puzzling over possible medical terminology.

We stared at each other for perhaps a second before Robby bolted. I heard him scream at someone, "Start the car!"

31

We never made it and will never make it. I hate ponytail. We had a fight and I cold-cocked him and drove and drove with him out like a light. He said I was an idiot and he should take me back to Ben Taub and lock me up again. My sister wouldn't like that I said and I said it again. I screamed it at him.

He screamed back and even spit in my face the little cock-sucker. Said it was my sister who'd put me there in the first place and I was too stupid and too doped up to get it through my thick skull. So I decked him. He stayed out and snoring a long time and I don't like driving in the dark with a nasty man snoring beside me. But people sleep on the sidewalks in Houston and they will tell Jelly where I am and she'll put me back in the hospital. I shouldn't have driven back here. Not here. Should have stayed in Beaumont where nobody knows me. I would have stayed in Galveston on the beach except he wouldn't take me there. Said his friend was meeting us in Beaumont. I didn't care. I wanted the beach. Except ponytail had a friend who knew me but I didn't like him either. Nobody really knows me. But they have spies everywhere and it's not safe to go inside anywhere cause they'll take me back. My sister will take me back. She hates me.

Ponytail made me go inside the café and get him a cup of coffee when he woke up and found me sleeping too. But I parked a block away so no one would see me. I was so very very very tired of driving. I didn't want to go inside but ponytail made me.

Bastard ponytail!! It was all a trick so my sis would see me and come after me to put me back in the hospital. She even looked scary when she saw me and I'm not scary and don't need to go back. Never go back. It's dangerous. Don't ever ever ever ever go back.

32

I grabbed up my things and hurried toward the front door. Maneuvering around the tables, I accidentally bumped a young man's chair. His coffee went flying. The girl with him jumped up, screaming as if she'd been knifed.

"I'm so sorry," I said, but was stopped from going any further by strong fingers squeezing my forearm. "Go get a rag. This is your fault."

"Calvin," I shouted as I jerked my arm free. "We need a towel over here."

My captor grabbed me again and held tight. Metal studs traveled up his left ear like sown seeds and one nostril sported what was supposed to pass for a diamond solitaire. His hair was dark and stringy, pulled tight in a scrawny ponytail. One glance at his girlfriend showed they were a matched pair.

Every eye in the room was on us and my heart sank. By now, Robby was long gone.

"If you'll let go of me, I'll get a towel. I apologize again. That's the best I can do."

With eyes telling me to leave, Calvin brought over a towel.

There was no sign of a speeding car when I stepped outside the café, my heart heavy with a new realization. Robby had run away after he'd seen me, and no one had pushed him. He was nobody's prisoner.

From years of practice, I shook off fears for Robby. If he wasn't someone's prisoner, he was willingly avoiding me and I felt mad enough to do the same. He was alive. I had a case to solve.

It was almost time for Juliet Ralston's afternoon smoking break, so I headed to the Alliance Insurance building off Westheimer, mentally reviewing questions as I drove. Perhaps Juliet had known LeeAnn's friend, Sandra Connor. The friend who'd taken the first opportunity to run away to Florida. Kind of like dear old Father.

The smell of cigarette smoke drew me around the corner of the insurance building and into a grassy quadrangle where workers sat on benches or leaned against pin-oaks shading the area. A small group of females huddled on a concrete bench. I asked the closest one if she knew the whereabouts of a Juliet Ralston.

She squinted up at me, lazily blowing smoke my way. "Who wants to know?"

"My name is Giles Faulkner. I've spoken with her about a mutual friend."

"What mutual friend?"

"Never mind," I said, nodding at a group of young men leaning against a tree. "They might be more helpful."

A loud chorus of hooting and hollering followed me toward the tree. One of the ladies yelled, "Watch out, John Henry, hottie's comin' after you."

The three young men wore grins on their faces. Picking the least leering expression, I addressed the tallest of the three. "Is Juliet Ralston out here by any chance? She told me I could meet her on a smoking break, but we've never met."

He nodded at a woman sitting by herself at the far end of the courtyard. Thanking him, I walked in that direction.

As I drew closer, Juliet's gaze at me narrowed. She looked away as if wishing I'd disappear. Even if the clique of rude women annoyed me, getting information out of a loner like Juliet Ralston might prove more difficult.

"You're the one that called me. Right?" Juliet flicked her cigarette on the ground and flattened it with the pad of her shoe before standing. She stuck her hand out and squeezed mine as if draining the last drop of juice from an orange. "Sit?"

I sat opposite and studied Juliet. Actually, we studied each other. She wore her brown hair cropped close to her head and appeared all angles with sharp jaw bones and a prominent brow. Her white button-down shirt was beginning to droop in the heat and the black slacks she wore were too loose to tell just how thin she was. With brown eyes leaning toward hazel, she wasn't unattractive, but then again, she'd never turn heads. A face quickly lost in a crowd.

I didn't want to engage in a staring competition of who blinks first and said, "You and LeeAnn Callahan were friends?"

Juliet held out her hand, palm up. "PI license?"

What difference should that make? I dug mine out. She glanced at it and handed it back. "I guess you're real, all right." She propped her elbows on the concrete table. "On the phone, I wasn't sure. You never know these days, right?"

I nodded.

"Yeah, you could say LeeAnn and I were friends of sorts. Only visited over lunch. Well, almost only."

I pulled out my tablet and pen. "Will you share what you knew about her? Her life, her friends, a boyfriend, perhaps, and what might have caused her to kill herself?"

Juliet snorted and pulled sunglasses from her white shirt pocket. They were oversized, making her resemble a cartoon insect. "I guess I can do that fairly quickly. She kept her life away from work to herself, only talked about her horse, and I was the only one here that ever had lunch with her. I had a horse as a kid is the only reason she had anything to do with me. Mine was a work horse, but LeeAnn came from money, from folks who paid big bucks so their little baby girl could win medals. Know what I mean? Now me? I got to earn my livin'. LeeAnn worked for fun. Liked to use her brain. Hard to imagine, isn't it?"

Nodding at the dark lenses across from me, I wished she would remove them.

"What about a boyfriend? She ever talk about one?"

"Not specifically," Juliet said.

"Did you ever see her with any bruises?"

"You mean like her boyfriend beat her up? Nah. No bruises I ever saw. But she had a boyfriend, alright."

"How do you know?"

My earlier wish that Juliet would remove her sunglasses was intensified by her next statement. "I'll get to that in a minute. It all fits together, you see. The fact that little lady never did herself in and I know 'cause," Juliet leaned toward me conspiratorially. "I'm the one she called to pick her up from the abortion clinic. Cried like a baby all the way to her place, know what I mean?"

"Did you ask who the father was?"

"Sure as hell did. Offered to take care of the bastard myself, but she wouldn't say a word. Said it would spoil her surprise if word got around. I tol' her I knew how to keep my mouth shut, but she just shook her head. Stubborn. Know what I mean?"

My neck was going to break from all my head nodding, fearful of stopping Juliet's flow. "Why wouldn't her abortion point to suicide if LeeAnn decided she couldn't live with herself?"

"Now don't go hoppin' ahead of me. I know cause once I'd helped her to bed that day, the afternoon of her abortion, I mean, she said the craziest thing."

Twin reflections of my face swam in her dark lenses, four eyes peering up from the bottom of a dark well. A cold breath moved across the back of my neck. "What did she say?"

Juliet grabbed my wrist, her voice husky and secretive. "She said 'if it takes me a hundred years I'll get that bastard. And when I do,' she says to me with the fiercest look I've ever seen on a human, 'I'm gonna fly to Paris to celebrate. It's the only thing I think about. How he'll be in jail and I'll be in Paris.'"

Several minutes later, I sat alone in my car. The air conditioner blew cold in my face while I dashed a few more notes. Once Juliet mentioned LeeAnn's abortion, my note-taking had stopped. Juliet had trudged back inside the building a few minutes after her revelation, but not before admitting she didn't know why LeeAnn had picked her, and not a closer friend, to call after the abortion. Juliet also had never heard LeeAnn speak of her supposed best friend, Sandra Connor.

Her lack of knowledge lowered my opinion of how much Juliet really knew about LeeAnn. It made sense to be leery of adopting Juliet's take on LeeAnn's state of mind. The abortion had been on February 24th, two weeks before LeeAnn dropped off the balcony. Plenty of time to sink into depression, decide life's not worth living. I was more determined than ever to interview LeeAnn's psychiatrist.

Driving away from the insurance building, I decided to try and catch Dr. Winthrop during office hours. Surely he wouldn't balk at referring me to LeeAnn's psychiatrist, whose name I'd noticed on a sign down the street from Winthrop's West Alabama office. The minute Keymap had spoken the name of LeeAnn's shrink, I'd remembered it. Unusual—*Hamblin Zoesky, Ph.D.* His proximity to Winthrop could indicate he knew him well enough to intervene on my behalf.

I paced, waiting for Dr. Winthrop to finish with his last patient for the day, when my cell rang from inside my briefcase. Caller ID flashed *caller unknown.* It could be Robby. I flipped it open, suddenly breathless. But it was Keymap.

"I've found your guy."

Robby! "Where is he and why was he running from me?"

There was quiet on the end of the line for a second too long. "I'm sorry, Giles. I didn't mean your brother."

I let his comment settle for a disappointed second or two. "Is it the man he ran away with?"

"No, not him either, although I have a couple of leads. Who is snagged and in-the-bag is the ME's lab guy. The cop who turned over

LeeAnn's possessions, her clothes, handbag, etc. to Boots, was at the ME's office after Dr. Doyle performed the autopsy. And this cop is a friend of mine. According to him, there's something that could still be at the lab. A little bit of info the detectives were told to drop. Something that makes my friend just a tad angry. He wants his name kept out of it, but the lab guy's willing to talk."

With a quickening pulse, I picked up my pacing. "Would you care to explain what this missing piece is about," I said, annoyed at his evasiveness.

"Don't get your feathers ruffled. He can explain. Here's name and number for you. Ready?"

The number for the lab worker was familiar, but with the addition of an extension I could now dial direct and avoid the ME's receptionist. His name should be simple to remember. Adam Franklin. Like two first names.

Before he could hang up on me, I asked, "How much is this information going to cost me?"

"Hmm, I'll have to think about that."

His tone was flirtatious enough to set my teeth on edge. "I'm serious. Since when do you work for free?" Before he could respond, I barreled ahead. "Why are you doing this, anyway? I didn't ask you to continue with my investigation."

"Relax, Giles. This one's on me."

But my mind was in fifth gear. "Last night. How come you knew Robby's nickname for me?"

Silence before a rough response, "You must have misunderstood. I've always called you Giles."

Disgusted, I flipped the phone shut. Liar. I sat, suddenly wondering why I couldn't just accept that Keymap wanted to help me. Probably because I'd grown too cynical from being a cop, then a PI, and before any of this, the older sister of a precious baby boy who'd never asked for his life to be so fucked-up.

33

Shaking off my self-loathing pity-party, I scribbled the lab guy's name and number. When sounds from the hall indicated Dr. Winthrop was escorting his patient to the front door, I hopped up and hurried into the hallway. Winthrop spotted me, his expression more confusion than delight.

"I know you're busy, but I need your help," I said.

His brow un-furrowed and he smiled briefly before shutting his front door and opening the door to his office. "Come on in. I've always got time for you, Giles."

Seated across from his desk, I explained my need for a referral to LeeAnn Callahan's psychiatrist, Dr. Zoesky. Winthrop made a tepee of his fingers, head bowed in thought.

"This puts me in an awkward position." He looked up at me. "If I call Hamblin, he might feel I'm pressuring him to cooperate with you."

That was the whole point, of course, but I remained silent, allowing him to ruminate awhile.

"You, in a way, are my patient, too," he added. "It's awkward."

"I've mostly consulted with you about Robby," I countered. "This is entirely different."

He nodded, staring into the distance, as if his final response would come from the air.

"How's the search for Robby coming along?"

I refused to change the subject. It was imperative I find out what really happened to send LeeAnn over the balcony. "Dr. Winthrop, the truth behind a young woman's death is at stake." The urgency, the growing frustration, in my voice was proof LeeAnn had hitched a permanent ride in my head, her young vitality now a shadow ghost. As a teen, she had helped handicapped children and now she was gone at the age of twenty-four. In an urn on Boots's mantle. I shuddered involuntarily and saw concern whisper through Winthrop's eyes.

"It is that important to your case?"

Winthrop was smarter than his comment, but I let it go. "Yes. It's that important."

He sighed loudly. "All right I'll do it, but he can always refuse by quoting patient privacy."

I held my breath as he dialed from the phone on top of his desk. "Hamblin? Winthrop here. I'm fine, fine. I have a young woman, Miss Giles Faulkner, in my office, someone I've known for several years who wants to speak with you about a former patient of yours. No, no. She's deceased. LeeAnn Callahan." He glanced at me with raised eyebrows in case he'd misunderstood her name. I nodded encouragement.

Winthrop continued to mumble intermittent yeses before hanging up. "Now," he said rising, "the ball's in your court." He pulled a pencil and a miniature spiral notebook from his shirt pocket, wrote down a number and passed it to me.

After thanking him profusely, he escorted me outside while we shared mutual worries over Robby's disappearance. I told him about my brother's note and his run from me at the café. We both knew his paranoia would only grow worse without his medications. Winthrop shook his head, called out good-luck as I settled behind the wheel. But then, Lady Luck could be extremely undependable.

Thank God I hadn't chosen, in the end, to follow in Winthrop's footsteps. As Robby was my witness, I was better at catching bad guys than straightening out those whose chance for a normal life leaned toward slim-to-none.

Instead of calling ahead, I figured I'd catch Dr. Zoesky before he left for the day. His office was located in a one-story vintage brick building two blocks north of Winthrop's. The front door opened onto a former screened-in porch with original tile floors and large picture windows instead of screens. Closed accordion blinds filtered the daylight.

The receptionist, a black-haired youth sporting a buzz cut and acne scars, was already reaching for his backpack when I entered. The paperback book he'd closed quickly, but not quickly enough, pictured a dark-haired hero tipping back a curvaceous blond damsel for a lusty kiss.

After pressing the urgency of my visit, the young receptionist reluctantly picked up the receiver, turned his back, and spoke with Dr. Zoesky. When he swiveled to face me, his lips didn't approve, but he said I could go inside.

Zoesky's office was huge, with the proverbial couch as well as two overstuffed chairs, a square mahogany coffee table between them. Kleenex boxes, captured in silver holders, sat atop every horizontal surface. The doctor had spared no expense with his furnishings. Oversized and overly carved. With velvet coverings for upholstery, the color scheme was soft rose and green, with pale green silk moiré covering the walls. Enough framed degrees for twenty people partially obscured the wall behind his desk.

Reminding me of the Assistant ME, he was writing when I entered and looked up briefly to point me toward one of the fat chairs opposite his desk before he resumed writing. I sank into a down-filled cushion.

After eight minutes, according to the grandfather clock behind his desk, he looked up and closed the file he'd been working on.

"How may I help you, Ms. Giles?" His accent was not American. Eastern European, perhaps. Dr. Zoesky looked in his early forties but was completely bald. His face was pale and round, with a small pouch of fat under his chin. His fingers splayed against the desktop were squat and stubby, startling as albino cigars. Meeting in the middle of his forehead, a slash of black eyebrows matched his black metal-framed eyeglasses. The bowtie under his white shirt collar was red and gold paisley. A navy blazer hung neatly on a mahogany butler's valet in the corner. Definitely GQ.

"I believe Dr. Winthrop mentioned my investigation into the death of LeeAnn Callahan at the request of her brother, Samuel Callahan."

"Miss LeeAnn Callahan," he said. "I perhaps remember, but must look for more of the complete memory to return." He rose and walked toward a gleaming file cabinet, pulled out a drawer and began flipping through files. "Yes I have it here."

When he turned, I noticed the incongruence of his long torso coupled with short legs. Sitting across from me he'd looked over six feet. The reality was more like five-eight.

He settled himself back at his desk, still studying LeeAnn's files, while my head throbbed from nervous tension. The ticking of the clock accompanied the pounding of blood in my temples.

"I'd really appreciate—"

"I will finish this in one little minute. Please wait on me."

Old grandfather clock said it was more like five minutes before he spoke again, removing his glasses and thumb-rubbing closed eyes before giving me a myopic stare, his round gray eyes almost without pupils.

He appeared reluctant, but finally spoke, "I remember her. I remember her death, and I also remember her talking of her brother. But, I believe her name for him was *Boots*." The way Zoesky pronounced it, Boots rhymed with *putz*.

"Yes. I thought if I called him Boots, you might not recognize his name." I was growing optimistic the doctor would share with me. I gave a small laugh, but his expression remained almost pained.

"One remembers the beautiful, does not one?"

My only response was a smile as I barreled forward.

"I'm anxious to verify rumors, if I can call them that, about her mental state."

His stare was unblinking as well as unnerving.

I ignored it while my former optimism receded. "The police say she was suicidal, depressed and that she killed herself. Her brother doesn't believe them and asked me to investigate."

Zoesky donned his glasses and looked away. "This file is privileged. My meetings with Miss Callahan are all privileged. Client and doctor, you see. How would you presume I am to talk with you?"

I shrank in the chair, deflated, before rallying. This was my one chance and I wouldn't leave without some answers.

"I thought Dr. Winthrop had explained that in order for me to discover the reason for this poor young girl's death, I must know the truth about her mental state." When he didn't respond, I pushed. "Dr. Zoesky, the young woman is dead, her parents are dead and her brother would definitely want you to share with me. It is not against the law for you to tell me. You don't have to talk to me, I know." And then, "Would it help if Boots signed a statement in support of your sharing information about his sister with me?"

"He is the one who ask you, no?"

"Yes. Boots Callahan hired me to find out the truth. He's devastated about LeeAnn's death, Dr. Zoesky. Won't you please help?"

"I do not like the recorder. You will not use one, agreed?"

My response, "Of course not," was whispered, the remnants of holding my breath. "I would like to take notes, if you don't mind."

With pale fingers he waved approval and again looked down at LeeAnn's file. "She was a young woman with many problems. None of them insurmountable, but not insignificant, either."

He spoke slowly, too slowly. I chewed on the inside of my cheeks to keep from rushing him along.

"Even though she was younger, her parents place her in responsible position for her brother. For awhile, she stay in Beaumont and try to curb the brother's tendencies, but then she move to Houston to put, how shall I say, distance between them. Her own life, I believe, grew more important than simply taking care for her brother. But the guilt. ”

“Was LeeAnn financially responsible for Boots?”

“Perhaps. More important was the emotional burden.”

I squirmed in my chair, felt heat rise to my cheeks. Too close for comfort. “So she would talk to you about feeling guilty over her brother?”

“Of course. Guilt is very powerful.”

Powerful enough to kill her? “Doctor. Did LeeAnn ever complain about physical pain? I was told she suffered constantly from back pain after a fall from her horse.”

Zoesky raised his brow as he again searched his notes. “No. I write nothing to that effect.”

“How about gambling or severe depression? Not guilt, I mean, but real depression?”

He sighed as if severely offended. “I know the difference, Miss Faulkner. On occasion she did grow anxious. I give her Zoloft. Not terribly strong medicine and it seem to help her. Miss Callahan did admit once to an involvement with a married man, but she laugh it off as doom to failure. I believe those were her very words.”

Again, his head was buried, searching his notes while I listened to the clock tick. I was growing irritated as well as frustrated. I’d learned nothing new.

“Was her anxiety ever serious enough for you to fear she would attempt suicide?”

“On the contrary. She enjoy her profession, her friends, and seem to have an active social life. She never ask me for medication and I only give Zoloft to help her in this transition away from her brother. After all, Miss Faulkner, Miss Callahan’s only real problem, other than her involvement with a married man, is difficulty with her brother.”

“This Boots is older, but in years only. His immaturity lead him to drinking and gambling. He sign her name, use her initials, on credit cards he secure, again, in her name. He is constant irritant in her life.”

Now this was new information. "Excuse me, doctor. Was Boots only an irritant to LeeAnn?" I asked, borrowing his term. "No filial affection or love between them?"

I should have kept my mouth shut. His response was long-winded and Freudian. I'd heard enough of that in college. Zoesky was not giving straight answers. At his next pause, I interrupted.

"Do you agree LeeAnn loved her brother? Otherwise, she would have turned him over to the police."

Zoesky nodded, "Of course, but I lean more to the obligation side of their relationship. In her eyes, she is only doing what her parents want in trying to keep her brother from harm's way. She feel, rightly or wrongly, responsible for him. She rescue him rather than allow him to fulfill the consequence of his actions."

I squirmed again, glad he wasn't my shrink. "Monetarily, you mean?"

He nodded. "I would say that, also. But this support cost her emotionally, too. She move to Houston to separate from her brother."

I wished he wouldn't keep using the present tense, as if LeeAnn and her problems were still alive. "You said she had many difficulties, doctor. Did she ever discuss attempting suicide when she was a teenager?"

"Hmmm. I will look to see." He flipped pages as I worried about the man's memory. Hadn't he already taken his time reading through the file?

He stopped and pointed at a page with his pen as if I could see for myself. "Here I have written that she tell me when she was sixteen she ran from home. But only briefly. Miss Callahan hitch a ride, I believe that is the correct terminology, to New Orleans. But she call home that very night so to not worry her parents and they send one of the help to retrieve her. She was back at home before the dawn. Not exactly suicide, but nevertheless, a call for help, would you not agree?"

"And that's all? She ran away once?" When he nodded, I said, "What about another psychiatrist? Anyone she would have seen in Beaumont?"

"Her parents send her to doctor there, but he is only family doctor. Not qualified to help with the young woman's mind, you see?"

"Do you have his name?"

"He is now dead. He was very old when the young woman visit him."

"So you didn't send for his records when LeeAnn first came to see you, which was?"

"She was twenty-one when first she came and the old doctor was already dead. His very foolish daughter throw out all the doctor's records when she close his office. Burn them, she said. Of course, you understand this is the woman rebelling against the father who is always busy with the patients and not the family, you see? I believe she got in great trouble over that."

"Is there nothing you can tell me about LeeAnn other than problems with her brother? Work issues?" When he shook his head, I added, "Did you know she was pregnant by her married boyfriend?"

Zoesky's wooly eyebrow rose to what would have been his hairline. "You know this for fact?"

"Yes." So far, I had only Juliet's word.

As he clicked his tongue in disapproval, a look of disappointment flashed across his face. "I say it is strange for a lady to come to me, pay for my expert advice, and then not tell me all of the truth."

He looked at me as if expecting an answer, but I had none.

"Perhaps," he said slowly, "this happen during her sabbatical."

"Sabbatical?"

"Yes. The young woman announce," Zoesky looked down and flipped toward the end of his notes, "in last week of December that she is taking a leave from coming to me. She seem almost happy. At least confident she can do without our weekly meeting."

"Did she explain herself, give you a reason?"

"She say to me that at last she get lucky and the new year is to be her best."

Some lucky new year. Falling a hundred feet, battering your head and breaking your neck.

34

So where did that leave me? With two male witnesses who swore LeeAnn had jumped, rather "dove," because she was in debt and feeling suicidal over a break-up with her boyfriend; Juliet claiming LeeAnn had had an abortion and wanted the boyfriend in jail; and Dr. Zoesky's confirmation of Sandra Connor's insinuation that Boots may not be the easy-going, loving brother he portrayed himself to be. Plus, Zoesky's belief that Boots had been LeeAnn's main problem, not back pain, gambling, or seeing a married man.

I needed a face-to-face with Boots, but decided first to head to the Methodist Hospital. If I was lucky, Huber's wife would have gone home for her evening meal, leaving the rodeo elevator guard and his kidney stones alone.

Fuming over the medical center's traffic jam and maddening multi-level parking garages with their infinite color-coded floors and alphabetized sections, I finally found a parking spot. It was in the blue section of the top floor, the uncovered floor that left cars baking in the sweltering heat, car door handles ready to inflict first degree burns when owners returned.

On the bright side, Methodist's frigid air-conditioning washed over me when I entered, and for once, I didn't reach for my jacket. It only took a minute to learn Huber was on the third floor, but another ten minutes to maneuver the halls, heading toward the yellow elevator signs and not the blue, green, purple or red ones.

Standing at Huber's half-open doorway, the smell of micro-waved dinners drifted toward me, evaporating my earlier hunger, my stomach now in revolt. I opened the door anyway.

Whatever was dripping in his left arm must be controlling any pain Huber was feeling. He lay mesmerized by a football game playing in silence on the wall mounted television, neatly tucked from armpit to underneath his feet by a pale blue blanket. His wrapped body lay like an ancient mummy's except for the large mound in the middle—his very modern-day stomach. From the looks of his bedside table, he'd consumed roast beef, mashed potatoes and gravy. A handful of green peas lay nestled on a smear of white starch layered with brown grease and bits of stringy beef.

Feeling invisible as I approached his bed, a slight snoring sounded from the other side of a blue cotton curtain, closed for the sake of privacy. According to the two charts hanging outside the door, Huber shared his room with a Mr. Appleton.

When the patient turned toward me with a quizzical look, I noticed his skin looked pasty gray, the color of mushrooms. He had mouse-colored thinning hair worn in a comb-over and pale plastic aviator glasses, a noticeable bifocal edging slashed the lenses. The glasses were dirty enough to obscure vision and I struggled against the urge to jerk them off his face and clean them.

"Mr. Huber?" I thought I'd double-check in case the snorer was the man I was after. When he nodded, I continued, "My name is Giles Faulkner and Captain Hightower from HPD suggested I visit with you about the death last March of LeeAnn Callahan."

His gray eyes remained blanks of pale, watery confusion.

"She fell from the eighth level balcony after Rodeo," I said. "Do you remember?"

He reached down, punched the off-button on the television remote and the screen went blank

"Who are you?" His eyes grew focused and wary.

I smiled broadly, wishing I'd brought flowers or candy. "At the request of her brother, I'm investigating LeeAnn's death and I was hoping you would share with me what you know."

"What I know?" His voice sounded hoarse as if he were not used to talking. He turned toward the bedside table and I quickly lifted a glass of water and held the straw to his lips while he drank. Finished, he sank back against his pillow. "I don't know nothing."

"But you were there, weren't you?"

"I told all I knows to the police."

I'd had a long day and didn't have the patience to try and charm Huber. "A young woman is dead and you're a witness to what happened that night. It's your civic, if not your professional duty to tell me what you know."

"I already did. You're not the police." His expression grew sullen as he picked at his blanket.

I switched tactics. "Mr. Huber. It's my understanding that you were absent from your post when LeeAnn fell to her death."

"So what? I get bathroom privileges."

"Of course you do. I'm just thinking you might have seen something you forgot to mention. That happens. We're all human. We can't be expected to remember everything at the scene of a horrible death like that poor girl endured. It's only natural."

"Damned tootin' it is."

I waited, asked if he needed more water or perhaps a Coke from the machine down the hall. When he agreed to a Coke, I dared hope he might cooperate after all.

When I returned, I poured the Coke into an empty Styrofoam cup stolen from the man sleeping behind the curtain and inserted a clean straw. "Want me to raise the head of your bed?"

He nodded and once I settled his pillow behind his back, he proceeded to drink the entire contents, slurping when he reached the bottom.

He sighed as he handed me the empty cup. "My wife says Cokes cause kidney stones. Stupidest woman on earth."

"I'm pretty sure it's hereditary. Not much you can do about it."
I hoped he'd consider my statement a truce of sorts. He started to
smile, but stopped himself.

Pulling an empty chair close to the head of his bed, I sat and
leaned toward him. A sour odor accosted me and I repressed the instinct to back away. "Mr. Huber. I'm in kind of a bind. I need to find
someone who'll tell me the truth, and I'm depending on you."

"Why'd anybody lie about it? That girl jumped over the side and
kilt herself. Nothin' more to say."

"That could certainly be what happened," I said. "It's just that if
there was anyone else up on the eighth level, you might have seen
them and they might be able to verify what happened. It would make
her brother rest easy, if you know what I mean."

"Yeah, I can see that. But when I got back from the john, there
was only the two fellas, Mr. Ewer and Mr. McGraw. They was mighty
upset. And I wasn't gone long, mind you. Damn kidney stones mean I
gotta drink liters of water while I'm standin' there by the elevator. Was
drinkin' like crazy. Lots of trips to the little boy's room, if you get my
drift. Had to pee in a damned strainer. Caught one, too, but it took two
more weeks to catch another. Now I got new ones that nothin'll help.
They gonna have to zap 'em tomorrow. What the hell? Been trying two
days to pass the buggers and it aint happenin'. Shoulda zapped 'em
today. Then you'd missed our little chat." His smile, showing crooked
teeth badly in need of brushing, held a trace of guile.

"So when you returned from the men's room, Mr. Ewer and Mr.
McGraw were where? On the balcony or in the corridor?"

"In the corridor. They tol' me what happened, said they'd called
security and it weren't long before a cop showed up."

"And before this, how much time had passed since the last person
had gone down your elevator and you left to go the bathroom?"

"Pretty long. I'd say twenty minutes. I took one old lady down
then nobody else came along. Figured by then all but the lady who
fell and Mr. Ewer out on the balcony had left the party suite. I guess

the other one, Mr. McGraw, came back while I was in the john, cause I'd taken him down earlier.

Huber's memory was better than average. "Mr. Huber, have you remembered all you can about that night? Anyone else who might have been in the corridor or on the balcony? Could any shadows on the balcony have hidden someone from view?"

"Naw. I went out there and looked. I stood beside the cop—can't remember his name—and saw that poor girl's body layin' there, skirt spread all around and her head all smushed. 'Twas an awful sight to see. Fact is, the old lady I took down the elevator earlier was standin' there, couldn't stop herself from screaming like a banshee. Didn't blame her a bit."

"So you saw nothing else?"

Without responding, Huber stared down at the blanket and again began picking at fluffs of blue fabric. The sound of snoring from the bed next to Huber's grew louder.

"Mr. Huber?"

He sighed loudly. "I guess there was somethin' I forgot."

My stomach tightened and I grabbed Huber's wrist. "What?"

He turned to me, startled at my gesture. I watched, fascinated, while his sweaty gray cheeks exploded with pink stripes like raw bacon.

"Sorry," I mumbled, withdrawing my grip. "What was it you forgot?"

His face screwed into a defensive glare. "Not like I really forgot. It was so gul-darned fast, I wasn't sure for months that I really saw him."

"Saw whom?"

"A man, tall man. Hurrying away down the corridor when I come back from the john."

"Did you recognize him?"

"Nope. But he turned real quick like and glanced back over his shoulder. He wore a cowboy hat. Brown or black. Prob'ly black. He had on jeans. Nice build. The kind ladies go ape over. The color of his shirt coulda been white. Or maybe beige." He flashed me a warn-ing look. "It'd do no good to tell the police this late in the game."

I nodded as of in total agreement.

"It was his eyes that finally made me believe I didn't dream it up," Huber said.

"What about his eyes?"

They was light colored. Lighter than most and kind of strange. From the distance, I couldn't tell if they was blue or green. Just un-usual. That make any sense?"

I kept a poker face as I dug in my bag for a business card, my mind in a whirl. Huber had described Boots to a tee. But what had Boots been doing there? And why hadn't McGraw or Ewer mentioned him?

Almost everyone coming to Houston Rodeo wore cowboy boots, but I had to ask. "Was he wearing boots?"

Huber nodded, "Black. I'm sure cause I'd uh noticed if they'd been a different color."

Again, black boots weren't unusual.

I passed Huber my card. "Here's my number. Will you please call me if you think of anything else? It could be very important."

He took my card reluctantly. "Well "

"Well what?"

"I'm purty sure I heard the elevator ding about the time that man was disappearin' round the hall."

A blip sounded on my radar screen. "What exactly are you saying, Mr. Huber?"

"I dunno It's jess that the elevator don't ding unless somebody sends it back up. I ask all the lease owners of the suites, you know, to do that. Get in the habit uh sendin' it back up when I punch 'em down."

"You mean you don't escort people down and then bring the el-evator back up with you?"

"Sure. Most uh the time. Not always. Certainly not when I didn't take 'em down in the first place. I'd been to the john, remember?"

I did remember. "Who has elevator keys?"

"All the rodeo head honchos and the cops workin' shifts. And guards like me."

Huber had confirmed what I already knew. I said thanks and good luck on his "zapping" procedure in the morning. He looked apprehensive as he nodded good-bye.

Talking to Boots was more imperative than ever. If he'd been on Reliant's eighth level the night his sister died, I needed to know the reason—and why he'd never told me.

35

Over the phone, Adam Franklin, the ME's lab assistant, had sounded like any young Texan, albeit one with a passion for Thai food. Heading west of downtown to Houston's version of Chinatown, I occasionally checked the rear-view mirror for a tail I hoped wouldn't be there. So far, so good. During the drive, remnants of an earlier white-hot sun turned a globular dusky-gold as it sank lower on the horizon. It would be dark soon.

Street signs were written in Asian script, sometimes duplicated in English, sometimes not. The far west end of Bellaire Blvd. was where the hardworking immigrants lived, whether Chinese, Vietnamese, Thai, or Indonesian. Warehouses, restaurants, and small store fronts nestled among gas stations and all-night 7-Elevens. This was what I cherished about Houston—its pockets of multi-ethnicity that reminded me this city was more than cowboys, trucks, and motorcycles.

I passed narrow residential streets turning off of Bellaire that were lined with modest houses, each fronted by a neatly-trimmed St. Augustine lawn and bordered by narrow strips of concrete driveway. A majority of these houses were paid for through the efforts of the entire family, children working for the family business from a young age.

Thinking of families reminded me of Zoesky's words about LeeAnn's caretaking her brother. Thoughts of families sat on the edge of my mind like a hungry buzzard, eager to have a go at me. I refused to dwell on my envy of relatives working together since, in both LeeAnn's and my case, we appeared to be the ones expending all the effort.

The six thousand block of Bellaire Blvd. whizzed by and I began rubbernecking for the restaurant Adam had chosen. Up ahead on my right, garish neon bulbs blinked *Thai Me To The Moon* I pulled in front and parked. Another glance in my mirror before I cut the engine convinced me no one had followed.

Inside, dim lighting and red paper lanterns likened this restaurant to every other Asian eating establishment in Houston, except for my greeting by a middle-aged Thai woman standing across from the entrance.

After spotting me, she bowed, displaying the top of her head— a thick black braid encircled and puffed like a cinnamon bun. Her posture of palms together summoned long-forgotten memories of me playing queen to Robby's servant, my skinny twelve-year-old self drowning in Mother's white satin wedding dress.

The Thai lady straightened from her bow and motioned for me to follow as if we'd already been introduced. Adam must have beaten me here.

She halted at the last booth against the far wall. When a young man turned and smiled up at me, I was sure my face showed surprise. Adam was young. Very young. With all the accoutrements of an American youth commonly found walking the hallways of Houston's high schools, the only giveaway to his heritage was his brown skin and dark, slanted eyes. That and his *wai* to the dark-haired woman whereby he raised his pressed hands up to his face, a sign of homage and respect.

With spiked, rigid hair dyed a bright yellow, it looked as if someone had sprinkled his scalp with seeds and he'd sprouted yellow grain in stiffened shoots reaching for the sun. Wearing a shirt dotted with red and pink palm trees, he was like an old black and white movie reincarnated in jarring Technicolor. By comparison, with my all-black outfit and black hair, I felt stodgy and drab.

Adam's earlobes sported round disks I knew from pop culture were in the process of making rather large peepholes historically favored by African tribesmen. I briefly wondered if this young person with wrists the size of baby birds, was really an ME lab technician.

I stood looking down at him, my escort having walked back toward the front. "Adam Franklin?"

"I know," he grinned. "I'm not as young as I look and, much to my parents disapproval, I had my name changed when I turned twenty-one. Thai names are too hard to pronounce. Besides, I was born here. Might as well sound American if you can't quite look it."

But he did look it. Every bit. I wondered silently just how long ago his twenty-first birthday had been.

Within seconds of my taking a seat across from Adam, a plate with four steaming egg rolls was placed on the table between us.

"I ordered these in case you're used to egg rolls," Adam said, slightly condescending, I thought, as he helped himself to exactly half.

I dug in, realizing as I wolfed down my two, that I was starving. When he recommended the *moo yang* and green beans with red curry paste, I nodded and chewed at the same time.

"I also want you to try the house specialty, squid in coconut sauce."

Squid? I wasn't so sure about that one.

Adam raised three fingers in the air. A young woman standing up front caught his signal, then disappeared behind a door leading, I presumed, to the kitchen. Everyone here must be a mind reader.

The restaurant began to fill with other customers, almost all Asian, and the hum of conversation, along with the smell of hot spices, filled the room. Their native tongue predominated as soon as they stepped inside, as if by crossing the threshold, they'd crossed a continent.

I grew thirsty, and with the assurance of a greater power sent to grant my every wish, a young waitress appeared and poured hot tea. I lifted my cup, and the smell of jasmine rose to my nostrils.

Adam delayed eating his last egg roll and began talking about his grandparents emigrating from Bangkok. His grandparents and parents, he said, worked hard at tailoring to send him and his twin sister to school. And now, since he was a third-year student at Baylor College of Medicine and wanted to help financially, he'd taken a part-time job at the ME's lab.

When I started to ask a question, he interrupted with a raised finger, the waitress reappearing with three steaming platters piled with barbeque pork, green beans covered in red paste, and squiggly creatures drowning in a pale sauce I took to be the squid. Her arched eyebrows at Adam were met with a shake of his head and she left us with two smaller plates to help ourselves.

The potpourri of spices and hot barbeque almost made me swoon. Adam heaped my plate and then his own and began using his chopsticks with aplomb. I opted for a fork and tried not to feel out-done. Appreciative silence followed while we both ate. Adam wasn't shy about portions, so I followed his example with abandon, trying to remember the last time I'd eaten anything other than fast food from a sack, hors d'oeuvres with Keymap notwithstanding.

After ten minutes and one attempt at the squid, which brought an immediate reaction from my surprised stomach, I pushed aside my plate and accepted another cup of tea. Adam continued feasting before he, too, pushed his plate away. Within seconds our table was cleared and another teapot appeared. If I'd been alone, would the service have been this efficient?

Cracking open my fortune cookie, I forged ahead. "My friend, Keymap, said you assisted the pathologist at LeeAnn Callahan's autopsy last March and that there was an irregularity you wouldn't mind discussing with me?"

"There was no irregularity in the pathology," Adam declared, emphasizing the last word.

Emphatic, I thought, for such a youthful-looking man who dressed antiestablishment to the extreme. His tone of unquestioned authority was unexpected and I sipped tea before speaking again. "All right. What was irregular?"

"The reaction of the police department was highly irregular. I spoke with a detective, who, of course, will deny his response if questioned. HPD wanted nothing to do with the tissue samples taken. They were in the middle of a high-profile audit of their DNA section. They're all paranoid."

I sat up straight, the combination of spices in my stomach rumbling so loudly I worried Adam would hear. I'd read about HPD lab informants being fired for no apparent reason. It seems there was cause for their paranoia. Before the question sprang from my lips, I glanced down at my fortune.

<u>Beware of gifts from strangers</u>

I crumbled the paper into a tight ball between my fingers. I didn't know what I'd expected, but not that tired cliché.

"What samples?" I prompted, dropping the fortune inside my briefcase and withdrawing my notebook and pen. We were finally getting down to business.

Adam leaned toward me, his tone dropping a notch. "Dr. Doyle jotted her findings on paper and expected me to repeat into the handheld recorder whatever she spoke aloud. Other doctors I've worked with dictate themselves while I follow orders and help with the cadaver.

"I've only done a few, so when she mentioned the woman's, I mean the body's paleness, I was startled. All bodies look pale to me. A quick run of the blood proved anemia. Dr. Doyle then examined the uterus. She said the endometrial tissue looked hemorrhagic, which would explain the anemia, so she scraped a sample for me to make up a paraffin block."

At my look of confusion, he explained the block of paraffin, made from a mold and hot wax, held samples almost indefinitely. "I secure it, label it and shelve it. After we finished the autopsy, she told me to let HPD know we have the sample. This autopsy's about two or two and a half weeks after her death. We get backed up as I'm sure you already know. I got the detective on the phone and he tells me the case is closed, they want no more samples. They're swamped, they're behind and dealing with an outside audit of the DNA lab. I tell him it looks like the body was pregnant within the last couple of weeks and he acts frustrated but says there's nothing he can do. Then a couple days ago, Keymap starts nosing around. Finds out I'm perfectly willing to talk to you." He settled back in the booth and reached for his tea cup.

"I can find out from Captain Hightower the name of the detective who investigated, so why not just tell me and save me the phone call? It should have been in the report, anyway."

"I gather from your lack of knowledge that the report was missing a lot of things."

My lack of knowledge? Great comment. "So how come the ME's report arrived at Hightower's office incomplete?"

Adam shrugged. "Ask the cops."

Sweat popped on my brow. As my heartbeat grew rapid, the burning in my stomach increased. I prayed fervently I wasn't getting ill. Taking small sips of hot tea, I realized Adam would not reveal the detective's name but had cracked the doctor's handwritten notes for me. "Paraffin block" and "hemorrhagic." My mind raced with possibilities of now finding the father. My bet was on Brad Ewer. I excused myself and rose to find the ladies room. Too much jasmine tea. A sudden wave of nausea hit and I chastised myself over practically inhaling that spicy food. Or was it the squid?

The building housing the restaurant looked as if it were built in the seventies. A restroom sign led me out a side door and down a long concrete hallway, dimly lit, and inhabited by garbage cans overflowing with bags of refuse. My heels echoed with a hollow ring, and as I walked, the sound of another patron joining me sounded from behind. Heavy steps, but the two signs jutting out from the wall up ahead showed both a men's room and a women's.

When the steps picked up speed, I heard someone call out, "Miss. Wait up. I have something for you."

I turned. The man was almost beside me when a driver's license photo flashed across my mind. The one who'd posed as Robby's cousin whipped his arm around my neck and pressed hard against my throat. The smell of garbage mixed with a sweet, chemical odor from the rag clamped tightly over my nose and I dropped into blackness.

36

I lay huddled against wooden slats, bouncing in a vehicle that sped along an obviously rutted road. The sound of traffic whizzed past. Surrounded by total darkness, my head ached and my stomach churned. It took a minute to recreate how I'd landed here and another to appreciate the fact that our dear cousin had mercifully not tied my hands or feet.

Struggling to sit upright, I stopped, rigid, at the sound of low, throaty growls. With shaking fingers pressed hard against the wooden floor, I waited for my eyes to grow accustomed to the dark. When they did, I almost cried aloud.

Two sets of yellow eyes blazed at me across from where I hunched. Thick silver chains hooked their collars to eyebolts in the wall of the hold. I strained to see just how long these chains extended. Long enough to reach me if they chose?

As one of the animals bared its teeth, I heard the swoosh of wood sliding against wood and slowly turned my head toward the sound. A pale sliver of light and a mouth appeared at the opening on my right. I guessed I was inside the hold of a cargo truck and someone's mouth was pressed against the opening between the cab and the cargo space. A low laugh was followed by a soft whistle.

"Those guys are keepin' you company. They're mighty hungry, too. That's Lone Star and Bluebonnet. Pit bulls are great companions. If they like you, that is." A harsh snort and the small opening slid shut. It was the same voice as my abductor. If the cousin could turn around and speak, who was driving the cab?

There were at least two men, depending on the cab's size. Just my luck. I began to shiver and bile rose to my throat. We turned a corner at frightening speed and I lost my precarious grip on the flooring. Groaning, I bent sideways, retching from deep in my belly. This continued until I was left in the throes of dry heaving, my stomach and rib cage sore and aching from the effort. Chains rattled and the dogs stood, barking furiously, lunging and pulling against their restraints, their nails scrabbling on the plywood flooring.

I glanced up and away from the stinking pile I'd managed to spew a foot away from where I lay. The animals, chains anchored, stood several feet apart against the far wall. For a brief moment, I thought they couldn't reach me until another sharp turn around a corner flung them toward me. Their collars strained from the effort to escape, fangs displayed, barking filling my ears, their fury as close to hysteria as I'd ever experienced.

Shrinking as close to the wall as possible, my body ached from constant shivering, as if in a fever. This shaking lasted for eternity, but suddenly the cacophony surrounding me stopped as the dogs stretched their necks over my oozing pile of vomit. Once more, my stomach protested and I turned my head from the sight, raising my hands to my ears to stop all sounds of their feasting.

A noxious sour smell overpowered the space and I began another round of dry heaves that left me too weak to sit upright. Would their dinner appease them so they wouldn't come after me? Had they used every inch of chain or could they still reach me? I again tried to calculate their range of motion and grew dizzy with the effort, the inside of the trailer spinning until my head landed hard on the floor and I closed my eyes. If they ate me, they ate me. I was too weak to care.

While dozing in and out of consciousness, instantly aware whenever my eyelids struggled open; I felt more than saw them watching me. At least they had stopped growling and lunging. Looked as if they enjoyed the Thai food.

How much time had passed? Perhaps an hour, depending on how long I'd dozed. The vehicle turned, slower this time, and drove over a far rougher road than before, braking occasionally. I sensed my journey was coming to an end. If the cousin had helped Robby escape Ben Taub, where was Robby now? Had he met the same fate I was heading toward? Or did my brother know and approve, perhaps right now driving me to my doom? I discounted that theory. Robby would never willingly harm me.

As we came to a stop, I remembered I'd had my briefcase with me on my trip to the ladies room. Unfortunately, I'd not retrieved my gun from its lockbox in the car. It was dark outside, dark inside, but I doubted the cousin had thrown my briefcase in beside me so I could make a cell phone call for help. New thought: had he already read my notes about the uterine tissue sample?

I'd memorized my abductor's face. Flat expression, eyes with nothing behind them. His menacing posture spoke volumes. It said I'll do whatever I'm told, as long as I get paid to do it. I'd seen men like him. In mug shots, behind bars, walking the streets of Houston. A chill ran through me. I had no idea what his plans were.

I ran through possible scenarios. My car in the parking lot would be a loud clue I'd been abducted. Surely Adam Franklin had alerted the cops when I didn't return. A new thought struck me. Was Adam in on this heist? But that would mean a host of others had played along. Too many, I hoped, to believe.

Or would Adam assume that I'd stiffed him for the bill? Surely not. Crap! Had he also been abducted?

The truck came to a shuddering stop. As the overhead door of my wooden prison was raised with a loud rolling sound, my teeth began to chatter uncontrollably. Oh, God. Surely someone was looking for me. Adrenalin would be in my favor, but I could muster up only so much fight without a weapon.

A flashlight beam arched across the interior, setting off a mad yelping and rattling of chains. A man hefted himself up and onto the flooring and then unlocked the dogs' chains from the bolts on the wall. Blood rushed to my head, heightened nerves stinging my fingertips. What now?

The man jerked the dogs from the cargo hold while all my senses slammed into emergency status. With an empty stomach, my body felt lifeless and limp, but the nausea had vanished and the danger light in my brain grew bright red. *You'll handle whatever's coming, Giles.*

Again, the man hoisted himself up and inside with a loud "Whoa, girl. You shore do stink!"

While being jerked upright, I felt dampness between my legs, the result of a bladder's unfulfilled destination sometime earlier. I might smell putrid, but the man who grabbed me under the arms and dragged me outside was no Mr. Clean. His breath was foul and his T-shirt reeked of fried chicken and stale beer. I wanted to tell him he was pretty rank himself, but held my tongue as he pulled me from the cargo space and dropped me on the hard ground.

Both animals lunged, but the man had wrapped their chains taught around a tree trunk. It wasn't the cousin who stood facing me. He must still be inside the cab. I felt a passing relief that Robby hadn't jumped out of the cab.

Except for the lighted pole beside an iron gate, it was pitch dark. We were in the country where nothing drowned the frantic, high-pitched chirping of cicadas. Soft breezes drifted underneath my jacket, across my neck and face, sending a mellow scent of pine needles my way.

The front door of the cab slammed and Mr. Cousin himself rounded the tail end of the truck before planting his fists on his hips, eyes narrowed in the straining light. "You don't look so hot."

"I don't feel so hot," I said, keeping my voice low and even, straining out fear before it could latch onto my reply.

"Know where we are?" he asked.

I looked around at the chain-link fence stretching for what appeared to be miles. A padlocked gate stood nearby. Beyond it, a gravel path curved between shadows of moss that hung from massive oaks while neighboring pines stood tall and black beside them, like sentinels. A distant bellow was followed by a small splash.

Yes. I'd been here years before on a field trip with my senior class. New girl in town, I'd moved with Robby to Houston when Father took a job as head of campus police at the University of Houston. I'd felt alone and singled out as a topic of gossip by the gaggle of girls who walked apart on our class excursion so many years ago. I would hate for this to be my final resting place.

Brazos Bend State Park, fifty miles from downtown Houston, was full of nature trails, lakes, rare flowering species, as well as birds and alligators galore. Signs warned to keep your pets on a leash at all times. Why were we here? If they were planning to kill me, my body would be discovered tomorrow when the park opened for guests. Then I recalled our guide saying there were 21 miles of hiking trails in this 5000 acre park. Maybe it would take longer than a day.

"Brazos Bend State Park?" I ventured.

"You're pretty smart, girl. But then, that's why you're here."

"Just why am I here?" I could hardly hear my own voice for the loud rushing in my ears and hoped I wouldn't faint. Weakness had more consequences than I dared dwell on.

Mr. Cousin grabbed up the chains of one of the dogs and smiled at me but spoke to his companion. "Help me throw her over the fence. Bluebonnet and I'll be right behind you."

It sounded as if all conversation was over. I glanced around. Could I outrun them? Hide in the woods?

"Don't even think about it unless you want me to let this here Bluebonnet off his chain. He loves a good chase." My life seemed full of mind-readers.

A combination of push-pulls and both men hefted me over the fence, where I landed on my back, struggling to pull breath back into my lungs. Mr. Cousin followed with the dog dangling from under one arm. Struggling upright, I felt the seam rip in my jacket armhole, but that was the least of my problems.

Cousin's partner grabbed my arms behind my back, and holding my wrists tightly, marched me away from the gate. We veered left at the first cross path with Bluebonnet jangling behind, his throaty growl reminding me we still weren't friends. My feet dragged in the dirt road, the consequence of an empty body filled only with terror at what lay ahead, the smell of pine no longer comforting.

We rounded a thick copse and there it was. The alligator lake. Across the lake, pale moonlight shone on gray snouts rippling the waters. Those creatures must never sleep. My shivering revved up a notch.

"I'm only goin' to let Bluebonnet here nibble on you a teensy bit. You'll be out cold and then we'll drag your skinny little legs in the lake here. Tasty for alligators, 'specially with the addition of a little bloody flesh. Don't worry. You won't feel a thing. Not till you wakes up."

As he approached, I caught a gleam from the hypodermic he withdrew from his pocket. "You should know better than stick your nose where it don't belong."

My mind exploded with an image of me, the gazelle, being torn alive by the pit bull, with only ripped and shredded skin and muscle left for the alligators to feast on. Buy yourself some time, Giles. Think of something. Quick!

"You mean I'm to stay away from LeeAnn Callahan's death?" I blurted out.

"I means what I means," he replied.

Encouraged I'd momentarily stalled my own demise, my voice came out stronger than expected. "What did you do with my brother?"

"Your crazy brother?" he asked, his voice sly and teasing.

"Where is he?" I demanded.

"He's spending time away from you, without his meds. But I've supplied him with a few of my own he seems to be enjoying." His laugh spurred me to action.

Yanking my wrists free, I took off running, a new-found energy surging through my legs. My heart pounded in my throat as I turned toward the front gate. Optimism soared until I was grabbed and jerked around. Screaming, I thrashed and kicked indiscriminately. He had me on my feet, hands behind me in an instant. Or so it seemed.

Stumbling, my wrists squeezed tightly behind my back, we arrived again beside the lake. Mr. Cousin yelled "Sic her" and released Bluebonnet's chain. As the dog dashed toward me, snarling, he became a blur of motion. I kicked out, made contact with the animals' chest and the dog flew sideways, howling in rage. Apparently hurting his pit bull was off-limits.

Mr. Cousin grabbed me by the throat, and, with me squirming as hard as I could, plunged the needle into my arm. As I jerked my elbow up, fluid dripped down my forearm. His cursing faded high above me while I slid. Mercifully, the pain of clamping teeth that seared deep inside my anklebone was short-lived.

37

other stood a short distance from the edge of the lake, a look of concern on her pale face. She held baby Robby in her arms and called out for me to wake up. Robby needed me. I shouted back for her to bring him to me, but she only shook her head, her eyes sorrowful and pleading. *You have to come get him. It's up to you, Jelly, I can't do it.*

That's stupid, I thought. Mother never called me Jelly. Only Robby. I shook my head as if my brains were dice and they'd tumble into something logical. I swatted at my neck and withdrew fingers covered in sticky liquid. It took a minute to realize I'd followed Mother's orders. I was awake.

Golden moonlight bathed the tops of majestic pines across the lake. The whine of mosquitoes, all on the same high C, grew louder. A sharp mosquito sting to my cheek, then another while I struggled upright. It was then I saw a small army of gray, knobby heads swimming in the moonlight, eyes like gray ping-pong balls in their sockets. They were gliding my way. I glanced down where my legs lay buried up to my knees in the lake. Their lake.

With my heart about to explode in my chest, I tried for a smooth retreat. Amazed I was alive, I willed myself to ignore the onslaught of bloodsuckers clouding my vision, not to mention the approaching alligators. Slowly, half-inch by half-inch, I scooted back up the bank of the lake, aiming for total silence. Not successfully, I realized, as stabbing pain tore through my right foot and up my leg. I stuffed down small cries that leaked, unbidden, from my throat. Surely Mr. Cousin kept his pit bulls in good health and I wouldn't lose my leg. I had to get out of here, away from those bug-eyed water creatures turned toward me, swimming slowly, as if deciding whether I was worth the energy.

Searching my brain for any facts regarding alligators until my head pounded, I became stuck over when did they feed? During the day, twenty-four hours a day, or only at night? My life might depend on it. But the only fact I could remember was that alligators were swift on land. Would they attack me, or was that mere curiosity I saw in their steady gaze?

I looked around for a large tree limb in case they opted for a chase, but saw none. Progress was slow, but now I was almost completely out of the water. Yet their eyes still followed me. Continuing my slow scoot away, it seemed hours before I grew brave enough to stand, wincing in pain, feeling fresh blood surge from my ankle. Now, paranoia about the bite turned to panic over bacteria from the lake feeding on my open wounds. Before taking time to deal with them, I needed more distance. A small wave lapped against the bank as one of the predators turned away, losing interest in my struggle. Still as stone, I watched the others join their leader.

I exhaled and promptly dropped hard onto the ground. This spot was good enough. Struggling out of my jacket, I pulled my cotton shirt over my head and using my teeth, tore strips in the fabric. Sometimes it paid to own a wardrobe of old clothing, soft and pliable.

After binding my ankle and calf, I slipped on my jacket, buttoned it and stood again, biting my lower lip against pain as I hobbled away, feeling the squish of water in my shoes, the wet fabric of my slacks painfully caressing my right calf with every step. I let it be. My mantra was to concentrate on escape.

Those two men knew my death was not inevitable, that I might escape. Yet they hadn't killed me outright. Why? This reinforced my opinion they were hired punks. Hired to scare me off. If they thought I'd be too frightened to continue investigating LeeAnn's death, they needed to think again. Bastards! I set my mind on not only surviving, but living to see those two creeps behind bars.

In order to keep up my courage, I aimed a litany of expletives to-ward my invisible captors, and with every limp up the path toward the gate, I substituted cries of pain with curses. Getting over the chain link gate that lay ahead of me would be tricky, but I never doubted I'd make it. My only doubt was in making it to the highway.

At least one agonizing hour later, I stood leaning against a fence-post on the shoulder of the highway, blood-soaked bandages around my ankle, listing slightly to avoid pressure on my right leg. Mosquitoes had followed me, stinging my neck, my arms. A few braved my cheeks and won out.

I stuck out my thumb, then chastised myself. No car in sight, Giles. Save your strength. I must have teetered there for at least thirty minutes, occasionally brushing away mosquitoes, before headlights loomed pale, shimmering against the dark skyline. Waving my arms with as much enthusiasm as possible, I contemplated running toward the middle of the pavement, but my first attempt had me seeing stars where stars shouldn't be. But my clothing matched the blackness around me and I had no white flag to wave.

Tears of frustration filled my eyes as the car sped past. A sob welled inside, smothering my chest. Was that the sound of braking? I turned and stared at twin brake lights shining to my left. Thank God! As the car U-turned and headed back toward me, tears plastered my cheeks. Surely these rescuers were good folks.

The car halted a few feet from where I stood. Both car doors opened and two men jumped out. My knees buckled. Please God, no Mr. Cousin and his demon partner. I squinted against light from their headlights and thought I recognized the man who'd jumped out the passenger side. It was Adam Franklin. Dear Adam. I wanted to hug his neck, but knew I'd topple at his feet if I tried.

But when Keymap rounded the front end of the car and called out my name, his deep voice strained with worry, my legs gave out beneath me.

38

I lay in the dark, sweat streaming while my body burned. Someone placed a cool rag on my brow and there was a whisper in my ear I only felt. With eyelids heavy as bricks, I tried, but could not open them to see where I was. Hurried movement buzzed around me like a fan whose energy I felt but not its cooling breeze. I feared I would suffocate in the burning flames that licked my cheeks, my eyes, and my chest. My right calf felt encased in bandages far too tight as the muscles throbbed painfully. My mouth babbled, but even my mother, standing close by my side, could not answer me. Everything was soft, still, and fiery. I felt a stick in my arm and tried to block it with my elbow, but it was only a wish as I lay, immobile, floating on flames.

❧

The first flutter of my eyelids revealed a narrowed view of a face leaning over me, soft fingers patting my arm. The sound of cooing, like doves, reached my ears. I felt loved and comforted and blessedly cool as I dropped off the earth again. Time was not a part of my universe as my eyes continued to open sporadically, then close as if my brain had emphatically refused all visitors. Sometimes it was dark and sometimes the light hurt my eyes, commanding me to close them.

When my eyes finally opened and refused to shut, I saw a tall figure in the corner, huddled over his cell phone, whispering as if he plotted something fearful. With a quickening pulse, I recognized Captain Lamar's voice. It took several attempts to clear my throat before he noticed me.

Hightower approached, wearing a goofy smile.

"You awake?" he asked, his voice solicitous. "You had me scared there for a minute. Your leg got infected," he added.

I immediately rose on my elbows to see if I still owned both legs, then dropped exhausted from the effort. The obvious swelling over my blanket indicated my limbs were intact. Struggling to recreate the reason I lay here incapacitated was like catching smoke, diaphanous and fleeting.

The captain scraped a metal chair close and sat. "Some of your shenanigans reached my ears. Keymap filled in the rest."

I groggily asked him to raise my headboard a little. A vision of bobbing alligator heads appeared, and, out of any logical order, of myself having dinner with Adam Franklin at the Thai restaurant. Then of my capture on the way to the ladies room. Like cartoon dialogue bubbles, images popped up, but logical reasoning remained out of reach. I realized Lamar was still talking.

"I owe you an apology," he said.

I focused on the captain. "An apology for what?" My voice was weak, but I needed to hear him admit I'd been right to investigate LeeAnn's death.

"You know what," he growled and reached out—as if to pat my arm? He seemed to be lacking a certain chip on his shoulder. "Those guys were hired thugs. Most likely their orders were to rough you up, scare you some." He paused, then spoke as if embarrassed. "I'm sure you figured that out already."

Scared me "some" ? I begged to differ. They'd scared the crap out of me.

"If anything had happened to you, I'd never forgive myself," Lamar said.

That made two of us.

"I just stopped by to check on you," Lamar added. "And, I thought I'd replace your cell phone as compensation."

Compensation? For what? Police incompetence or for my being laid up in the hospital?

Lamar dropped a ruby-red Blackberry on my lap. "I had them keep your same phone number. In the meantime, I have my folks hunting the guys who did this. Not so difficult until they wised up and tossed your briefcase in the bushes off Interstate 10, a couple of miles outside Beaumont. Your cell phone was how Keymap located you. He was less interested in the moving vehicle than when your cell stayed put for over thirty minutes. Smart man. But being able to afford tracking equipment didn't hurt, either." He rose and mumbled it was time he left.

My mind seemed awakened as if from a dormant state. Now that I was safe, I grew more interested in where the cousin had headed. Beaumont. Boots and LeeAnn grew up in Beaumont. Coincidence? He'd also mentioned something about Keymap being able to afford tracking equipment. I'd never thought of Keymap as well-heeled. It was time to rethink a lot of things.

"By the way," Lamar added, his hand on the doorknob, "those fingerprint guys I sent to your apartment turned up nothing but your own. Someone obviously wore gloves."

I thought of Robby. For him to plan a raid on my office and bring gloves was hard to believe.

"Any leads on where Robby is?" I asked, fearful of the answer.

Lamar appeared to hesitate. "We'll find him," he said.

I'd heard that before. My thrill over Lamar's remorse was swamped by worry over my brother. Just keep him safe, I prayed. I'll handle anything else that comes my way, God, just bring him home safe.

39

Morning sunshine streamed across my loathsome breakfast tray. I hated red Jello and Tapioca pudding. From outside my room came the sound of wheeling carts and enticing smells, headed for those allowed eggs and bacon. A real breakfast.

Sometime during the night, my IV had been removed as well as the other apparatus I was grateful to be without. I felt stronger with only a slight ache in my leg. It was time to leave. Where was Keymap?

Glancing at the bedside table, I spotted the white envelope Lamar had given me before leaving the day before. From your neighbor, he'd said. Apparently, he'd seen Santa outside my apartment and she'd said Keymap had called her. Santa couldn't wait around for me to wake up, so she'd given the captain an envelope for me. I vaguely remembered tossing it aside and dropping back against the pillow. I'd planned on only a short nap until the cheery breakfast nurse had awakened me thirty minutes ago.

I opened the envelope, feeling the bruised spot on my hand from the IV. I smiled at Santa's down-sloping scrawl. Her note was written in green ink.

> *Giles. I hope you believe me when I tell you how sorry I am about the tea. I meant what I said. I'll never ever ever do that*

again! I have thrown out my box of you-know- what. Please
get well and tell me I'm forgiven.
     Santa

I was reaching for the telephone to call her when a mousy-looking girl in baggy jeans opened the door. A large sketch pad protruded from underneath her arm. As she approached, she clicked her tongue several times like a disapproving kindergarten teacher.

"Oh my dear, I am soooo sorry to disturb your breakfast but the captain said to get right over here. I'm Amy, HPD artist, and I'll just sit right down here in this chair and whenever you're finished, I'll let you describe away, if that's okay. Gosh, I rhymed." She flipped open her pad and stared at me from behind horn-rimmed glasses perched on the middle of her small nose.

I told her I was finished with breakfast and then clarified that it was the "cousin's" partner I was being asked to describe. Pictures of the imposter himself were already posted.

Thirty minutes later, the portrait she'd drawn was as close as I could recall. Having this creep stare out at me from the page was unsettling and comforting at the same time. She had his likeness dead-on.

Standing, she replied to my thanks, "You were easy to work with. Not many people have your memory for detail."

After the sketch artist left, I heard raised voices and my door burst open. When I recognized Keymap, my throat closed and tears threatened, as if we were replaying my rescue from Brazos Bend. Get a grip, Giles. If you break down, I'll deny you Snickers for the rest of your life.

The good nurse Ratchet was right behind him, scolding him for entering against her orders. "She needs her rest, sir, and it's time for her pain meds."

Keymap turned his most ingratiating smile on her and I saw her eyes flicker. His voice was smooth as silk. "How about if I wait outside until you're through with the patient and then I promise not to stay longer than five minutes."

Her dark brown eyes melted under his grin and, holding open the door for him to leave, said gruffly, "All right, but just five minutes, you hear?"

As I zeroed in on possible signs of bodily distress, I realized I didn't need or want pain medication. My leg throbbed, but nothing unbearable. I just wanted to go home.

"How are we feeling today?"

"Actually, I'm not in pain and I'd like to speak to the doctor."

Too late, I noticed her long white coat and brass nameplate with "Dr. Messenger" engraved in block letters.

She caught me looking and said, "How can I be of assistance?"

"When can I leave?" Better cut to the chase now that I'd shown my idiocy.

"I'll run some labs today." She reached over and carefully pulled back the blanket covering my leg. I glanced at the swollen shape of mummy wraps around my calf and ankle. She lifted my leg and began to unwrap. I didn't know whether to look or not, but then I'd always been nosy.

While she gently probed the wounds on my leg, I took a peek. There was swelling around dark lines of stitching which looked worse than it felt. "You're healing nicely," she said, reminding me of my worry over how many teaching nights I'd missed.

"How long have I been here?"

"Three days. This is the morning of your fourth day."

I was struggling over which day of the week it was, when she spoke "It's Thursday morning."

For a wild moment, I wondered if I could talk her into letting me teach tonight's class. I'd missed Tuesday night.

"We'll get a fresh bandage and draw your blood. Then we'll see how soon you can leave."

"Is today a possibility?"

She appeared to consider it. "Do you have anyone at home?"

"Yes," I lied. Did a cat count?

"We'll see," she said, reaching in her pocket as her beeper erupted. She left the room and never looked back. If hospitals could dismiss a woman the day after her mastectomy, why was I still here?

When Keymap entered, I flew into overdrive, raising my headboard upright. "As soon as they replace my bandage, will you get me out of here?"

He shook his head. "You spent twenty-four hours in intensive care and I'm not going to be responsible for a relapse. Besides," he continued, "I already called the school. Captain Hightower replaced you, so no hurry on that score."

How casually Keymap delivered that blow to my ego. "He was just here yesterday!" I protested. "Why didn't he mention that little fact to me? Crap!"

"In the future, I'm going to stick close," Keymap said, ignoring me. "I came by to say you might not always know where I am, but I'll keep up with you. I'm aware you can handle yourself, but I'd like to think you're smart enough to know when you need help."

I tried frowning at his comment but a bite on my forehead demanded scratching. My vigorous attempt only made it itch worse.

There was a brief pause before Keymap added, "My five minutes are up."

He leaned over me and frowned. "Looks like you got a bad case of pimples, woman." Then he laughed, while I scratched my cheeks, suddenly all my bites itching at once.

His smile left me cold. I'd foolishly begun a fantasy in my mind where he was in my apartment, at my bedside, refusing to leave me alone. Actually, that would drive me crazy. But a little solicitation wouldn't hurt. Instead of sitting in my visitor's chair, taking my hand in his, and treating me like a woman who'd been abducted, mauled by a pit bull and almost attacked by alligators, Keymap turned to leave. "Anything I can do for you before I go?"

Hell, no, I thought.

40

Santa hovered while I sat on the living room couch. Her need to be forgiven was starting to get on my nerves as she brought me pillows, my mail, a tuna sandwich and coffee she'd brewed herself. "Sure there's nothing more I can get you?" Her bright eyes looked down at me.

"No, really. Thanks again for picking me up."

"No problem." She headed toward the door with a cheery wave of her hand as if she'd just made a new friend. Before leaving, she turned toward me, an impish grin on her face. "Did you know I considered working with you as a PI? Now don't look so horrified. Watching you lately, I decided it was far too dangerous." Giggling, she shut the door behind her.

Santa as partner would be a worse nightmare than lying drugged and wounded with my feet in an alligator lake. Summoned to my hospital room, Santa had brought clothes from my closet along with her eagerness to please. The nurse might have thought we were a couple. I didn't care. Santa fit the bill of the "someone at home" so the doctor would let me go.

The first thing Santa assured me once we were settled in her car was that she hadn't seen or heard from Robby. What I wouldn't acknowledge was that I'd rather Robby be lying on her floor, drunk with opium tea. At least he'd be safe.

After scooting my back upright against the sofa, I propped my leg on the coffee table, cradled by a green pillow with a red-Christmas tree cut-out, courtesy of my neighbor. Curled beside me Suzy snored loudly. I wore jeans, cotton flannel shirt and black Keds with wool socks. Houston's weather had decided to do a one-eighty while I was inside the hospital and it was almost chilly outside.

Sipping coffee and chewing on Santa's tuna fish sandwich, I rifled my stack of mail until I found what I was looking for—a Beaumont return address.

I ripped it open. There was the Last Will & Testament of Boots's parents and of LeeAnn Callahan. After one read-through, I grew energized and hastily threw the remainder of my sandwich on the coffee table before hobbling to my office for a yellow highlighter. I couldn't believe what I'd just read. On the balcony the night of Brad's cocktail party, J.D. McGraw had hinted at the monetary axe LeeAnn held over her elder brother's head. I hadn't been sure this was true until now.

The kitchen phone rang and for a second, I considered not answering. Then again, it might be about my abductors or my brother, or both. I hobbled into the kitchen and picked up the receiver.

"This is Giles."

"I'm right sorry those critters didn't do you more damage," a muffled voice spoke. Before I could respond, the man continued. "If you keep on nosing in other folks' business, you can kiss yer little brother goodbye." The line went dead. Even muffled, I'd recognized my abductor's voice.

With a pounding heart, I dialed Lamar. Angie said he was out, but in response to the urgency in my voice, said she'd find him and have him call as soon as possible. But then, I was in no mood to wait. I'd hunt down that creep without the captain's help.

Picking up the receiver, I punched the recall button, immediately spotting the 409 area code. Beaumont .With my pulse beating like a metronome against my throat, I dialed the number. When the caller picked up, I was startled into a brain-dead response, quickly apologizing for dialing a wrong number. A perky female voice had answered, "Tilman, Durst, and Brewton Insurance Company. How may I direct your call?" That was Ramsey Tilman's company he'd founded back in the sixties. Boots's uncle.

Taking a deep breath, I dialed Boots. He told me he was in Beaumont. Sounding puzzled about why I would drive so far just to talk to him, he said I'd find him at home. Questioning Boots was imperative, but first I needed to make a phone call or two.

Several Houston PI's were known to specialize in insurance investigations following a questionable death. I dialed Tim Bridgeway. He picked up, but turned out to be unhelpful. I then called Sal Klepper who told me to check with Morty Silverstein.

Morty picked up on the third ring.

"I don't believe it! Long time, no hear," Morty said, his booming voice so loud I pulled the phone away from my ear.

"How are you, beautiful?"

Morty was a jokester who dealt in serious stuff but remained, on the surface at least, unfazed.

"I'm fine, Morty. And yourself?"

"I know you didn't call me 'cause you miss my bod," Morty said.

I had to laugh at that one. Morty was as round as he was tall and I imagined his bald head a twin of his obvious round paunch. At his son's Bar Mitzvah several years ago, he and his wife were embarrassingly proud of their son and each other.

"I need your help. Do you know anything about an investigation over LeeAnn Callahan's fall from a Reliant Stadium balcony last March? I'm looking into the death and her will mentions a life insurance policy among her estate assets."

A low whistle came over the phone. "Seems like her brother got his hooks into you," he said.

My pulse did a little jig. "Why do you say that?"

"Yours truly was called on that one. Policy was taken out by Tilman, Durst, & Brewton. Know it?" I nodded and Morty barreled forth as if he could see me. "They do mostly automobile but some life and property. LeeAnn's deal was a piece of cake 'cause of the two-year Texas law."

I knew what he meant. By state law, no life insurance would pay on death by suicide within the first two years following its purchase. "So LeeAnn's policy was less than two years old?"

"You got it. Her brother with the stupid name was more than pissed the police seemed sold on suicide."

"Boots got in touch with you?"

"Insurance company passed him on to me. I had to get right rude, if you get my drift. Sent him a copy and that shut him up. His uncle, old man Tilman, is one of the company founders. He blew a gasket over the stink Boots made."

"When did Boots first contact you?"

"April Fool's day." He bellowed loudly. "But the suicide ruling only became final a month ago. Never so glad to be rid of anyone in my life. Anything else you need, sugar?"

"Yeah. A huge favor, Morty. Can you fax me a copy?"

"Only for you."

I thanked him, gave him my fax number and hung up. I returned to my office and pushed the control on my printer to allow for fax. Pacing the room, waiting for the hum to begin, I remembered my forgotten lunch.

Back in the kitchen, I stood at the sink and finished my sandwich, poured out the cold coffee and refilled my cup. How much money could be involved for a loving brother to start inquiring about life insurance ten days after the death of a beloved sister? Licking tuna fish from my fingers, I heard the sound of the fax and hurried back into my office. The policy was four pages long. Pretty standard stuff. The only shocking part was the amount: $500,000. Why would Boots be upset about half-a-mil when he'd inherited several million when his parents died?

By now Suzy was picking up on my frenzy. She started a yowl of protest when I grabbed my car keys. I found my new cell phone as well as my pistol and handcuffs, just in case. I stuffed these in my bag along with copies of the wills, LeeAnn's insurance policy and, after a trip to the freezer for a Snickers bar, limped out the front door, locking it behind me.

While I waited for the elevator, I pulled out my cell and dialed Keymap's beeper.

41

Beaumont was a flat, boring drive out Interstate 10, ninety miles east of Houston. Marsh lands, rice fields and belching refineries dotted the landscape as I pushed my Civic to the speed limit and a little beyond. I hadn't bothered to change clothes or shower and I could still smell the odor of antiseptic on my skin. I didn't care. Pondering over parents who'd made their younger child trustee over their older son's share of their wealth, I wondered if this was favoritism to the extreme or wise judgment. Not knowing for sure, I had to admit I was leaning toward the latter.

Police sergeant Irma Doyle said Boots had been a wild teenager, gambling and wrecking cars. During our first meeting, Boots had mentioned he was seven years older than his sister. Same age difference as me and my little brother. LeeAnn had died at age twenty-four. That made Boots around thirty-two. Time enough to have grown up and left bad habits behind.

Had my brother grown more stable with age? In truth, he'd gotten worse. But he had mental issues where Boots appeared perfectly sane.

I lowered the window and allowed the breeze to relax my nerves. It was mid-afternoon and outside a crystal blue sky was striped with sporadic gray plumes whipping upward from refinery chimneys. But the view only made me think of Boots and the oil-moneyed rich. Had he killed his sister over money? On LeeAnn's death, he'd inherited outright millions. I'd had a chance to read just enough of LeeAnn's will to discover Boots would inherit his sister's share from their parents' death, as well as her life insurance policy. But not if she took her own life.

Had he hired me just to get her life insurance? Did half a million mean that much to him even after his inheritance? Would he have risked exposing himself by hiring me if he'd killed her?

Was it Boots the elevator guard had seen walking away from the balcony? But then his description of a tall, pale eyed gentleman wearing black cowboy boots and hat could fit hundreds of rodeo attendees. I realized, as I drove, that I should have looked into the liquidity of Brad's insurance company. Hammerly was involved in several law suits. Did they stand to lose millions? Enough to tempt Brad and J.D. to partner with Boots in the demise of his sister? Split the inheritance? But if that were the case, Boots never would have hired me. Unless he was so much in the hole, he needed that money badly. Badly enough to risk discovery.

Needing a diversion, I tuned the radio to a country and western station. Soon I was singing along with Wynona Judd—"You Are My Strongest Weakness." We belted it out together. Until, that is, my unruly mind jumped to Adam Franklin. Why hadn't I called the ME's lab assistant before leaping at the chance to track the cousin and question Boots?

Wynona's warbling stopped abruptly when I shut off the radio. From outside, the roar of speeding trucks and semi-trailers invaded my ears. I rolled up my window and tried to recall Adam's phone number. My old phone stored all my phone numbers. Perhaps Lamar hadn't realized I would have been far more grateful for my old cell than a fancy Blackberry.

Within a minute or two, the first three digits came to me, but were the last four one-nine-three-eight or one-nine-three-six? Aware that I should stop before dialing, I pulled over in the right lane and slowed. The Blackberry sat perched on my thigh, my fingernail going for the tiny squares, ending with a three-eight. A cleaning service answered. As I hung up, I veered off the interstate and idled while dialing the number ending in three-six. When Adam's voicemail answered, I silently congratulated my memory and left him a message. If I could discover the father of LeeAnn's aborted baby, I'd be that much closer to solving the case.

Another fact from LeeAnn's will. If she had children at the time of her death, her life insurance stipulated her child or children would inherit, and not Boots. Sorry, brother. I now have progeny that comes before you. If Boots had known about her pregnancy, but hadn't known of her abortion, he would have had another reason to want his sister dead.

But what about the green-eyed monster? Jealousy weighed heavily in murders. Could the one who'd helped LeeAnn over the balcony be a jealous boyfriend? What about a jealous brother growing up with parents who trusted their sensible daughter more than their son?

I preferred to think of Robby as over-protective rather than jealous. After he picked a fight and broke the arm of my high school sweetheart, I managed without a love interest. But our father had not shown similar restraint.

Robby and I had joked about Father's girlfriend. She was a secretary in the Safety Department at the University of Houston where Father was chief of campus police. He would leave our small house smelling of English Leather, his thinning gray hair slicked against his head. Never did I think he'd remarry. My mother had been the perfect soul-mate, the soft voice to his gruff nature. I'd often blamed my father's genes for the unstable young man my brother had become.

Father called late on a Wednesday, just as I was leaving for evening law school class. I'd interspersed psychology classes with law, knowing that in order to be a good defense attorney, I'd need both. The only problem with all these classes was that I still needed to earn money. We had yet to qualify Robby for social security disability and his treatments were expensive.

According to our father, police work was admirable, and I should forget law school and stick to catching bad guys. I'd long given up arguing with him. Robby was his son, but I'd witnessed the violent disconnect between them and filled the role of grounder against their lightening. As years passed and my goal not yet half-attained, the more resentful I became. Robby couldn't help himself, but Father was a different animal.

He sounded out of breath. "G.L I'm bringing Maybell home with me after work. Sevenish. Can you have dinner ready? Do we have gin?" He chuckled. "Can't believe I have a woman who hates beer and loves martinis."

I noted the "have a woman" part and cringed. "I've got contract law class tonight. Did you forget?"

He breathed heavily into the phone but said nothing.

"Father?"

"Do you mean to tell me you're not going to be there when I need you? Maybell is very excited about meeting you two."

"Can't she come over tomorrow night?"

"No. She can't come tomorrow night. We need to talk to both of you, and I want you there. Are you telling me you're letting me down? You won't accommodate me this once?"

I didn't know whether to laugh or cry. "This once" times a thousand would be more like it. Robby had taken his meds, was scribbling happily in his bedroom, and I needed to leave for class.

"I've got to go to class tonight. I missed last time when Robby was upset over his visit to the shrink. Remember?"

"I can't believe this. I choose to believe you'll change your mind and have your fabulous lasagna waiting for us. I know you will, honey. You love your father too much to desert him tonight."

He hung up. I went outside and sat in the car. I even turned on the engine. But instead of driving to class, I drove to the corner grocery store. My only rebellion was to buy the cheapest gin from the liquor store. This woman and my father had been dating for over two years, and he had to pick tonight.

I prepared Robby that Father and his girlfriend were likely to announce their engagement over dinner. He only shrugged and told me to close his bedroom door behind me. I straightened the living room while the lasagna was in the oven, then sat reading my contract law book until Father and Maybell came through the front door, laughing like teenagers.

Maybell leaned against Father, breathing heavily. She looked around, caught my eyes on her and winked. "Well, you must be G.L.!" She looked up at Father and playfully hit his shoulder. "You didn't tell me you had a beauty for a daughter." She turned back to me, "Can you believe this man has never showed me a picture of his children?"

I had no trouble believing her. I'd never seen a picture of her, either. Her hair was dyed the color of eggplant and pulled into a cow pile on top her head. Her lipstick was bright orange, and kiss-smudged around the edges. Her figure most resembled one of those round columns used to support large public buildings.

I rose and came forward, my hand outstretched. She broke away and came speedily toward me, arms wide and proceeded to bury me inside her bountiful bosom. I feared her cloying perfume would upset my stomach, and quickly pulled myself away. "Glad to meet you," I said.

Maybell was finished with me, her small eyes searching the living room. "Where's the boy?" she asked, her tone accusing as if I'd purposefully hidden him from her.

Father's jovial response was frightening, as if an alien now ruled our father's body. "He's the artist in our family, right G.L.? He's most likely in his room. I'll go get him." And I was left with Maybell.

"May I fix you a martini?"

"Now aren't you the sweetest thing," Maybell crooned. "But I prefer to fix my own, so just show me the way."

I stood and watched Maybell's preparations. A soft sigh floated through the kitchen when she spied the Gordon's on the counter. "I don't suppose you have any other gin on hand?"

"Sorry," I said, but wasn't. The woman's dreamy expression and slight sway over the sink told me she'd already imbibed that evening.

When Father returned with a sullen-looking Robby in tow, I figured the jovial alien had escaped for good.

"Robby," his voice like a warning from the doorway, "meet Maybell. Maybell, this is my son, Robby."

Maybell twirled, the gin bottle still in her hand as she rushed toward my brother. "You darling," she cried. "You're even better looking than your sister, you handsome thing." She slung her arms around Robby's neck and planted a fat orange kiss on his mouth.

I sucked in my breath as Robby lurched backwards, his face full of loathing. He swiped his mouth and glared. "Get away from me."

"Now, Robby," Father grabbed his arm. "You be nice to my Maybell."

"Your Maybell," Robby sneered. "You can have her." He turned as if to leave.

Father stepped back and slugged Robby in the jaw, watching as his son staggered, his skull hitting the doorframe. After crying out, Robby reached toward the back of his head and withdrew bloody fingers. I yelped and stepped toward Father when he stopped me with his outstretched arm.

"You're not going anywhere, G.L. I'll handle this."

He again grabbed for Robby's arm, but met Robby's fist on the side of his ear and went down. Maybell shouted that Robby was a bastard and should be put away. I didn't know who to help, Robby or Father. I chose Robby.

But he'd have none as he pummeled hard against Father's chest. Maybell and I both screamed and bent down to protect Father. In a rage, Robby pounded our backs with his fists. This gave Father a short respite and he staggered to his feet, using the wall as leverage. A surge of panic and I stood, pulling Robby out the kitchen door. I was shaking but managed to talk him back inside his room, promising I'd return with a bandage for his head.

Feeling more mentally bruised than physically injured, I headed back to the kitchen. Maybell held a bag of ice to Father's temple. They both stared at me with vacant eyes. I figured their silence was not a show of shyness, but of how shocked they were.

I sank onto the kitchen chair. Father took the ice bag away from Maybell and joined me at the table.

"We're leaving tonight. We'll be married in the morning. I turned my letter of resignation over to the department last week. That was my news. I'm nine months past qualifying for retirement. Maybell and I are moving to Florida. You're better at managing Robby than I've ever been. I don't want anything from the house. It's all yours."

I sat, stunned. Nothing he'd said was a surprise except for the part about moving out of state and leaving me responsible for Robby. I was twenty-five and Robby was eighteen. Fine and dandy to say he would take nothing from the house. We had nothing worth taking.

"Robby's now certified for social security disability," Father said. "Got notified today. I'd hoped we could have one final decent meal together." He rose and flung the baggie of ice into the kitchen sink.

"Guess not." Without another word, they left the house arm in arm.

That was ten years ago and neither Robby nor I have seen him since. Six months later I dropped out of law school. Robby's behavior had grown more and more extreme and his disability payments weren't nearly enough.

Would my brother kill for me? Of course he would, but not unless he thought my life was at stake. Would he kill me for any reason? No. But all brothers were not the same.

42

Beaumont's city limit sign focused me away from ancient memories and morbid thoughts. By chasing down my abductors and interrogating Boots, was I goading "Mister Cousin" into hurting my little brother?

Less than thirty minutes later, I found the Beaumont Chamber of Commerce. A friendly woman interrupted her knitting of a blue baby blanket to hand me a downtown map and instructions for reaching both Tilman's insurance company and Boots's home two miles northeast of town.

I headed to the insurance company, eating a perfectly defrosted Snickers bar on the way.

Directly off Main street, Tilman's one-story, red-brick building that stood beside a Stop 'n Go was in stark contrast to the Hammerly Insurance sky-scraper offices in Houston. I pulled in, parked in front, and limped inside to the sound of a tinkling bell.

The young girl chatting on her cell phone behind a shiny laminated desk had brown curly hair and a small round face with traces of acne scars dimpling beneath a layer of cosmetics. When she saw me, she whispered into her cell, snapped the lid closed and looked at me as if I'd interrupted something important.

"Hello," I said. "My name is Giles Faulkner. I'm from Houston and am trying to locate this man." I withdrew a photocopy of the cousin from my purse and handed it across the desk. She took it, a puzzled frown on her face that no girl should assume while wearing too much makeup.

"Why're you asking me?" She handed back the photo.

"I think he may have been here earlier. Was he?"

"Depends. He done something bad?"

Patience, Giles. "Not necessarily. He may have been witness to an accident."

She appeared to perk up. "You work for an insurance company?"

I smiled and nodded, mentally crossing my fingers.

"Which one?"

Hoping she wouldn't ask for my business card, I rattled off the name of a contact I had with a small property insurance company on the west side of Houston. "I do contract work for Tim O'Quinn at Memorial Insurance of Houston."

"Ohhhh. That's nice." She smiled, exposing a purple molar nestled like a grape toward the back of her mouth.

"So," I continued, "did you see the man I'm looking for this morning?"

She nodded. "You're not dressed for work."

I shrugged. "I dress casual for subcontract work."

"You have a business card on you?"

I looked remorseful and shook my head. "It's really so stupid, but I changed purses this morning and only realized half way here that I'd left all my cards at home."

She hesitated while my mind invented. "I met Ramsey Tilman once, years ago. My hero," I said, with a slightly humble and ingratiating tone of voice. I felt like Uriah Heep as I continued, "Such a remarkable man. You must be really smart to have been chosen to work for his company."

She brightened and sat up taller, allowing me to see the pink line of makeup where it stopped at her chin. "Well, I almost never made a C in high school."

"Did this man introduce himself?" I said, holding up the cousin's picture while furtively searching the desk top for a name plate. There it was. Jenny Berkeley.

"Jenny," I added lamely while she appeared lost in thought.

"Yeah. He did say who he was, but I didn't write it down. I think it was "GL" or "GS" or something like that. Come to think of it, I don't recall his mentioning any last name, you know?"

"What brought him here to your office?" I hoped she'd notice the "your" and be pleased.

"He just wanted to use the phone," Jenny said. "But," she quickly added, "He promised it wouldn't be long distance."

My hi-rise in Houston would qualify as a long distance call. "Did you stay, dial the number for him?"

Jenny's face grew pinker than her makeup. "I had to use the ladies room. Right then. Female thing, you know? My boss doesn't like us using the answering machine, so the man promised to answer the phone while I was gone cause Joanne called in sick and wasn't here. He even repeated our company name, just to be sure he knew how to answer it, you know?"

"So you heard none of his phone call?"

Jenny shook her head.

"What about the car he drove?"

She brightened. "He had a cool car. Parked next to where you are," she pointed outside through the picture window. "A red convertible, maybe a Chevy, or maybe a Ford. I didn't get too close a look, but it looked pretty new."

"Was he by himself?" I asked.

"Oh," she said with the surprise of sudden memory. "He did say he was looking for a friend. Asked if I'd seen him, but I hadn't."

His partner-in-crime? "Did he give you a description of the man he was looking for?"

She appeared to think a minute. "Just said he had black hair and was about his height."

That wasn't his partner. He'd had dirty blonde hair and was several inches shorter than the cousin. Looked like Robby had run off unexpectedly. I didn't know whether I should worry more or less.

"Thank you so much, Jenny." I flashed a smile, reached in my purse for a piece of paper and scribbled my name and number. "If you think of–"

"I know. If I think of anything else, I'm to call you, right?"

Right. Thanks to TV cop shows. "I'd appreciate a call if you do see a dark-haired man around here."

I started to leave but remembered one more question. "Were you working here several years ago when LeeAnn Callahan, Mr. Tilman's niece, also worked here?"

She nodded eagerly. "All of us here thought she hung the moon." Her face fell. "So sad how she died."

"Were you two close?"

She shook her head. "LeeAnn worked in the claims department. My friend, Cheryl, who worked closely with her, said she was smart as a whip. Everybody loved her. In spite of her connections, you know?"

"Would you say she and her uncle were on friendly terms?"

He eyes shone with fervor. "Mr. Tilman thought the sun rose and set on that gal. He had no children of his own, you know. He took LeeAnn to lunch whenever he was in town—Mr. Tilman spent a lot of time in Austin. When LeeAnn decided to move to Houston, I typed up the reference letter he wrote about her skills and all. It would'a got any girl a top job at any insurance company in Texas. Or anywhere, for that matter." She shook her head mournfully.

"Could you tell me where I might find Mr. Tilman?"

Her eyes flitted to her lap then back to me. "He's not available."

"Do you know where he is?"

"He's out of town. That's all I can say. Sorry."

"Thank you, Jenny," I said, and left to the sound of the same tinkling bell, my right ankle throbbing.

Choosing three miles as a good radius, I toured the surrounding hotels and motels, now including a picture of Robby with that of the cousin. No luck on my brother, but at my third stop, about a mile from the insurance building, I found where the cousin had stayed. A clerk behind the motel desk remembered him. After checking the sign-in sheet, I verified he was still using my name: "G.L. Faulkner."

The motel clerk was young enough to be impressed by my PI license. At least impressed enough to loosen up. The cousin had checked in two days before, alone. That morning, he'd checked out at noon, paid with cash and gave no permanent address, explaining he was not settled yet. The motel had his car license number, and the desk clerk identified his vehicle as a late model red Mustang. His room had been cleaned out, and after double-checking with the maid, the clerk reported nothing was left behind.

After jotting the Mustang's license number and thanking the clerk, I limped outside to the car. Pain shot up my leg, now more piercing than throbbing, and I cursed myself for not bringing even an aspirin with me. Seated behind the wheel, I dialed Lamar. When Angie said he was still in a meeting with the mayor, I told her it now appeared my abductor had abandoned the truck van and now drove a red Mustang. I gave her the license plate number and Angie promised to pass this on to Lamar.

Feeling a small sense of accomplishment, I headed toward Boots' address, stopping along the way for aspirin. I chewed as I drove.

What were possible reasons for the cousin deliberately choosing to call from Tilman's office building? He could have called from his motel room or the Stop 'n Go next door to the insurance building, or anyplace else along his escape route. Unless he wanted me to know where he was. Perhaps to point me in the direction of the man who'd hired him—Mr. Tilman. Or Tilman's nephew, Boots?

But if he'd deliberately led me to Tilman's insurance company, why warn me about harming Robby if I kept prying?

Tilman himself, who'd been close to his niece, had no obvious reason to want LeeAnn dead. He was a wealthy man in his own right. LeeAnn had worked for his company while living in Beaumont. According to the receptionist, Tilman and LeeAnn had shared mutual respect and affection. I'd seen the smiling photo of LeeAnn and her parents standing beside an elder-looking Tilman, all with their arms around each other. But no Boots. Certainly Boots had been reluctant to talk about his uncle. Why?

43

Several minutes later, I turned onto a farm-to-market road, barbed-wire fences lining cow pastures on both sides. The smell of freshly cut hay crept inside the Honda and I again rolled my window down. A mile or so later, I spotted a free-standing white mailbox with <u>Callahan</u> written across it in black scroll lettering. A painted iron statue depicting a grinning black boy for a hitching post spoke of the age-old prejudices that still abound in east Texas. Boots's iron gate was open and I turned in, scrutinizing the vista at the end of a long gravel drive.

Wheat acreage surrounded a white clapboard, two-story house with a faded red barn about a hundred feet away. LeeAnn had stood there with her horse, smiling for her brother's camera.

The sky above was a painful, piercing blue. I tooted my horn to let Boots know I was coming, thinking I could drive up this road forever, smelling country air filled with sweet hay and clover. Drawing closer to the house, I spotted four dormers atop the roofline, each aimed in a different direction. A slate roof extended over a deep wooden porch supported by multiple white columns that marched around the house. Early twentieth century would be my guess.

Boots strode outside and stood waiting on the front porch as my car came to a stop. Dust from the gravel tickled the back of my throat and my exit from the car was accompanied by a round of sneezing. Boots's expression as he came down the front steps appeared welcoming.

He noticed my gimp. "You okay?"

I nodded and he placed his hand under my elbow, guiding me up the steps to a rocking chair. He sat beside me, eyes filled with concern.

Looking incapacitated in front of my client was not part of my plan. "This is a beautiful house," I said.

"Yep. Sure is. Built in 1910. I'd give you a tour but there're a couple guys painting the downstairs."

Only then did I notice the back of a white beat-up van parked on the other side of the house with a <u>Gutierrez Painting</u> sign across the rear doors.

"That's okay," I said. "Perhaps another time."

"So tell me why you're limping."

"Two men took me on a ride in the country. One of their dogs took a dislike to me and chewed on my leg awhile. The men enjoyed that. It'll be fine," I added, not liking the excitement that sprang to his eyes.

He leaned closer. "Is this over you looking into my sister's death?"

I stared out at fields of wheat bending in unison, feeling the cool breeze against my flushed cheeks. Did I have a fever? I turned toward Boots and nodded. "Yes. Someone doesn't want me snooping. Any idea who?"

"Shoot. If I knew, I wouldn't need you, now would I?"

His tone of condescension was hard to miss. I was beginning to see Dr. Zoesky's point that LeeAnn's biggest problem was her brother.

The pains in my leg were growing stronger and I felt suddenly parched, as well as the need to stall and gather my thoughts. "Do you have any cold water?"

Boots looked startled and then guilty as he rose to his feet. "Sure thing. Should' a offered you something right away. Beaumont's a far piece from Houston."

He disappeared inside the house and I began to mentally priori-
tize my questions. Drinking the entire glass once he returned took
another minute or two. He stood over me as if ready to snatch my
empty glass and refill it.

"This is fine," I said. "Thanks."

He remained standing.

"Sit down, Boots. Please."

He did, but scooted his rocker a bit closer to mine. "Tell me what
you've learned and about the men with the dogs."

I did as he asked, ending my recap with the police finding me after I dragged myself to the main highway. The police part was not exactly true, but close enough. I mentioned Robby's possible abduction
from the mental ward by a man posing as our cousin; that he was one
of my abductors, and that the same man had placed the threatening
phone call from Tilman's office in downtown Beaumont.

"You think those guys killed my little sister?" Boots asked.

"No," I shook my head. "I think they were hired to scare me off
the case." Before he could ask another question, I said, "I'd like to
meet your uncle."

Instantly, Boots's demeanor turned wary and he drew back.
"Why?"

"For one thing," I said, "he could tell me about LeeAnn. Give me
a different perspective."

"I gave you all the perspective you need," Boots said, frowning.
He wore black cowboy boots which reminded me of another question
for later.

"Where's your uncle now?"

Boots scratched his head, tilting backwards until his rocker leaned
against the house. For a full minute, he appeared lost in thought. "I
guess it won't hurt to tell you." He swung forward, stopping the mo-
mentum of his chair by stomping his boots against the porch flooring.

"My uncle's a private man. His staff knows, but the word in Austin
among the legislators isn't out yet. He wants it to stay that way."

Filled with curiosity, I swallowed a sneeze and waited.

"He had another stroke. He's resting in a rehab kinda spa place near Austin. Last I spoke with his nurse, it'll be months before he's ready to leave. Speech lessons, hell, walking lessons if you must know."

"That sounds difficult to keep quiet," I said.

"Not if you're the Great Tilman, it aint." Boots spat on the porch as if ending an unpleasant topic.

"I gather you two weren't close," I said.

"You got that right. Anything else you want to know?"

"Yes. Why did my abductor choose Tilman's insurance company to place his threatening call to me? Why not a pay phone? Why not his motel phone?"

"You're the detective."

I let his comment hang in the air, felt his body tense, his good nature evaporate.

"I'm trying to be, Boots. That's why I read a copy of your parents' and your sister's Last Will and Testament."

He jumped up and stalked to the nearest porch column, his empty chair now rocking a ghost.

When he spoke, his voice was filled with venom. "Why'd you do that?"

"You're a rich man, Boots."

"So? I was rich when my parents died."

"Oh? Your sister was trustee over your share. Are you saying she passed it all on to you immediately on their death?"

Boots shook his head as if I'd greatly disappointed him. "Whether she did or didn't has nothing to do with how my sister died."

"Does the fact she'd been pregnant have anything to do with her death?"

As if I'd fired a gun in the air, he pounced and with two giant steps, was in my face. "Who told you that?" His breath was hot and his mouth curled into a snarl. I half expected him to grab my collar.

Silently, I stared back, his eyes darker blue than I'd ever seen them. His breath was ragged and he stayed hunched over me for a few seconds before straightening, his eyes now focused on the horizon. As silence descended, I listened to the distant lowing of cattle.

When he spoke it seemed intrusive, shattering my limbo.

"You'd best tell me who told you."

"How did you find out, Boots?"

"Who said I knew?"

"Just admit it. You knew."

"So what if I did?"

"For starters, I have a copy of her life insurance policy. If LeeAnn decided to keep the baby, you'd lose out on her life insurance money. Which you'd lose out on, anyway, if the police ruling of suicide remained on the books. You know Texas law. Her policy was taken out less than two years prior to her death. Is that why you hired me?"

"You're walking on thin ice, lady," Boots said.

"Did you talk her into an abortion, Boots?"

That wasn't exactly the way I'd intended to question my client. Whether I was disappointed or truly suspicious didn't matter. Boots was no longer the devastated, grieving older brother I'd identified with. He stood to gain from his sister's death.

I'd already dug myself into a hole, so when all I got from Boots was a look meant to kill, I dug myself deeper. "You know the father's identity, don't you? You were there the night LeeAnn was killed, weren't you?"

I couldn't hear his teeth grind, but I saw his jaw working and imagined he wanted to slug me.

"Get off my land, lady! You're fired! Get it? I'm firing your ass!"

Boots grabbed my shirt and lifted me out of the rocker. "I want your final written report and any money comin' back to me, you better send post haste."

He marched me down the porch steps. The sound of an approaching vehicle caught us by surprise. With his hand still on my shirt, Boots and I watched a white vehicle encircled in a shroud of dust speed toward the house. When the HPD police car screeched to a halt, Boots eased his grip. We watched Lamar Hightower pile out the passenger side.

Lamar grinned our way and headed toward the porch.

"Now aren't I the lucky one? I get to see my beautiful ex-officer by accident, when all I expected was to talk to this ugly guy here." His look was that of a man telling a funny joke.

"Thought you'd want to know we're reopening your sister's case." He glanced from Boots toward me, his eyes widening as he noticed Boots's fist on my collar.

Boots let go, but reached behind to the small of my back and shoved, hard. I stumbled down the steps, crying out as my ankle twisted painfully and I fell.

"You can stay, captain, but I want her gone or I'm calling my own cops!"

Boots turned on his heels and marched back toward the house shouting, before he slammed the door, "Come inside captain, but not before you get this bitch off my property."

Lamar helped me to me feet, mumbling under his breath. "I'll help you to your car."

He settled me in the front seat, leaned down and snarleld, "What was that all about?"

I told him my suspicions about Boots's need for money, and the elevator guard's statements of seeing a man of Boots's description leave the scene of the crime. I didn't mention LeeAnn's pregnancy.

Lamar's sympathy for my indignities at the hands of my now-ex-client didn't extend as far as letting me off the hook. He flung facts at me. There were three witnesses to Boots's whereabouts the night LeeAnn died. Two were women Boots met at a party thrown by a friend. The three of them ended up at Sammy's Bar and Grill on Louisiana Street. The bartender remembered Boots, his female guests and the time of night. When LeeAnn fell to her death, her brother was buying his fifth round of whiskey for women who would later reward him for his generosity.

Lamar ended with a challenge, "The only way Boots could be involved is if he hired Brad Ewer and J.D. McGraw to throw that girl off the balcony. You gonna tell me you support that theory?"

I remained silent, digging my nails into my thighs in a feeble effort to redirect pain away from my ankle. Lamar wasn't through. "I've reopened the Callahan case. I thought we could work together on this. I came here to assure Boots we'd keep you in the loop. But not now. I'll lock you up if I catch you snooping."

Almost as if he didn't trust himself to say anything further, Lamar straightened, took a few steps away before doubling back to my car window. "You okay to drive?" His voice held an undertone of sympathy.

Pressing the accelerator, I tore off, eyes straight ahead, stinging with tears. I preferred the captain's anger.

44

onytail was asking for it. In my face, asking for it. Jerk! I was writing on the wall since I'd run out of paper for heaven's sake. He said he'd stop giving me pot if I didn't quit. I said shove it up your ass and ran away. I ran and ran and ran and ran until I got to the freeway. A lot of running.

No money on me. I'm very very tired and I'm very very hungry. So I wrote a wheel of choices on my palm. Dr. Winthrop said writing is good. And writing a wheel of choices is even better. One always has choices, young man, he says. I wrote all my choices on my palm and stared at it with the sounds of cars buzzing in my ears. Then it came to me that after being mean to me Jelly is always good to me and even if she bugs me about my medicine she is family and even if the government pays her to spy on me she spends the money on me and pays me to take pictures and spy on other people which I really like. So. I'll head back to her place and this time without stupid ponytail who stole all Jelly's papers and now since I drew the wheel of choices I know ponytail is a spy, too, but he doesn't love me like Jelly loves me and so I can hold out my thumb and hitch a ride back to Jelly and she may report this to the government but she loves me and says I am all the family she has and she will give me something to eat.

I am very very tired and very very very very hungry.

45

In the spirit of Scarlett O'Hara, tomorrow was another day. I awoke late morning, but without the leg pain I'd had in Beaumont. The doctor said I could swim, but no jogging until she checked me out, which wasn't for another two weeks. I blamed a lack of exercise for my ennui of body and soul.

After a thirty-minute swim, I stepped on the elevator, still wrapped in my terrycloth robe. I took it slow up the stairs to the bathroom, washed my hair, applied antibiotic to the stitches, and re-wrapped my ankle and calf. Once dressed in navy slacks and a white shirt, I pulled on thick socks and tennis shoes. Suzy wrapped herself around my ankle and howled, reminding me to feed her.

Downstairs in the kitchen, I stroked Suzy's back while she attacked a pile of chopped liver. The poor cat spent most of her time alone. But then, so did I.

Even with the swim, my spirits stayed in the pits. I kept seeing the captain's face as he flung Boots' alibi at me. But everything he said should have been in the police files. Had he removed information on purpose? Or was I being paranoid again?

I left the hi-rise in search of a new computer. If the captain thought he'd scared me away from this investigation, he didn't really know me.

Three hours later, I was back at my desk, only a little tired and achy. My new portable computer was smaller and faster than the old one, and I was good-to-go on the internet. Chicken nuggets, a couple of aspirin, and a cup of coffee promised I'd be perky in minutes.

First on my list was a final written report to Boots and calculation of how much of his retainer I'd used up. After double-checking my moral Geiger counter, I charged Boots for my new computer. It was LeeAnn's investigation that got the old one stolen. If time proved me wrong, I'd reimburse him and asterisked a post-script to that effect.

Calculating my medical insurance payments, I realized I still owed the hospital a goodly amount for my four-day stay. Boots should pay for that, too. Re-adding for the third time, I allowed myself a deep breath. Boots was in debt to me by $229.75. An amount I was willing to forego. Not that I had any choice in the matter. I placed report and invoice showing "paid-in-full" in an envelope. After addressing and stamping it, I took it downstairs and shoved it through the outgoing postal slot.

Back at my desk, I entered Ramsey Tilman's name and read his history: ten years in the Texas House of Representatives and six of those as chair of the state insurance committee. I had switched to the Chronicle archives when my cell interrupted.

It was Adam Franklin, my little Thai assistant medical examiner with the American name and mode of dress. "I got your message. Sorry it took so long for me to get back to you. How're you feeling?"

"I'm fine. Not sure I ever thanked you for coming to my rescue at Brazos Bend."

"You can thank Keymap for that. One call to my contact at HPD and they went east looking for you while Keymap picked me up and we headed west."

Not anxious to rehash my alligator experience, I continued, "I was hoping to ask you more about the paraffin block. If I managed to get a hair or toothbrush, or cigarette butt from Brad Ewer, could you run his DNA against the tissue samples?"

Adam paused a beat too long before responding, "I knew when I met you at the restaurant it would come to this. I don't want to be responsible for another attack against you. How do you plan to get a sample without getting caught?" He lowered his voice, "I wish I'd never gotten involved in the first place. You could have been killed."

"But I wasn't, Adam. You want LeeAnn's murderer to go free?"

"You don't know she was murdered," Adam said.

"If you don't think anything is suspicious about her death, then why did you bring the samples to my attention?"

"Because the police didn't do their job."

"That's right. And now, I'm doing my job, which is to find out who fathered her baby." When no response was forthcoming, I added, "I absolve you from any responsibility. If I get in trouble, I'll never mention your name."

"And if you end up dead?"

"Then I sure won't mention you name."

Silence.

I sighed loudly, desperate to get my point across. "Are you Buddhist, Adam?"

"Yes."

"Then just look on my death as an opportunity for me to return to a higher level of enlightenment."

❧

I dialed Brad Ewer's house and his wife answered, "Hello?"

"Cathryn? This is Giles Faulkner. I wanted to thank you for the lovely evening last Friday. Keymap and I enjoyed it a great deal." Now, more than ever, I wished I knew Keymap's real name.

But instead of demanding who Keymap was, she mumbled something polite. I rushed ahead, "I'm going to be in your neighborhood and wondered if I could stop by and talk a bit about LeeAnn Callahan?"

"I'm sorry. I have nothing to say."

"Yes, but I know she worked at Hammerly and knew your husband. You attended the rodeo party the night she died, correct?"

"I'm out the door for an appointment and will be out most of the day. Perhaps another time." She hung up the phone.

Hmm. She was leaving the house. But someone of Cathryn Ewer's status would have a maid.

Quickly changing clothes, I pulled on my television repair shirt with its large logo on the pocket, khaki green cargo pants, and black workman boots whose laces I couldn't pull quite as tight around my ankle as the last time they were used.

After strapping a tool belt around my waist, I pulled television repair business cards from my desk drawer, and headed for the elevator. All this paraphernalia was only in case I got caught by a maid. Inside my pocket was a very-illegal but handy tool which unlocked any human-made security device that could be opened with a key.

In less than ten minutes, I pulled off Kirby and onto Lazy Lane, parking a yard from the gated entry of Brad Ewer's River Oaks mansion. It wasn't long before a silver Lexus convertible came zooming out, top down. I barely had time to drop against the floor board after catching an image of Cathryn Ewer's blond hair blowing free.

Adam had reluctantly agreed to start DNA testing, but only if I brought him a sample today. I looked at my watch. Three p.m. Anxious to get him something before he changed his mind, I was out the car door, heading toward the Ewer's driveway, when the ring of my cell sounded from inside my pocket.

It was Keymap. "Sorry to be so late returning your call. I'm out of town. What's up?"

With no desire for a lengthy discussion, I told him I'd been fired, but that Adam would perform a DNA against a Ewer sample which I hoped to soon have in my possession.

"Where are you?"

"On Lazy Lane, outside Ewer's house," I said.

He groaned a little too loudly. "Don't do this. You need back-up. Can't you wait till I return? One more day won't hurt. Besides, I can easily get you one of Brad's cigarette butts. You'll get yourself caught going inside."

"Check you later," I said, and punched the off button.

At the property entrance, a decorative iron gate dipped low enough in the middle for me to climb over.

Hurrying up the drive, I reached the front door, breathing hard. As I looked inside glass-panels flanking the massive wooden front doors, I saw no one. But the distant sound of a vacuum meant the maid was somewhere on the first floor.

In less than a minute, I'd unlocked the door and slipped inside. Adrenaline pushed me into overdrive and, after closing the door, I crouched and listened, my pulse rushing blood to my head. The maid vacuumed the big party room beyond the massive front entry, loudly singing a Pavarotti aria above the noise.

Still crouched, I headed up the winding stairwell on my left. Behind a mahogany paneled door on my left, I discovered Brad's home office, almost as large as the one downtown except without the view. A large mahogany desk stood against the wall on my left while floor-to-ceiling bookcases and a wall-mounted flat-screen television appeared opposite. A dark red leather sectional sofa rounded the far corner for easy television viewing.

One quick look and my heart sank. The maid had already cleaned; a strong smell of lemon wax and gleaming white porcelain in the attached bath told me nothing of Mr. Ewer would be found here. At least, not to the naked eye. A spotless Waterford ashtray sat atop Ewer's desk, and a quick investigation showed the trash can was emptied. I slipped out the study door, feeling relief over the continued noise from below.

The Ewer's master bedroom was positioned around the corner. Picture windows looked over the back of the house and the wooded bayou beyond. It appeared equally as large as the party room below. A quick dash around the room, and my heart was still thumping out of my throat. Too clean. Already done. The huge bathroom with his and her walk-in closets might be more fruitful. It wasn't as if Ewer were bald.

Dark suits and sport coats lined one wall of Ewer's closet, starched shirts the other. Shoving jackets apart, I searched among them, looking for a stray hair. I even shoved my hand inside the pockets, hoping for a cigarette butt. Unfortunately, Ewer was too fastidious or too wealthy to collect half-smoked cigarettes.

Suddenly, the house grew quiet. The vacuum was no longer running and the singing had stopped. I scurried back out into the hallway, holding my breath. Murmurs wafted up the stairwell. The maid was talking on the phone.

Back inside the closet, I cursed myself after spotting a rheostat. Light would certainly help, Giles. Once the space was lit, I scanned hanging jackets for a pale color, more likely to show a darker stray hair. The edge of tan ultrasuede caught my eye. I held it up to the light and, swiveling it on its hanger, spotted a small, dark hair clinging to the collar. Quickly removing it with tweezers from my belt, I placed the hair inside a small zip bag, also from my tool belt, and replaced the jacket.

Back at the top of the stairwell, I was about to descend when the front door flew open and Cathryn Ewer entered. Crap! She said she'd be gone all day.

"Roberta," she called out, slinging her bag onto the entry loveseat. All she had to do was crane her neck upward and she'd spot me. I took one tentative step backward, my heart slamming painfully. Would she remember my face from all those party guests? I'd still have too much explaining to do.

Cathryn continued away from the front doors and back toward the party room, her sandals clicking against the tile floor. I must move. Now.

"Dios! Que pasa?"

The voice came from behind me. A quick glance—female wearing black uniform, feather duster and startled brown face—and I'd been snagged. Instead of replying, I took off. Stupid, Giles, to think Mrs. Ewer would employ only one maid.

I silently praised the rubber soles on my work boots as I executed a sharp turn on the stairwell, running for all I was worth. From behind, the maid screamed loudly, using Spanish hysteria unfamiliar to my limited vocabulary.

Even my ankle didn't hold me back as I dashed out the front door. From behind, the sound of Cathryn's heels on tile urged me faster. Instead of heading down the visible, long driveway, I turned and fled to the side of the house, veering around back. I'd have to flee toward the bayou. Thick undergrowth would do a good job of hiding me, but it would also delay my trip to the ME's building.

Frantic female voices came from the front of the house while I dashed toward a clump of azalea bushes. I didn't think they'd seen which direction I fled. Pain shot from my ankle as I scrambled for cover and landed on my stomach.

Peeking around, I saw no one and sprang up, panic driving me as I rushed on through low undergrowth, thick with ferns and azaleas, toward a bank of oak trees reaching for the sun. Beyond the trees, the bayou flowed, its waters swollen from recent rains. I hoped that water was all it was filled with.

Alligators be damned, I hurried down the slope toward the bank, fighting bushes that grew from ankle to waist. I followed the bayou's course upstream and away from the Ewer's house. Thick foliage kept me from seeing where I could climb up the bank and out onto the neighbor's property. Later, I'd worry how to get to back to my car.

Traversing a winding five minute walk along the bayou, branches scratching my hands and face, I figured I could risk a peek at what lay above. With aching leg muscles, I climbed upward, grabbing at limbs. Almost at the top, I flattened against the ground and peered over the ledge at a sprawling red brick monster a hundred yards on my right. Surprisingly, a bridge appeared on my left with cars zooming past. I'd made it to the bend in Kirby Drive where, if you kept going straight, a bridge led you onto Shepherd Drive.

I was farther from the Ewer's than I'd thought. Crouched like a monkey scrounging for dropped bananas, I scooted toward the direction of street traffic before venturing to stand upright.

The bayou ran underneath the bridge. Reaching it, I climbed up the bank and headed south, keeping to the shoulder of Kirby Drive. From behind, the sound of a siren grew closer. My instinct was to scramble back down and hide. Instead, I continued ten or twelve feet to a large oak tree and slipped behind it, waiting for the siren to pass. A police car whizzed past and turned right two streets up ahead. Lazy Lane

Feeling relatively invisible behind the oak's low spreading branches, I stripped off my shirt, turned it inside out, and pulled it back on. I left a few shirttail buttons undone and tied the tail ends at my waist. The underside of the logo stitching was almost invisible, and inside out, looked considerably cleaner. The tool belt was too expensive to dump so it stayed on my waist. I would stash it in the trunk of my car.

While sticking to the shoulder of Kirby, I walked a few minutes before turning right into Lazy Lane. I had my story in place. Approaching Ewer's house, I saw no patrol car. The officer was probably talking with Cathryn Ewer and her maids.

Annoyed over my limping gait, I headed to my Civic. If I only had a new car with one of those remote entry keys, I'd be inside it in a flash. Instead, I pulled keys from my pocket just as a policeman exited the Ewer's entry gate and spotted me. He shouted.

Beside my car now, I inserted the key, plopped in the seat and turned the ignition. The officer started to chase me, hesitated, then ran back up the drive, presumably to his car.

Executing a U with one hand, I reached down with the other, unbuckled my tool belt, and stuffed it underneath the passenger seat. I retrieved my cell and small billfold from the glove box, and glanced in the rear view mirror at the twirling red lights now out the gate and gaining on me.

Swirling lights flashed in my rear-view mirror. I turned right onto Kirby then edged slowly toward the curb.

With both hands on the wheel, fingers of my right hand clutching my small wallet, I waited for the police officer to reach me. Only when he leaned over and knocked on my window, did I move to lower it. He needed to see my hands at all times.

I hated to think I was perfecting my lying skills, but it couldn't be helped.

"What's up officer?"

"Need to see your license, Ma'am," he growled. After snatching it from my fingers, he straightened. "I don't like having to chase you down."

"I apologize. I had no idea it was me you were shouting at or I would have stayed put," I said, smiling brightly.

"I want you to pull your car further off the road," he said, "and put on your emergency blinker."

I reached my hand out to retrieve my ID, but he just shook his head. "Pull over and then exit your car nice and easy, if you don't mind."

Staring at my ID, the policeman walked a few feet away and spoke into his walkie-talkie. He'd know the truth in about fifteen seconds. Instead of appearing surprised when he clicked off, he only said, "I'll be just a minute."

Traffic on Kirby slowed and I imagined swiveling stares as drivers ogled my predicament.

By the time his female partner came jogging around the corner, I was burning hot. Sweat stung open scratches on my face and hands and my armpits were sticky. Only after his partner performed a thorough pat down, embarrassingly thorough, did she declare me free of weapons.

"Let's go," she said and led me over to the patrol car where she shoved me down in the back seat. No one spoke as we turned off Kirby and back onto Lazy Lane.

Perhaps my appearance would confuse Cathryn. She'd only seen me in a strapless black dress escorted by Keymap.

We pulled up the drive. The female officer told me to stay put and exited the car after her partner killed the engine. He got out and opened the back door, keeping a hand on my arm as he helped me out.

At the bottom of the entry steps, Cathryn and two uniformed maids stood talking to the female officer. As we approached, all chatter ceased.

By that time I'd sneaked a look at my captor's name plate: B Yardley .

"Any of you recognize this woman?" Yardley addressed them.

One maid looked doubtful. The other wore a triumphant expression, speaking rapid-fire Spanish to the female officer who nodded with total understanding. Cathryn's reaction needed no interpretation.

"This woman, officer, is Giles Faulkner, a private investigator." Her voice rose in volume with every word. She practically spit out the remainder. "She called me earlier and wanted to come to the house and talk. I told her I was leaving and would be gone all day. Which I would have been if I hadn't needed to come back and search for a credit card. My return was the only thing that scared her away."

Not exactly true, but I wasn't in a position to argue the point. Just then I felt a trickle ooze down my forehead. My hair had covered a scratch on my forehead that only now had decided to ooze. Crap! I was a cooked goose.

Yardley turned to me and said, "You're lucky these ladies verified nothing's missing from the house. Can you explain yourself before I book you for breaking and entering?"

I frantically searched my memory for an attorney to call. Instead, what came out of my mouth was far calmer than the frantic activity in my brain. "I'm on a case. Call Captain Lamar Hightower, Homicide Division, and he'll explain."

My heartbeat grew stronger as I shoved shaking hands inside my pants pockets. You fool, Giles. Lamar won't come to your rescue. In fact, he'll tell the cops to put you behind bars.

Yardley's face was expressionless as he instructed his female partner—he called her Francis—to keep an eye on me. Then he turned and walked back to his car. Standing beside these women while Cathryn shot daggers at me made me wish I were in jail. Not really, but Yardley's return a few minutes later was more than welcome.

"Francis," Yardley said. "Stay behind and get Mrs. Ewer's and her maids' signed statements while I drive Ms. Faulkner back to her car." He grabbed my arm and we walked away.

"Are you just letting her go?" Cathryn shouted. Yardley stopped suddenly, turned and walked back. I heard him ask if she wanted to press charges against me. That Cathryn's name would undoubtedly be in the newspaper if she chose to do so. They conferred several minutes in an undertone before he returned and led me out the entry gate.

He opened the back door of his car and waited, silently, while I settled in the seat.

More silence for the minute drive back onto Kirby Drive where he drove off the road and parked behind my Honda. When I reached to open the door, he stopped me. "I don't need to lecture a fellow police officer. Even one who's left the force. But you're one lucky PI."

I couldn't resist the bait. "She won't file charges?" I ventured.

"That's not the half of it."

Curiosity wouldn't let me stop. "What did the captain say?"

Yardley leaned closer, eye to eye contact. "He said to tell you that's your last get-out-of-jail-free card."

46

As I headed toward Old Spanish Trail and the ME's office, I hoped Cathryn wouldn't blame her maids. It wasn't their fault. From watching Cathryn, I doubted she spoke much Spanish. All Texans should learn Spanish. We'd soon be a majority Hispanic population. Why fight it?

I glanced at the clock on my dashboard. A quarter to five—only fifteen minutes before Adam left the lab.

With one minute to spare, I pulled in the ME's parking lot. Adam Franklin stood outside the side entrance, glancing at his watch. His hair—brass-colored spikes—was hard to miss. I started to honk my horn, then thought twice. No need to advertise. Turned out it wasn't necessary. My Honda parked outside the Thai restaurant that fateful night must have been imbedded in his brain.

He saw me and waved, hurrying toward me as I pulled in front. After stopping the car, I reached under the seat for the tool belt. Opening the car window with one hand, I burrowed inside one of the belt pockets with the other and withdrew the bagged sample.

"This has got to be Ewer's hair," I said. "His wife would never let her roots go this dark."

"Where did you lift this from?"

"Jacket collar," I answered, rather smugly.

"Then how do you know it wasn't from one of his honeys?"

In spite of knowing Ewer's reputation, Adam had obviously never seen the man's guest powder room before.

"Because," I replied, "the gentleman prefers blondes."

Adam looked doubtful. "Give me a few days."

I waved him off and he trotted back to the building.

Back home, I stripped, slathered alcohol over my cuts, pulled on my sweats and resumed an online search for any information about the lawsuit between Hammerly and the Fenley Group. After more than an hour, I was about to fix a martini for medicinal purposes when I came across a blurb about an out-of-court settlement between the two companies.

Reading it through, I recognized the attorney's name representing the Fenley Group and had to smile. Justin Lane. He'd been a fellow student in several of my law school classes and had pursued me until, one night, I broke down and told him all about Robby, ending with our father's abandonment. That was our last date. After that, I'd convinced myself I was emotionally unfit to have a boyfriend. What was my excuse, now?

Picking up the phone, I dialed information and let them send the call through. Justin was probably married with children. A woman's voice answered, sounding beleaguered. I heard a child crying in the background. Bingo.

She gave me Justin's office number. One reason not to marry ambitious attorneys is that they're never home. I dialed and Justin answered, sounding equally stressed.

"Justin? This is Giles Faulkner. Remember me?"

"Who?" he asked. So much for the 'Gee I've missed you' response.

"Giles Faulkner. We were in a couple of law classes together. It's been almost ten years, so I can't expect—"

"Giles! My heavens, girl. How are you?"

That response was much nicer. "I saw your name in the paper. You negotiated a settlement between Hammerly and the Fenley Group."

"Yeah, yeah. What's your interest?"

Now he sounded like an attorney. "You may not remember, but I dropped out of law school. I'm a PI now and on a new case. In a round about way, it involves the CEO of Hammerly. He and his chief counsel were both witnesses to a death last March during rodeo."

"Yeah, I remember. What's that got to do with the settlement agreement?"

"Maybe nothing. But I wondered if you'd share with me whether Hammerly took a beating on the settlement. It's the Hammerly part that interests me."

Pause. "Can you give me half-an-hour then meet me someplace for a drink? I'll tell you what I can."

I hesitated, thought about his assertive tactics so many years ago, then dismissed it. He and I were both a lot older. Plus, I was ninety-nine percent sure he was married and instinctively gave him credit for being a faithful husband.

"You name it," I said, before adding I needed an hour lee-way to get dressed. That was a lie, but I'd suddenly remembered Logos, Ltd., the entity that wrote monthly checks to LeeAnn. I wanted a fifteen minute search on the web while it was still on my brain.

The search took less than five. One interesting fact about Logos Ltd.: it was an oil, timber, and farming company whose partnership interests were held by LeeAnn's parents as well as Ramsey Tilman. LeeAnn's generous monthly checks were most likely dividend payments for her deceased parents' interest in the company. Since LeeAnn had been trustee over Boots, I wondered if Boots's share had been included in LeeAnn's checks. That could explain why her lifestyle, although not penurious, lacked evidence of lavish spending. Unless, of course she was a heavy, but secretive gambler. I didn't have time to use a search program for LeeAnn's credit rating, but wrote a mental note to do that when I returned home.

Hotel Derek was located at Westheimer near the 610 Loop that ran an inner circle around Houston. When the hotel appeared ahead on my right, I turned in. Traffic around the hotel was congested, with scurrying valets and cars lining the circular driveway. Parrot-colored bouquets of flowers in tall brass urns flanked the hotel's beveled glass front doors.

Valets tended to stall out my Civic. Besides, I needed the $8.00 almost as much as they did. This was my litany as I looked for street parking several blocks away. One U-turn later, I found a spot on the street, pulled over and parked.

After ordering a martini with a twist, I looked around the dimly-lit room, crowded with suited, shiny lawyer types. Laughing over their latest trial won by whatever means. I could have been one of them, but had long ago lost the desire.

Anticipating this swanky hotel crowd, I wore a white silk blouse and an altered-to-fit deep burgundy suit of Aunt Eunice's. One of those affairs that can go dressy or not, depending on what you do with it. I even wore the only black leather pumps my foot didn't protest over. Even with a slight limp, I felt almost prissy, not counting my ankle bandage.

As the bartender shoved a martini toward me, I noticed two men, jackets slung over their shoulders, leave a corner booth. I pushed through the crowd, feeling piggish as I scooted into its expansive padded leather seat. From this vantage point, I could easily see those who entered.

My glass was almost empty when a man hurried inside the bar, craning his neck around the crowded room. Feeling cheery, I stood and waved until he caught my eye. Even if his blond hair was thinner,

Justin hadn't changed that much. I only hoped the same was true for me.

Smiling, he slid inside the booth. "Still drinking martinis?"

He hadn't made any motion toward an air kiss or a hug. Perhaps he remembered that about me as well. "Yep," I said. "Some things never change."

"Your brother's situation. That changed any?"

When I shook my head, he sighed. Scooting out, he stood and walked over to the bar, not wanting to wait, apparently, for table service.

He returned a few minutes later with a beer and mug. He poured the bottle slowly into the iced mug, turning it golden amber. "Sorry to hear that about your brother." And then as if he'd been rude, "Man, I've been married too long. Want a refill?" He pointed to my martini glass.

I shook my head. "Nope. I'm happy."

"Are you? Happily married?" he asked, his eyes somber above the rim of his mug.

"Happily unmarried." My response sounded purposely cheerful.

He set his beer down, laughing. "Good for you."

"When I called your house, I heard a child crying?"

Justin grinned, "Yeah. Susie's a year old. Smart as a whip—"

He looked puzzled when my laugh interrupted. "My cat's named Suzy."

He held up his mug and motioned me to do the same "Here's to our little Susies."

We clinked glasses and drank, mine now empty. I pushed it away, leaned forward, arms resting on the table top and said, "Okay. Formalities over. Tell me about Hammerly."

"Wellllll," he furrowed his forehead and puckered his mouth, reminding me of this familiar gesture from our law school days. "Hammerly and Fenley settled, as you know. The sum wouldn't interest you. Less than a mil. But Fenley did get TSP's list of contributors. Know about them?"

I knew he referred to the non-profit organization, Texans for Sound Policy, behind the smear campaign against the Fenley Group.

"Was Hammerly a contributor?"

"Not the main one, but certainly significant. Fenley Group went away happy this was exposed. Hammerly got its hand slapped with a fine."

I leaned back in the booth and frowned. "Is that it?"

The din in the bar was a mere notch below rowdy. Motioning me closer, Justin hunched over the table, cocking his head until his mouth almost touched my ear. "Both Ewer and McGraw are being targeted by the FBI."

Startled, I switched position until my lips were now almost in his ear. "Why?"

He continued our head dance. "Did you valet?" Justin asked before downing his beer.

"I'm down the street a couple of blocks."

"Maybe your car would be best," he said, already sliding out of our booth.

* * *

The two of us sat inside my car, windows up, air conditioner blowing.

"I trust you can use my information for your own purposes and not reveal your source or have to prove up anything by me," he said.

"Sure. I promise," I said, my curiosity about to burst an artery.

"This is all rumor. You know how that goes. Feds are buttoned up, asking questions, poking around. But when word finally gets out, there's usually some truth behind all the rumors. Too many connections among law enforcers, too many opportunities for a leak." He loosened his red silk tie, and inspected his nails. They looked as if they'd just been buffed.

I was about to get pesky over his unnecessary preamble when he spoke, letting each word stand on its own.

"The rumor is stock fraud." At my look of shock, he said, "Not a word of this to anyone and that's all I'm going to say."

While my brain scrambled to land this news into its proper slot, he turned the door handle. I grabbed his arm "Wait. How long has this been under investigation?"

Justin opened the door and placed one foot outside on the pavement. "I started hearing about it maybe ten months ago. Somewhere in there. Gotta go." He was all the way out, holding the door open with one manicured hand when he stuck his head back inside. "By the way, you're as tempting as ever. I'll meet you for a drink anytime. As long as it's not business." Then he was off, hurrying back toward the hotel.

Ignoring his flirtatious invitation, I sat in shock over his news. Stock fraud? That was federal prison time. That was lose-your-wife time. Go-crazy time. Avoiding that was enough to kill for. But how did LeeAnn fit into this?

I burned a U and headed toward Westheimer. Passing Hotel Derek on my left, I glanced over and my heart sank. Brad Ewer stood at the edge of the curved drive, watching me drive past, his arms crossed, his face screwed into a scowl. His eyes seemed to burn into mine.

Crap! Had he seen me with Justin? He couldn't know what we'd talked about, or could he?

47

Home less than ten minutes, I was pulling on my sweats when the lobby buzzed that a Mr. Brad Ewer was downstairs and was it alright to send him up? I hesitated. By now he knew I'd broken into his house. My emotions urged me to slip my gun inside my waistband, while my brain said Brad wasn't here to kill me. I hoped. Instead of arming myself, I said, "Tell Mr. Ewer I'll be right down." The lobby was a better place for a confrontation, if that's why he'd come.

I descended the elevator, my pulse racing. The concierge pointed a finger toward Ewer at the opposite end of the lobby, pacing beneath the painting above the fireplace.

From across the room, I saw his mouth moving as he muttered to himself, his hands clasped behind his back. Uh, oh.

"Mr. Ewer," I spoke up, wanting to give him a few seconds to take a deep breath, calm down for whatever it was he had to say to me.

He heard me and swirled, his eyes hard as flint. "You." He took giant strides toward me and grabbed my arm, pulling me closer. Venturing a guess at such close range, I'd have to say his blood pressure was far too high.

"Yyyou!" he struggled to spit out the word. "You take one more step inside my house and I'll . . . I'll . . . "

I wrested out of his grasp, determined not to show he was hurting my arm and took a step back. "Shall we sit?" I walked toward a pair of chairs near the center of the lobby, a round table between them. I remained standing beside one of the chairs. I wouldn't sit unless he did.

He walked close behind me, stopping only when I did. I faced him and said, "I find your proximity to me offensive. Back off!" We both stood our ground. Out of the corner of my eye, I saw the concierge staring.

Ewer's heavy breathing, his closeness, his forward stance was intended to threaten me. It didn't.

And then, he decked me.

୬

The next I knew, a shaft of morning sunlight stabbed my eyelids where I lay in bed on top of the covers. Suzy began a licking frenzy against my cheekbone. My head felt the size of a pumpkin, bruised and throbbing. I tried to raise my head off the pillow. Mistake.

A thick bandage encircled my head, confusing me until my memory surfaced of the concierge carrying me upstairs—a female doctor bending over me, her hair smelling of shampoo and murmuring I'd cut my head against the table when I fell.

After several attempts to sit up, I managed an upright position, my head in my hands while leaning back against the headboard. After less than a minute, a piercing ring from the bedside phone split my head in two.

It wasn't the phone, but the buzzer from downstairs. "Dr. Camron is on her way up."

"No. Really, I'm fine. Tell her I'm fine." But there was nobody on the other end.

The concierge let the doctor inside my apartment. She hurried up the stairs and into my bedroom, looked in my eyes, examined the back of my head and left me three pain pills to take when needed. I was headed for the shower, head throbbing, when the bedside phone rang.

"This is Giles."

"You sound like the night of the living dead," Adam spoke. The little Thai Assistant ME spoke too loudly for my tender ear.

"I am the living dead," I croaked as I struggled to talk without moving my jaw.

"What happened?"

"Hangover," I lied. "Any news on the sample?" In spite of the pain, my heart was thumping with abandon over possible DNA results.

"Yeah," he said. "Negative. Sorry. Worked overtime, too Sure it wasn't a hair from the wife or girlfriend?"

At that point, I couldn't be sure of anything. Nor was I positive I could utter another word.

"Thanks. Later." I hung up, now seriously focused on pain relief. Scrapping the idea of a shower, I shuffled back toward the bed and swallowed one of the doctor's pills.

When I awoke, the clock said noon. My screaming head-ache felt slightly abated, and my jaw only protested when I tried to move it from side to side. The message button on the phone beside the bed blinked insistently. I sat on the edge of the mattress and reached across to punch playback. There were two messages.

"This is Sandra Connor calling for Giles Faulkner. I understand from a man called Keymap that LeeAnn's brother hired you to investigate her death. He said you sent him to interview me, but still I'd rather send what I have directly to you. You'll understand when you get it. Please don't try and get in touch again. You'll soon have everything I ever had from LeeAnn. I just want to be left alone."

Patience was never my long suit. I started to head downstairs and check my mail when I heard the middle of my second message. The voice belonged to my sometime savior who'd lately been missing in action.

"Giles? It's Key. Just got a call from Sandra Connor. Apparently she was feeling the need to unburden. She couldn't get a hold of you on the phone. Told me you'd be getting a FedEx package today. An "important package" were her exact words. You're at home, so don't know why you're not answering your phone."

Even if I felt brain-injured, I caught his remark about me being home. How did he know? I could easily be away, in my car, in jail, whatever. I wasn't wired or I'd know it.

Moving tenderly, I took the stairs one at a time and checked outside my door. No package. After calling the front desk, they promised to let me know when it arrived.

Suzy howled, rubbing frantically against my ankle. After feeding her, I toasted bread, buttered it and tried to eat. Failed miserably. Toast wasn't worth the pain of chewing. Instead, I brewed a cup of tea .Why was herbal tea always more comforting than coffee?

I tried not to let my anger at Ewer explode. It would do my head no good. Besides, I had entered his house uninvited. More than once. I wondered what the building staff had done after he socked me. Handcuffed him? Somehow, I doubted it. He'd most likely been escorted to his car and warned not to show his face again.

With tea in one hand, an icepack against my jaw with the other, I went inside my office and logged onto the computer. After almost an hour of attempting, one-handed, to enter findings and fit puzzle pieces together about LeeAnn's death, I let my aching head and twitching eye convince me to head for the couch. First I opened the travel book of Egypt and retrieved Mary Nelson's instamatic photos of the guests at Brad's sky-box party.

With a fresh bag of ice and clutching the pictures, I plopped heavily on the living room sofa. Where had I heard about LeeAnn gloating over putting her lover behind bars? I spread Mary's photos on top of the coffee table. When I remembered LeeAnn's co-worker, Juliet

Ralston, who'd driven LeeAnn home after her abortion, my spontaneous cry, "ah, ha!" brought an instant stab in my jawbone and tears to my eyes.

Why hadn't I immediately thought of LeeAnn's vow when Justin told me about the FBI targeting Brad and J.D.? LeeAnn must have known what the FBI didn't know yet, but was trying to find out. She had, after all, worked for Hammerly before leaving for a job at Alliance. Had she left Hammerly because she knew about stock fraud? Did Brad and J.D. know she could incriminate them? Then again, the FBI had been wrong before.

I was ruminating over the various ways to perpetrate stock fraud when my Blackberry rang. It was the captain.

"We think we've got the man who posed as your cousin, Giles. Your abductor. Maybe Robby's, too. Can you come downtown now for a lineup?"

Nothing could stop me. Full of excitement, I stood quickly and just as quickly dropped back onto the couch, my head bursting with tiny black stars, the room spinning. I decided to treat myself to a cab ride downtown.

It took half an hour to make it to police headquarters. Ten of that was spent attempting to change clothes without dropping my head from an upright position. The sight of my face in the bathroom mirror was a shock. With a swollen jaw, a blood-filled right eye, and a blossoming purple bloom against my temple, I decided makeup was futile. I'd only look as if I were trying to hide a beating. The truth, actually. Perhaps not teaching classes on family abuse was a good thing for now.

After paying the cabbie, I stepped out across the street from headquarters. Orange cones cordoned off the entire block. Two abandoned bright yellow bulldozers perched atop the street's broken blacktop as if waiting for a choreographer to set them in motion. Downtown workers bustling along the sidewalk probably enjoyed the break from construction noise as much as I.

Once inside the building, I repeated the requisite screening requirements, but this time, the receptionist said I was to meet the captain on the fifth floor.

The elevator opened to the overpowering smell of fresh paint. Stepping off, I wondered who'd chosen the wall color. Puke green would have been at the bottom of my list. At least it was spotless. Across the hall, a view of closed doorways ran the length in both directions.

From my left, I saw Lamar heading toward me. When he reached me, he stared, alarm spreading across his face. "What happened?"

"My face met a fist," I said.

"Whose fist?" He sounded ready to kill someone.

"Your good friend and good citizen, Brad Ewer."

He clinched his jaws, eyes narrowing into slits. "Want to press charges?"

"Right. And then his lawyer will ask me what I was doing posing as a repairman inside his house? I think that's called 'unlawful entry.'"

Lamar shook his head, forcing his face back into non-committal status. "When did this happen?"

"Last night."

"How're you feeling now?"

"Shitty," I said.

Lamar held my arm gently and led me down the hall, muttering something to the effect that he should have put me in jail. We stopped outside a closed door mid-hallway and he said, "You know the routine. Take all the time you need."

My heart hammered as I went through the door. The room held a long, narrow wooden table with three wooden chairs positioned behind it. The chairs faced the opposite wall of solid glass for viewing lineups. Fluorescent ceiling lights cast a yellow tint over the room, but behind the solid glass partition, the lighting was stark blue-white. I'd been in interrogation rooms before, just not this particular one.

Lamar introduced me to the only person seated at the table. He was the sergeant who, Lamar said, had caught up with my assailant at a Lake Charles motel room. The officer looked to be in his twenties with dark straight hair cut short, and a flattened nose. He sat military straight, chewing on a toothpick.

The captain closed the door. We three were the only ones in the room. The young officer's name was Smithy. He shook my hand after I sat down. "It'll be just a minute, I'm told," he said.

After Smithy shot his third surreptitious look my way, I leaned toward him and whispered, "I ran into a wall."

Lamar stood beside the table until the door cracked open. A young officer poked his head around. "Ready, Captain?"

"We're ready," Lamar said, and took the seat beside me.

The only door leading into the glassed-off room opened and a line of five men shuffled inside. A voice over the speaker system told them to spread out and look straight ahead. My assailant stood second from the right, hands clasped behind him, his face unmistakable. With greasy hair pulled back in a thinning ponytail, his overly large ears appeared plastered to the side of his head as if someone had flattened them. His familiar smirk was mixed with a nervous flitting of his eyes. I knew he couldn't see me. He knew I could see him.

"Second from the right," I pointed.

"Second from our right," the Captain echoed, followed by instructions over the speakers for the man to step forward, out of line-up. He did.

"That's him," I said.

"Positive?" Lamar asked.

I nodded and the captain scraped his chair back. "I'll walk you to your car."

"Wait. I want to know about Robby. He knows where my brother is. I want to be there when you interrogate him."

Lamar didn't answer. Instead, he led me out into the hallway and turned to thank Smithy. The two men shook hands and Smithy hurried toward the elevator. I called out a "thank-you" to his back.

He turned and waived his acknowledgment with a satisfied grin. "You're the one called in the Mustang's plates," he shouted back.

I really did love the police. I just didn't want to be one of them.

Turning to Lamar, I tried again. "Please. At least let me listen from the hall, write down questions for you to ask."

He looked unhappy, but staring into my face would make anyone wince. "Okay. Follow me."

48

My abductor went by several names. Twice he'd been arrested for drunk driving, once for identity theft, twice for assault, and last for suspected armed robbery. Nice fella.

I stood in the hallway outside a much smaller interrogation room with one-way glass panes on either side of the doorway. Lamar sat opposite the man whose real name was Williford Henson, aka Willy. A tape recorder sat on top of the table. I'd scribbled a few questions for Lamar on a piece of paper now placed beside the recorder.

After turning it on, Lamar read Willy his Miranda rights and began. "You've been ID'd by the woman you abducted, Mr. Henson. Kidnapping is a federal crime. You could get fifty years, or life. Maybe be out in time to select your own coffin."

When Willy didn't respond, Lamar glanced down at my questions before continuing. "You've also been identified as visiting Robert Faulkner shortly before he escaped from Herman Hospital's mental ward. Two kidnapping charges and you'll die behind bars."

Henson glanced up, then away, his reply garbled.

"Speak up, Mr. Henson." Lamar's voice rose a notch but remained in the polite zone.

"I said, I don't know nothin' about any of that and I want to call my lawyer." He bent over and gave a loud sneeze.

I grinned. Gotcha, you creep!

"Haven't booked you on anything, yet." Lamar said.

"Then I kin leave?"

"Not quite yet." Lamar leaned forward. "You cooperate with us, and I'll think about reducing kidnapping to aggravated assault. Several years versus a lifetime behind bars."

"Cooperate how?"

"Lead us to the person who hired you."

"I think I'll take my chances on a lawyer," Henson said.

Lamar leaned back in his chair, withdrew a pack of cigarettes from his shirt pocket. The captain didn't smoke. He held the pack out toward the prisoner. "Want one?"

Henson hesitated before accepting a cigarette and a lit match from Lamar.

Giving the prisoner time to smoke, Lamar looked on with a benign expression before he spoke again. "Listen up. If you think the jerk who hired you is coming to your rescue, you ought to re-think."

Henson drew the last of his cigarette just as Lamar reached for the tin ashtray and flicked it across the table. Snuffing out his cigarette butt, Willy blew smoke above Lamar's head. "Don't know his name, anyhow."

I could feel the tension from out here. A police officer I'd never seen before had drawn up beside me, also listening. My body was humming and for once, the pain in my jaw and head took a back seat.

"How'd he contact you?" Lamar asked.

"A buddy of his. I was at The Hitchin' Post, drinking beer."

"When was this?"

"Saturday night 'bout eight eight or ten days ago," he said.

"Can you identify this buddy?"

"Nope. Never seen him before. Never said his name or his friend's name, neither, in case you're full of hypothesizing and all."

"What about your partner in the kidnapping of Ms. Faulkner? Where's he now?"

Henson shrugged. "He took off. Said he was traversin' to Mexico. Demanded half, but I only gave him a thou. He took the van and I had to buy a car. No reason it should come out of my share. Besides, I planned it. It was my deal, not his. And I want what you said in writing."

"What? My promise to reduce the charge to aggravated assault if you cooperate? It's on tape."

"How do I know that's all I need?"

"You don't," Lamar said. "You just have to trust my word. Would you recognize the go-between if you saw a picture of him?"

Willy nodded.

"I need you to speak out loud," Lamar said.

"Yep. I would."

"What about an artist's rendering?"

Willy looked confused, so Lamar rephrased his question. "I'd like our police sketch artist to sit with you and draw while you describe this man's features until you're satisfied with the likeness. Could you do that?"

Willy pointed to the pack of cigarettes. Lamar's gesture said he could help himself. The prisoner picked up the book of matches Lamar threw on the table and lit up. "So I can go see this artist now?"

"She'll come to you." Lamar scribbled on a sheet of paper before looking back at Willy. "How much money were you given and what were your instructions?"

"The man gave me half, three grand, and said I'd get the other half when the little woman quit nosing around LeeAnn Callahan's death."

Somehow I was disappointed to be worth only six-grand.

Lamar leaned across the table, "How was he supposed to contact you?"

"Said he'd find me. Not to worry."

"Why the trip to Beaumont? Why place a threatening call to Ms. Faulkner from there?"

"Jes to scare her some. I wuz thinkin' if I got her frettin' over her brother, that I'd give it a day or two to gesticulates, you know, and then call back and ask for big bucks to return him." He pulled smoke from his cigarette, cheeks sunken like a cadaver. "I'm no dummy. The rest of my money might never come my way and whaddo I do 'bout it? Nothin'!"

"So," Lamar said, "what happened to your scheme to ransom Robert Faulkner?"

"Gul-durned fool took off. Knocked me over and took off."

"Where and when? Did he take off in a car?"

"Motel 6 off I-10. The idiot took off on foot a couple a days ago."

"You still haven't answered why Beaumont and not someplace else?"

"Cause I thought he might uh run there. Hitched a ride."

"Why would you think that?"

"Cause one time when he'd had too much to drink, Robby tol' me he knew somebody who had a relative livin' there. Some big muckety-muck who owned an insurance company and was a big powerhouse in the Texas Legislature. Like Robby was hot stuff jes by association." He ended with a huge sneeze.

I stood, stunned. Two unrelated thoughts flew into my head at the same time. Willy sneezed just like the person who'd Tasered me at LeeAnn's storage facility. The more urgent thought was how could Robby possibly know Ramsey Tilman? And if he knew Ramsey, the relative could be none other than LeeAnn Callahan. Or could it be Boots?

I leaned against the glass wall to steady myself. Suddenly, everything changed.

When Lamar discovered I'd arrived by cab, he offered to drive me home.

Neither of us spoke while I sat, like a stone, in the passenger seat. Perhaps I was feeling the same as someone who'd just witnessed a head-on collision, or a building explode into flames, or a child knocked twenty feet from the impact of a speeding car. No shock, no anger or denial. I merely breathed and waited to feel something, anything.

"You hurting?" Lamar asked.

I didn't respond. What does a person do when everything true turns false? When what you took for granted grows suddenly meaningless? I felt naked and more unsure of my place in the world than I'd ever felt before. If my brother wasn't who I thought he was, then who was he? Who was I?

Now the drawing I'd discovered in his empty hospital room made sense. It <u>was</u> of LeeAnn Callahan. And the guard's description of the man walking away, down the corridor with the startling, pale eyes? My brother.

I began to shake, but gritting my teeth was out of the question. So was crying. I was too numb for tears, anyway.

Lamar pulled off of Kirby, into the circular drive of the hi-rise, and stopped the car. "Please, Giles. Take a pain pill and go to bed. You're asking for a breakdown, little girl."

Without responding, I got out and walked through the revolving door of the building. I stayed beside the sign-in desk until Lamar drove off. Unwilling to go up to my apartment, I walked back outside and asked the parking attendant for my Honda. I should have searched Robby's room more thoroughly a long time ago.

※

Mrs. Cathcart seemed unnaturally horrified at my presence, until I remembered what I looked like.

"My goodness, child. What happened to you?"

"Nothing major," I said. "I'm here to inspect Robby's room, if that's okay with you."

"Of course. You pay the rent, honey, you can come anytime."

I followed her toward the back of the house to Robby's room. When it looked as if she intended to stay, I turned.

"I need to do this alone, Mrs. Cathcart."

I shut the door behind her and got to work. Robby's bags of pills were inside his bathroom. Pills he needed. An aspirin bottle stood above the sink, and after checking the contents, I swallowed three. There was nothing underneath the toilet lid, or the shelves filled with towels, and no other drugs but aspirin.

Inside his bedroom, I discovered more drawings of LeeAnn Callahan at the back of his desk drawer. Renderings in colored pencil and in charcoal that captured her both off and astride her horse. The sketched backgrounds were either of the Houston Rodeo arenas or its horse stalls. Rodeo took any and all volunteers, and my brother did know horses. How else could he have met LeeAnn?

Underneath Robby's bed, a black cowboy hat rested alone, leaving a dust-free outline on the floor when I grabbed it. LeeAnn's initials were stitched on the inside label. I sat heavily on the floor beside his bed, the smell of girl-sweat and hay wafting from the hat on my lap. No tears came. No sobs of "I can't believe this is happening." After a few minutes, I left, shutting the door behind me. With the black hat tucked underneath my arm, I hurried away as if it might scream like a story book character, alerting everyone to its theft.

Now that you have evidence that places your little brother at the scene of the crime, Giles, what next?

49

B ack in my apartment, I picked up the kitchen phone to order a pizza for supper. It was my younger self telling me I needed to eat something. As a child, whenever I grew upset, Mother would say that eating would settle me down. Of course, I'd been a skinny kid and she probably just wanted me to eat, no matter my mental state.

I buzzed downstairs and alerted the front desk about my pizza. There was always a staff member willing to carry take-out food to an apartment owner. Checking my billfold, I made sure I had a couple of dollars for the tip and twelve for the pizza.

After fixing a cup of hot tea, I walked into the living room and peered out at the blanket of white clouds perched high in the sky, poised as if waiting to be enveloped by an eerie green sky forming beneath.

I opened Aunt Eunice's large armoire and clicked on the TV weather channel. Another hurricane in the Gulf could turn our way. If it did, it was a day away from Houston. So far, the worst storms of the season had bypassed us, but now, with Hurricane Lola threatening, we may have congratulated ourselves too soon.

Swiveling rapidly in the easy chair, I stared blindly out the window. A barrage of emotions raged through my mind, along with a powerful need to lash out at Robby. How could he do this to me?

How could he be so sneaky? My thoughts ranged those of any parent whose child had turned into a stranger. It should have been easy for me to laugh at myself. I hadn't given birth to Robby. But I wasn't laughing, and nothing made sense.

Robby had never killed any living creature. Yes, my brother had a quick temper and used his fists, as he'd shown in Dr. Winthrop's group session recently. But LeeAnn had fallen to her death. What had Codger said? It was a calculated push, not a powerful shove that had sent LeeAnn over the balcony railing. If it were possible for Robby to shove LeeAnn off the balcony, he would have done it in a rage, unaware of the consequences.

In spite of a steady diet of aspirin, my temples continued to pound. I stretched out on the couch, conjecturing on leads that could point to someone other than my brother as a murderer.

LeeAnn had known about the stock fraud, had threatened to expose Ewer, and he'd killed her. But if the hair sample I'd snatched from Ewer's jacket had been his, he hadn't fathered her child. So could he still be the boyfriend LeeAnn had sworn she'd put behind bars? What about J.D.? He was chief counsel for Hammerly. He'd go to jail along with Ewer. Tomorrow, I'd somehow get a sample from J.D. Perhaps Keymap could retrieve one of the man's cigarette butts. Did Keymap know J.D. as well as he did Ewer?

The ring of my doorbell interrupted my thoughts. I paid for my pizza plus tip, and carried the box back into the living room. No plate, no fork. Setting the box on the coffee table, I pried back the lid and picked up a steaming slice topped with pepperoni, jalapeno and melted cheese. Chewing carefully, and taking longer than ever to eat, I eventually managed to make a pig of myself. Cold pizza was good for breakfast, so when I finished three slices, I put the remainder in the refrigerator.

While washing grease from my fingers, I heard the phone ring. I dried my hands and picked up the kitchen receiver.

"I heard what Ewer did to you," Keymap said. "Don't worry. I'll take care of his sorry ass as soon as I'm back."

"Who told you about that? Where are you?"

"Tallahassee airport and word gets around. By the way, I talked Sandra Connor into giving me that package. I'll be there in three hours. Want to wait up?"

"Of course." I hung up the phone, excitement mixed with irritation at his one-up-man ship. What was inside this package from Sandra? Hopefully nothing to further implicate Robby. I buzzed the front desk to let them know I expected Keymap in a few hours.

I glanced at the clock. Eight p.m. He'd be here by eleven. With an effort at discipline, I planned to go over all of my notes again. But before heading into my office, I'd take another look at Mary Nelson's snapshots, those she'd taken at the rodeo sky-box party the night LeeAnn died.

Ten minutes later, I was still staring through a handheld magnifying glass at a picture of two girls, both in profile, one talking, one listening. The photo was grainy, but not so poor you couldn't identify them. LeeAnn was the one with wavy blond hair cascading from under her black cowboy hat. In profile, her mouth appeared to be twisted in disapproval, her eye squinting at the girl talking.

The young lady speaking to LeeAnn was hatless. I'd seen her before, but where? Her hair was light brown, straight and cut on the diagonal—shorter in the back, sweeping longer toward her chin, cupping where the hair tucked slightly underneath her strong jaw line. She appeared animated, caught with her pretty mouth open, neither happy nor sad.

The Chronicle sometimes featured high-profile Houstonians attending exclusive parties. I spent the next hour and a half in my office, on-line with back issues of the paper. I found a snapshot of Brad Ewer wearing a tux standing beside his wife, Cathryn, in a long evening gown. Also a younger J.D. when he was made chief counsel at Hammerly, his tall, severe-looking wife at his side. The two couples were frequently photographed together at social events.

In one photo taken at Houston Rodeo over a year and a half ago, Brad and Houston's mayor stood side by side as Brad awarded a blue ribbon to the ecstatic young owner of a prize steer during Houston Rodeo.

About to give up, I scrolled down when suddenly it was as if I'd pulled the lever and three sevens popped up. Four photos among many attendees at a Muscular Dystrophy fund-raising event last June showed the young woman I sought. Her shorter hair-style at the rodeo party had thrown me.

Peggy, J.D.'s daughter, stood between father and step-mother, posing with her lips planted on her father's cheek, both parents beaming proudly at the camera. In another shot, Peggy stood beside her father, his arms around her, her head tilted up toward his face. Another photo caught Peggy near the right corner of the image, her father square in the middle. She gazed at J.D. with a wistful, almost longing expression as he leaned over to hear whatever a small boy of perhaps seven, sitting in a small wheelchair, was saying to him. In all of them, Peggy's hair hung in waves to her shoulders, similar to the style I'd seen her wear at Brad's recent cocktail party, only a few inches shorter.

The last newspaper photo was of her laughing, head thrown back, where she sat at a table among other privileged young ladies.

I shut down the computer, leaned back and rubbed my eyes. So Peggy and LeeAnn knew each other. What did that prove? But J.D.'s daughter had been at the sky-box party and talked to LeeAnn. She could have returned during the guard's bathroom break. I had no motive, but added her to my list of suspects.

Pulling out the center desk drawer, I grabbed my hastily scratched notes from the police files. I'd added another dead bolt to my front door, but still felt this drawer was a lucky hiding place. What that said about the thief who'd ransacked my office, I wouldn't dwell on. Desk drawers would have been my first place to search.

The doorbell rang just as I glanced at the time. Keymap wasn't due for another half hour. I glanced through the peephole but saw only the back of a black jacket. Keeping the chain secured, I unlocked the front door and cracked it open, fearful for a second that Ewer had snuck past the front desk and was back to slug me again.

Whirling around, Keymap grinned. "I'm glad to see you're finally being cautious."

I slid off the chain and let him inside. "You're early."

"We had a tailwind."

"As in a hurricane tailwind?" I asked.

He just shook his head "It's coming our way, though. Don't suppose you have any gin in the icebox?" In spite of his sexy baritone voice, he sounded tired to the bone.

His black silk shirt was pulled from his jeans and there were smudges of purple beneath his eyes. A black backpack drooped from his left shoulder to the point it was in danger of sliding onto the floor. His obvious weariness awoke tenderness in me. Just in time, I stopped myself from giving him a hug.

"Sure," I said and gestured for him to walk ahead of me into the kitchen. So I could admire his tight-fitting jeans? Slow down, Giles.

His pack hit the kitchen floor with a thud. Turning, he placed both hands on my shoulders.

"Let me have a look." He cupped my chin and turned my head toward the ceiling light, emitting a low whistle of appreciation. "That's a beaut, all right."

Not the sympathetic comment I'd hoped for. When he dropped his hand, it left heat against my skin. As if sensing my awkwardness, Keymap retrieved a lemon from the fridge, peeled it like a pro and plopped the yellow curls in our glasses.

We settled in the living room, he on the sofa and me in the easy chair opposite. He appeared in no hurry to show me Sandra's package. But then, he probably needed to drink his martini first.

A silence descended as we listened to the wind, the clink of ice in our glasses while we sipped. I wasn't surprised when he rummaged in his backpack and retrieved a CD. Again making himself at home, he ambled to the stereo before returning to the sofa.

"Wassenaer's Concerto Grosso. Eighteenth Century. Cool stuff."

The sound of strings floated in the air, but I'd had enough of his procrastination. Tired or not, he needed to hand it over.

I set my drink on the coffee table, feeling almost normal as the pain in my jaw and head receded. "What did you bring me?"

Keymap's drink must have de-stressed him. He smiled slyly, "It's worth a lot."

"I'll pay you! Just show it to me."

Expelling an exaggerated sigh, he reached in his backpack. "Guess I couldn't expect to find you in a playful mood."

He withdrew two large manila envelopes. He kept one and passed me the other. The name "Sandra Connor" swooped across the front, underlined with a flourish from a black felt-tip pen.

I opened it and withdrew a typed letter, signed and notarized. It was addressed to the FBI and dated February 2nd. I read quickly. LeeAnn stated that she had been asked to notarize the execution of options to buy 50,000 shares each of Hammerly Insurance and Trust at a stated price per share by stockholders Brad Ewer and J.D. McGraw. They had executed these options January 3rd, backdated the paperwork to July 14th of the previous year, and resold these shares on January 31st of this year.

Keymap watched me closely and when I was finished and almost out of my chair, he said, "I've already checked. A year and a half ago, those shares were selling for a little less than half what they are today. When they sold those shares, each man pocketed over a million each."

"And the other envelope in your hand is a copy of the stock option she mailed to herself, signed and return receipt directive, correct?"

"I'm impressed," he said. "Yep. Proving beyond a doubt that those two men broke the law. Jail time. All the FBI needs to put them behind bars is right here."

"So the two men somehow discovered what she'd done but had no idea where this evidence was kept, maybe tried to get it out of her on the balcony that night, and when she wouldn't give, shoved her over."

"Sounds logical to me," Keymap said. "According to Sandra Connor, LeeAnn gave her both envelopes, saying under no circumstances to turn them over to anyone. Not the police, not the FBI, no one. It was only for back-up in case she needed it down the road."

"But then LeeAnn died. Why didn't Sandra go to the police then?"

"Until a month ago, she was involved in a child custody battle with her ex. Didn't want any bad publicity."

I took a sip and let this information sink in. No reason LeeAnn couldn't have had a single parent as a best friend. I moved on. "Sandra said she was going to FedEx me a package. Is this it?"

"This is it. Caught her at a good moment, I guess. Called her since I was close by on other business. Just to check in. She said she'd been getting threatening phone calls, warning her that if she had anything from LeeAnn Callahan in her possession, she'd better return it to Brad Ewer. When she mentioned she was sending it to you, I convinced her you'd get this sooner if she let me carry it back to Houston tonight."

I wasn't sure I approved. Any bill he might give me for this added service would go unpaid. I hadn't asked him to follow up with Sandra, but that potential conflict could wait. "Were the threatening calls from a man or woman?"

"A woman."

Thinking aloud, I said, "It could have been Janet, Brad's first lady at the office. She'd be capable of that. Protecting her boss."

"That means Ewer would have told her."

"Not necessarily. Maybe she figured it out for herself. She's bound to be privy to the company books."

"There's so many ways to hide that kind of crap it's unbelievable." Keymap jumped up, raising his empty glass. "Want another?"

I did and I didn't. "How about half?" I held mine out. He grabbed it and returned to the kitchen, talking louder as he prepared our drinks.

"Tell me what you've been up to while I was gone. Looks like you got yourself in a pile of trouble." He returned to the living room with two martinis. Mine looked more than half-full. With a smoothness that startled me, he removed the paper and envelope from my lap and settled himself on the sofa.

I frowned, debating for an instant whether to snatch them back. Instead, I replied to his comment.

"Not a 'pile of trouble' as you call it. I got inside Ewer's house. And," I jutted out my face, trying to play cute, "obviously paid for trespassing with a banged-up jaw."

Keymap locked his eyes onto mine. He wasn't buying it. "I worried about you the entire time I was gone."

The CD stopped. I couldn't look away from him, his parted lips made darker against a sliver of white teeth. Tremors skipped up my spine. If an invisible connection between two people could be struck by lightening and the charge pass through both bodies, it would have burned us alive. I blushed and looked away. His presence was too intense, too larger-than-life for comfort. How had he insinuated himself into this case, and my life, so smoothly? Too smoothly. And now he was taking ownership of evidence I needed.

"I can take care of myself, Keymap."

He leaned back

"Sure you can." He studied me for a moment before dropping his head. "You know, I was eighteen when my father remarried. Mother left us when I was ten. It's too much of a cliché, but she really did run off with the yard man. He strangled her two years later and is still behind bars.

"For several years my dad buried himself in his oil company. During those years, I grew up pretty fast, or so I thought. When I turned sixteen, Dad began to notice me. Began focusing his attention on me, all his devotion, if you will, being his only child. Sometimes I soaked it up and sometimes I resented the hell out of him. So when all that changed with his new wife, I figured it was as good a time as any and left home." He looked up at me as if he was a professor in class and I was his student.

"Sometimes Giles, we are our own hangman. Don't get me wrong. I did fine. After two years of drugs and too much booze, I joined the marines. Won't go into that, but I came out with a career. And a missing foot."

He pulled up his left pants leg, showing a black sock around an ankle too thin to be flesh. Especially on a man his size. I tried not to act shocked or surprised, but I was both. No wonder his gait was irregular.

"Now, I work only for those I want to work for and on my own terms," he said, jerking his pants down over his ankle. "I make good money. Get to the bad guys before they get to me. After a few fiascos early on, I learned when to cry for help. To use my contacts, old buddies from my marine days. Sometimes, I simply can't go it alone."

"I heard you had three wives in three different states."

His eyes seared into mine. "I'm not going to grace that stupid rumor with a response." He patted the seat beside him as if he were calling a dog.

I ignored him.

"Giles, listen to me." He leaned forward, arms resting on his thighs. "I want to help you."

I cleared my throat. "Thanks, and when I needed your help, I asked, and you did your job and then gave me a bill. I expect you'll do the same for those envelopes you brought. Fine. I'll pay you so there'll be no question as to ownership."

"What about facing Ewer with what you know?" He waived the other envelope in his hand before dropping it back on the sofa. "You want to do that alone?"

When I didn't respond, he spoke again, softly this time, "And Robby?"

My heart stopped and I grew instantly alert. "What about Robby?"

"I heard the police want to question him about LeeAnn's death."

He might as well have slugged me in the stomach.

"Wake up, Giles. You want to get yourself killed over your brother?"

"Just because the police want to question Robby doesn't mean he's guilty. Or haven't you learned that yet?"

He let an awkward silence grow before he spoke again. "Your loyalty is touching."

His eyes bore into mine before they softened, a small appraising smile on his lips.

I felt as if he were stripping me naked. Blushing, I looked away first.

"Why isn't a beautiful woman like you married?"

For a second, I sat stunned, but when anger exploded inside my head, I sprang out of the chair. "What is wrong with you men? Marriage equals happiness? Since when? Ask me how many married men hit on me and I'll tell you the answer to that stupid question!"

His expression said he wasn't fooled.

"It's Robby, isn't it? You're so busy caring for him, you have no time for yourself. I repeat my question. Are you willing to die for him?"

Arms crossed, clutching my elbows, I paced. I always thought better on my feet.

"Why not? I should be you? You don't have anyone you'd die for, do you? You probably started that rumor about wives all over the country."

I stopped and stared at him. An image of my brother behind bars replaced that of Keymap. Robby, guilty of murder in the first degree. Dropping my head, I fought back tears.

"Hey," Keymap murmured. "Look at me. You okay?"

When his voice sank into that intimate bedroom croon, I lost all composure. Swamped by a numbing sensation, I sat hard in the chair. Something about his tone and its affect on my body was alarming. Turning my face away, I nodded hard that yes, I was okay. But my head throbbed anew, and this sudden agony grew overwhelming. I covered my face with both hands and sobbed, unable to hold it to-gether any longer.

Before I knew it, he'd hurried around the coffee table and grabbed me up in a quick, tight hug. My spine tensed and it must have felt like he was hugging a tree.

Easing up, he pulled back enough to take my face in his hands as gently as if I were priceless china. Before I could object, he began planting soft kisses along my jaw line until he reached my forehead. Closing my eyes with one thumb, he tenderly kissed my eyelids until my face burned. When he pressed his cheek against mine, his stubble pleasantly tickled my skin. My body flushed.

Mentally, I was upstairs in the throws of passion with this hunk, when the invasion of facial hair against my cheek grew from pleasur-able to slightly irritating, almost painful. The spell was broken and it was all downhill from there.

I slid out of his arms. "Don't," I said. "You should leave now." I shuddered, stifling the sound of my own harsh breathing. I couldn't get involved with a man I knew nothing about, who made a point of being mysterious.

Keymap reached for me. "I understand, Giles."

But I'd already pulled out of reach of his force field, feeling more alone than ever.

"You can't possibly. Please go."

He stood silent, looking at me for what seemed forever before he turned away. With my back to him, consumed with regret, self-pity, and feeling like a hard-hearted bitch, I heard him rustling around, perhaps retrieving his precious CD before finally shutting the door behind him. It took a minute for me to calm myself, forget the look on his face as he'd drawn away from me—a mixture of sadness and cynicism—but when I did, I hurried over to the couch.

He'd taken the evidence with him.

50

Several times during the night, I awoke with my heart racing. What had frightened me? The wind? From inside the building, its low howl was barely discernable. I went to my bedroom window and looked across the street where oak trees swayed, their limbs moving in a gentle, melodic rhythm. Nothing scary. I watched as the first rays of the sun turned a smoky haze in the sky to salmon.

More than once during the night, I'd turned on the bedroom light and, to still my mind, flipped through Aunt Eunice's atlas. She loved showing me places she'd seen, the odd ends of the earth where one or another of her husbands had taken her.

"I want you to see the world, Giles," she'd said to me more than once. "Your mother never did." When she added that I needed to be tough, she hadn't meant overbearing like my father. Aunt Eunice's edict was for me to stand up for myself, put myself first. But then my aunt never had a handicapped brother. Eunice's only sibling was my mother, who'd grown up to be a soft-spoken woman with very different dreams. In the last months of her life, my mother had whispered more than once that all she ever wanted from life was there, under our roof.

I wasn't like my mother and I'd be damned before I'd turn into my father. But what was I to do about Robby?

On my second cup of morning coffee, the phone rang. It was the Terminator, disguised as Brad Ewer.

"I owe you an apology, Ms. Faulkner. I'm in meetings all day but wondered if I could stop by on my way home this evening and bring you a little something. Something to show how sorry I am."

I stifled the impulse to reply nothing would make up for his assault, but only because I wanted to talk to him, too. "That would be fine," I replied and hung up.

As of last night, both Keymap and I were privy to information we were required by law to turn over to the federal government. Neither of us wanted to end up in prison, so I would not be recording any conversation with Ewer over stock fraud. For a moment, I wondered if Keymap was a strictly-by-the book detective and had already turned LeeAnn's proof over to the feds. My stomach soured at the thought. I couldn't let them arrest Ewer for fraud without knowing who had killed LeeAnn.

Surely my brother was innocent. For him to be in possession of LeeAnn's cowboy hat proved he'd been there that night, but not that he'd shoved her over the edge.

Dressed in sweat pants and T-shirt, I sat on the sofa and watched the television report on hurricane Lola. It appeared that Galveston, as well as other coastal towns, was in for a killer storm. Forty-eight hours ago, Galveston Island had started mandatory evacuation.

Our mayor warned Houston residents to collect water, batteries, and board their windows if possible. The thought of being in this hirise during a category three hurricane didn't appeal to me, but if it struck Houston, we now had until midnight to prepare.

Houston's city populace should be off the streets and hunkered down within a couple of hours. At this late date, an evacuation order would mean evacuees stuck on the freeways, running out of gas and patience. Our building could withstand any level of hurricane winds, or so we were told. Lola might be its first test.

Robby was out there somewhere, perhaps joining the idiots who gave hurricane parties on coastal beaches, only to wash ashore days later, their partying days over for good. He'd gone over a week without meds, which meant there was no predicting his behavior.

Thinking I should take this storm threat seriously, I followed our mayor's prudent advice, and joined Houstonians standing in line for water at the grocery store and then fuel at the gas pumps.

An unbelievable five hours later, I was back, exhausted, inside my apartment. Waiting in long lines, I'd had plenty of time to plan my strategy for a Ewer confrontation. Anyone facing federal prison was bound to be unstable. After retrieving my gun, I sat with cleaning solution and pipe cleaners, the barrel resting on the coffee table. I had no intention of using it, but this preparedness frenzy of mine demanded a clean weapon.

The update on hurricane Lola was not good news. It was headed in a 60 mile-wide swath straight for Galveston and downtown Houston. I hoped it wouldn't scare Ewer away from our appointment.

I was swabbing the bore of the gun barrel when my doorbell rang. Leaving it, I cracked open the front door and slid off the chain to greet a panic-stricken Santa.

"Giles!" She hurried inside. "Can I stay here for the night? I'm petrified of hurricanes!" She practically shook with fear, her arms crossed over her chest, her complexion drained of color.

"Hey," I gave her a quick hug. "We're fine for now. Lola won't hit for another six hours."

"I won't be any trouble," she pleaded.

"I'm expecting a visitor any minute now, Santa. Why not come over in two, three hours? I need to meet with this man alone."

"Is Robby coming?"

"Not Robby."

"Oh. I'm sorry. So could I just go upstairs until the man leaves?" She looked morose enough to cry.

I gave her another quick hug, kept one arm around her and led her across the hall and inside her apartment, murmuring that I was sorry, but this meeting called for privacy.

Santa's television blared predictions of doom and destruction. I switched it off while she wrapped herself in a blanket, leaving only her small fiery head exposed where she huddled in the corner of her sofa. If she'd stuck her thumb in her mouth, she'd resemble a red-headed Linus. "Want me to fix you some hot chocolate?" Her air-conditioner setting would keep raw meat fresh.

She nodded, so I scrounged around her kitchen for milk and Nestles, mixed the two in a cup and set it in the microwave. After bringing her the steaming cup, I sat beside her and waited until she'd drained the last bit.

"You okay now?" When she nodded, I rose. "I'd really appreciate you waiting until eight o'clock before you come over. We'll have a slumber party."

She turned large pleading eyes toward me. "Okay. But I doubt I'll get much sleep."

I left her and returned to my apartment. The door stood open a few inches, but then I hadn't locked it after leading Santa away. I closed and secured the lock and returned to my gun-cleaning after muting my television set. A wide swath of green and red swirls on the screen left no doubt Lola headed our way.

Thud. The noise repeated itself, at first a slow repetition before picking up speed. Sounding as if it came from the kitchen, I snapped the loaded cylinder shut and with the gun inside my waistband, rose, pulling the hem of my T-shirt down as I moved slowly toward the kitchen.

Robby stood, bent over the refrigerator, legs braced and arms hugging both sides as he repeatedly banged his head against the metal door of the freezer. I could smell his body odor from where I stood. Uttering a cry, he whirled, lunged toward me and buried me in a fierce hug.

Almost gagging, I returned his hug and began to cry. "There, there. It's all right. Everything's going to be all right." We were like children again when I, struggling to be strong for my baby brother, would end up crying with him over his hurts. As youngsters, we fearlessly expressed tidal waves of emotion—outrage, shock, sorrow, pity, even unbridled joy—so unlike our adult selves storing years of buried feelings, layer upon layer, hidden underneath deep pools of emotional protection.

I stuffed my tears as Robby sobbed, his body heaving. Pulling against his arm, I cajoled him up the stairs where I turned on the hot shower and handed him a clean towel. We were too exhausted to talk.

From outside the closed bathroom door, I heard the clunk of his shoes hit the floor, one at a time, and then his belt buckle rattle against the tile. After the shower curtain signaled a metallic swoosh, I hurried into my bedroom just as the concierge buzzer sounded. Knowing it announced Ewer, I punched the intercom and shouted in passing that I expected a visitor and to send him up.

Since Robby occasionally spent the night, I kept a change of clothes in the back of my closet. A minute later, with his T-shirt, jeans, and underwear under my arm, I cracked open the bathroom door and one-armed them through the steamy fog and onto the toilet lid.

Downstairs in the kitchen, I made a pot of coffee and fixed Robby a peanut butter sandwich. He looked as if he hadn't eaten in days. On second thought, I fixed two sandwiches and boiled two eggs. Robby loved soft-boiled eggs slathered in pickle relish. I set the table while my mind whirled. Above me, the shower stopped. I flung open the refrigerator, remembering the box of hypodermics for whenever Robby turned manic. It was imperative that I anticipate the need to calm Robby and not wait too late. Retrieving one, I shoved it deep in my pants pocket.

When a couple of minutes passed and he still hadn't come downstairs, I walked up to investigate. The front door bell rang. Ignoring it, I checked the bedroom, but it was empty. Except for the laundry room, which I quickly examined, there was no other place Robby could be.

I knocked on the bathroom door before trying the handle. It was locked.

"Robby? Are you dressed? I've fixed you something to eat."

Silence.

I knocked again. "Robby? Please open up."

Again the doorbell sounded. I couldn't let Ewer leave. At least I knew where Robby was and, hurrying downstairs, tried to convince myself he wouldn't take the blade out of my razor and slit his wrist. My aspirin bottle was low due to recent heavy use—not enough pills left to kill anyone.

After sliding off the chain, I opened the front door. J.D. McGraw, Ewer's lawyer, grinned as if arriving for a date.

"I wasn't expecting you."

"I know. But Mr. Ewer had to go home. His wife's frightened of hurricanes." He sniggered, wanting my agreement that she was foolish.

Instead, I snarled, "So am I."

Turning away, I walked into the living room. We sat opposite each other, J.D. on the sofa, me in the easy chair. "Are you here in your official capacity as Ewer's attorney? He afraid I'll sue him for assault?"

"No more than you should fear his taking you to court for unlawful entry."

He had a point there.

"On the contrary, Mr. Ewer wants to apologize for the injury he inflicted on you. He also wants to dissuade you from the misguided notion he had anything to do with LeeAnn Callahan's death."

"And how will he do that?"

"Mr. Ewer," J.D. said, reaching inside his jacket—

The cop in me reacted instantly. I jumped from my chair, grabbed his thumb and jerked it backward. He grunted in pain, and as he bent forward, I grabbed his hand up and behind his back. "Stop right there."

J.D.'s eyes widened with surprise. "You think I came armed?"

With my left hand, I motioned for J.D. to stand while squeezing his wrist with my right. Tensions crackled between us as the stakes jumped more than a notch. As if on queue, winds howled around the building as if every brick were in pain. From outside something crashed with a metallic crack. The view from the picture window showed a block of house lights suddenly extinguished. Surely our building had back-up power.

After frisking J.D. one-handed, I let go and warned him to sit while I backed away and stood beside the easy chair.

Making a show of his disappointment in me, J.D. sat and shook his head slowly while he rubbed his thumb. "May I retrieve something from my pocket now?"

I nodded and he withdrew a bulging white envelope and handed it over. "Mr. Ewer would like you to accept this gift as an apology."

I took the envelope and looked inside. Thousand dollar bills more than two inches thick. He didn't want to kill me, after all. He just wanted to bribe me.

"In case you're wondering," J.D. said, "that's a hundred thousand. I'd take it if I were you, especially since you can investigate till the cows come home, and you won't find any evidence against Mr. Ewer."

"Then why pay me?" I said. "In fact, why pay someone six thousand to scare me off?" I threw the envelope down on the coffee table. "If you and your boss are innocent, you wouldn't risk this much money."

He leaned back, his eyes squinting as if viewing me from a distance. There are those who show emotion by fidgeting, flushing red in the face, or turning away their gaze. J.D. did none of these, unlike his cohort, Brad Ewer, whose feelings toward me had been all too obvious.

J.D. stared, his body language relaxed. "I thought you were smarter than that. You have nothing to implicate either of us and you never will." He unfolded himself from the couch as if from a nap. "You'd be a fool not to take this. It won't be offered again."

"Good," I said, "Because I have enough proof to put you both in jail."

Picking up the envelope, he held it out as he walked up beside me. The smirk on his face flashed so briefly I might have imagined it. After calculating the distance to my front door, I figured he could easily stop me.

He bent down to whisper in my ear. "You could disappear, you know. In South America you could live like a princess on a hundred grand. Or if you chose some place slightly more expensive, we might consider upping the ante." His breath was hot on my cheek and I shrank back, my heart skidding.

"You must not have heard me," I said. "I have proof of your guilt."

He stepped closer, backing me against the chair. His eyes danced with amusement when he spoke, as if to a child or an idiot. "Why not show it to me then? I might decide it's worth paying extra for. But mind you, not because of any guilt on my part, just for smoothing purposes. You know. Avoid trouble." He reached out and touched my nose lightly, completing his fatherly advice persona. His eyes flicked down at my waistband. When he glanced back at me, his eyes were wide with recognition. Had he been close enough to feel my gun?

A shout rang out.

"Get your hands off my sister!" Robby ran toward us and before J.D. could react, Robby had his throat in a strangle-hold. "I'll teach you a lesson, you filthy animal!"

J.D. jerked back, his arms and legs paddling wildly as they both dropped to the floor. "Let go of me, you crazy bastard!"

"Crazy, am I?" In one swift movement Robby flipped J.D. on his back and, straddling his chest, reined blows against J.D.'s face and chest. I pulled at Robby's shoulders as hard as I could, but he shook me off. While I screamed for him to stop, the underdog lawyer grabbed Robby by the neck with both hands. Robby continued to flail away at J.D.'s face. Suddenly J.D.'s head dropped against the floor, eyes closed, body flaccid. Great. Robby had knocked him out. Now what?

For my brother to switch from avoiding me at Café Artiste, to protecting me from a man with no obvious intentions toward harm, was not surprising.

I reached for the syringe in my pocket, but Robby stood and grabbed my arm. "You having a fling with that man or what?" I saw tears in his eyes as his face flushed with anger. He squeezed my arm and shook me until my teeth rattled.

Trying to control myself I reached out and steadied my free hand against Robby's cheek. "Of course not. Listen to me, Robby. Let go of my arm and I'll tell you all about him."

Robby appeared confused as he stared down at his fist around my arm.

"Please sit with me," I said. "Will you?"

He shook his head no and glanced at J.D. unconscious on the floor. When he turned back, defiance threatened to overtake his confusion. "What's he doing here? Tell me now. No sitting down."

"I fixed you two sandwiches and I have boiled eggs and pickle relish. Let's sit at the kitchen table, okay?"

His dilemma proved short-lived as he shrugged, letting go of my arm.

With Robby seated across from me, I explained my involvement in LeeAnn's death. During my monologue, I watched as his face crumbled and he stopped eating.

"I killed her, Jelly. I shoved her down and she died." He began to sob.

I swallowed a lump the size of a football, jumped up and hurried around the table. With my arms around him, I wanted to ask a million questions, but suddenly, an strong arm grabbed at throat, pulling me away. Robby jumped up, fighting an expression of total surprise, followed by a fury that stopped his tears.

With one swift motion, J.D. reached around me with his other arm and withdrew my gun, aiming it at Robby. "I'd stay right there, if I were you."

When Robby attempted to jump across the table, J.D. loosened his grip around my neck. I tried for the gun, but J.D. fired. He must have missed. Robby tackled him around the waist as I wrestled free. J.D. turned and fired again. Pain pierced my calf, spinning me around.

When I dropped, the kitchen floor hit my nose. I smelled pickle relish and naively reasoned that if I could still smell, my nose wasn't broken.

Barely able to turn my head, I witnessed J.D. struggling to heft Robby. A kitchen chair lay toppled against the floor, one of its legs broken. My brother sat slumped on the floor, his left shoulder spurting blood through his white T-shirt. J.D hadn't missed after all.

"I think it only fitting we head up to the roof," J.D. said, finally pulling Robby to his feet, "or your big sister'll get the next shot through the back of her head."

Robby nodded.

"We'll find out if you like going the way LeeAnn did, head first," J.D. said as he dragged Robby to his feet.

I tried to call out but my voice stuck in my throat. As if J.D. had erased me from his mind, he only grunted as he and Robby stumbled out the front door, leaving me to watch tiny rivulets of blood trickle onto the kitchen floor, my nose throbbing, my calf screaming for attention.

51

Panicked over what J.D. would do to my brother and fighting off tears of pain, I struggled onto the one upright kitchen chair. My calf felt as if a cannonball had blown through it, but proved to be only a gouge of profusely bleeding flesh as the bullet had sped elsewhere. A quick attempt to assess damage to my nose hurt like hell.

As quickly as I could, I wrapped my leg with the linen napkin I'd set out in honor of Robby's return. I had to get up there, *now*. My head reeled from Robby's confession. The better part of me said he was delusional. He hadn't killed LeeAnn. Or had he?

As I hobbled to the front door, wondering what to use for a weapon, since I owned only one gun, I spied the chair's broken leg. Solid wood. It would have to do.

The intercom buzzed. "Miss Faulkner? A Miss Peggy McGraw is here. She says her father is visiting and she'd like to come up."

Feeling a new trickle of blood on my upper lip, I swiped it against my sleeve. "I'm headed to the roof. Call the police. An armed man's up there holding my brother captive."

I added, surprised I'd remember at a time like this, "Call Santa Henderson and tell her to stay inside her apartment." They'd probably warn all the tenants, for those not already huddled inside a closet. This building was supposed to be hurricane proof. We'd soon find out.

I grabbed handcuffs from a bag in the front closet and stuffed them beside the hypodermic in my other oversized pocket. My brother was wounded, so I doubted he'd need the injection, but J.D. might.

Forced to hobble at a maddening, slow pace down the hall, I finally rounded the corner leading to the roof. I'd tell J.D. his daughter waited for him downstairs and maybe he'd regain his composure without sedation. But I'd refused his bribe and bragged I had evidence to put him behind bars. Why should he act rationally? Somehow, I'd get my brother and my weapon back, even if I had to crawl up to the roof.

The door handle leading to the roof was broken and dangling. I pushed against the door, the wind fighting me until it suddenly flew open. I glanced around the roof. Strong winds whipped my clothing. A curtain of stinging rain made it difficult to see beyond the roofline. It was as if I stood atop the only building left in the city.

I blinked rapidly as a low concrete wall came into view. Spanning the roof's perimeter, the wall wasn't high enough to allay my fear of heights. My heart skidded erratically.

When a sodden Peggy appeared at my side, I jumped. My voice sounded strange in my ears, half-frightened, half-angry, and surprised as hell.

"What are you doing up here?"

"Where's my daddy?" she shouted.

Leaning close, I tried a recap of events, aiming to sound calm and reasonable. "Your father came to see me at an unfortunate time. My brother's been missing for over a week from a mental ward and he finally returned. They're both up here. Your father has my gun. He shot my brother. I'll take care of this. You go back down and wait for us."

She whined, "What's the stick for?" Her crimson-painted lips pouted like a spoiled child wearing her mother's make-up.

I did a mental about face. Perhaps she could be of some use. "Follow me. Maybe you can talk some sense into your father." I limped away.

Huge air compressors dotted the landscape of the roof's gravel surface. Small outdoor-lighting fixtures shone as if through a fog along the bottom of the concrete ledge. Not great light, but better than none.

I'd exited the stairwell near the middle of the roof, but even so, my head grew light and my heart continued its amateur tap dancing. With gritted teeth, I fought the urge to run back down to the safety of my apartment.

The roof compressors were tall, but not tall enough to hide J.D. and Robby. Had they both fallen over the ledge? Could I force myself to walk over and look below for evidence? I shuddered. Not yet.

Struggling against the gale, my clothing soaked, I moved ahead, shouting for Peggy to keep behind me. The sound of tree trunks cracking, or perhaps transformers blowing, shot through the howling winds. The sky seemed to grow darker by the second.

I made my way to the closest compressor, five yards to my right, and searched its perimeter. No luck. The biggest unit on the rooftop sat near the far concrete ledge. Heading toward it, I braced myself by bending at the waist, protecting my eyes from bits of gravel thrown by the wind.

As I rounded the big compressor, my heart jumped in my throat at the sight of both men seated with their backs against the unit. My pistol was on J.D.'s lap, his finger around the trigger, the barrel pointed toward Robby. Robby sat slumped, eyes closed.

Peggy rushed to her father, screamed, and dropped down, wrapping her arms around him. I bent for my gun.

J.D. was too quick, raising it up at me.

"Don't try anything or I'll shoot. And drop that stick."

I did as he asked.

"I only want to take care of Robby," I shouted.

J.D. nodded at Robby slumped to his left.

Robby's face was pale and his eyelids flickered. I noticed his T-shirt. Earlier, only the shoulder of his shirt had been soaked in blood. Now the entire front glistened in the low lighting, its color an iridescent red. I bent to feel his pulse, barely beating. Hot anger surged through me. J.D. had done that to my brother. The bastard!

"He's bleeding to death." I said. "You've got to help me get him downstairs."

"I'll help you with your brother," J.D. said, struggling to untangle Peggy and rise. "I only meant to scare you two. Your brother shouldn't have attacked me."

"You did a lot more than scare him." I stood, shaking. "He's bleeding out!"

Peggy wiped at her eyes as she glared at me. "This is all your fault!"

"Actually, baby girl, it's my fault," J.D. said. Or that's what I thought I heard him say. Somewhat louder, he added, "Besides, I'm not the one that's hurt."

While the winds and rain lashed at us, J.D. stood gazing at Peggy. His voice, when he spoke, sounded stronger, more intense, as if he were a lawyer speaking his last appeal to the jury and Peggy was the only juror that mattered.

"Robby killed LeeAnn because she laughed at him. Said Robby was nuts and he'd never be her boyfriend."

Startled, I screamed out, "I don't care!" Turning away, I tried to lift Robby. "Just help me get him downstairs. Can't you see he's dying?"

"You handle it," Peggy snarled. "Daddy and I are leaving."

"Sorry, baby girl." J.D. said. "I'm helping."

"You can't, Daddy! Let's get out of here!"

"It's better for all of us if Robby lives. I shouldn't have waited this long to get help. I never intended to kill him, only to scare him. He might have confessed, don't you see?" He peered at his daughter as if imparting a silent, but urgent, message. "You leave before the winds get any worse. Now!"

He shoved my gun in his back pocket and bent over Robby.

Peggy moved in, pulled the gun from J.D.'s pocket and turned toward me.

With a rush, I felt blood drain from my head. If I died, Robby died.

"None of this would have happened if not for you," Peggy screamed. "You're a bitch, questioning my father and Brad. You're the one who needs to die."

In spite of both hands on the grip, Peggy's arms wavered in the winds. Rain plastered her hair to her head, enhancing eyes turned wild with fury.

Peggy might hit anything or nothing. My knees trembled as I stepped away from Robby. I couldn't let her get away with murder. Plunging my hand deep in my pocket, I jockeyed the hypodermic for an easy withdrawal.

"Give me the gun, Peggy," J.D. said. "You don't want anyone else to get hurt."

He stepped toward his daughter, his hand out. "This has got to stop. Now. Hand it over."

Peggy's attention was focused on J.D. Easing myself closer to her, I began to slip the rubber tip from the end of the hypodermic.

"Robby's the killer," Peggy said. "Let him die. I . . . I saw him that night." She stared, waiting as if expecting her father's praise. "He had LeeAnn's black cowboy hat in his hand hurrying away." Her eyes darted frantically between her father and me.

I froze, still frantic over Robby, but not fogged enough to miss her point. She'd been there. But after Robby had left. Neither Brad nor J.D. would have concocted a suicide scheme to protect my brother. But they would do it for J.D.'s daughter. Photos of her adoring gazes at her father flashed across my mind. Had Peggy known about LeeAnn's pregnancy?

I turned on her. "You were there! It was you who shoved LeeAnn over, not my brother. He'd already left!" I wasn't sure she heard me above the roar.

"Get Robby, Daddy." Peggy's screaming grew desperate, "Do it for me. Together we can throw him over the wall."

"I'm sorry," J.D. said, his voice firm. He turned to me, "I'll help you get him downstairs."

As he turned, my plans shifted instantly from the hypodermic, which was tricky at best, and reached for the table leg, hefting its rounded end. My timing couldn't have been as slow as it felt because, after I slung it like a boomerang, it twisted furiously through the air.

The wind directed it straight at Peggy's arm. It hit her wrist. She cried out and dropped the gun, but not before it fired a loud *thwack* into a distant metal compressor. Moving fast, she retrieved the gun before I got to it and, fighting the wind, attempted to swing the barrel toward me.

J.D. stepped between us, reaching for the weapon. The gun fired, spinning J.D. back toward me, a look of astonishment on his face before he fell at my feet.

Part of his head was missing. Bloody matter oozed from the fractured skull, the force of the rain spreading it outward. I turned away, struggling against nausea, expecting a bullet in my back.

Peggy screamed, and when I looked back, had thrown herself against her father's prone body. I could hit her over the head, but every second mattered. I hurried to my brother, wet hair whipping my face, and squatted in front of him. His closed eyelids were still. I lifted his wrist and held his hand. It was cold and pale.

Suddenly, shoved from behind, I belly-flopped beside by brother, my T-shirt little protection against the gravel.

Peggy straddled me, her long fingers squeezing my neck. Panic drove red rage through-out my body. Palms against the gravel, I thrust upward, jerked my legs in, and with the aid of sheer panic, flipped us both over onto our sides. Peggy clung to my back like a monkey.

As I gasped for breath, my chest heaved. Black spots danced in my eyes. But once on our sides, like spooning lovers, Peggy's grip loosened. I jerked away, rolling over gravel until I put distance between us.

As I stood on rubbery legs, Peggy rushed me.

Ramming her head into my stomach, she propelled me backwards, straight toward the edge of the concrete wall. I flailed for balance. I would not be thrown over the wall like LeeAnn. I would see Peggy behind bars. I would live to save Robby.

Vision blurring, gasping for breath, I panicked as the wall around the rooftop drew closer. Terrified, I had only one choice. Collapsing my legs, I sent us down in a heap. Before Peggy could recover, I scrambled upright.

She grabbed my ankle.

I kicked out, trying to jerk free. Struggling for balance, I reached in my pocket, grabbed the needle and plunged it in her neck. It wobbled. She batted it free with one hand. Her other hand held tightly to the sole of my tennis shoe as I hopped backward on one leg. My heel began to slip and as Peggy fell back, she held only my shoe in her grip.

I turned and dashed toward J.D.'s body. My gun was there somewhere.

Spying a faint, metallic gleam, I lifted the dead weight of his arm and grabbed my weapon. The raging wind, stinging rain, and the sound of cracking timbers disoriented me as I whirled around, my heart racing.

Her blood-red mouth open in a silent scream, Peggy was rushing toward me. I staggered back, adrenalin surging. She stood between me and rescuing Robby. The cop in me had kept count. There was one cartridge left. Hopefully, one was all I needed. She was perhaps three feet away and closing in on me. Winds battered my shooting arm, threatening to throw off my aim. Using both hands for leverage, I raised the gun and fired.

Shivering, I stared at Peggy's fallen body. Walking closer, I saw the bullet hole between her eyes. Incredible. I couldn't have managed that shot if I'd tried.

It was over. I collapsed beside Robby. Afraid to test his pulse, I sat motionless. Robby would wake up. When we were children, he would feign sleep until I tickled him. "Fooled you," he'd giggle and I'd pretend to be surprised.

The wind suddenly died and the rains stopped. Snuggling closer, I took Robby's head and leaned it against my shoulder. I looked up just as the heavens opened into a perfect hole, the eye of the hurricane. The moon, round and yellow, shone down. Nothing stirred.

Slumped beside me, Robby was also still. I grabbed his hand and squeezed with both of mine. Couldn't we stay here forever, my brother and I?

Within minutes—it could have been longer—I heard the *whup-whup* of helicopter blades approaching from the east. Out of nowhere the name S76 came to mind. Coming toward me was a large S76 copter like I'd seen on television, sent to rescue stranded victims during a hurricane or a flood.

The helicopter's wings blew gales in its path. Watching, I placed one arm around Robby's shoulder and whispered. *This big black bird will land on the roof here. Men will come hurrying to our rescue, little brother. I'll duck my head and climb inside but you'll be with me. They can't make me leave you. I'll never leave you.*

52

Hurricane Lola turned out to be a category two. If that was a two, I never wanted to experience a three. Many parts of Houston were without electricity for weeks, as the city struggled to clear roads of broken limbs, some from hundred-year-old oaks. Unfortunately for Galveston Island, it took the majority of Lola's destruction, with beach houses leveled and downtown businesses completely flooded.

I missed the hurricane's aftermath. My world had ended. Why should I care about anyone else's?

My nose had to be re-broken and set and the wound in my leg cleaned, packed and bandaged. Good excuses for remaining prone, curtains drawn. Many nights I awoke sweating from dreams of a large, red mouth about to eat me alive.

Santa was a constant presence. She'd turned into someone I'd never seen before. Bossy, dictatorial, ever watchful as she forced pills down my throat and made me sit in a chair while she changed my sweat-soaked sheets, my clothing. Visitors left with her promise I'd call when I was better.

After three weeks, Santa showed me a note from Dr. Winthrop. If she didn't succeed in getting me up and eating solid food, Dr. Winthrop wrote, he would hospitalize me. I hated hospitals. His threat became my incentive to try and sit upright for longer periods of time each day. Eventually, I made it downstairs where I could view the world from the living room window, swallowing as much of Santa's offerings as I could keep down. Wearing a robe and wrapped in a blanket, I sat and shivered. Where had the heat gone?

Santa saved newspaper articles portraying me as a heroine for solving LeeAnn Callahan's death, a case the police were accused of abandoning. Tantalizing me with these stories, Santa agreed to show me the papers only when I could eat and keep down three meals a day. We had our first argument then, but I won out. She couldn't declare what amount of food constituted a meal. Only me. She gave in after two days.

Apparently Keymap had showed up within days of Robby's death and Santa turned him away. Waiting weeks until I routinely came downstairs to sit, Santa finally handed me Keymap's handwritten note. I couldn't have been more surprised. He wanted me to know that his father had been Aunt Eunice's third husband. My aunt had instructed him to stay away from, but keep track of, yours truly. I wasn't always cautious enough, she'd told him. And, she knew I'd resent Keymap if he revealed her instructions to me. And he hadn't "stayed away" from me after all. Before tossing Keymap's note, I had to admit pleasure he'd promised me a nice meal when he returned from overseas in several months. Good. Lots of time to think of a response to his news.

During the coming weeks, I sat with newspapers stacked at my feet, reading voraciously about the aftermath of my investigation into LeeAnn Callahan's death. The mayor publicly vowed to hire more detectives for cold cases. Again, the crime lab was in for criticism. One day, Santa handed me the phone. It was Lamar. He asked me, very politely, if I would consider returning to police work. I declined, with humor. Santa, thus encouraged, shoved over a stack of phone messages for me to return. Cold cases to investigate.

Brad Ewer, hoping the Feds would lighten his fraud sentence, was singing like a bird. The Feds weren't promising, and neither, Lamar said, was HPD. Brad told him how Robby had appeared on the smoking balcony like a love-sick puppy. LeeAnn scorned him and Robby had pushed her down, but not off the balcony. Instead, he grabbed up her hat as if he couldn't leave without something that belonged to her.

A little later, when J.D. showed up looking for his jacket, he and LeeAnn were quickly reduced to passionate embraces, their usual 'can't keep their hands off each other' routine that had been going on for months. Brad thought they had broken off their relationship, but obviously they hadn't. Unfortunately, Peggy appeared in time to catch LeeAnn perched on the balcony railing, her skirt bunched, her father embarrassed.

Brad stated that Peggy had screamed something about how LeeAnn would never give birth to her father's baby as she rushed forward, shoving LeeAnn to her death. If only Peggy had known that LeeAnn, by that time, had already undergone an abortion.

J.D. begged Brad to go along with the suicide story. Promised he'd get help for his daughter. Later, J.D threatened to expose their stock fraud if Brad failed to protect his daughter. No one believed this, since J.D. would be incriminating himself along with Brad. What a price J.D. had paid for perhaps loving his daughter a little too much. Or was it just pride?

Right before Thanksgiving, I got a call from Randy Tilman, Boots' uncle. He wondered if I knew of Boots's gambling habits, his drinking and womanizing. His uncle had severed contact with Boots years before. I was certain all Boots wanted was his sister's insurance money. Almost made me not want to cash the huge check he sent along with a bonus for my "excellent work."

Not long ago, I read about a state legislator who'd started looking into Houston Rodeo's net profits versus dollars spent on scholarships. Minority groups had begun complaining they didn't get a fair shake in the bidding for vendor contracts, and the money spent on

Rodeo's office furniture was investigated and published to wide criticism. Rodeo had more than one problem on its plate.

Dr. Winthrop tries to help me deal with Robby's death. I loved my brother and tried to protect him. That would have to be enough. The *enough* part of Winthrop's mantra is still difficult.

I've also had difficulty with Winthrop's take on the lack of seriousness of Robby's "Midnight Disease." Without his compulsion to scribble, Robby might have sought me out more, been more communicative. His need for such a solitary pursuit left my brother vulnerable to dream up a relationship with a woman who had no romantic interest in him. His fits of writing left him more paranoid, depleted his energy, and certainly added to his withdrawing from me. There are bi-polar individuals, who, with this as their only mental issue, take medication and carry on useful, productive lives. I try not to dwell on this line of thinking. It's counter-productive and I fight it. But I can't easily discount it.

I'm selling Aunt Eunice's hi-rise apartment and taking Suzy with me. I found a small bungalow in the Heights and soon I'll be its new owner. My aunt's permission came to me in a dream. Or so I told myself. Suzy will adapt.

Santa thinks she'll sell out and move into my neighborhood. I find that strangely comforting.

There was a sparse turnout for Robby's memorial, which was postponed so I could attend. The small chapel at the edge of the cemetery was stark, its walls whitewashed. Pale wooden folding chairs stood in rows and a large brass cross hung against the front wall. Robby's group therapy folks were there, led by Dr. Winthrop. The Cathcarts came. Both of them. And Father came. I hardly recognized him. With stooping shoulders, he was almost completely bald, his complexion ghostly, jowls drooping. His wife, he told me, had died a little over a year ago. I almost felt guilty for not answering his weekly phone calls.

Heading down the cemetery slope following the service, I heard Father call out.

"G.L., stop." He drew up beside me, panting, and placed his hand on my shoulder. "Would you, uh, come to Florida for a visit sometime?"

I watched as his expression grew hopeful.

"Sure. Sometime."

"Should I, uh, stick around for awhile? Keep you company?"

"That's not necessary."

"Sure would be good if you could come see me."

"Yeah. I know."

He reached out, patted my arm, his eyes turned away. "You're busy, I know. I could, uh, come visit you. Maybe. Sometime."

I nodded, silent.

"Well." He patted my arm one more time. As he walked away, I noticed how his jacket flapped around his small frame. Maybe I would visit. Buy him a new suit.

Continuing down the slope where Santa waited for me, I craned my neck toward the sky and, for an instant, noticed a canopy of deep green oak leaves lit by the sun. Their transformation to bright, spring green resembled the tender shoots of new growth. A mirage, for sure. But nice, nevertheless.

Marcia Gerhardt is an award winning author and playwright. She was a winner of the Ft. Bend County Short Story Contest and was a finalist in the 2002 Writer's League of Texas manuscript contest. Her novel also placed in the Pacific Northwest Writers Association mystery writers' competition. She won The Liam Callen Award for fiction writing at the Willamette Writers Conference, 2002, Portland, Oregon. Her play, *Pie*, was produced as part of the Rice University Play competition. She lives in Houston and Portland with her husband and dog.

Marciagerhardt.com

27030578R00185

Made in the USA
Columbia, SC
22 September 2018